I0662496

Also from Indigo Sea Press
by Pat Bertram

More Deaths Than One

A Spark of Heavenly Fire

Light Bringer

Grief, the Great Yearning

Daughter Am I

By

Pat Bertram

Deep Indigo Books
Published by Indigo Sea Press
Winston-Salem

Deep Indigo Books
Indigo Sea Press
PO Box 26701
Winston-Salem NC 27114

Second Deep Indigo Books edition
published February, 2017.
Deep Indigo Books, Moon Sailor, and all production
design are trademarks of Indigo Sea Press, used under
license.

For information regarding bulk purchases of this book,
digital purchase and special discounts, please contact the
publisher at indigoseapress.com

Cover design by Pat Bertram

Manufactured in the United States of America
978-1630663681

For Jeff

Forever

Chapter 1

"Who were James Angus Stuart and Regina DeBrizzi Stuart?" Mary asked, trying to ignore the mounted heads of murdered animals staring down at her from the lawyer's wood-paneled walls.

Conrad Browning took off the silver-framed eyeglasses that matched his full head of hair and peered at her. "You don't know who they were?"

"No. Until I got your letter, I'd never heard of them. Since they're Stuarts and so am I, I thought they might be distant relatives, but why would they leave me everything they own?"

Mr. Browning cleared his throat. "It's simple. They were your grandparents."

Mary shook her head. "I don't have any grandparents. My father's parents died before my birth, and my mother's parents died shortly after."

"Be that as it may, James Angus Stuart and Regina DeBrizzi Stuart were your grandparents. They had one son, Peter Thackery Stuart, who married Gwendolyn Jane Smith. They, in turn, had one daughter. Mary Louise Stuart. You."

"I don't understand. My father told me they were dead."

Mr. Browning shuffled through the papers on his massive black walnut desk. His age-mottled hands moved slowly, as if weighted by the six turquoise rings he wore.

"Ah, yes. Here it is. According to the note appended to this file, your father had a falling out with his parents."

"How did my . . . my grandparents die?"

"Shot. They had been bound and gagged, and the house ransacked. The police have no suspects. It seems to have been another senseless act of violence."

She swallowed to keep the lump in her throat from turning into tears, not wanting to cry in front of Conrad Browning. He appeared to be a kindly older man, but he was a lawyer, after all.

Besides, she'd never known her grandparents, so how could she feel sad?

"Did you know them?" she asked.

"I must have met the Stuarts, but I don't remember." The brown leather chair groaned as he leaned back and steepled his fingers. "I wrote the wills twenty-five years ago and never revised them."

She bit her lower lip. So they had known about her all along. It didn't seem fair she'd only heard about them a few minutes ago.

Mr. Browning droned on about probate and the small trust fund her grandfather had established to pay any inheritance taxes. She tried to listen, but her mind struggled with the realization that her father, her stern, upright father, had lied to her.

"James and Regina Stuart died two weeks ago," Mary said casually.

Whatever reaction she had been expecting, it wasn't her father's bland, "Please pass me the potatoes, Gwen," or her mother's calm, "Certainly, dear. Anything else?"

Mary glanced at each of her parents in turn. "Is that all you have to say?"

Gwen's brow furrowed. "Watch your tone of voice, young lady. You might not live here anymore, but we're still your parents."

"I find out you've been lying to me my whole life, and *you* reprimand *me*?"

Mary's fiancé Bill Spindler, a handsome, dark haired man of medium height, swallowed the mouthful of food he'd finished chewing twenty times. Mary knew it was twenty times because he always chewed every bite twenty times.

"This is a lovely meal, Gwen," he said. "You outdid yourself." He cut a tiny piece of roast beef, then turned to Mary. "Who's been lying to you?"

She nodded toward her parents. "They have. They told me my grandparents were dead, but they aren't. I mean, they are now, but they weren't."

"You're not making any sense." Bill put the forkful of meat into his mouth and chewed.

When Mary found herself counting his jaw movements, she averted her eyes. "A few days ago I got a letter from an attorney telling me a James Angus Stuart and a Regina DeBrizzi Stuart named me in their wills. Today, at the reading of their wills, I discovered they were my grand-parents. They've been alive all this time, and I didn't know it." Looking at her father, she drew an unsteady breath. "Why did you tell me your parents were dead?"

Pete dropped his napkin by his half-filled plate and stood. "They were dead," he said quietly. "Dead to me." Then he left the dining room.

"How come you didn't tell me the truth, Mom?"

Gwen's mouth thinned. "I didn't know they were alive."

Becoming aware of her trembling legs, Mary put her hands on her knees to still them.

"What about your parents?" she asked. "Are they really dead? Or are *they* alive, too?"

Gwen frowned at her. "You never know when to let well enough alone, do you?" She rose and followed her husband out of the room.

A feeling of helplessness washed over Mary. This hadn't gone at all the way she'd envisioned.

"What did they leave you?" Bill asked, cutting off another tiny piece of meat.

Mary gave him a blank look.

"Your grandparents. What did they leave you?"

"Oh. Everything they owned, including their farm, where they raised my dad." She shoved a few stray peas around her plate. "I thought he grew up in Denver. I didn't know he was a farm boy."

"I did."

She sighed. "Why am I not surprised? He's talked to you more in the past few months than he's talked to me in my entire life."

"What are you going to do with the farm?"

"I don't know. The lawyer said they already have an offer for it."

Bill set his fork on the table and dabbed at his lips with his napkin. "Great! Now we can get married. We always planned to wait until we had enough money for a sizeable down payment on a house."

Mary winced. *You're the one who always planned to wait,* she told him silently. Aloud, she said, "The lawyer let me have the key. I'm going out there tomorrow to take a look."

"What time?"

"About nine."

He nodded. "I can fit that in. You want me to pick you up? Or are you going to drive?"

She hesitated, not knowing how to tell him she wanted to go by herself. "I'll drive," she said at last.

"What a dump," Bill said when Mary pulled in front of the old farmhouse.

Much as she wanted to defend it, Mary had to admit, if only to herself, that the place had seen better days. The once white paint peeled, the porch roof sagged, and the shutters hung at odd angles, giving the house a rakish appearance.

She couldn't imagine that the house had ever been charming, not even when new. It was a plain, two-story structure, the kind small children draw. The few scraggly bushes did little to soften the graceless lines, and it had no lawn, just bare dirt dotted with clumps of weeds. The house's one pleasant feature appeared to be the stand of old cottonwoods shading it.

"I sure don't envy the new owners," Bill said. "It will cost a fortune to have those trees cut down."

Feeling like a mother whose child has been insulted, Mary stared at him. "What do you mean, cut them down?"

"They're old, brittle. The first strong wind to come along will uproot them, probably destroying the house in the process, though that won't be any loss. I'm surprised it hasn't already happened. Out here on the eastern plains, high winds are the norm."

"Well, I know one thing," she said. "I'm not going to cut down those trees. I don't understand why people hate trees so much. All they do is destroy them, it seems." She got out of the car and spread out her arms. "The first thing I'm going to do is plant more trees, lots of trees."

Bill scrambled out of his seat and slammed the car door. "You're not thinking about keeping the place, are you? I thought we decided—"

"No. You decided." Mary took a deep breath. "Smell that clean air. And listen—no traffic."

Rolling his eyes, Bill shook his head. "You barely make enough to support yourself. How are you going to manage the taxes, insurance and upkeep for this place? From the looks of things, your grandparents didn't have much money to leave you."

Not wanting to hear any more, Mary ran up the porch stairs. She fumbled with the keys, pushed the front door open, and paused, thinking there should be a drum roll to mark this momentous occasion. Then she stepped into the house. Her house.

She sucked in her breath as she stared at the mess in the living room. Not one inch of space remained untouched. Furniture had been overturned, cushions ripped apart, lamps shattered. Glass crunched beneath her shoes, and wisps of white stuffing clung to her black jeans.

Tears stinging her eyes at the thought of her unknown grandparents caught in such violence, she checked out the rest of the house. The old-fashioned kitchen that no one had remodeled in forty years. The two bathrooms with rust-stained fixtures. The dining room, the den, the four bedrooms, all of which looked as chaotic as the living room.

"There you are," Bill said when she returned to the living room. "I thought you'd hurt yourself walking around in here. The inside is worse than the outside, and outside was ghastly. You're not thinking of keeping this rat hole, are you?"

"I don't know. Maybe."

"One thing's for sure, whoever put in an offer for this place isn't buying it for the house. It's a catastrophe waiting to happen. How many acres are there?"

"Eighty, I think the lawyer said."

He nodded reflectively. "Not bad. You should be able to get a good price, enough so we could buy our house outright, though with mortgage rates so low, it doesn't make a lot of sense."

"If I gave up my apartment and moved out here, I could save money. Then maybe I could afford the taxes and whatever."

"You'd have a ninety mile commute one way. The gas alone would cost more than you're spending for your apartment."

"Maybe I could rent out the land."

"I don't understand why you're being so stubborn about this. The best thing for us—you—is to get rid of the place as quickly as possible."

Mary turned away, unable to look him in the eyes. She didn't understand it either. In fact, she hadn't known she could be stubborn. She considered herself to be wishy-washy, usually giving in to preserve the peace. So why this desire to keep the house? She certainly didn't feel any affinity for it. If anything, its decrepitude repulsed her.

"God damn it," Bill said. "Why won't you listen to reason? The place is crumbling to bits. It won't take much for the whole thing to crash on top of your head. Look." He thumped the wall. A chunk of plaster fell to the floor. "See what I mean?"

Mary pointed to the wall. "What's that?"

"A hole. Believe me, there will be a lot more of them, too."

She shook her head. "No. There's something inside. I think I caught a glimpse of metal."

"There's nothing." Reaching behind him, he ripped out a handful of plaster. "See?"

Mary stared open-mouthed into the hole. Instead of the

dining room, which should have been on the other side of the wall, there was a windowless room not much bigger than a walk-in closet.

"What are you looking at?" Bill turned around. "What the—?" Within minutes he had ripped away enough of the plaster so they could squeeze through the struts.

Once inside, they could barely move around. A folded rollaway bed, a shallow wooden cabinet, a metal desk and chair took up most of the available space.

"A secret room," Mary breathed. "It's like something out of Nancy Drew or the Hardy boys."

"It's a storage area," Bill said.

"Then where's the door?"

"Probably behind the gun cabinet."

"Can't be there. How could someone have dragged the cabinet in front of the door once it was closed? There must be a hidden entrance somewhere."

Bill raised his right shoulder in an indifferent shrug. "Maybe it is a secret room. So what?"

"I think it's romantic."

He snorted. "You would."

She jerked her head around to stare at him. "Did you say gun cabinet?"

"Yes." He reached over and tugged at the double doors of the wooden cabinet. "See? Guns."

She took a step back. "Ooh. I hate guns."

He didn't seem to hear. He ran his fingers over a long, sleek rifle, and something akin to awe sparkled in his eyes.

"It's beautiful," he said.

"Oh, ick. How can you say that?"

"Look at it. It's either a refinished old west lever action rifle, or a handmade replica, complete with a hardwood stock, engraved brass receiver, and blued octagonal barrel."

Mary leaned closer to peer at it, then drew away again. "Looks like a plain old rifle to me."

"Oh, wow! Look at this one. A Chicago typewriter!"

"Typewriter?"

"It's a nickname for the Thompson submachine gun.

7

You've heard of a Tommy gun, right?"

"In old movies."

"Well, you're looking at the real thing."

But Mary wasn't looking at the gun; she was looking at Bill. She'd never seen him get so excited about anything.

"How do you know so much about guns?"

"I had a collection of miniature weapons when I was a boy. I wonder what happened to them. I think I'll call Mom, see if they're packed away somewhere."

As Bill exclaimed over the other guns in the cabinet, Mary searched the desk. Most of the drawers held typical office supplies, but the bottom drawer contained a locked metal box. She found the key in a small glass bowl full of paper clips and rubber bands.

"What do you have there?" Bill asked, looking over her shoulder.

She palmed the key. "A box. I'll take it home, see if I can find a way to open it."

"You should take the guns, too. They're worth a small fortune."

She shuddered. "I wouldn't be able to sleep with them under the same roof."

"Then I'll take them."

"No!"

He raised his eyebrows.

Averting her gaze, she mumbled, "I'm not allowed to take anything until after probate."

He looked pointedly at the box she hugged to her chest, but merely said, "Then we'd better do something about the hole in the wall. Don't want someone walking off with the few valuable things in this place."

After cleaning away the plaster, they moved a tall bookcase in front of the hole.

"I suppose it will do," Bill said, sounding doubtful. "You're sure you want to leave the guns here?"

"Positive."

* * *

Mary sat cross-legged on her bed and slowly unlocked the metal box. She told herself not to expect too much, but she couldn't help feeling a rising excitement. Taking a deep breath, she lifted the lid.

Money! Maybe enough so she could keep the house.

She spread the cash out on the bed and counted it. Though it looked like a lot, the bills were small denominations—fives, tens, a few twenties—and added up to about three thousand dollars, nowhere near what she would need. Swallowing her disappointment, she set the money aside and rummaged in the box again. She discovered a small stack of snapshots—young men in old-fashioned clothes, older men in more modern attire. She studied the pictures, but could not guess which of the men, if any, was her grandfather.

Looking in the box once more, she found a small black address book with faded entries and two gold coins—a ten-dollar gold piece and a five-dollar gold piece.

Her pulse quickened. Real gold! Except for jewelry, she'd never seen gold before. She picked up the coins, and smiled. They had a satisfying heft to them, not at all like ordinary money.

Still clutching the gold, she reached into the box for the remaining items—four envelopes yellowed with age. Three of the envelopes held Christmas cards, the personalized kind with family photos. Mary recognized herself as a small child standing beside her parents. The fourth envelope contained a birth announcement for Mary Louise Stuart. All the envelopes were addressed to her grandparents in her mother's distinctive handwriting.

Mary's hand trembled as she took the envelopes out of her purse and laid them on the table in front of her mother. Although she had wanted to dash over to her parent's house last night to demand the truth, she had decided to be mature about it and calmly discuss the situation after a good night's sleep. So today, before noon, she'd stopped by her father's plumbing supply business where her mother worked as office manager, and invited her to lunch at a nearby sandwich shop. She waited until after they ordered—spinach and avocado salad for both of them—but she couldn't wait any longer.

Gwen grimaced at the envelopes. "I hoped they hadn't saved them."

"Well, they did."

"I can see that." A touch of impatience crept into Gwen's voice. "What do you want from me?"

"The truth. You said you didn't know they were alive."

"This is between your father and his parents. It has nothing to do with you."

"But they were my grandparents." When Gwen remained silent, Mary asked, "What were they like?"

"I never met them, and Pete never talked about them." She touched one of the envelopes with a forefinger. A faint smile curved her lips. "I was young, in love. I thought if Pete's parents saw how much we cared for each other and our new baby, they'd soften toward him. Maybe they did, I don't know. But he didn't soften toward them. I stopped sending the cards when I realized Pete would consider it a betrayal."

When their salads came, Gwen ate two bites, then pushed her plate away. "I wish you'd drop this whole thing. You have no idea what it's doing to your father."

Suddenly weary, Mary said, "Fine, I'll drop it."

And, for the moment, she meant it.

Chapter 2

Mary gripped the black address book in her left hand and held the receiver with her right. The phone rang three times, then a deep voice on the other end of the line growled, "Yeah? What do you want?"

"Mr. Randaccio?" Mary said.

"Who is this?"

"My name is Mary Stuart. I'm the granddaughter of James Angus Stuart. I wondered—"

"Never heard of him." The line went dead.

Mary stood outside the row of attached houses on Zuni Street and checked the address again. It was definitely the right place.

She hesitated, glancing at the blistered gray siding, the clumps of weeds growing out of the buckling sidewalk, the cardboard box full of empty bourbon bottles on the curb next to a neatly tied bag of trash.

Hearing Bill's voice in her head calling her every kind of fool, she heaved a sigh. Maybe she was acting foolish, but what other choice did she have? Her father refused to talk to her about his parents, her mother claimed to know nothing, and most of the addresses in her grandfather's little black book were either out of date or out of town.

She squared her shoulders and made her way to the front door.

When she pressed the doorbell, she could not hear it ring inside the house, so she knocked. Then she knocked louder.

The door jerked open. "What do you want?"

The voice was the same as the one she had heard on the telephone yesterday—a deep growl that seemed incongruous coming out of the mouth of the little old man scowling at her.

"Mr. Randaccio?"

"Who wants to know?"

"Mary Stuart. I'm looking for information about my grandparents, James Angus Stuart and Regina DeBrizzi Stuart."

"Never heard of them." He slammed the door.

Mary saw a curtain twitch in the front window. She knocked once more, but the old man did not come to the door again.

The next morning when she knocked on that same door, the same man yanked it open and greeted her with the same question. "What do you want?"

Mary held up a bottle of bourbon, the brand of all the empties she had seen yesterday.

The old man's gaze shifted from her face to the bottle. After a moment, he disappeared into the murky interior of the house, leaving the door open. Taking that as an invitation, Mary stepped inside. In the dim light, she could see a tiny living room with a few pieces of shabby furniture and not much else. The place smelled musty, as if it had been closed up for a long time, but it seemed neat and clean.

She heard the opening and closing of a cabinet in a room off to her right, and followed the sound. The old man set two spotless glasses on the scarred wooden table. Without glancing at her, he motioned for her to sit, then waited until she perched on the edge of one of the mismatched chairs before settling himself in another.

Mary set the bottle in front of him. He poured a small amount of bourbon into her glass and a hefty amount into his. She expected him to toss it back, but he drank it slowly, savoring it as if it were a fine wine.

Steeling herself, she picked up her glass and took a tiny sip. She managed to keep from choking as the harsh liquor burned its way down her esophagus.

She curved her lips into something she hoped resembled a smile and nodded at the old man, who watched her with narrowed eyes. When she took another tiny sip, some of the stiffness seemed to seep out of his body, and he turned his attention to his own drink.

Trying to be discreet, she looked around the dollhouse-size kitchen. Dingy and outdated, it appeared to be scrupulously clean; she could detect a faint odor of disinfectant and dish detergent beneath the ambient mustiness.

She glanced at the old man. With his sparse white hair neatly combed, his lavish mustache well groomed, the cuffs on his yellowing shirt frayed, he looked as tidy and as shabby as his house.

After a few more sips of the bourbon and a last look around, Mary rose. The old man capped the bottle and pushed it toward her, but she left it on the table. He followed her through the house and stood at the door while she negotiated the buckling sidewalk.

As she drove away, she could see him still framed in the doorway.

Good. She hadn't spoken a single word to him during the entire visit, and her silence seemed to be rousing his curiosity. Maybe tomorrow he would open up and she would finally learn about her grandparents.

For the third day in a row, Mary knocked on the door of the decaying row house. The old man opened it immediately.

She held up another bottle of his brand of bourbon.

When he stepped aside to let her enter, she caught a whiff of after-shave. Though still threadbare, his pants and shirt looked freshly ironed.

He led the way into the kitchen. They drank in silence for several minutes, then he blew out a breath.

"Who did you say you were?"

"Mary Stuart. James Angus Stuart was my grandfather."

"Don't know him."

"Oh." Mary felt as if he'd knocked the air out of her. "But he had your name in his address book."

He poured a finger of bourbon into his glass, took a sip, and gave her a sidelong glance. "He did some work for me once."

"What kind of work?"

"Why don't you ask him?"

"I can't. He's . . . he's dead. So is my grandmother."

Staring at his drink, the old man tipped his glass this way and that. "I didn't know." After a moment he gave himself a little shake and sat up straight. "He restored an 1860 cap and ball revolver for me." A smile flitted across his face. "Sure was a thing of beauty."

Mary shrank back in her chair. "A gun?"

"Of course, a gun. Your grandfather was a gunsmith, didn't you know?"

"No. I don't know anything about him. I never got to meet him."

"He seemed like a nice guy."

Mary gave a humpf of unamused laughter. "That tells me a lot."

The old man narrowed his eyes. "Why does this mean so much to you?"

Mary took a sip of her drink, and for once welcomed the spreading warmth. "I don't know," she said at last. It sounded lame, but it was the truth. She *didn't* know. She wished she could do what her parents wanted and forget the whole thing, wished she could do what Bill wanted and sell the farm, but something inside of her she couldn't name would not let her. One thing, though. She didn't believe her grandfather was a nice guy, otherwise his son, her father, wouldn't have repudiated him so totally.

"Sorry to have bothered you." Mary rose to her feet. Remembering the photos in her purse, she dug them out and laid them on the table. "Do you know any of these people?"

He looked through them, giving each a cursory glance. Eying the last picture, he blinked. "Crunchy?" He held the picture to the light and peered at it. "Well, how about that?"

"What?" Mary said, curling her hands into fists to keep from grabbing the picture.

"Nothing."

"You recognized someone."

"No one you'd know."

14

"Who is he?"

"You don't give up, do you? He's an old wrestler from Milwaukee called Crunchy." He slid the picture toward her. "Fellow on the left."

Mary studied it, but the snapshot was so grainy she could only see a block of a man with masses of dark hair.

"He looks huge," she said.

"He wasn't, really. Less than six feet tall, but broad in the shoulders, with thick wrists and forearms, and fists as big as a man's head."

Mary got out her grandfather's address book and paged through it. "There's no Crunchy here. What's his real name?"

"Viktor Zamoyski."

She turned to the last page. "Here he is. Lambert Avenue in Pueblo. I wonder if he still lives there."

"Could be. Why?"

"I thought I might go see him."

The old man shook his head. "Not a good idea."

"I don't care," she said in a voice that surprised her with its firmness. "I was the only kid in my school without any relatives—no aunts, no uncles, no grandparents, no cousins. Now I discover my grandparents were alive all along. After all these years of not knowing them, I have to find out who they were."

The old man gave her a considering look. "Crunchy won't talk to you," he said after a moment.

"How do you know he won't talk to me?"

"He doesn't like to talk to anyone. His parents came from Poland, and they raised him speaking Polish. When kids at school made fun of his poor English, he would give them a hammer blow to the head, a crunch punch. Hence his nickname. He dropped out of school at a young age. The way I heard it—" The old man stopped abruptly.

"The way you heard what?" When he didn't respond, she said, "You can't stop there. What were you going to say?"

He shrugged. "The mob found him wrestling in small venues, took him out of Milwaukee, and set him up in

Chicago where he made a good living." The old man paused. "You sure you want to hear this?"

"Yes," Mary said, wondering if she really wanted to learn about someone with ties to the mob.

"Sometimes Crunchy went with the mob guys on collections. He stood there, not saying anything, not doing anything. Occasionally he had to crunch someone, but it seldom went that far. When he got too old to wrestle, the mob sent him to Pueblo as part of a job lot of forty to fifty men, to be a strikebreaker for Colorado Fuel and Iron. Later, after the unions formed and took hold, he worked as muscle for the unions against the company."

Mary frowned at the snapshot. "How did my grandfather know someone like him?"

"I don't know."

"I'm still going to see him."

"I told you, he won't talk to you." Then his eyes lit up. "Hey, I could go with you. He'd talk to me."

"I appreciate the offer, Mr. Randaccio, but—" She stopped when she saw him wince. "What's wrong?"

"Nothing. I don't like being called 'Mr. Randaccio,' not by a pretty girl. It makes me feel old."

"What should I call you?"

"I used to be known as Kid Rags."

"Okay, Kid Rags, but I don't think—"

"It's still early. We could go now, be back this afternoon."

"I can't today."

"Then tomorrow morning. What time should I be ready? Eight o'clock?"

Mary opened her mouth to tell him she wasn't going anywhere with him at any time, but the look of pleading in his eyes stilled her tongue.

Hoping she wasn't making the final, fatal mistake of her young life, she said, "Eight o'clock will be fine."

Chapter 3

Kid Rags stared out the car window, frequently craning his neck to look at something they passed, but he made no comment on whatever had caught his interest. When Mary had seen him standing outside his house dressed in a dark blue suit with a matching homburg and a red bow tie, her first inclination had been to drive on by— what did this dapper little old man have to do with her?—but her car, a tan Toyota Corolla, seemed to have stopped of its own accord. After a few agonizing attempts at conversation, she too had fallen silent.

It wasn't until they neared Pueblo that Kid Rags finally spoke. "Do you know where Lambert Avenue is?"

"On the west side of town. I do a job at a warehouse near there every year." Seeing his questioning glance, she added, "I work for an inventory company. We travel all around the state taking inventory for various businesses."

"That's a job?" he asked, his tone dubious.

Mary gave a little laugh. "You sound like Bill, my fiancé. He doesn't think it's a real job, either. Says there's no future in it. He wants me to work for his accounting firm, but I like what I'm doing. We work like crazy during our peak season, but when business is slow, like now, I have a lot of free time."

Thinking of Bill, Mary frowned. They had a repeat of that same old conversation last night, along with another discussion about the house. He hadn't been too happy when she admitted she still hadn't contacted the lawyer about selling it. Good thing she hadn't mentioned her planned excursion to Pueblo with Kid Rags—he would not have understood and would have tried to talk her out of it.

"I think this is it." Kid Rags pointed to a pale yellow building that looked like an old hotel. It had a forlorn air, as if long abandoned, but as Mary pulled up to the curb, she noticed an old man and an old woman sitting on rocking chairs on the long veranda, staring off into the distance. A sign on the front lawn advertised rooms for rent.

Kid Rags stepped out of the car, smoothed his mustache, adjusted his bow tie, ran his fingers around the brim of his hat, then headed for the front door. Though his steps were unfaltering, Mary had the impression he didn't feel as self-confident as he acted.

She got out of the car and caught up to Kid Rags as he asked the two old people where he could find Crunchy. The man stared straight ahead without responding, but the woman gave Kid Rags a coquettish smile.

She patted the chair next to hers. "What do you want with an old goat like him? You'd be better off talking to me."

Kid Rags tipped his hat and winked at her. "Maybe later."

"Is Viktor Zamoyski here?" Mary asked.

The old woman glanced at her, then turned away. "Second floor. First door on the right."

Kid Rags opened the front door and ushered Mary inside. A broad, once elegant staircase creaked and groaned beneath their feet as they climbed to the second floor.

A man who could only be Crunchy answered Mary's knock. Though his skin hung loosely as if he'd lost a lot of weight, he still looked imposing. His dark hair had streaks of gray, but it was thick and grew low on his forehead.

He stared at them, saying nothing.

"Hello, Crunchy. It's me. Kid Rags."

"Hey, Kid." Crunchy slapped the smaller man on the back, sending him reeling.

Recovering his balance, Kid Rags gestured toward Mary. "This is Mary Stuart."

Crunchy turned to Mary and held out his hand. Resisting the urge to hide her hands behind her back, she gingerly reached out. His hand engulfed hers, making her feel like a little girl. To her surprise, his touch was gentle.

"Hello, Lady," he said softly, dark eyes twinkling at her from beneath heavy eyebrows.

"Hello, Crunchy."

Crunchy drew her into the room and settled her in an

armchair upholstered in a dark green nubby fabric. He offered Kid Rags the desk chair, then he leaned against a wall, arms folded across his chest.

While the two men spoke briefly about people with names like Ratsy and Joe the Barber, Mary surveyed the room. It was fairly large, but bare. In addition to the desk and the two chairs were an iron bedstead with a sagging mattress and a bedside table with a lamp and a clock radio. A braided rug partially covered the scuffed wooden floor.

Hearing her name, she turned her attention back to the two men.

"Mary's trying to find out about her grandparents," Kid Rags said. "His name was James Angus Stuart."

Crunchy shook his head. "Don't know no James Agnes Stuart."

"What about Regina DeBrizzi Stuart?" Mary asked.

"Don't know her neither."

Mary took the photographs out of her purse and showed them to Crunchy. "You're in one of these snapshots. See? Here's you. How could they have a photo of you if you never met them?"

Crunchy's brow furrowed. "Don't know no James Agnes Stuart." He riffled through the pictures, squinting at them, then he showed one to Kid Rags. "Lefty Louie?"

Kid Rags studied the picture. "I think you're right. Lefty Louie. I heard he's living in an old folks home in Alamosa."

"Heard that too," Crunchy said.

"Who's Lefty Louie?" Mary asked.

"A guy from the old days," Kid Rags said. "He used to have a ranch near Monte Vista."

"Maybe he could tell me about my grandfather. What home is he in?"

"Guardian Angels," Crunchy said.

Mary rose. "Thank you for your help, Crunchy. Sorry to have bothered you."

"No bother."

Crunchy put on a shapeless tan sweater with brown elbow patches and followed them outside. When Mary paused by her car to say good-bye to him, he lumbered past her and climbed into the back seat.

Mary looked at Kid Rags.

He shrugged. "Obviously he wants to come with us to Alamosa."

"But we're not going to Alamosa."

"Don't you want to talk to Lefty Louie?"

"Yes, but I planned on calling him. It's not worth going all that way so someone else can tell me they don't know my grandparents."

"Who's going to tell Crunchy? Not me."

Mary peered through the window. Crunchy stared back at her.

All at once she felt a giggle well up inside her. Biting her lip, she told herself there was nothing funny about the situation, but she couldn't help smiling.

"I guess we're going to Alamosa," she said.

They stopped at the first gas station they came to in Alamosa. Mary filled the tank. Crunchy hovered near her, glaring at anyone who looked her way. Kid Rags went in search of a phone book.

"Guardian Angels is a short distance from here," he announced when he returned. "Take a right at the next corner and go about three blocks."

Guardian Angels Home for Senior Citizens, a sprawling, one-story brick building, looked new and the grounds well kept. Paved pathways meandered around formal flowerbeds, and wicker chairs were grouped under young shade trees.

They found Lefty Louie watching television in the bright and cheery community room. He smiled broadly at the sight of them.

"Sure, I knew James Stuart," he said after the three men caught up on their news. "Because of him I moved to Colorado."

"What was he like?" Mary asked eagerly.

Lefty Louie ran his fingers through his wisps of white

hair, making them stand on end.

"James was . . ." He ran his fingers through his hair again. "He was swell," he said at last.

"That's it?" Mary asked. "That's all you can tell me?"

"I liked him," Lefty Louie said. "He was a stand-up guy." He turned to Kid Rags. "You should go talk to Teach. He knows words. He can tell her about James."

Kid Rags tilted his head to one side. "Teach? I didn't know he's still around."

Lefty Louie nodded. "I understand he's got himself a nice little business."

"Who's Teach?" Mary asked.

"Carlo Santucci," Kid Rags answered. "He and your grandfather were partners once, or so I heard. Lefty Louie's right—Teach certainly knows words. He talks more than anyone else I ever met."

Mary dug her grandfather's address book out of her purse and found Carlo Santucci's address. "Tombstone, Arizona. That's a ways from here."

"Not really," Lefty Louie said. "Take two eighty-five south to Santa Fe, then get on Interstate twenty-five to Interstate ten, and that will take you to Arizona." He tugged at his hair. "I always wanted to see Tombstone."

"Why don't you come with us," Mary said impulsively. "We'd love to have you."

His eyes lit up. "Really? You mean it?"

Mary glanced from him to Kid Rags and Crunchy, who gazed at her with identical expressions of hope flitting across their faces. Pushing aside her misgivings, she said, "Sure. Why not?"

Lefty Louie jumped from his chair. "I'll go get packed."

"We'll wait for you out by the car," Mary said, wondering why Crunchy and Kid Rags suddenly seemed so still. Maybe they were worried about being unprepared for the trip. "We can get anything we need along the way," she assured them, but neither would look at her. All at once, she understood.

"This is my mission," she said carefully, "so it's my

responsibility to pick up the tab."

"We can't let you do that," Kid Rags protested weakly.

She gave him a considering look. "Tell you what—I'll pay for everything, and we can settle later."

"You have that much cash on you?"

"No, but I have plastic."

Lefty Louie came outside, hands empty, hair standing on end. He shifted from foot to foot and wouldn't look anyone in the eyes.

"I can't go," he mumbled.

"Mary's paying," Kid Rags said.

Still not looking at anyone, Lefty Louie flicked his wrist in a dismissive gesture. "It's not that."

"What's wrong?" Mary asked. "Won't they let you leave?"

Crunchy curled his hands into fists. "Want me talk to warden?"

"No, no. Don't," Lefty Louie blurted "We're having fried chicken tonight, and movies and popcorn afterwards."

"What about if we come back for you tomorrow?" Mary asked.

"Tomorrow we're having meatloaf." He turned and shuffled back to the home. He opened the door. Looking back at them, he said, "I did want to see Tombstone," then he disappeared into the building.

After a long moment of silence, Crunchy said, "We still going, Lady?"

Mary smiled at him. "Yes, Crunchy, we're still going."

"Good." Kid Rags patted his belly. "What's for food? I'm hungry."

Mary woke and stretched. She lay in bed for a few more minutes, listening to the semis pulling out of the parking lot. She smiled to herself. How strange to find herself in a motel at a truck stop somewhere on I-10—maybe Arizona, but probably still New Mexico—and two old men she didn't know in the room next door.

She sat up with a guilty start. Here she was lolling in bed when they were probably starving, although given the amount of food they'd put away at dinner, they shouldn't need to eat again for another week.

She got out of bed, took a quick shower, dressed in the off-white peasant blouse and underclothes she'd washed in the sink last night, then pulled on her black jeans and tennis shoes.

When she left the room, she found Crunchy sitting in a chair beside her door, glowering at all who passed by.

"Have you been out here all night?" she asked.

He jumped out of his chair and twinkled at her, but made no other response.

She gazed back at him, not knowing whether she felt flattered or smothered. "You didn't have to do that," she said. "I can take care of myself, and you need your sleep."

Crunchy folded his arms across his chest. "Don't need much sleep."

"I bet you could use some food."

Kid Rags appeared at the door of the next room. "Did someone say food?"

Mary laughed and led them to the diner where they'd eaten the night before. She nibbled on a piece of toast and a scrambled egg while the two old men stuffed themselves with ham, eggs, hash browns, sausage biscuits, pancakes, juice, and uncountable cups of coffee. Hoping neither of them would have a heart attack while in her care, she paid the bill and escorted them out to the car.

Mary pulled up in front of a large cream-colored Victorian house with dark green gingerbread trim. If Teach lived here, he must be doing well for himself. Then she noticed the row of mailboxes and realized the place had been converted into an apartment building.

A middle-aged woman in cut-offs and a halter-top weeded the garden bordering the house. Brushing her auburn hair from her forehead with the back of a gloved hand, she straightened and gave them a questioning glance.

"Carlo Santucci?" she said in answer to Mary's query. "Yes, he lives here, but he's not in right now. He went for a walk a while ago."

"Do you know where we can find him?"

"Try Allen Street." The woman pointed to her right. "It's that way."

"Thanks," Mary said.

As they headed back to the Toyota, the woman called out, "You can leave your car here if you want. You'll have a hard time finding close-in parking."

Mary hesitated a moment, but decided the old men might not survive a walk in the heat. Ninety-nine degrees in May. She hated to think what Tombstone would be like in July.

She found a parking space half a block away from Allen Street, then they headed on foot for the historic district where gambling halls, saloons, and houses of prostitution had once abounded. The illusion of an old western mining town was marred by all the people wearing garish tee shirts imprinted with pictures of Wyatt Earp, and clutching snow cones or drinking from oversized paper cups.

One old man, however, did fit the image. He wore jeans and a white long-sleeved shirt with a western string tie, a leather vest, boots, and a cowboy hat. Round, wire-rimmed glasses framed bright eyes, and he had the beginnings of a beard, as if he couldn't be bothered with shaving every day. He was talking to a young couple who gazed raptly at something nestled in his palm.

"Let's go see what he's showing those folks," Kid Rags said.

"I don't think we should—" Mary began, but Kid Rags had already walked away. She shrugged and followed him, Crunchy close on her heels.

"My grandpappy dug it out of this very building," the cowboy was saying when Mary approached. "If you look close, you can see the bullet hole."

"Awesome," the young woman said. "One of Wyatt Earp's own bullets."

"Well, now, I can't rightly say it came from Wyatt Earp's gun. There were a lot of bullets flying that day my grandpappy said."

"How much do you want for it?" the young man asked.

"I'm not sure I want to sell it. It's all I have to remember my grandpappy by."

"Five dollars?" the young man said. "Ten dollars?"

"One of the actual bullets from the shoot-out at the OK Corral ought to be worth a lot of money," Kid Rags said.

"I'll give you twenty dollars for it."

The cowboy glanced at him. "Now that's a mighty fine offer."

"Twenty-five," the young man said.

"Thirty," Kid Rags countered.

Thirty dollars? Mary tried to catch Kid Rags' eye. No way was she going to give him thirty dollars for a bullet.

"Thirty-five," the young woman said.

The cowboy took the young woman's right hand, dropped the misshapen piece of metal in it, and closed her fingers over it. "If I didn't need the money so bad, I wouldn't part with it, but I'm glad it's going to such a lovely young lady."

The young man counted out thirty-five dollars and handed it to the cowboy.

The cowboy stuffed the bills in his vest pocket. "Much obliged."

The young couple hurried off, heads together, laughing.

Mary sighed with relief. At least she didn't get stuck with the bill.

"They seem to think they got the better of you," Kid Rags said.

"That's how it should be." The cowboy's face broke into a huge grin. "Gee, it's great to see you, Kid Rags. How long has it been?"

"Too long. Teach, I'd like you to meet Mary Stuart, James Stuart's granddaughter. And this is Crunchy, an ex-wrestler from Chicago."

After shaking hands with both Crunchy and Mary, Teach

asked, "How is James?"

"He passed away not too long ago," Mary said.

Teach shook his head. "I'm sorry to hear that. He was a good man."

"Mary didn't know her grandparents," Kid Rags explained. "She wants to find out what they were like."

"Well, you came to the right place," Teach said. "I knew your grandfather well." He checked his watch. "It's getting on toward noon. Why don't we pick up some sandwich fixings and go to my place where we can talk in private."

Suddenly afraid of what Teach might have to say about her grandfather, Mary could only nod.

Chapter 4

"How could you bear to part with the only thing you had that belonged to your grandfather?" Mary asked when they were all munching sandwiches in Teach's kitchen. The large rooms of his apartment seemed small because of the books stacked everywhere—on shelves, on tables, on the floor, on the kitchen counters.

"Even if it was only a bullet," she added.

"There's more where that came from." Teach lifted the top of a ceramic cookie jar sitting in the middle of the table, reached in, and pulled out a handful of metal blobs. He let the pieces of lead clatter back into the ceramic jar, then stuck two fingers in his vest pocket and took out a ten-dollar bill. Handing it to Kid Rags, he said, "Here's your share. Usually I get about fifteen dollars per bullet."

Kid Rags plucked the bill out of Teach's hand, carefully placed it in his wallet, and continued eating his ham and cheese sandwich.

Mary's mouth fell open as she stared at Teach. "You're a con man!"

Teach raised one eyebrow. "You say that as if it's a bad thing."

"Well it is. You cheated those people."

"No, I didn't. I gave them exactly what they wanted— romance, excitement, memories. And don't forget, they thought they were taking advantage of a poor defenseless old man."

"It's still not right," Mary said.

"You don't get it, do you?" Teach rolled one of the bullets between his fingers. "It's all one great big con."

"What is?"

"Everything. Life. Love. Happiness. The OK Corral. Wyatt Earp."

Mary shot a questioning glance at Kid Rags who shrugged and busied himself constructing another sandwich.

"Wyatt Earp was a con man himself," Teach said. "He and a mysterious character named Dave Mather got caught pulling the gold brick swindle in Mobeetie, Texas, and they were run out of town."

"Gold brick swindle?" Mary asked.

Kid Rags groaned. "Don't egg him on. Now we're going to learn more about gold swindles than we ever wanted to know."

"I wanna know," Crunchy said.

Teach grinned at Kid Rags. "You're welcome to wait in the living room."

Kid Rags waved his sandwich. "I haven't finished eating yet."

Teach leaned back in his chair. "They plated lead bars and sold them as solid gold. A simple swindle, but lucrative. A warrant had also been sworn out for Wyatt Earp in Oklahoma territory for horse stealing. And he got kicked off the police force in Wichita, Kansas because he refused to pay the fine for being a pimp—he had one or two prostitutes working for him in a place behind the saloons. Back then, law enforcement officers didn't get paid much. They made their money off fines—licensing fees, really—and since he worked as a police officer, Wyatt Earp thought he didn't have to pay the fine. The marshal disagreed, and fired him."

Mary frowned. "Is this true?"

Teach nodded. "Every word. The point I'm trying to make is no one gets rich off telling the truth. People beg to be conned. They want life to be more than it is. Would people come all the way here to Tombstone if they knew the famous shoot-out at the so-called OK Corral wasn't much of a gun battle? Of course not."

Kid Rags took a bite of his third sandwich and chewed as if the meal were all that interested him, but Mary could tell he listened as intently as she and Crunchy.

"Little of the legend is true," Teach continued. "The fight didn't take place in a corral, but in an alleyway next to Fly's Photographic Gallery. Wyatt Earp's brother Virgil was the town marshal. Wyatt was merely his deputy. Two dozen

Daughter Am I

bullets at most were fired, and one or two of the men the
Earps shot didn't have guns. The whole thing was an
inconsequential feud between two inconsequential rival
gangs, but the fable—the lie—is much more compelling than
the truth.

"We want the pretty lies, and the lies we tell ourselves are
the most compelling of all. We tell ourselves love comes to
each of us and lasts forever. We tell ourselves we're
civilized, that only soldiers, legendary heroes, psychopaths,
and psychotics have the ability to kill, but the fact is we all
retain that deadly instinct somewhere deep inside us."

Mary shook her head. "Not me. I could never kill
anyone."

Teach studied her for a moment. "Maybe. Maybe not.
Nowadays, few of us are put to the test. All I'm saying is
that life is a lie, a con. If you ever doubt yourself, the whole
thing falls apart because you can no longer bear yourself.
The way I see it, the secret of life is to control the con, not
let it control you."

Kid Rags let out a bark of laughter. "You're as full of hot
air as ever, Teach. Give it a rest. You're boring Mary and
Crunchy."

Crunchy looked up from his sandwich. "You bored,
Lady?"

Mary smiled at him. "No, not in the least."

"Me either. His words feel good to my ears."

"And anyway," Kid Rags said, acting as if he hadn't been
interrupted, "Mary's more interested in finding out about her
grandfather than listening to you spout half-baked
philosophies."

"And my grandmother," Mary said. "She also died before
I got to know her."

"What did you want to know?" Teach asked.

"Whatever you can tell me. I don't know anything about
either of them."

"Well, your grandmother was beautiful. Not pretty—she
had too much character in her face for that—but beautiful.
She had blond hair as a young woman, and wide-spaced gray

eyes."

"Blond hair?" Mary asked. "DeBrizzi sounds like an Italian name."

"There were a lot of blond Italians in Northern Italy. Your grandfather had reddish-brown hair and brown eyes. He was of average height, but stocky. He could be moody at times—friendly and expansive one moment, cold and withdrawn the next—but for the most part he appeared even-tempered. He was also the sort of man who, if he wanted to, could slam the door on a subject and not speak of it again."

"Sounds like my father," Mary commented. "Why didn't he and my grandparents get along?"

"They never mentioned it, and I never asked."

"How do you know my grandparents?"

"Your grandfather and I once planned on going into business together, but it didn't work out."

"What business?"

Teach shook his head.

"Look," Mary said. "I've figured out my grandfather wasn't a saint. You might as well tell me."

"Well, your grandfather did a favor for a man called Lefty Louie—"

"She met Lefty Louie," Kid Rags said. "We stopped by to see him before we came here."

"How is he?"

Kid Rags shrugged. "Different. Old."

Teach snorted. "Aren't we all?"

"What favor?" Mary asked, but Teach was taking a sip of water and seemed not to hear.

Teach set his glass back on the table. "Since Lefty Louie didn't have any cash at the time, he paid off your grandfather with a gold mine located near Crested Butte."

Mary's eyes grew round. "It must have been a big favor."

"Not really. The gold mine was worthless. Played out. Lefty got it for practically nothing. A friend of his had made a fortune mining similar places for crystals like rhodochrosite, and he thought he'd do the same, but he found nothing in that gold mine except rotting timbers and the bones of an unlucky miner or two."

"Why would my grandfather want a worthless old mine?"

"He knew I was looking for one."

"Why did you want one? Oh, don't tell me. Let me guess. A scam."

Teach nodded. "That's right."

Kid Rags took a hip flask out of his back pocket. "Listening to Teach is thirsty work. Anyone want a drink?"

Mary shook her head, but the men all took long swigs. When they emptied the flask, Teach rose and got a bottle of whiskey and three clean glasses out of a cupboard. The men toasted one another, Mary, her grandparents. Then Teach pushed aside his drink.

"I read about a guy who paid eight hundred dollars for a worthless emerald mine in South America. He sold shares in it, declaring that it was operating and producing emeralds valued in the millions, and he bilked people out of five hundred thousand dollars before anyone discovered there were no emeralds.

"I didn't want to do anything that big, but I thought I could make money by selling shares of a gold mine for a relatively small piece of change."

Kid Rags turned to Mary. "That's Teach for you. Twenty minutes of worthless information before he finally gets around to answering your question."

"Nothing came of it," Teach continued. "Before the share certificates were printed, I had to leave town in a hurry, and somehow we never got back to it."

"What happened to the gold mine?" Mary asked.

"I imagine James kept it."

"In that case, it belongs to me. Wow! A gold mine."

"A worthless gold mine," Kid Rags pointed out.

"I know, but still . . ."

Teach's eyes gleamed. "You and I could go into business together. We could make a fortune."

Mary toyed with her empty glass, trying to think of a tactful way to discourage Teach, but in the end all she said was, "No, thanks. Now I understand why my father did not get along with his father. My father would not break the law under any circumstances, wouldn't even consider bending it."

"Maybe that's not the reason for their estrangement," Teach said. "Maybe it's the result."

"Whatever." She stood and started cleaning off the table.

"Sit. Sit," Teach said. "I can do that later."

"It's the least I can do to pay for your hospitality."

Teach smiled.

Mary narrowed her eyes. "What?"

"James was like that, always wanting things to balance out."

"My mother says I have a childish sense of justice, but I don't know what that means."

"It means you're goodhearted," Teach said.

Mary blushed, and ducked her head.

"You okay, Lady?" Crunchy asked, glaring at Teach.

"I'm fine, Crunchy. Just not used to compliments."

"Oh. Okay."

Mary finished clearing off the table, leaving only the glasses and the whiskey bottle. There was no food to put away; they'd eaten every crumb.

"Are you going to show Teach the pictures?" Kid Rags asked.

"Oh, I forgot." Mary opened her purse, which she'd slung across the back of her chair, and pulled out the packet of snapshots.

Teach studied each picture. When he finished, he went through the stack a second time. He gave a start, then bent down to peer more closely at one of the pictures.

He frowned. "This doesn't make any sense."

Mary craned her neck, trying to see the picture. "What doesn't?"

Teach pointed to one of the men in the photograph. Though two others stood in front of the man, partly hiding him, Mary could still see most of his distinctive face. His black hair formed a sharp V in the middle of his forehead. His thick black eyebrows were inverted V's. His cheeks were gaunt, sunken, and his eyes were shadowed, making them look like burnt holes.

Mary shivered. "Who is he?"

"Iron Sam. Also known as Butcher Boy."

Kid Rags grabbed the picture. "Jeeminy Christmas. How did I miss him? The Butcher Boy himself."

Teach shot him a look tinged with disbelief. "How *did* you miss him? You have such a good eye for detail."

Kid Rags shrugged. "But a terrible memory for faces."

"Butcher Boy?" Crunchy said. "Let me see."

Kid Rags slid the picture across the table, poured himself another drink, and gulped it.

As Crunchy studied the picture, his hands curled into fists.

Teach took a deep breath. "He was a stone killer. I never knew James to associate with people like him."

"Well, my grandfather was a gunsmith," Mary said.

"Iron Sam did not appreciate collector quality weaponry. He probably disposed of more guns in a year than James made in a lifetime."

"So how did my grandfather know him?"

Teach drew the photograph toward him and stared at it. "That's what I can't figure out."

"Could my grandfather have blackmailed him or something?"

"James was a stand-up guy," Teach said. "He would not have resorted to anything so underhanded."

Kid Rags poured himself another drink. "You could go ask him."

Mary stared at him, confused. "Ask who? My grandfather?"

"No. Butcher Boy."

"I can't believe you'd suggest that," Teach said. Then he added, "Iron Sam wouldn't agree to see her. He hates women, remember?"

"We could go with her."

Teach snorted. "Yeah, right. I can see you waltzing into Leavenworth and asking to see Iron Sam."

Kid Rags slumped in his chair. "You got a point."

"Ain't going to no prison," Crunchy said.

Mary put her hands on her hips. "None of us are going."

Teach nodded. "Good thinking. Butcher Boy is not someone to get involved with. He's a strange character. When he was three—"

Kid Rags rolled his eyes. "Oh, no. Not another lecture!" He pushed the whiskey bottle toward Mary. "You should have a drink. If this keeps up, you're going to need it."

Mary pushed the bottle back. "I'm fine, really."

"Me too," Crunchy said.

Kid Rags poured another dollop of whiskey into his glass. "Good. More for me."

"Butcher Boy's real name was Samuel Bornstein," Teach said. "The story goes that one night the sound of someone moving around the house awoke his father. He went to check it out and found three-year-old Samuel standing over his brother David, a knife in his hands. His father took the knife away from little Samuel and asked, 'Why?' 'I hate David,' Samuel said. He seldom spoke after that. He rebuffed companionship, finding ways to live within himself. He sought dark places—cellars, closets. He liked the dark. Supposedly still does.

"After Samuel's father died, his mother married a butcher—a kosher butcher, actually—who hated him. On his seventeenth birthday, Samuel told his mother and stepfather he was leaving home. They said, 'We'll get the door for you.' When they found out he had become a hit man for the Cleveland Syndicate, they sat Shiva for him as if he had died and not his victims."

"Jeez," Mary said.

Teach nodded. "A fine specimen of humanity. I heard that he once said, 'I love all of God's creatures, but I love killing them more.'"

"Isn't he the one who killed Carmine the Snake?" Kid Rags asked.

"So they say." Teach turned to Mary. "Calling Carmine a snake is an insult—to snakes. By all accounts, Carmine

Rastelli was a crude and vicious creature who considered himself God's gift to women. He raped the wife of a connected guy, and when the guy caught him with his pants down, Carmine the Snake killed both the guy and the wife. That happened forty years ago. Iron Sam has been credited with the hit on Rastelli.

"A lot of killers begin to lose their taste for killing after a while, but Iron Sam never did. The Syndicate managed to keep him out of prison for a long time, but when he got caught after doing a contract hit for a Detroit automaker, they washed their hands of him. He's spent the last thirty years in Leavenworth."

"You sure know a lot of reprehensible people," Mary said.

Teach held up his palms. "I don't know them. I know of them. Big difference."

Mary rose. "It's getting late. We've used enough of your time."

Teach stood and bowed over her hand. "The pleasure was all mine." As they walked to the front door, he asked, "Where are you off to next?"

Mary gave a little laugh. "Home. I've had about all the adventure I can stand for a while."

"Aren't you planning on going to Prescott to see your cousin Robert before you leave Arizona? He grew up with your grandfather. I'm sure he'd be willing to talk to you about him."

Mary's eyes lit up. "I have a cousin?"

All the way from Tombstone to Phoenix, Teach and Kid Rags bickered good-naturedly about how Mary and Robert Stuart were related.

"Robert's father and James's father were cousins, so that makes Robert and James first cousins once removed."

"No. Second cousins."

"So what does that make Mary's father and Robert? First cousins twice removed? Third cousins? Second cousins once removed?"

"I have no idea. All I know is that Mary and Robert are cousins."

"How do you figure?"

"According to the dictionary, a cousin can be a relative descended from one's grandfather or from a more remote ancestor in a different line."

"I don't think they're related. The connection is too far back."

"If you go back twenty generations, everyone is related to everyone else."

"See? Proves my point . . ."

Their voices lulled Mary, almost putting her to sleep. Wanting to get to Tombstone as quickly as possible, she'd driven late into the night yesterday, and hadn't gotten nearly enough sleep. She glanced behind her and was pleased to see Crunchy dozing. She shied away from thinking about how he spent the night keeping watch outside her room, and instead thought about the upcoming meeting with her unknown relative.

What should she call him? Uncle? Cousin? Robert? Well, she had Teach along to make the introductions, even though Teach said he couldn't count on Robert remembering him since they'd met only once or twice.

"Are we there yet?" Kid Rags asked. "I'm hungry."

Crunchy's eyes opened. "Me too."

"The next exit is six miles," Teach said.

When Mary got out of her air-conditioned car at the truck stop, the heat slapped her in the face, but the others didn't seem to notice the scorching temperature.

Teach offered to pump the gas for her. When she declined, he followed Kid Rags into the convenience store. Crunchy, as usual, stood guard while she filled her tank. Going inside to pay, she found Teach heating sandwiches in the microwave and Kid Rags piling bag after bag of snacks on the counter along with a six-pack of beer.

"They don't carry bourbon," he said, as if that explained the heap of food.

Mary added fruit and bottles of water to the provisions, then handed over her credit card.

For a long time afterward, the only sounds in the car were the rattling of bags, the popping of beer tabs, an occasional belch. Mary noticed that while Kid Rags and Crunchy gobbled everything in sight, Teach ate sparingly, though he did drink his share of the beer.

After choking down half of a mystery meat sandwich, Mary passed the second half to Kid Rags who swallowed it practically whole.

They reached Prescott in the late afternoon.

"Wow," Mary said, gazing at Robert's residence. The house was all glass, flagstone, and rough-hewn timbers, set in a garden that looked vaguely Japanese though it featured exotic cactuses rather than Bonsai trees.

Kid Rags let out a long, low whistle. "I'll bet this set him back a pretty penny."

"He can afford it," Teach said. "His wife's father owned a chain of department stores in northern Wisconsin, which she inherited. She sold them for a fortune shortly before the national discounters moved in and put them out of business. The new owners took her to court, thinking they had been cheated, but nothing came of their lawsuit."

They all got out of the car and headed for the house. Catching a glimpse of yellow, Mary drew in a sharp breath.

Crunchy moved closer to her.

"What?" Kid Rags asked.

Maybe nothing, she wanted to say, but the words stuck in her throat. Feeling sick to her stomach, she took a few more strides forward, then stood staring at the broad yellow tape lying crumpled across the porch steps.

CRIME SCENE, the plastic strip said. *DO NOT CROSS.*

"What do you want?" a voice demanded from behind a bush in the yard next door.

"I'm here to see Robert Stuart," Mary said.

"Who are you?"

"I'm his . . . he's my . . . he's my cousin."

"Oh." A man of indeterminate years, carrying a baseball bat, stepped away from the bush.

A querulous female voice came from inside the man's house. "Who is it?"

"Some relatives of the Stuarts, Mom."

"Well, you be careful, Sonny."

"Yes, Mom."

The man crossed his yard, still clutching the baseball bat. "We're all on edge after what happened to the Stuarts."

"What did happen?" Teach asked.

The man gestured to the house. "Someone broke in, trashed the place, and shot Robert Stuart and his wife dead."

"Is anyone in custody?" Teach asked.

The man hefted his bat. "The cops don't have a clue. What are we paying them for if they can't keep us safe in our own homes?"

Mary listened to this exchange as if from a long way off. Robert and James and their wives all killed?

The daylight seemed to dim. She thought a cloud had drifted in front of the sun, but when she glanced upward, she saw clear skies. Wishing she had thought to bring a coat, she wrapped her arms around herself, but she couldn't stop shivering.

Crunchy took off his sweater and draped it over her shoulders. She tried to smile at him, but only managed a slight baring of her chattering teeth. He led her to the car. Once seated inside, she folded her arms on the steering wheel, rested her forehead on them, and forced herself to breathe evenly.

A few minutes later, Teach and Kid Rags returned to the car.

"He doesn't know anything," Teach said.

Mary remained motionless for a while longer, then she raised her head. "I didn't tell you, but my grandparents were also shot by people who broke into their house and ransacked it. A senseless act of violence, supposedly, but I don't believe it."

"Neither do I," Teach said. "It's too much of a coincidence."

"What are you going to do?" Kid Rags asked.

"I don't know," Mary answered, and that ended the conversation until they returned to Tombstone.

"I'm going to talk to Samuel Bornstein," she said, pulling in front of Teach's apartment house. "Maybe he would know why someone wanted to kill them."

"Not a good idea," Teach said.

Kid Rags let out laugh. "That's the wrong thing to say. It will make her more determined."

"Maybe it's not a good idea," Mary said. "Maybe he won't talk to me. Maybe he doesn't know anything. But I have to try."

"See?" Kid Rags said. "What did I tell you?"

"Then I'm coming too," Teach said.

Mary shrugged. "Fine. You can all come if you want. But with you or without you, I'm going to Leavenworth."

Chapter 5

Mary brushed her teeth, splashed water on her face, then slipped out of her filthy clothes. She collapsed on her own bed, and soon fell asleep.

The sound of a knock penetrated her dream. She jerked herself awake and stared around her sunlit bedroom. Morning already? It felt as if she'd fallen asleep moments ago.

Yawning, she struggled out of bed, put on her robe, and went to answer the door.

"Dad? What are you doing here?" She wiped her suddenly clammy hands on her robe. "Is everything okay? Nothing's happened to Mom, has it?"

He curled his lips into a smile, but his eyes remained serious. "Do I need a reason to visit my only offspring?"

"No, but you've never come to see me before."

"Then it's high time I did. May I come in?"

"Yes. Sure." Cheeks growing warm, she stepped aside to let him enter.

As he looked around her living room, she was acutely aware that it needed a cleaning, though he seemed not to notice. He nodded toward her brown over-stuffed armchair.

"So that's where it went. I wondered what happened to my favorite chair."

"Mom gave it to me." Then, frowning uncertainly, "Do you want it back?"

"No. Your mother hates that chair, always wanted to get rid of it. I'm glad it's still in the family." He slumped in the chair and, closing his eyes, let out a long sigh. After a moment he opened his eyes and gave her a piercing stare.

Heart thudding, she hung her head. Reminding herself she was a grown woman, not a disobedient child about to be punished, she forced herself to meet his gaze.

"Your mother's worried about you," he said. "You haven't been answering your phone."

Mary stole a look at the blinking light on her answering machine and remembered she hadn't bothered to check her messages when she got home last night.

"I went out of town."

He raised his eyebrows. "I thought you didn't have to work this week."

"I don't."

He studied her in silence for a moment, and all at once she understood that he didn't know how to speak to her. When had they grown so far apart? She remembered the long walks they took together when she was a child, the bear hugs she gave him when he came to tuck her in at night.

A sharp pain lodged beneath her sternum. The years passed so quickly. She noticed, for the first time, her father's receding hairline, the deep crinkles at the corners of his brown eyes. Soon he would be as old as Kid Rags, Teach, and Crunchy.

Tears stung her eyes at the thought of her father living alone in a dingy hovel, and she vowed she would not let that happen.

Realizing the silence was stretching out awkwardly, she opened her mouth to speak, but he held up a palm to forestall her.

"I don't want to know what you're doing," he said. "Whatever it is, I know it's something you feel you have to do. I thought you should be aware you're upsetting your mother."

"I don't mean to."

He heaved himself out of the chair. "That's all I came to say."

"I'm glad you stopped by," she said. "I planned on calling you later anyway to tell you I'm going to be away for a few days."

He stared at her for a moment, then shrugged. "I don't understand what you're trying to accomplish, but I suppose you know your own mind."

You are so wrong. I don't know anything.

He walked to the door, paused with his hand on the knob

for a second, then turned to face her.

"I love you," he said softly.

She swallowed. "Oh, Dad. I love you too."

He opened the door. "Be careful, okay, honey? You don't know what you're getting yourself into."

After her father left, Mary took a long shower to wash off the grime of her travels. Blow-drying her chin-length honey blond hair, she was pleased to see that it, at least, hadn't gone limp with exhaustion.

She and the rest of the crew had left Tombstone yesterday before any trace of dawn touched the sky, and they drove straight through to Denver, stopping only for food, gas, and a short detour in Pueblo so Crunchy could pack his battered old suitcase. She'd settled Crunchy and Teach in a motel in west Denver, then dropped Kid Rags off at his place. She planned to pick them up at noon to give everyone plenty of time to rest, but she hadn't been able to sleep as late as she wanted.

Well, one good thing about having no deadline—she could stop as soon as she got too tired to drive.

She packed two suitcases and sat at the kitchen table to eat a bowl of cold cereal. A knock on the door startled her. She dropped her spoon and went to answer it.

Bill greeted her with a kiss, then leaned back and peered into her face. "Are you feeling all right? You look tired."

She tried to smile. "I am tired."

"Me too. Do you have any coffee? I could use a cup."

"I didn't know you were coming, so I didn't make any. I've got instant."

He winced. "I'll get a cup on my way to work. I stopped by to make sure you're all right. You didn't return any of my calls."

"I wasn't home."

He shook his head. "You're the only person I know who doesn't own a cell phone."

"Yeah, well, I'm not interested in getting brain cancer."

she said, wondering how many times they'd had this same conversation. Not wanting to hear his standard response about that being an urban legend, she added quickly, "I'm about to eat breakfast. Why don't you come keep me company?"

He looked at his watch. "I think I have time."

In the kitchen, he poured himself a glass of orange juice, then sat opposite her. "So, what have you been doing with yourself lately? You haven't gone back to that old house alone, have you?"

Mary pointed to her mouth. When she finished chewing and swallowing, she said, "I went to see some people who knew my grandparents."

Bill gave her a long look. "I don't understand you. You know it's upsetting your parents, yet you're persisting in this quixotic quest."

"Someone killed my grandparents before I got a chance to know them. For once in my life I'm going to do what I want to do—no, what I have to do—without worrying about upsetting other people."

He finished his orange juice, rinsed the glass, then leaned against the counter. "I understand you think this is something you have to do, I just don't understand why you feel that way. It seems to me you're complicating your life unnecessarily when everything is falling into place."

"Maybe I don't want everything to fall into place," Mary said quietly. "For you, A plus B always equals C. What if it sometimes equals D or E or F?"

Bill didn't say anything, but while she finished her cereal, she could feel his gaze resting on her. When she got up to rinse out her bowl, he looked at his watch again.

"I have to be going. How about dinner tonight?"

"I'm sorry. I can't."

Just then, another knock sounded on the door. Glad of the interruption, she went to answer it.

An old man stood there grinning at her. He had a long, sharp-featured face, the kind that looks old when the person is young, and ages slowly so the person looks young when old. He was clean-shaven. Not having seen him without his whiskers, it took Mary a moment to recognize Teach.

"We've come to pick you up," he said.

Mary stared at him. "How did you get here?"

"Happy drove us."

"Happy? Who's Happy?" She grabbed her purse off the table by the door. "Never mind. I'll go see for myself."

"Who is this guy?" Bill asked.

"His name is Teach. He knew my grandparents. Teach, this is Bill Spindler, my fiancé."

The two men eyed each other, but Mary didn't stick around to find out if they shook hands. She ran down the stairs and dashed outside, then stopped short. A small gray bus was parked haphazardly, one wheel on the curb, the back end sticking out into traffic. Crunchy, arms folded across his chest, leaned against the bus. Kid Rags stood next to him, adjusting his red bow tie. Both watched a short, skinny old man who brandished his small fists and bounced around like a bantamweight prizefighter. Effie Werner, an elderly woman who lived in Mary's apartment building, backed away from him, clutching her hissing cat.

"You calling me a liar?" the skinny man said in a high, excited voice.

"Deny it all you want," Effie said, tears in her eyes, "but I saw you almost run over my precious baby."

"You insinuating I'm a bad driver?"

"Insinuating nothing. I'm coming right out and saying it. You're a terrible driver. What's more, you're a menace to society."

Head held high, Effie bore her pet into the building.

The man stopped bouncing and let his arms drop to his sides. Now that he stood relatively still, Mary could see he was skinnier than she'd first thought. A gray slouch hat tilted toward one eye, but the baggy pants cinched high above his waist and the bright flowery shirt several sizes too large marred the jaunty effect. His hands shook uncontrollably. Parkinson's disease?

"You must be Happy," she said.

Frowning, Happy patted his torso. "Must I be happy?" His voice deepened to what Mary assumed was his normal tone. "Can I be happy? Can anyone truly be happy?"

"His name is Barry Hapworth," Kid Rags said, flicking a bit of lint off his navy pinstriped suit jacket. "For several obvious reasons, everyone calls him Happy."

Mary glanced from the bus to Happy. "Were you driving this thing?"

Happy puffed out his meager chest. "Sure was."

"And did you almost run over Mrs. Werner's cat?"

"I'll take the fifth." Happy paused for a fraction of a second. "A fifth of bourbon."

"Did someone say bourbon?" Kid Rags removed the flask from his hip pocket, took a swig, and passed it around.

"Who are all these people?" Bill asked from behind Mary.

Mary turned, wondering how she could explain the situation, but Teach saved her the trouble and made the introductions. Arms still folded across his chest, Crunchy nodded to Bill, then stepped close to Mary. Happy punched the air, but stopped when Bill showed no inclination to fight.

Kid Rags shook Bill's hand. "You're a lucky man."

"What are you all doing here?" Mary asked. "I was supposed to pick you up. And why is Happy here?"

"Happy is a friend of Kid Rags," Teach began, but Kid Rags interrupted him, saying hastily, "Not a friend. Just a fellow I know."

"Happy knows someone who knows Iron Sam," Teach continued, "and since we knew your car wasn't big enough for all of us, we accepted Happy's offer to drive us in his bus."

"Who's Iron Sam?" Bill asked, sounding plaintive.

"Butcher Boy," Kid Rags said.

Bill's eyebrows drew together. "Butcher Boy? Mary, are you sure you know what you're doing?"

Mary laughed, suddenly feeling lighthearted and carefree. "I haven't a clue."

Bill blew out his breath. "I don't understand what's

gotten into you."

Crunchy stepped in front of Mary. "He bothering you, Lady?"

"No, Crunchy, he's worried about me." She giggled. "As you can see, Bill, you have nothing to be concerned about. Crunchy will take care of me."

Crunchy raised a fist in the air and brought it straight down like a pile driver. "I crunch anyone who bothers her."

Bill looked anything but reassured.

Happy bounced on the balls of his feet. "Hey, we going or what?"

"Do you have a license?" Mary asked, looking for an excuse to keep Happy from driving.

"No. Why?"

"I can drive," Kid Rags said.

Mary turned to him. "Do you have a license?"

Kid Rags smiled. "Sure do. Looks like the real thing, too. Want to see it?"

Rolling her eyes, Mary shook her head.

"I could use a license," Teach said.

"Me too," Crunchy chimed in.

"I'll see what I can do," Kid Rags said. "You want one, Happy?"

"No. Been driving all my life without one. Don't see any point in getting one now."

Mary put her hands on her hips. "Well, that settles it. I'm driving. I'll be right back. I need to get my things."

Trailed by Crunchy and Bill, Mary hurried back upstairs to her apartment. There was a small scuffle when both men grabbed her suitcases, but she gave one to each of them to carry.

Eyeing the luggage, Bill asked, "How long are you going to be gone?"

Mary shrugged. "I don't know. As long as it takes."

After stowing the baggage behind the last seat, Bill gave Mary a quick, self-conscious peck on the cheek, and said, "Take care of yourself."

"I will."

Bill hovered nearby while Happy told Mary how to operate the bus, then he climbed down and stood on the curb. As she drove away, she could see him still standing there, shaking his head.

Chapter 6

"So where are we going?" Mary asked.

"York, Nebraska," Teach said. "It's a small town about fifty miles this side of Lincoln. Take I-twenty-five to seventy-six, which will merge into eighty on the other side of the Colorado border, then keep going until you see the turnoff for York."

It took all of Mary's concentration to maneuver the bus through Denver's traffic. Though the vehicle looked small from the outside, from the inside it seemed huge. Behind the driver's seat were four rows of double seats divided by a wide central aisle. The ceiling rose high enough so they could stand upright and walk around, which Happy did with some frequency, trying out first one seat and then another. Crunchy, as usual, sat behind Mary. Teach sat across the aisle from him, and Kid Rags dozed on one of the back seats.

When they were on the highway, well away from the city and its congested streets, Mary asked, "Who are we going to see?"

"Wallace Brown, AKA the Scourge," Teach said. "Happy thinks he might be able to get us in to see Iron Sam."

"The Scourge? Sounds spooky."

"By all accounts he was. Like Iron Sam, he worked for the Cleveland Syndicate. He was the liaison between the bosses and the hit men. The bosses kept as many people as possible between them and the muscle. The government called them cutouts, the Syndicate called it insulation, but it amounts to the same thing."

Thinking of Bill's favorite TV show, Mary said, "But in *The Sopranos* . . ."

Teach snorted. "The Sopranos were low level punks. The bosses *never* got their hands dirty. Nor did their lieutenants. I don't know if you're old enough to remember how when the Teflon Don, John Gotti, got arrested, they made him out to be a major crime boss but, like the Sopranos, he was a low-level punk. The Syndicate did not admire men who stuck out their own necks when there were plenty of others willing to do it for chickenfeed. To get ahead, men had to show proof of brains and the ability to delegate violence. Nowadays the bosses don't meet in the back of bars and barbershops. They meet in boardrooms. They run Fortune Five Hundred Companies. They control billions of dollars."

"So what's the difference between them and any other major corporation?"

Teach chuckled. "By gum, you're as smart as your granddaddy. To answer your question, there isn't any difference. The big corporations indulge in the same sort of criminal behavior the Syndicate does, and the Syndicate operates their businesses like all the other corporations do. A perfect example of the Hegelian dialectic—thesis plus antithesis bringing about synthesis."

Mary laughed. "Yeah, right." After switching lanes to avoid ramming into a tractor entering the highway, she said, "So this Scourge was a big deal in the Syndicate?"

"Definitely. Whenever you saw the Scourge, you knew something bad would happen. He was the voice of the bosses."

"The voice of doom," Happy intoned from the seat behind Teach.

"Then how come he ended up in a place like York, Nebraska?"

"He was on the lam." Happy moved to another seat. "He planned to stay at a safe house run by Jimmy Boots when he—"

"Jimmy Boots?" Crunchy asked. "We going to see Jimmy Boots?"

"Jimmy Boots passed away," Teach said. "I thought you knew."

"No." After a beat Crunchy added, "He was my friend. He treated me good."

"Everyone dies," Happy pointed out. "Life is something you suffer through on your way to death."

Not knowing how to respond, Mary let several seconds

tick by before she asked, "Safe house? Like the witness protection program?"

"A lot like that," Teach said, "but it had nothing to do with the government. These safe houses strung from coast to coast, many in places you wouldn't connect with the mob, like Sun Valley where the California boys took refuge and Saratoga where a spa offered accommodations for large groups. They were usually run by people on the periphery of the underworld, such as friends, relatives, small time gangsters who were clean—guys with no criminal records, no warrants. It was a touchy situation for the lamster. To keep the safe house operator loyal, he had to pay more than the law would because usually the operator worked both ways."

"Jimmy Boots didn't," Crunchy said. "When a scab got hurt bad in Pueblo, Jimmy Boots let me stay with him until the cops got paid off, and he didn't tell nobody even though I didn't have no money."

"That's right," Teach said. "He didn't inform on anyone, and he wasn't a cheap hustler who demanded huge payments."

"About the Scourge," Mary prompted. "You said he planned to stay at the safe house. What happened?"

Happy moved back to the seat behind Teach. "He stopped off at York to have a drink, met a dame, and moved in with her. Never left, not even when he got the all clear."

"After Iron Sam was arrested," Teach explained, "the Syndicate feared he'd give up his contact, and since they couldn't take a chance on the Scourge being compromised, they sent him out of town. Iron Sam didn't utter a word, though. The way I heard it, the cops tried everything they knew. They coaxed, cajoled, threatened, used whatever physical violence they could get away with. Through hours of grilling, he remained poised, completely contained, with no show of emotion. He always acted polite, but not once did he so much as admit he knew what day it was. He knew enough not to parry with a questioner. The guys who do are easy prey for the investigator, because a reply, no matter how obtuse or offhand leads to another question. Iron Sam said nothing at all. He just sat there, hour after hour, day after day, for fifteen months, looking at them in deadpan silence when they asked him a question."

"Jeez," Mary muttered, wondering what she was letting herself in for.

She passed a rusty pickup, then glanced back at Teach. "Yesterday you said Iron Sam had been hired by a Detroit automaker, but if he never broke, how did anyone find out?"

"A newspaper reporter who thought it strange that a hit man would kill a little guy in glasses—a nobody—investigated and managed to piece the whole story together. They published the article in one edition of one paper before it got quashed. It turns out the little guy in glasses had invented a new automobile, one that runs on free energy. He believed the earth acted like a giant dynamo generating and storing electricity, and he found a way to tap into that energy.

"Over the years there have been many such inventors, but the industrialists managed to get their hands on the patents and bury them. There is no way anyone is ever going to be allowed to manufacture a car that costs substantially less than the market will bear, particularly one that needs no fuel whatsoever.

"The little guy in glasses refused to give in to intimidation, and even though the bankers wouldn't have anything to do with him, he managed to find several private investors. Before he could begin manufacturing his vehicles, he was killed."

"I've heard of stories like that before," Mary said, "but I didn't know if they were true."

"It happens more often than most people realize. The Syndicate made a lot of money by hiring out hit men to so-called legitimate businesses that wanted their competition to disappear. There were some branches, though, like the Brooklyn branch, that kept their services strictly for the use of the Syndicate. They were paid a flat yearly salary rather than per job. Murder by retainer, so to speak."

"I'm hungry," Kid Rags announced from the back of the bus.

"Me too," Crunchy and Happy both said.

"I could eat a bite," Teach drawled.

Mary turned off at the next exit where they could get food and gas. She filled the tank, then drove to one of the ubiquitous fast food restaurants. Herding her charges toward the building, she realized Happy was missing. Turning back, she saw him clambering from the bus, his now untucked shirt billowing in the breeze. One of his pant legs rippled, and she heard a muffled *thunk*.

Happy grabbed his right foot and hopped around on his left, howling. "My toe! I broke my toe!"

"Well, no wonder," Kid Rags said, scooping up a metallic object. "I thought I told you to leave the piece behind."

Mary held out a hand. "Let me see." She sucked in her breath when Kid Rags carefully laid a small gun on her palm. "What the heck is this?"

"A gun," Kid Rags said.

Teach leaned over to look at it. "It's an Astra Cadix thirty-eight special snub nose revolver with a two inch barrel and a five-shot cylinder, to be exact. Made in Spain."

Happy let go of the foot he had been holding. "It's my gun. Give it to me."

"No." Mary shuddered to think of a gun in the possession of someone whose hands shook so much he couldn't tie his shoelaces properly.

"What are you going to do with it?" Kid Rags asked.

Mary stared at the weapon. "I don't know. Throw it away."

Happy rushed at Mary, but Crunchy caught hold of his shirt and yanked him back.

Happy curled his hands into fists and waved them around. "You can't throw it away. It's mine."

Teach stroked his chin. "It's of good quality and workmanship. It would be a shame to throw it away, Mary, particularly since it's clean."

Brow creased, Mary glanced at him. "What do you

mean?"

"It's untraceable." He pointed to a gouge on the side of the gun. "See this? Someone who knew what he was doing removed the serial number. Most people think you can file it off, but the metal beneath the numbers is compressed when the numerals are stamped in, and an application of an acid will bring it out."

"Then it's illegal? All the more reason to throw it out."

"Someone might find it and use it."

Mary sighed. "Maybe you're right." She tucked the gun into her shoulder bag. The strap strained with the extra weight.

"Give it to me! I need it." Happy tried to lunge for her purse, but Crunchy still had hold of his shirt.

"I'll give it to you when we return to Denver but until then it remains in my purse."

Happy's shoulders sagged.

Seeing something akin to panic in his eyes, Mary felt sorry for him. "Tell you what. If you ever need it, if you're ever in danger, I'll give it back to you, okay?"

Happy nodded, but he would not look at her.

"Now can we go eat?" Kid Rags asked.

A dark-haired girl was half-heartedly filling a napkin dispenser when they approached the counter. She turned toward them, eyes blank, as if she were looking right through them.

"Can I help you?" she asked in a bored monotone.

As Kid Rags began to order, the door opened. The rank odor of perspiration and unwashed socks preceded a group of teenage boys into the restaurant. One boy carried a basketball under his arm. All wore low-slung baggy shorts and torn tee shirts with sweat stains beneath their armpits. They jostled each other and made rude remarks punctuated by overloud laughter.

Kid Rags raised his voice. "Four cheeseburgers, two orders of fries, two apple pies, and a large Coke."

The girl set about filling the order. Returning to the counter, she wiped her forehead with the back of her hand as if she had finished a monumental task. "Anything else?" she asked with a casual glance that took in Mary and the old men.

Crunchy stepped forward and pointed at Kid Rags. "I want what he got."

The girl's plucked eyebrows drew together as she looked from Crunchy to Kid Rags and back to Crunchy again. After a moment, she shrugged, went to get the food, then dropped it on the counter. "Is that all?"

"I'd like a chicken sandwich and a glass of water," Mary said.

"What about you?" the girl asked, directing her question at Happy.

Happy gazed at the lighted menu.

The girl tapped her long, elaborately decorated fingernails against the side of the cash register.

"Come on, Gramps," one of the boys called out. "We don't have all day."

"Ignore them," Mary whispered to Happy. "Take all the time you need."

Happy reached into his shirt pocket, pulled out a pair of eyeglasses with thick lenses, and held them in front of his eyes.

"Are those glasses or Coke bottles?" the same boy jeered.

"This is a fast food restaurant," another said. "Fast. Get it?"

Happy tucked his glasses back in his pocket. "I don't know if I want a cheeseburger or chicken nuggets."

"Get both," Kid Rags said. "I'll eat what you don't finish."

"He must have a tapeworm," the first boy said to his buddies, who laughed and muttered a few comments Mary couldn't hear.

"Okay, then," Happy told the counter girl. "I'll have a cheeseburger, chicken nuggets, apple pie, and a large Coke."

"It's about time, Gramps."

While Teach gave his order—a chicken sandwich and a small Coke—Happy turned around to face the boys.

"What are you looking at?" snarled the boy with the basketball.

Crunchy moved away from the counter and, folding his arms across his chest, positioned himself to protect Mary.

"I'm trembling all over," the boy said.

Happy clenched his hands into fists. "Didn't anyone ever teach you to be respectful of your elders?"

The boy furrowed his brow. "No," he said at last.

All of the teenagers dissolved into giggles.

Happy bounced on the balls of his feet and jabbed the air with his fists. "Then it's time someone did."

The boy with the basketball shivered theatrically. "Oooh. I'm really scared now."

Happy stopped bouncing, and thrust a hand toward Mary. "Give me my gun. I need to shoot these punks."

"No one is going to shoot anyone," Mary said.

"But you promised—"

A young man wearing a nametag that stated MANAGER hurried toward them.

"No guns allowed," he said breathlessly, interrupting Happy. "I'll have to ask you to leave."

Mary widened her eyes. "Guns? What guns?"

The manager scratched his head. "I heard him say . . ."

Mary looked at each of the old men in turn. "Do any of you have guns?"

"No," chorused Kid Rags, Crunchy, and Teach.

Happy frowned. "But—"

Kid Rags kicked him on the ankle.

"Oh, right," Happy said. "No guns."

Mary showed her palms. "See?"

Tightening his lips, the manager stood by while the girl rang up the sale and accepted Mary's money.

Teach and Kid Rags grabbed the bags of food. As Crunchy escorted her outside, Mary could hear the boys laughing, cheering, and slapping palms.

Teach and Kid Rags exchanged glances and small smiles. "What?" she asked.

Teach grinned at her. "You did that nicely, deflecting the manager's attention to us. You have the makings of a good con man."

"Con person," Kid Rags said.

"Thanks, I think. I didn't plan it. I blurted out the first thing that came into my head. I'm not good at acting, but I had to do something to protect Happy."

"Why did you have to protect Happy?" Kid Rags asked. "You're the one carrying the concealed weapon."

Mary's stomach lurched. Imagining the sound of prison doors slamming shut behind her, she hugged herself around the middle, bent forward, and tried to breathe.

"You don't look so good, Lady," Crunchy said. "You okay?"

No, I'm not okay. I'm going to be spending the rest of my life in prison. Will my parents come visit me? Will Bill? An involuntary moan escaped her lips. Maybe she should return to Denver, buy Teach a bus ticket to Arizona, and forget the whole thing.

Unbidden, the image of her grandparents' ransacked house rose in her mind. If she quit now, she'd never know what kind of people her grandparents were, never know what they had done to inspire such violence, never know why her father had disowned them.

She straightened her shoulders, took a deep breath, and said, "I'm fine. Really, I am."

Chapter 7

"Was Jimmy Boots my grandfather?" Mary asked.

She and the old men were eating pizza in a restaurant in Kearney, Nebraska after checking into a nearby motel. Three rooms! Good thing she had thought to bring the cash from the secret room as well as her credit cards.

Teach looked up from his plate. "What makes you ask that?"

"Something you said this morning."

"Me?" Teach poked himself in the chest. "Something *I* said?"

"Yes. When Crunchy asked if we were going to see Jimmy Boots, you said he passed away. Then you added, 'I thought you knew.'"

"So?"

"Well, you just met Crunchy, right? How would you know what he knew if we hadn't talked about Jimmy Boots, and the only two men we talked about who passed away are my grandfather and his cousin Robert."

Kid Rags laughed. "I think she's got you, Teach."

Teach shook his head. "I can't believe I made such an amateurish mistake."

"Why did you lie to me? Everyone's lied about my grandparents my whole life, and I'm sick of it."

Crunchy edged away from her, and for the first time his eyes didn't sparkle when he looked at her. "I didn't lie. I don't know no James Agnes Stuart. You never asked me about Jimmy Boots."

"I didn't lie either." Kid Rags sounded as unfriendly as when Mary first met him. "I just didn't tell you the whole truth. We didn't come from nice suburban neighborhoods where things are relatively safe. For our own protection, we had to learn not to talk about ourselves or anyone else."

Mary frowned. "But you told me about Crunchy."

"Nothing that wasn't public record."

"The lives we lead necessitate secrecy," Teach said. "People today don't respect other people's privacy—where they came from, what they did. You young people have grown up with the Internet where everyone's life is out there for anyone to delve into, but that's not our way."

Crunchy nodded. "Don't tell nothing to nobody."

"Jimmy Boots was your grandfather?" Happy asked. "I didn't know."

Mary toyed with her pizza. "I still don't understand why you couldn't have told me about my grandfather."

"We didn't know you," Teach said.

"You were nothing to us," Kid Rags added. "We didn't owe you anything."

Mary recoiled as if she'd been slapped. Looking at each of the men in turn and seeing the reserve in their eyes, she realized they still weren't comfortable with her. Well, to be honest, she didn't feel comfortable with them, either, but she needed their help if she were ever to discover the truth about her grandparents.

She took a bite of pizza more for something to do than because she wanted it. After she washed it down with a sip of water, she took a deep breath. "Was my grandfather Mafia?"

"No," Teach answered. "There is no Mafia in this country."

Mary stared at him, speechless. "Of course there is," she said at last.

Teach poured himself another beer from the pitcher in the center of the table, then leaned back. "The Mafia began in 1282 when the Sicilians rose up against their French rulers. Supposedly, the motto of that rebellion was *Morte alla Francia Italia anela,* which means 'Death to the French is Italy's cry.' Afterward, the rebels formed a secret organization to protect poor Sicilians. It took its name from the first letter of that motto, hence MAFIA."

Kid Rags took out his flask and spiked his beer. "Sure you don't want any, Mary? This is the only way to survive when Teach gets on his soapbox."

"I'm fine."

"Sometime during the nineteenth century," Teach said, "The Mafia reversed their goals and hired themselves out to rich landowners who needed help with keeping the peasants in line. Eventually the Mafia extorted money and goods directly from the peasants. The Mafioso came to this country with the first wave of Italian immigration at the end of the 1800s. By 1910, Mafia gangs were in most major U.S. cities. This was the true Mafia—a closed corporation of pure Sicilians demanding the blood brother initiation and the dread code of *Omerta*. They waged bloody battles against one another and preyed mostly on their own kind as all criminals did in the beginning. Italians preyed on Italians, Jews preyed on Jews, blacks preyed on blacks.

"This continued until September 1931 when, in a single night, a syndicate of Jewish-Americans and Italian-Americans executed more than forty of the old-world 'Mustache Petes' all across the United States. The murders of these Mafia leaders were carried out in such a way they were never linked. That ended the Mafia—the clannish, Sicilian Mafia—as a major force in this country."

"You're wrong," Kid Rags said. "They didn't do it all in one night, and it didn't end the Mafia. There are still gangs of Sicilians in parts of the country."

"But they are only localized groups like the fictional Sopranos. The Syndicate had national power and, unlike the Mafia, they let other ethnic groups into their ranks. The idea of the Syndicate being strictly Italian is pure Hollywood tripe. Some branches, like the Cleveland Syndicate, were primarily run by Jews."

"I thought the Syndicate and the Mafia were the same thing," Mary said.

"No. It went by many names—the Syndicate, the Outfit, the Mob, the Arm, the Combination, the Office—but it was not the Mafia. It was a cartel, a confederation of independent business concerns working toward a common goal—profits. A board of all the regional bosses made the decisions.

"In the beginning, a gang's effective control was limited

to the neighborhood. When telephone and automobiles became prevalent, they expanded their control and dictated to city political bosses. Better roads and commercial airlines led to regional operations and ultimately to the national alliance, where they could get into bed with federal government employees, some of whom rose to power along with the Syndicate."

Kid Rags made himself another drink and passed around the flask. When Teach poured a small amount of whiskey into his mug, Kid Rags laughed. "Even you can't take yourself straight, can you?"

"Is there something you'd prefer to talk about?" Teach asked.

Kid Rags spread his hands. "I have nothing to say, but maybe Crunchy or Happy would like to get a word in edgewise."

Happy jerked his head up. "You talking about me?"

"Kid Rags thought you might have something to say," Mary explained.

Happy gave Kid Rags a suspicious look. "Whatever he said, I didn't do it."

Mary felt a giggle well up inside her. She clamped her lips shut to keep it from escaping.

Crunchy peered at her. "You okay, Lady?"

"I'm fine, Crunchy."

Teach took a sip of his drink. "Should I continue?"

Kid Rags let out a theatrical sigh.

Happy shot another suspicious glance at Kid Rags.

Mary and Crunchy nodded for Teach to proceed.

"By the 1950s, with the advent of the jet, a new breed of gangsters had developed. Many of these gangsters were the sons of the bootleggers and had been raised in luxury. Others were recruited from the best business schools. They were multi-lingual, well educated, sophisticated, at home anywhere in the world. They moved into banking and investments. Syndicate money financed some of the biggest mergers and acquisitions in the 1950s and 1960s. They got into manufacturing. They bought all kinds of real estate, including some of the tallest buildings in Manhattan. They built resorts and casinos in places like Las Vegas and the Bahamas. They had a say in the running of a major airline. They created banks. You see, they had so much money—money beyond comprehension—the hard part was trying to figure out what to do with it all. In the end, they got so big and powerful, they disappeared into moneyed society like the robber barons did.

"Take the Kennedy's for example. Joseph, JFK's father, was a bootlegger and a stock swindler, but today that doesn't matter except to add romance to the family history.

"People talk as if the Mafia and the Syndicate are still active today, but the Syndicate phased out the American Mafia, wealth phased out the Syndicate, and now new gangs of all races and nationalities have taken their place."

"You said my grandfather wasn't Mafia, but did he work for the Syndicate?"

"He did minor jobs for them when he was young, but when he ran the safe house, he didn't actually work for them, though most of his 'guests' did."

"Was Lefty Louie one of his guests? Could that be the favor my grandfather did for him?"

"Yes."

"Oh." Mary picked at her now cold pizza and wondered what it had been like for her father growing up in a house frequented by gangsters on the run.

Men like Iron Sam.

As if he read her mind, Teach said, "I still don't understand why James had a picture of Iron Sam. His guests were usually the less violent types."

"Could someone in the Syndicate have killed my grandparents?"

"It's possible, but I doubt it. He really was a stand-up guy who treated his guests well, and besides, it's been many years since he took in any lamsters."

"Were you one of his lamsters?"

Teach gave her a long, considering look.

She felt her cheeks grow hot. "I shouldn't have asked."

"I wasn't a lamster," he said at last. "I met your grandfather when he still lived in Chicago."

"Did you grow up together?"

"No. I was born and raised in Pittsburgh. My father worked as a steelworker, and that's what I thought I'd be. The thing I remember most about my father is that he loved to read travel books. More than anything, he wanted to see exotic places. He planned trip after trip, and saved what money he could, but it seemed as if every time he managed to get enough money together, one of us kids would get sick, or would outgrow our clothes, or the jalopy he drove to work would need repairs. 'That's okay,' he would say, 'I can go after retirement.'"

Teach drew in a deep breath. "He died of a heart attack three weeks before he retired."

"I'm sorry," Mary said.

Teach nodded. "Me too. By then, I was out of high school and working in the steel mills, but the day after we buried him, I quit work and went on the road. I hitched a ride and found myself in a small town in upstate New York. I was broke, but that didn't worry me. I thought I could do odd jobs to get enough for a meal and a bed, but no one wanted to hire a transient. I was wandering around town, hungry and tired, when a cop stopped me and demanded to know who I was and what I was doing. Since I had no money, no job, no identification—at the time I didn't know how to drive so I didn't have a driver's license—he arrested me for vagrancy.

"It shocked me. I didn't know a person could be thrown in jail for not having money or a job. I realized then it made no difference whether I obeyed the law or not, and since I had no intention of doing what my father had done—wasting his life working for a big company—I decided to become a gangster. When they released me, I hitched a ride to Chicago.

"I didn't know you couldn't go to a gangster and apply for work, but I lucked out and happened to meet your grandfather, who was running errands for a local mob boss at the time, and he put in a good word for me.

"It didn't take me long to realize working for the mob was like working for any other big business. The bosses made all the money while the rest of us did all the work and took all the risks. I did manage to get a grubstake together, mostly by pulling the weeping act."

Mary had been so mesmerized by his story that she had a hard time bringing herself back to the present to ask, "What's the weeping act?"

"I'd go into a bar, find a rich-looking patron who'd drunk too much, then burst into tears. In those days, I could turn the tears on and off whenever I wanted to. I'd start blubbering that my wife was dying and my sister was in the hospital, and I didn't know what to do or where to turn for financial assistance.

"Once I got enough money together to leave Chicago, I never pulled the weeping act again. I decided it wasn't right using people's kindness against them, particularly since there were plenty of greedy, conniving individuals out there for the plucking.

"After I left Chicago, I stayed in touch with your grandfather. I was best man at his wedding, but you probably knew that."

Mary shook her head. "I told you, I don't know anything about my grandfather."

"He was a good friend. I don't think he wanted to do the gold mine scam, but he knew I needed the money, so he went along with it. He didn't say anything, but I know he felt relieved when it fell through.

"You see, he had this idea he wanted to make the farm a self-sustaining, legitimate enterprise. Don't ask me why—I never could understand it. It seemed too much like work to me."

Mary laughed at the sour face he made. "What's wrong with work?"

"I don't believe in it."

Her eyes opened wide. "I've never heard anyone say that before."

"Why would you? This country is steeped in the

Protestant work ethic, and it's almost sacrilegious not to believe in work."

Mary glanced at Kid Rags, Happy, and Crunchy, none of whom had uttered a word for a while. All three appeared to be dozing.

Teach laughed. "Looks like I put them to sleep."

Kid Rags' eyelids popped open, and he jerked himself upright. "Sleep? Who's asleep? Not me."

Chapter 8

Mary nibbled on a hangnail and glanced around while she and the old men waited for someone to answer her knock. If the Scourge had socked away a lot of money from his Syndicate days, she couldn't see any indication of it. The unostentatious ranch-style house looked like the others on the outskirts of York, though perhaps a few more acres surrounded it.

"Yes?"

Mary gave a start and turned to face the old woman standing on the other side of the screen door.

"Is the—" Mary stopped. She felt silly asking if the Scourge was home, but for the life of her, she couldn't remember his real name.

Teach stepped forward and touched the brim of his cowboy hat. "Good morning, Ma'am. Is Wallace Brown at home? We'd like to have a word with him."

The woman laid a liver-spotted hand on her chest. "What do you want with my husband?"

"Who ith it, my love?" A rotund little old man wearing plaid Bermuda shorts and a pink polo shirt appeared at the door beside the woman.

"Hello, Wallace," Happy said.

Mary bit back a giggle. This was the Scourge? This gnome of a man with twinkling eyes and a lisp?

Wallace peered through the screen at Happy. "Do I know you?"

"Don't you remember? We used to work for the same outfit."

The woman's face lit up. "Oh, how nice. Won't you come in?"

She made a move to open the door, but Wallace put out a hand to stop her.

"That won't be necessary. These folks are leaving."

"Hey!" Happy protested. "What's the big deal? All we

want is some information about Butcher Boy."

"The supermarket in town has a nice butcher," the old woman said, "but you can't call him a boy. He has to be forty."

Wallace patted the woman's arm. "Let me handle this, sweetie." He opened the door, slipped through, and closed it behind him. Motioning for Mary and her gang to follow, he headed toward the road.

"This your bus?" he asked.

"Yes." Happy frowned. "You don't remember me?"

"Of course I remember you."

Wallace climbed aboard the bus; the others trooped in behind him.

"My wife doesn't know about my work with the Syndicate," Wallace said, "and I want to keep it that way."

"What did you tell her you used to do?" Teach asked.

"I told her law enforcement, just neglected to mention whose law." He tilted his head to one side and studied Teach. "I don't believe I've met you."

Happy made the necessary introductions, then said, "We need to talk to Butcher Boy. We were hoping you could help us get in to see him."

"I doubt he'd talk to you. I understand he hasn't spoken much since being sent to prison. Didn't talk much before that, either."

"We'd appreciate any help you can give us," Mary said.

"Why is it so important to speak to him after all these years?"

Mary explained about her grandparents' murders and about how she'd found a picture of Iron Sam among their effects.

Wallace raised his eyebrows. "That's all you have connecting him to your grandparents?"

Mary felt her cheeks redden. "I know it sounds silly, but I thought maybe he could tell me about my grandparents, maybe give me an idea of why someone wanted them dead."

"Even if I wished to help you, I couldn't. I don't know where he is."

"Leavenworth," Happy said.

Wallace shook his head. "I got a card from him the other day. He wrote, 'I'm out.' Nothing else, not even an address."

Mary dropped into a seat. "So that's it. End of the trail." She sighed. "It was a long shot."

Wallace was leaving the bus when he stopped and slowly turned around. "Speaking of long shots . . . I heard that Lila Lorraine used to write to Samuel. Maybe she knows how to get in touch with him."

Kid Rags' eyes gleamed. "Lila Lorraine? Really? Where can we find her?"

"Omaha, I think." He waved to his wife who still stood in the doorway. "I better go back before she thinks I've been kidnapped."

"Thanks for your help," Mary called out, but Wallace, hurrying toward his house, seemed not to hear.

She rose to her feet. "How far is Omaha?"

"A hundred miles or so," Teach said. "Why?"

"To go see Lila Lorraine, of course."

Kid Rags smoothed his mustache. "But we don't know where she lives."

"Yes we do." Mary rummaged in her purse and brought out her grandfather's address book. Holding it aloft, she said, "It's in here."

Teach grinned. "That sly old dog."

"She sure was pretty." Kid Rags sighed. "It's hard to think of someone like her getting old. She's probably as ugly as sin now."

Crunchy raised his fist above Kid Rags' head. "Don't say bad things about Lila Lorraine."

Kid Rags backed away. "No problem. I didn't realize she meant so much to you."

Crunchy lowered his arm. "Well, she does. She was nice to me. So were Gina Dale and Cokey Flo."

"Everyone was nice to you in those days," Kid Rags said. "We were afraid we'd get crunched if we weren't."

Crunchy folded his arms across his chest. "Being afraid of getting crunched is not the same as being nice."

"What are we all standing around for?" Happy grumbled. "Let's go if we're going."

Mary parked the bus in the mostly empty visitors' lot of the Wide River Senior Citizen Residence, a large gray concrete block with no aesthetic appeal. She got out of the bus and choked on the thick concentration of diesel exhaust from two nearby highways.

"This air is going to kill us," Happy said, coughing. "One minute of an idling diesel engine produces more carcinogens than you could get from smoking two thousand cigarettes."

"Then we better go inside." Mary headed for the building.

A young woman with cornrowed hair sat behind a counter. She looked up when they entered.

"May I help you?"

"We'd like to see Lila Lorraine," Mary said.

"Who should I say is calling?"

Crunchy leaned against the counter. "Tell her Crunchy."

Wrinkling her nose, the young woman dialed the phone. When she replaced the receiver, she looked surprised. "She says you can go up. Apartment three-oh-two."

An old woman with a halo of pale orange hair, wearing a purple warm-up suit and an array of bright necklaces, waited for them when they got off the elevator on the third floor. Beneath the woman's clownish makeup—the smeared lipstick, the round spots of rouge on her wrinkled cheeks, the penciled-on eyebrows that didn't match—Mary could see a pleasant face with a sweet smile.

Bracelets jangled as the woman held out a hand, which Crunchy enveloped in both of his.

The woman gazed at him. "Is it really you, Crunchy?"

Crunchy's lips twitched, the closest Mary had seen him come to a smile. "It's me. You're still pretty, Lila Lorraine."

Lila Lorraine ducked her head. "Oh, go on with you."

"It's true," Crunchy insisted.

Lila Lorraine smiled at him, then glanced over to where

Mary, Teach, Happy, and Kid Rags waited. "Aren't you going to introduce me to your friends?"

Crunchy named the three men, pointing at each in turn.

Lila Lorraine smiled at Happy, gave Kid Rags a puzzled glance as if she knew him but could not place him, then held out her hands to Teach.

"I didn't recognize you in your western duds, Teach. How have you been?"

After Lila Lorraine and Teach got reacquainted, Mary let herself be drawn forward.

Lila Lorraine's eyes widened when she heard Mary's name. "Oh, my dear. It's so lovely to meet you. You look exactly like your grandmother did at your age."

She gestured toward an open doorway framing a room filled with knickknacks, frilly pillows, and scenic pictures. "Won't you come in? We can talk over a nice cup of tea."

"You knew my grandmother Regina DeBrizzi Stuart?" Mary asked when she and the men were seated in the woman's crowded living room.

Lila Lorraine moved around her tiny kitchen; a breakfast bar separated it from the living room.

"I knew her well. We've been friends since we were young girls." She filled the kettle with water, then set it on the stove. "I'm so pleased you finally got to meet her." Her voice faltered as she seemed to become aware of the unnatural stillness in the living room. "What's wrong?"

"I never got to meet her," Mary said quietly.

Lila Lorraine frowned. "I don't understand." From the way she slumped against the stove, though, Mary was sure she did.

Crunchy rushed over to Lila Lorraine and led her into the living room.

After she collapsed into a chintz-covered armchair, she looked at Mary with watery eyes and repeated, "I don't understand."

"She and my grandfather were killed," Mary said. "I didn't find out about them until I got a letter from a lawyer saying they mentioned me in their wills." She went on to tell

Lila Lorraine what little she knew about their deaths and those of her cousins, ending with her belief that all four had been murdered.

"The reason we're here," Teach said, "is that Mary found a picture of Iron Sam among her grandfather's effects, and she wants to go talk to him. We heard that you used to correspond with him. Did he tell you where he's staying now that he's out of prison?"

Lila Lorraine wiped her eyes. "Yes. Blossom View Chalet in Leavenworth. I still have the card he sent telling me he got out."

The teakettle screeched. Mary jumped up and went into the kitchen to turn it off. Following Lila Lorraine's instructions, she took spoons out of a drawer, thin china cups and saucers out of one cabinet, a canister of tea and a sugar bowl out of another, piled the items on a tray and set it on a coffee table in the living room.

"Why don't you pour, my dear," Lila Lorraine said.

When Mary finished serving the tea, Kid Rags took out his hip flask, spiked his tea, then passed the flask around. Lila Lorraine dosed her tea as enthusiastically as the men did. Only Mary refrained.

"It's amazing how that flask always seems to be full," Mary commented.

No one responded to her feeble attempt at humor.

Lila Lorraine took a sip of her tea. "I don't understand what you expect to gain from talking to Iron Sam."

"Maybe nothing. But I would like to hear what he has to say about my grandparents." Mary stared into her cup. "Ever since we learned that Iron Sam is out of prison, I've been wondering . . . do you think he could have killed them?" She glanced up. All were looking at her as if the thought had not occurred to them.

Lila Lorraine took another sip of tea, then set the cup on the table. "I don't know why he would have, but I don't know why anyone would have. Everybody liked your grandparents." She brushed away a tear. "I think it's so brave of you to try to find out who killed them."

Mary shook her head. "You've got it all wrong. I'm just trying to find out who my grandparents were. I'd be scared to death if I met the killer. I mean, the guy's murdered four people that I know of."

Crunchy folded his arms across his chest. "I'd protect you."

Happy bounced in his chair, sloshing his tea. "And I'd shoot him."

"Iron Sam's a killer, Mary, and you're going to meet him," Kid Rags pointed out.

"I know. Just thinking about it gives me the shivers. To be honest, I'm not sure why I'm doing this."

Lila Lorraine patted her hand. "We all deal with grief in our own way."

"Grief? How can it be grief? I didn't know my grandparents."

"The loss of something that never was can be as devastating as any other loss," Teach said.

"In America, one person dies every sixteen seconds," Happy intoned. "That's five thousand, four hundred bodies each day or nearly two million deaths a year."

As usual when Happy made one of his pronouncements, there was a moment of silence.

Then Lila Lorraine sighed. "I'm sorry I can't offer you anything to eat. If I had known you were coming, I'd have baked some cookies."

"No problem," Teach said gallantly. "We're not hungry."

"Speak for yourself," Kid Rags muttered.

"We have to be going soon," Mary said.

Crunchy lumbered to his feet. "Can Lila Lorraine come?"

"Sure, if she wants to."

Lila Lorraine patted her hair. "Oh, I couldn't."

"We got lots of room," Crunchy said.

Mary drained the last of her tea. "We'll be spending the night in Leavenworth, but we should be back tomorrow. If you can come, we'd love to have you."

Lila Lorraine started to rise. In an instant, Crunchy moved to her side and helped her out of the chair.

"I'll have to make a phone call to let the girl at the front desk know I'll be leaving," Lila Lorraine said, sounding distracted. "Then I'll have to pack a few things."

She went into her bedroom and closed the door. When she opened it several minutes later, Mary expected her to inform them she couldn't go, but she said, "Will someone help me with my suitcase?"

Chapter 9

Crunchy settled Lila Lorraine in the seat behind Mary, then sat in the seat behind her. Teach sat across the aisle from Lila Lorraine, Kid Rags sat toward the back of the bus and, as usual, Happy moved from empty seat to empty seat.

Mary stopped at a fast food restaurant with a drive-up window, ordered enough to feed a small army, then headed south on I-29. She ate a hamburger while she drove, and thought about her grandfather.

"I don't get it," she said, wadding her sandwich wrapper. "My grandfather associated with gangsters, did errands for them when he was young, gave them asylum when he got older, and alienated his son, yet the general consensus is that he was a stand-up guy liked by all."

"That's right," Crunchy said. "A stand-up guy."

"What don't you get?" Teach asked.

"Well, how come you call him a good guy when he obviously wasn't?"

"Good and bad aren't necessarily determined by what side of the law a person is on," Teach said. "Gangsterism is funded mostly by fine, upstanding citizens who use the services it provides. The truth is, vice has always been a growth industry. During the depression, boys starting out had few opportunities, so a lot of them worked for the mob. Some boys welcomed the lifestyle—it gave them money, excitement, the chance for possible advancement—but others, like your grandfather, were nudged into it by circumstances."

"Jimmy's father died when he was twelve," Lila Lorraine said, "leaving Jimmy to support his mother and two baby sisters. He sold newspapers, shined shoes, and delivered groceries, but couldn't make enough money to pay the bills, so he started doing errands for local mobsters and eventually became a numbers runner. They liked using boys because, if they got caught, the courts were fairly lenient, but Jimmy didn't get caught."

Mary swallowed, trying to imagine a twelve-year-old boy bravely shouldering a man's responsibilities. At twelve, she had whined and procrastinated whenever she had to do her few chores.

"People are never one thing," Teach said. "I once knew a guy, one of the nicest people you could ever meet—kind, courteous, soft-spoken. He took good care of his invalid wife and their three adopted children. He didn't drink or smoke. He wouldn't let his daughters use lipstick or wear short skirts, and he criticized movies for contributing to the lax morals of the youth. Before retiring at the age of fifty-seven and living out the rest of his long life as a happy, well-respected man, he charged fifty dollars for a murder and twenty dollars for roughing up someone. Of course, that happened a long time ago when money still had some value."

Although Mary expected it, the punch line still made her gasp. "A hit man?"

"Sure. Hit men have families and go to church. A lot of gangsters carried crucifixes or Stars of David in their pockets along with their revolvers."

"Jeez," was all Mary could say.

Teach chuckled. "Even I had my share of skirmishes on the right side of the law. I once spent a couple years as a deputy marshal in a small town in Missouri."

"You did?" Kid Rags came forward and slid into the seat behind Teach. "This I've got to hear."

"There's not much to tell. And anyway, I thought you didn't like hearing my stories."

"I can make an exception this once."

"I want to hear," Crunchy said.

Happy plopped next to Kid Rags. "Me too."

"Well, if you insist . . . It all started with a poker game I operated in a sleazy motel on East Colfax in Aurora back in the early sixties. I needed to get a stake together to finance the gold mine project, and I was doing well when in walked some of Joseph Mannelli's men. Since Joseph Mannelli owned a piece of most of the gambling in Denver in the 1960s and 1970s, I thought his guys were coming to shake me down, but to my surprise they each pulled out a wad of bills and said they wanted in. I presumed they were toying with me because guys in the know don't gamble—it's a sucker's game. The odds are with the house even when the game is on the up and up.

"I'd been playing with a deck of cards that looked unmarked to the naked eye, but when someone wore a special pair of contacts, as I did, the markings were as plain as day—it was like playing with the deck face up. I decided I'd better play it straight. I even cracked open a new deck of cards with the name of a reputable manufacturer on the wrapper, but it was for show since those cards were marked too.

"Mannelli's guys drank so much they didn't have the foggiest idea of what they were doing, and they kept losing big time. I had visions of being given a Newport nightgown and dropped in a deep mountain lake, so I started dealing them winning hands. Trouble was, they all kept discarding the wrong cards, and I kept winning.

"We'd been playing draw poker, so I switched to straight poker, thinking they couldn't lose, but darned if those guys didn't keep folding when they were about to rake in the pot. That concrete blanket began to seem mighty real to me."

Mary let out a breath she didn't know she'd been holding. "What did you do?"

"I kept dealing them winning hands. They kept drinking and losing. By then, the other players realized something strange was going on, and they took off. Only Mannelli's boys and me stayed. Finally, they got so drunk they all passed out. I scooped up the winnings and left town."

"Couldn't you have left the money there?" Mary asked.

"I thought about it, but the first guy to wake would have pocketed the cash and blamed it on me, and I would still have been in the same position. Besides, I needed the money so I could lay low for a while. I drove east and kept on going until I started nodding off, then I got a motel room for the night. I hung around that backwoods town for a while thinking if I didn't know where I was, no one else would either."

Kid Rags nodded. "Good idea. So then what?"

"I struck up a conversation with a guy in a local bar, and we got on well. Turned out he was the marshal with a problem he didn't know how to deal with. A band of gypsies had descended on the area like grasshoppers, picking the place clean. All the storeowners knew who was doing the shoplifting, but no one could catch the gypsies in the act. The marshal asked me if I wanted a job staking out the little department store. Not having anything else to do, I agreed. Being a grifter myself, I was able to finger the shoplifters and explain exactly how they plied their trade. A few were arrested, the others left town, and the marshal offered me a job as deputy." He murmured, "It was a nice town," then fell silent.

By now Mary knew enough not to ask personal questions, but her curiosity got the better of her. "How come you didn't stay there more than a couple of years?"

Teach remained quiet for so long she thought he wouldn't answer. Then he heaved a sigh and said, "The usual. I met a girl, the prettiest little gal I ever saw, but I was getting bored and restless, and she didn't want a drifter, so she married the boy next door, and I took off."

"Wisdom comes with age," Happy grumbled, "too damn late to do any good."

"Isn't that the truth," Lila Lorraine said softly.

The mile markers flashed by. No one spoke.

Lila Lorraine broke the silence. "I wonder what Iron Sam is like now."

"It's hard to figure," Teach replied. "Prison sometimes exacerbates convicts' vicious tendencies. On the other hand, age does tend to mellow people, if only because they're too tired or weak to act on those tendencies."

"I heard about a guy who spent most of his life in prison," Kid Rags said. "When they finally let him out on parole, he found himself alone. No relatives. No friends. No money, either. And it was winter. He walked the streets, looking at the world that had passed him by, and he missed the warmth, food, companionship, identity, and routine he'd left behind when they released him. He broke parole so he could go back and live out his last years in prison."

"It happens," Teach said. "Did you know John Bell?"

"The bank robber they called Ding Dong?" Kid Rags asked.

"Right. He got old, sick, had a few months left to live. He went into a bank in Sierra Vista, robbed the teller at gunpoint, then sat on a couch in the lobby, lay the money and the gun on the seat next to him, pulled a sandwich out of a pocket, and started eating. By the time he finished his sandwich, the cops showed up. The young cop who cuffed him asked, 'Why did you do it?' 'I didn't want to die alone,' Bell answered. Then he added, 'I wanted to do one more bank, to go out practicing my profession.'"

"Jeez." Mary glanced behind her. "Don't you guys know any stories with happy endings?"

Kid Rags lifted his shoulders. "That was a happy ending."

"There are no happy endings," Happy said. "Everyone's story ends in death."

After a moment of speechlessness, Mary blurted out, "Do you think we'll be safe talking to Iron Sam? I still want to do it, but the closer we get the more nervous I feel."

"There's nothing to be afraid of," Happy said. "Unless, of course, someone's put out a hit on you." He made a sound like the grinding of gears, and Mary realized he was laughing.

"Iron Sam has a reputation for being an out-of-control killer," Happy continued when he got hold of himself, "but he isn't. Jacob Levy, one of the guys in the Cleveland Syndicate, hired him to hit Turk the Weasel, who was muscling in on Levy's territory. To make sure the message got across to anyone else with the same idea, he had Iron Sam do the whole family. When the Syndicate found out, they weren't too happy about it, so Levy swore he told Iron

Sam to just take out Turk. You did not mess with Levy if
you valued your life, so no one contradicted him, but the
truth is that Iron Sam was only following directions."

"How do you know that?" Teach asked, sounding
dubious.

"I was the wheelman on that job." Happy flexed his
fingers. "There was no better wheelman than me. Those
steering wheels were so big and I was so small I needed to
be good. I'd never of been able to handle a car in a tight
situation, so I made sure I never got in a tight situation." He
snorted. "In movies they always have high-speed chases, but
in my whole life, with all the jobs I did, I never once got
involved in a high-speed chase. I didn't need to. Before a
job, I'd drive the entire getaway route eight, ten, maybe
twelve times until I knew every inch of those streets, the
alleys, the through driveways. If I had been wheelman when
Iron Sam did that last hit, he'd never of been caught."

Mary rotated her head and shrugged her shoulders to
work out the stiffness while she searched her mind for
something to say, but she could not think of anything
remotely appropriate.

Because of road construction delays, they didn't reach
Leavenworth until evening. Deciding to wait until morning
to talk to Iron Sam, they checked into a motel, getting three
rooms right next to each other. Crunchy, carrying Lila
Lorraine's bags, escorted her into the room she was to share
with Mary. Happy tried out the beds in the other two rooms,
Teach set off to find a newspaper, and Kid Rags remained in
the bus, refilling his flask from his stash of bourbon.

Mary paced in front of the bus to stretch her legs and
wondered how her elderly companions could be so chipper
when all she wanted to do was crawl into bed.

The bearded trucker who had been in line behind her at
the motel registration office parked his rig, climbed out of
the cab, and headed for the opposite end of the motel. At the
last moment he veered in her direction.

"What's a babe like you doing with all those old geezers?" He made a motion as if to cup his crotch, but his stomach protruded so much he could only gesture in the general vicinity. "Why don't you let me show you what a real man can do?"

Mary backed away from him, shaking her head.

"Hey, baby, I just want to show you a good time." He grabbed her arm and yanked her toward him.

Heart pounding, Mary tried to pull away.

Laughing, he wrapped his arms around her, pinning her elbows to her sides. She brought her knee up, aiming for his groin, but his low hanging belly prevented her from getting close. She stomped his foot as she dropped her leg.

"A feisty one," he said, still laughing. "I like that."

She kicked him in the shin. He lowered his hands to her buttocks and drew her closer.

Crunchy charged out of the motel room. The trucker loosened his grip slightly. Mary managed to jerk herself free as Crunchy grabbed the much bigger, much younger man and threw him against the bus. The trucker slipped but, bracing himself, he regained his balance.

"That the best you can do, old man?"

Crunchy punched him in the nose. The truck driver staggered back, shaking his head and looking confused, then he rushed at Crunchy.

Happy bounced on the balls of his feet, waved his small fists around, and yelled in a high-pitched voice, "Shoot him, Mary! Shoot him!"

Kid Rags climbed out of the bus, gripping a bottle of bourbon. He got behind the trucker, who was bending over while grappling with Crunchy, and thunked him on the head with the bottle. The glass cracked. Drenched in bourbon, the trucker crumpled to the ground and lay still.

Kid Rags kicked him. "Damn you. That was a brand new bottle of bourbon."

Crunchy put an arm around Mary's shoulders. "You okay, Lady?"

Taking deep gulps of air, Mary nodded.

"Why didn't you shoot him?" Happy demanded, still prancing around. "You shoulda shot him. What's the good of a gun if you don't use it?"

Mary stared at him for a moment, not having any idea what he meant, then she remembered the gun in her shoulder bag. How could she have forgotten all about it?

Happy kicked at the ground, mumbling to himself, "I would of shot him if she hadn't taken my gun from me."

Lila Lorraine led Mary toward their motel room. "You better come sit down, dear."

Mary glanced back, shuddering. "What do we do about him?"

"Nothing. See? He's already trying to get up."

"Have a little trouble, boys?" Teach asked, returning with his newspaper.

"Lot of good you were," Kid Rags growled.

Teach laughed. "Looks like you did fine without me."

Later, in a nearby restaurant, Mary pushed her dinner around the plate, too queasy to eat. She could still feel those strong arms around her, could still smell that hot, acrid breath. Aware that the elders gazed at her in concern, she looked up and smiled at them.

"I'm fine, really," she said, as much for her benefit as theirs. She ate a bite of her broiled fish, then set down her fork. "I did everything I knew how to do, but it didn't faze him."

"I never understood the problems women have trying to defend themselves until I got old," Crunchy said. He made a fist and stared at it. "I can't crush hardly nobody no more. Most everyone is bigger and taller and stronger than me."

The others nodded in agreement.

Mary sighed. "Maybe I should take self-defense classes."

"Could be," Teach said, "but a lot of women and small men find that those classes only serve to give them a false sense of security."

"All you need is a gun," Happy said. "Guns are great

equalizers. There used to be an inscription on the Colt revolver that said, 'Be not afraid of any man no matter what his size. When danger threatens, call on me, and I will equalize.' I memorized that," he added.

"You could spit," Kid Rags offered. "I knew a kid once—Spitting William we called him. He was a powder puff puncher, couldn't fight worth a damn, and he got picked on. He started chewing a combination of plug tobacco, cloves, and hot pepper, and he'd spit the mixture into the eyes of anyone who got in his way."

Mary giggled, thinking of spitting spicy tobacco juice into the shocked eyes of the trucker, and suddenly they were all laughing so hard they clutched their sides and gasped for breath.

Chapter 10

"How do you know Iron Sam?" Mary asked. She couldn't sleep, and from the sounds in the next bed, she could tell that Lila Lorraine was awake, too.

"We had a fling once," Lila Lorraine said. In the darkness, Mary heard a sigh. "He was such a handsome devil."

Mary shivered, remembering the face in the snapshot. Devilish, certainly. But handsome?

"I thought he hated women," she said aloud.

The bedsprings creaked. "Oh, he did. Probably still does. But, like all men, he had needs."

"Why did you go out with him?"

Lila Lorraine giggled, sounding like a teenage girl. "I can't actually say we went out. Mostly we stayed in." Then she sighed again. "I was stupid. I thought he needed a good woman—me. I didn't know then that you can never change a man. He is what he is, and you either accept it or move on."

Mary fell silent for a moment, then she asked hesitantly, "Did you have a . . . a fling with my grandfather?"

"Oh, heavens no. What makes you think that?"

"I found your name and address in my grandfather's little black address book."

Mary heard Lila Lorraine sniff and wondered if she were crying.

"Your grandmother had macular degeneration." The woman spoke with a tremor in her voice. "She couldn't see things close up, couldn't see to read or write, so your grandfather acted as her secretary. Gina and I were friends for most of our lives—"

"Gina?" Mary broke in. "Gina Dale?"

"Yes. Your grandmother took Gina Dale as her stage name. How did you know?"

"Crunchy mentioned it. He said you and Cokey Flo and Gina Dale were nice to him."

"Well, he was nice to us. When he didn't wrestle or do odd jobs for the mob, he worked at The Joker as a bouncer, protecting us girls from the customers. He was so gentle with us, like a big teddy bear. He took it hard when Cokey Flo died of an overdose, but how he expected to protect her from that, I don't know."

Mary's mind seethed with questions, but she kept her mouth shut, not wanting to interrupt the stream of reminiscences.

"Cokey Flo and I were born in Chicago, but Gina came from a small farming community in Wisconsin. She wanted to be a dancer. Since she had no formal training, none of the dance companies hired her, so she worked at The Joker as a showgirl.

"Dale was her middle name, that's how she became Gina Dale. I made up my name—I couldn't do much with Alice Myrtle Plotkin. I don't remember the name Flo chose, but she had such a bad drug habit, someone started calling her Cokey, and it stuck.

"Gina didn't have a willowy dancer's body, and she wasn't well-endowed, but when she danced, she was riveting. I'd walk out on stage, and everyone would call out my name. Gina would walk out, and everyone would hush. Men always fell in love with her. She had eyes only for your grandfather, though. Jimmy Boots tended bar at The Joker. He got his name from the fancy cowboy boots he wore. Did anyone tell you about them?"

Lila Lorraine didn't wait for a response. "By the time he and Gina got married, he wasn't doing many jobs for the mob—he was too low on the totem pole. And he didn't intend to be a bartender for the rest of his life, so when Gina decided they should save to buy a farm, he went along with it."

Lila Lorraine giggled. "The rest of us girls read magazines like *True Romance*, but not Gina. She read *The Farmer's Home Journal.*

"When Gina got pregnant and stopped dancing, she thought they wouldn't be able to afford a farm, so she tried to put it out of her head. Then Cokey Flo died, and Gina became determined not to raise her child in such a dangerous place. She searched the ads in the *Farmer's Home Journal* and found a farm she thought they might eventually be able to afford. It was way out west in Colorado, and she didn't think Jimmy would want to move so far away from Chicago, but Jimmy loved her and would have done anything to make her happy, even move to Venus if she wanted, so he promised to get the money together to buy the farm. She didn't question where it came from. She was so grateful to be out of the city.

"Jimmy had a hard time getting used to the desolation. He'd sit on the porch and watch the road in front of the farm, staring at those miles and miles of empty nothingness, waiting for someone, anyone, to come along.

"Then a friend of his from the old days, a loan shark by the name of Lefty Louie, got in trouble and had to leave Chicago for a while, so Jimmy invited him to come stay with him and Gina and baby Pete. Lefty Louie was impressed with Colorado and pleased that Jimmy didn't extort a fortune from him for letting him hide out on the farm, so he passed the word along. At first, they didn't get a lot of visitors, but as more and more of the action moved to Las Vegas, the farm became something of a way station.

"I don't think Gina liked running a safe house for mobsters since they were one of the reasons she wanted to get out of the city, but she could see how much it meant to Jimmy, so she never said anything."

Lila Lorraine fell silent. After a moment, she began breathing deeply and evenly, occasionally letting out a gentle snore.

Mary stared at the ceiling, trying to imagine her grandparents when they were young and in love. Then she too drifted off to sleep.

Blossom View Chalet looked like an army barracks and smelled like a hospital. The only flowers Mary saw were in rooms occupied by children with the resigned faces of the elderly or elders so frail they seemed no bigger than children.

"What is this place?" Crunchy asked in a loud whisper.

"A hospice," Teach said, consulting a brochure he'd picked up at the front desk. "It's where terminally ill people go to die."

"Oh." Crunchy edged closer to Mary and stared at the floor, but the others looked around with wide, fearful eyes as they walked down the long corridor to Iron Sam's room.

"Nomadic peoples," Happy said, "like Mongols and Native Americans, abandoned the terminally sick and the infirm—young or old. They left them behind when they moved on."

"Doesn't seem as if we've made much progress, does it?" Teach commented.

"At least we bury them," Kid Rags said. "Or cremate them. We don't leave them for the vultures."

"Maybe we should," Teach countered. "That's what the Parsi's in India do. They believe if you dispose of a body by fire, or bury it in the soil or at sea, you defile those earthly elements with carrion."

Mary groaned. "You're all beginning to sound like Happy."

Happy puffed out his chest and strutted as if he'd been given a compliment.

Lila Lorraine shuddered. "It's this place. Even Iron Sam deserves better than this."

Still puffing out his chest, Happy said, "When people are cremated, the organic compounds are destroyed by fire. What's left are inorganic minerals and trace metals. The part we preserve, the so-called ashes, is the inorganic being that never lived in the first place."

Mary let out a sigh of relief when she spotted Iron Sam's room number. The morbid talk, here in this place of dying, gave her the creeps.

When she heard no response to her knock, she opened the door and stepped inside. In the dim light, she could see that both beds were unoccupied. Turning to leave, she caught a glimpse of a man sitting motionless in a shadowy corner.

"I can't see anything," Happy complained.

Lila Lorraine went to the window and threw open the curtains.

Mary blinked in the sudden brightness, then blinked again when she saw Iron Sam. He seemed to be the personification of the inorganic being, as Happy called it. His skin looked ashen. Charcoal bags hung below slate eyes. His hair, still thick, still with the deep widow's peak, had faded to pewter. The only hint of color in his face was the gold tooth visible between slightly parted gunmetal-gray lips.

He glanced up as they entered, but no other part of his body moved. Nor did he speak.

"Hi, Sam," Lila Lorraine said.

The slate eyes shifted toward her.

"It's me. Lila Lorraine."

Iron Sam nodded, the merest inclination of his head.

Happy stepped forward. "Remember me? Happy?"

Again the tiny nod.

Mary wondered if he were paralyzed, but if so, wouldn't he be in a wheelchair instead of an ordinary wooden chair?

Any compassion she might have felt withered when his eyes met hers. Feeling like a bug impaled on a pin, she gazed at him, unable to look away, unable to move a single muscle. After what seemed like a long time, but must have been only seconds, he turned his attention to Kid Rags, leaving her feeling limp and very thirsty, as if her vital fluids had been sucked right out of her.

With nonchalance Mary could only marvel at, Kid Rags pulled out his flask and offered it to Iron Sam. When Iron Sam nodded toward the plastic cup sitting on the bedside table, Kid Rags poured two fingers of bourbon and handed the cup to him. He sniffed it, inhaling deeply with closed eyes, then took a mouthful and held it a moment before swallowing it. His lips twitched—a smile perhaps?—then he took another sip.

The alcohol fumes mingling with the hospital odors and the stench of decay emanating from Iron Sam's pores turned Mary's stomach. She swallowed hard, then swallowed again, knowing she shouldn't show weakness in front of Iron Sam, and somehow she managed to get her queasiness under control.

He flicked a look in her direction, as if sensing her struggle, then concentrated on his drink once more.

"My name is Mary Stuart," she said when she could no longer stand the heavy silence. She introduced Kid Rags, Crunchy, and Teach, then explained about her grandparents' deaths.

"What can you tell me about my grandparents? You might have known them as Jimmy Boots and Gina Dale."

Iron Sam looked at her with no show of interest.

Kid Rags poured another two fingers of bourbon into the plastic cup, but Iron Sam didn't touch it.

Happy moved about the room, bouncing on the beds, fiddling with the curtains, picking things up and putting them down.

Between Iron Sam's stillness and Happy's restlessness, Mary's nerves felt as if they were stretched to the breaking point. Suppressing an urge to scream, she fished the pictures out of her purse, riffled through them for the one of Iron Sam, then laid it on the bedside table.

"Where did you get that?" he rasped in a gravelly voice.

"I found it with my grandfather's things."

"I don't remember your grandfather." Except for the movement of his lips, Iron Sam remained immobile while he spoke—no flinches, no shrugs, no gestures.

"Jimmy Boots ran a safe house on the eastern plains of Colorado," Teach said. "Perhaps you stayed there at one time."

Iron Sam made no response.

"Is there any place around here we can get something to eat?" Kid Rags asked. "I'm hungry."

Grateful for an excuse to terminate the uncomfortable and unproductive interview, Mary said, "Maybe we should go."

"I saw a coffee shop not far from here," Teach said.

"Would you like to come with us, Sam?" Lila Lorraine asked. Then, flustered, "I mean, if you can."

Iron Sam's wide shoulders had given Mary the impression he was still powerfully built, but when he stood, she could see how emaciated he'd become—his clothes hung on him with all the finesse of garments on a wire hanger. Although his pale yellow pullover shirt seemed crisply new, it smelled musty and was faded along the fold lines as if it had been packed away for a long time. Shivering, she wondered if he'd been wearing that very shirt when he was arrested.

Iron Sam tossed back his drink, shuffled along behind them to the bus, then struggled to climb the two low steps into the vehicle.

"We can turn the steps into a ramp or an elevator," Happy said.

He showed Mary where the controls were, but by that time Iron Sam had heaved himself into the bus and was settling into a seat well apart from the others. All the way to the coffee shop, he stared out the window and spoke not a word.

At the restaurant, the waitress led them to a large corner booth and handed oversize menus all around.

Though they'd eaten breakfast a short time ago, Kid Rags ordered a breakfast platter, as did Crunchy. Lila Lorraine, Happy, and Teach ordered coffee and doughnuts. Mary ordered hot chocolate. When Iron Sam's turn came, he stared at the menu as if he couldn't comprehend the bewildering array of selections. And maybe he couldn't, Mary thought. He probably hadn't eaten in a restaurant for many years.

"He'll have the scrambled eggs," Lila Lorraine told the waitress. "Make sure they're well done. Also crisp bacon, unbuttered toast with jelly, and tea. Oh, and apple juice if you have it."

Iron Sam stared at Lila Lorraine. Mary felt like putting her arms around the old woman to protect her, but then Iron Sam's mouth curved into something resembling a smile.

"You remembered," he said.

Lila Lorraine smiled back at him. "You're a hard man to forget, Sam."

The meals Mary had eaten with the elders had not been raucous affairs, but they had been filled with the sound of Teach telling stories, Kid Rags teasing him, Happy making pronouncements that were anything but happy, and Crunchy putting in a word now and then. Now they were all as silent as Iron Sam.

When their meals came, Iron Sam huddled over his plate, one arm circling it protectively, and immediately began shoveling food into his mouth.

Mary averted her gaze, not wanting to be caught staring, but she couldn't help sneaking an occasional peek. The pang of compassion she'd been holding at bay washed over her as she got a glimmer of what it must have been like for him being incarcerated all those years almost without end.

Back at the hospice, after Iron Sam dragged himself off the bus, he turned and looked at Mary with a hint of craftiness in his eyes. "If you come back tomorrow, I might be able to tell you something about your grandpa."

Before Mary could answer, a heavy-set nurse with tightly permed hair scurried outside, pushing a wheelchair. Wheezing, she bundled Iron Sam into the chair. As the woman wheeled him into the building, Mary could hear her shrill voice scolding him for leaving the premises without permission.

Mary blew out a long, low, "Jeez."

"Are we going to come back tomorrow?" Lila Lorraine asked.

Turning sideways in her seat, Mary caught the worried expression on the old woman's face. "Is there any reason we shouldn't?"

"No. It's just . . . oh, it's so silly."

"Tell me," Mary said gently.

Lila Lorraine rummaged in her purse and pulled out an amber container, the kind typically used for prescription drugs, and handed it to Mary. "I thought I packed my blood pressure medicine, but I grabbed my sleeping pills by mistake. The bottles all look alike, and the printing is too small for me to read . . ." Her voice trailed away.

Mary returned the bottle to her. "We'll go back to Omaha. If road construction delays aren't too long, we can be back here in Leavenworth before dark."

"We don't have to go to Omaha," Kid Rags said.

"Oh?" Mary raised her eyebrows. "You have a better suggestion?"

"Yes. She can stop taking the pills."

Lila Lorraine sucked in her breath. "I couldn't do that."

"Why not? I did. Those quack doctors made me take so many drugs, I had a hard time choking them down. The stuff they gave me for high blood pressure took away my appetite, but since they said I couldn't have salt or alcohol, it didn't seem worth the trouble to eat. Then I got depressed, so they prescribed anti-depressants, which I got side effects from, so they prescribed more drugs. One day I decided the hell with it and stopped taking all those pills, and believe me, I felt a whole lot better, especially when I got my appetite back."

"Don't listen to him, Lila Lorraine," Mary said. "He's ninety years old and eats and drinks like he's nineteen."

"Ninety? I'm not ninety." Kid Rags appealed to Teach. "Do I look ninety to you?"

"You don't look a day over eighty—I mean seventy," Mary said hastily, "but that's beside the point."

"Beside the point?" Kid Rags huffed. "Not to me it isn't."

Lila Lorraine dropped the sleeping pills back into her purse. "Maybe he's right. My next-door neighbor Edna took all sorts of heart medication. She decided she didn't want any more pain and suffering, so she stopped taking her pills and waited to die, but she didn't. Die, I mean. She ended up having to starve herself to death."

"How long did it take her to croak?" Happy asked, bright-eyed.

Crunchy frowned. "You need to take your pills, Lila Lorraine. I don't want nothing bad happening to you."

Lila Lorraine smiled at him. "That's sweet of you,

Crunchy, but one more day shouldn't hurt me. I didn't take them last night or this morning and I feel . . . I feel . . ."

"What?" Mary asked.

"Hungry," Lila Lorraine finished, sounding surprised.

Kid Rags adjusted his bow tie. "See?"

Chapter 11

After swimming lap after mindless lap, Mary pulled herself out of the motel swimming pool.

Lila Lorraine, lounging in a chair by the side of the pool, held out a towel. "You're very good. Did you swim competitively?"

Mary mopped her face. "No. My dad said I was good enough, but that I didn't have the killer instinct." Toweling her hair, she added, "I never wanted to win as desperately as the other kids, and when I did win, I felt sorry for the losers. I don't understand all the emphasis on winning. I mean, people say we're a nation of winners, but since there can only be one winner, that makes everyone else losers, right?"

A rumble of laughter came from behind the newspaper Teach was reading at a nearby table. "Smart girl," he said.

Mary sighed. "Bill agrees with my father. He says I lack ambition."

Teach peered over the top of his paper. "Ambition is another word for greed."

"Whatever it is, I don't have it. I don't see why some people have to have so much more than everyone else. Things should be even. You two live in okay places, but Kid Rags and Crunchy live in hovels."

Teach laid his newspaper on the table. "Kid Rags told me Happy lives in a hotel for transients."

"See?" Mary said. "I read somewhere that two percent of Americans own fifty-four percent of the total assets in this country, ten percent own eighty-six percent, and fifty-five percent have zero assets or a negative worth. If things were fair, maybe Crunchy and Kid Rags and Happy wouldn't live the way they do."

She draped the towel around her shoulders, then plopped into a chair. Leaning back and stretching out her legs, she blew out a breath. "I wish I could do something."

"You *are* doing something," Lila Lorraine said. "This trip

is a big something—one last adventure for us."

Mary sat up straight and looked around. "Where are the others?"

Lila Lorraine reached over and patted her knee. "You sit back and relax, dear. They're fine. Crunchy found an exercise room where he can work out, and the Bobbsey Twins are wandering around the parking lot looking at cars."

Kid Rags and Happy trudged into the pool area.

"Talk about street-smart people," Kid Rags said. "We found two cars with keys still in the ignition."

"There's a lot of ugly vehicles on the road today," Happy grumbled. "And the colors are so drab. Whatever happened to all the American heavy metal cars of the fifties and sixties? Those were beautiful machines."

Later that evening, when the two women were in their room getting ready for bed, Mary asked Lila Lorraine if she'd ever been married.

"No. Came close once or twice, but that's about it."

"I used to want to get married," Mary said, "but now I don't know what I want. I thought I was a finished product, but I'm finding out I'm not—there's more to me than I ever knew." She opened her wallet and showed Lila Lorraine a picture of her fiancé in his soccer uniform. "Everything is so clear to Bill. He knows what he wants and where he's going. I used to find that attractive since I don't have a clue about myself."

Lila Lorraine moved in close to get a better look at the photograph. "Nice pins on that boy. How can you think about letting go of a good-looking guy like him?"

Mary jerked her head up. "Whatever gave you the idea I'm letting him go?" She dropped her gaze back to the picture. After a moment, she said softly, "Maybe I am. Maybe I need more than a good body and a pretty face. Looks are a poor basis for a long term relationship."

Lila Lorraine chuckled. "You sound like your grandmother. She told me the same thing a very long time ago, but I didn't believe her. It took me a lifetime of bad men, bad relationships, and bad memories to find out she was right."

Mary took one last look at the photograph, then closed her wallet. "I don't know what's gotten into me lately. Bill and I do have a good thing going. And my parents like him. My dad especially. They have a lot in common, both being into sports. My dad was on the swim team in college and won a whole cabinet-full of trophies. Bill played soccer in college and still plays whenever he can—he's on a team sponsored by his athletic club. It's like he's the son they never had."

Lila Lorraine gave her a sharp look. "Even I know marrying to please one's parents is not a good idea."

"Oh, it's not just for them. Bill doesn't make me weak-kneed, but we're comfortable together. And don't we all have to settle in the end? Isn't that what maturity means?"

"Your grandparents didn't settle. They loved each other deeply their whole lives."

"People say relationships were easier back then."

"No. We didn't have as many choices as you young people have today, but relationships have never been easy."

"Lately I've been wondering if Bill is having doubts, too. He doesn't seem to be pleased with the decisions I make. Or rather, don't make. He's unhappy with me because I can't make up my mind about selling my grandparents' farm. He's also unhappy because I won't agree to start working at his accounting firm, but I think it would be horrible. Then he'd always be passing judgment on me and finding me less than adequate."

"Doesn't sound like it bodes well for your marriage." Lila Lorraine climbed into her bed and turned off her light.

Mary pulled back the covers and stared at her empty bed. "No, it doesn't, does it?"

In the morning when Mary entered the hospice accompanied by her entourage, she found Iron Sam sitting in one of the waiting room's uncomfortable-looking chrome chairs with thin orange plastic cushions. A tattered brown paper grocery bag, the top rolled down like an oversize lunch bag, rested on his knees.

Although his expression didn't change when he saw them, Mary detected the faintest relaxation of his facial muscles.

"Hello, Sam," she said quietly.

He inclined his head a fraction of an inch, then struggled to his feet, grasping the paper bag.

"I'm going to be visiting with my granddaughter for a few days," he informed the gum-popping young man at the reception desk.

The young man stared at him, furiously working his jaws. "But . . . but . . ."

Lifting his chin, Iron Sam shuffled toward the door.

"If you're spending the night," the young man said, "you'll need to get packed."

Iron Sam held up the paper bag. "I am packed."

"Don't forget you have an appointment with your parole officer the day after tomorrow."

Iron Sam acted as if he didn't hear.

Mary's gaze met Lila Lorraine's. "Granddaughter?" she mouthed silently.

Lila Lorraine pointed at Mary and mouthed back, "I think he means you. He has no family."

Feeling as if she'd completely lost control of the situation, Mary hurried after Iron Sam to seek an explanation, but when she caught sight of the forbidding look on his face, the words died in her throat.

"Where do you want to go?" she asked after everyone settled in the bus.

"Kansas City," he answered, giving her an address on West 46th Street.

No one spoke until a mile beyond the exit to Lansing when Happy announced, "Someone's following us."

Chapter 12

Mary wanted to slam on the brakes, but she gripped the steering wheel and forced herself to continue driving at a steady pace.

"See that dark blue Pontiac Grand Am three cars behind us?" Happy said, holding his glasses to his eyes and peering through the back window.

Checking the rear view mirror, Mary could see the car Happy mentioned. As she watched, the Pontiac dropped back, letting other cars get between it and the bus.

She relaxed her grip on the steering wheel. "He must not have been following us after all."

"He doesn't have to stay close since there's no immediate turn-off," Happy said, "but when we near the next exit, he'll close the gap again. He's been doing that since we left the hospice."

As one, the elders all turned to Iron Sam.

"Never saw him before in my life," he rasped.

How would he know? Mary wondered. The vehicle remained too far back for them to get a good look at the driver.

"So what do I do?" she asked.

"Nothing," Happy answered. "There's no way this old bus can outmaneuver a new car."

"Don't worry," Teach said soothingly. "I doubt he's going to try anything. This highway is too public."

Glancing in the rear view mirror and seeing the dark blue car following far behind, Mary couldn't help worrying. What did the driver want with them? For that matter, what did Iron Sam want?

When Mary pulled up at the address Iron Sam had given her, Happy, trailed by Kid Rags and Teach, disembarked and headed for the Grand Am, which stopped about a block away. Apparently catching sight of the old men, the driver peeled away from the curb, turned a corner, and sped down a side street.

Crunchy stayed close to the women, though Mary could tell he would have liked to go with the men.

Iron Sam stared at the building, which housed a gourmet coffee shop.

"Aren't you going to get out?" Mary asked him.

"No." The single clipped word sounded like a grunt.

Happy climbed back into the bus. "He got away." He jabbed the air with his fists.

Good, Mary thought, appalled at the idea of such ancient men having gone off to confront possible danger.

"If I'd of had my gun," Happy added darkly, "things would of been different."

Kid Rags appeared at the door of the bus. "Anyone want coffee?"

"I don't drink no sissy coffee," Crunchy said.

Happy bounced on the balls of his feet and continued to shadow box. "I could use some caffeine."

Mary declined. Iron Sam, still staring impassively at the coffee shop, made no response.

When Kid Rags and Teach returned with three Styrofoam cups of coffee, Iron Sam said, as if to himself, "This used to be a smoke shop. Imported cigars. Best in the world. The owner was a friend of us."

Mary stared at him, wondering what he meant by "us", then chills ran up her spine and down her arms, giving her goose bumps, when she realized he meant the mob. The Syndicate.

Could Iron Sam be trying to renew his contacts with the Syndicate? Whatever he wanted, she doubted it had anything to do with her grandparents.

She rubbed her arms and tried to sound carefree. "What next?"

"Food," Kid Rags said.

Their brief conversation, during lunch at a diner shaped like a trolley car, centered on the Grand Am. They concluded that somebody wanted to avenge one of Iron Sam's victims. Iron Sam, huddled over his plate, rapidly shoveling chicken fried steak, mashed potatoes, and salad into his mouth, did not join in the speculation, did not even seem to hear what the others said.

Mary studied him covertly and wondered what was going on inside his mind.

By evening, she still didn't know his agenda. They had traveled from place to place, getting farther away from the hospice, looking for bars and tobacco shops that were long gone. Occasionally she caught a glimpse of the Grand Am, but it stayed well away from them.

They ate dinner at a steak house on the outskirts of Moberly, Missouri. Mary gave a guilty start when she realized she had forgotten all about Lila Lorraine's lack of medication.

"How are you feeling?" she asked.

Lila Lorraine put aside the fork she had been using to pick at the small salad she ordered, and massaged her temples. "I'm getting a headache, but I'm sure I'll be fine after I rest for a while."

Mary glanced at her watch. "There's no way we'd be able to make it back to Omaha tonight, but we can make a start."

"Oh, no," Lila Lorraine said. "You mustn't go back on my account."

"Do you have your doctor's phone number? Maybe we can have a prescription called in to a drug store around here."

Lila Lorraine nodded. "That would be good."

When Mary finally got hold of the doctor, the woman refused to issue a prescription, saying Lila Lorraine needed to make an appointment first.

"I don't think she believed me," Mary said, giving a snort of unamused laughter. "I think she thought I was running some sort of scam."

Lila Lorraine patted her hand. "Don't worry, dear. I'm sure I'll be fine."

* * *

Later, Mary was driving down the highway in search of a motel for the night, when a Missouri State Patrol car came alongside the bus. It kept pace with them for what seemed like a long time while the officer studied them and their vehicle.

After the cruiser finally pulled ahead and disappeared into the distance, Happy let out his breath in a loud whoosh. "Sheee. That was close."

Mary jerked her head around. "What do you mean?"

"Nothing."

She gave him a suspicious look. "Is there something you're not telling me that I should know?"

"Hey, look out!" Kid Rags yelped.

Mary faced forward and slammed on her brakes in time to keep from rear-ending a stalled SUV.

Teach stood at the motel door, hat in hand. "May I come in?"

Mary glanced over at Lila Lorraine sleeping uneasily in the far bed, put a finger to her lips, and whispered, "For a second."

Teach slipped into the room and laid his hat on the credenza next to Mary's purse. "I came to find out how Lila Lorraine is doing."

"Not well. Tell the others we'll be going back tomorrow."

"They'll be disappointed."

Mary hunched her shoulders. "Can't be helped. And anyway, I've probably learned all I'm going to about my grandparents."

Teach picked up his hat. "We'll keep it quiet next door so we don't disturb Lila Lorraine."

True to his word, Teach and Kid Rags, who shared the room next door, were silent. The only sound was the faint scraping of Crunchy's chair as he changed position.

Mary tried not to think of the old man keeping his lonely vigil outside her door. He did sleep part of the night, she had discovered, but he was there when she went to sleep and again when she awoke in the morning. Although she still felt uncomfortable with him guarding her, tonight she appreciated the buffer between her and Iron Sam.

She shivered, thinking of that too silent, too still man. She had never met anyone who kept his hands and body motionless while he talked. When he talked, that is, which he seldom did and then only in short, clipped sentences.

She would never wish for Lila Lorraine to be ill, but she was secretly glad of the excuse to cut the excursion short. After dropping Iron Sam off at the hospice tomorrow, she wouldn't have to see him again, though he'd probably be in her head for many years to come. As Lila Lorraine had said, he was a hard man to forget.

Still thinking of Iron Sam, and mindful of his fearsome eyes that seemed to bore right through her, she lay on top of the bedspread fully clothed, sure that sleep would elude her.

A loud crash awakened her. She jumped up and went to the window. Pushing aside the drapes, she saw the gray bus backing away from a dumpster. She glanced at the credenza where she had dropped the keys. Her purse and the motel key were still there, but the bus key was gone.

She ran to the door and yanked it open. Happy, Kid Rags, and Teach clambered out of the bus talking, laughing, and careening into each other. Iron Sam, as silent and impassive as ever, trailed them.

"Hey, Mary," Kid Rags called out before she could say anything. "Guess what? We won't have to go back tomorrow!"

He came to her and, with a flourish, handed her an immense bottle of pills.

"What's this?" she asked, eyeing the men.

"Lila Lorraine's blood pressure medicine."

"Where did you get it," she demanded.

Happy puffed out his chest. "A pharmacy."

Feeling as if she herself would soon have need of the pills, she screeched, "You robbed a pharmacy?"

"We didn't rob it," Kid Rags said. Before Mary's own

blood pressure could return to normal, he continued, "We burgled it."

Mary slumped against the doorframe and gaped at them, speechless.

"We used a glass cutter," Happy said, then added quickly, "but don't worry—we didn't steal the cutter. We bought it at a discount store that's open until midnight."

Kid Rags ran his fingers around the brim of his hat. "We thought you'd be pleased."

"Pleased?" Mary glared at him. "What did I ever do to make you think I'd condone criminal behavior? And you," she said, turning to Teach. "I would have thought you were too smart to get involved with something as foolish as this. And you!" She pointed a trembling finger at Iron Sam. "If you're trying to get back into prison like Ding Dong Bell, that's one thing, but you have no right to pull these others in with you."

Catching sight of Kid Rags' grin out of the corner of her eye, she rounded on him. "What are you laughing at?"

"Nothing. It's been a long time since anyone's cared what happens to me."

"I don't care," Mary said crossly.

Kid Rags' grin broadened.

"I wasn't trying to get back into prison," Iron Sam said suddenly, as if the cork had blown on the words he'd bottled up over the years. "I was trying to get killed. Sitting in a death house wasting away by inches is no way for a man to die. I lived by the gun. I should die by the gun." He glanced at Teach. "What is it you cowboys say? Die in the saddle?"

Teach nodded. "Or, more commonly, die with your boots on."

"Right," Iron Sam said. "I wanted to die with my boots on. But we were in the pharmacy such a short time—"

"These pills weren't locked away with the narcotics and barbiturates," Kid Rags explained.

"The cops didn't show until we were driving away," Iron Sam finished as if Kid Rags hadn't spoken.

Mary put a hand to her throat. "Did they see you?"

"Maybe," Teach said, "but I don't think so."

"Go get packed." When no one moved, Mary waved them away. "Go on. Get packed. We have to leave before they come looking for you."

Mary went over to the bed where Lila Lorraine slept. She shook the old woman's shoulder. "Wake up, Lila Lorraine. We have to get out of here."

Lila Lorraine sat up and rubbed her eyes. "What's happening?"

Mary thrust the bottle of pills at her. "Kid Rags, Happy, Teach, and Iron Sam robbed—burgled—a pharmacy, so we need to take off right now."

Lila Lorraine hugged the bottle to her chest. "Wasn't that sweet of them."

"Yeah," Mary said, gritting her teeth. "Real sweet."

Chapter 13

No one spoke as Mary got on the highway going east, but she thought she detected a collective sigh of relief at not having to turn back.

"We can't go much farther," she warned them. "This is just the fastest way out of Missouri."

"How come we can't go much farther?" Kid Rags asked. "We got plenty of blood pressure pills for Lila Lorraine."

Mary winced. "I don't want to talk about that."

"How come we can't go much farther?" Kid Rags repeated.

"We have to get Iron Sam back to the hospice tomorrow in time for his appointment with his parole officer."

"I'm not going back," Iron Sam announced.

Mary turned around to give him a questioning glance. "I thought you didn't want to go back to prison."

"I don't. That's why I'm not going back. I've broken parole. If my parole officer finds out I left Kansas, he'll send me back to the joint."

"How will he find out?" Kid Rags asked.

"Yeah," Crunchy said. "We're no rats."

Happy jumped out of his seat. "Maybe he was the one following us in the Grand Am."

"I doubt it," Teach said. "Parole officers usually aren't that dedicated. Unless they're vindictive."

Iron Sam stared out the window. "I only met him once."

Mary heard a distant siren. Her palms sweated so much she could barely grip the steering wheel. As the siren got louder, she realized it was coming toward them. By the time she finally saw the flashing lights when the other vehicle topped a small hill, her legs shook uncontrollably and her breath came in short gasps.

Not only was Iron Sam going to be caught and sent back to prison, she'd be accompanying him. Moistening her lips, she added up her crimes. Carrying a concealed weapon.

Receiving stolen merchandise. Aiding and abetting an escaped felon. And probably several more she couldn't begin to guess at.

The wailing vehicle drew nearer.

She slowed, ready to pull off to the side of the highway.

Then all at once the vehicle whizzed past.

An ambulance.

She wiped her palms on her black denim-clad thighs and tried to still her trembling legs by sheer force of will, but mile after mile flashed by before she finally got herself under control.

She glanced back at her passengers, planning to make a facetious remark to lighten the atmosphere, but no one seemed aware that they'd averted a potential disaster. Teach, Kid Rags, Happy, and Lila Lorraine all slept. Iron Sam stared out the window. Crunchy gazed down at his shirt, his lips curled in the faintest of smiles.

Mary turned her attention back to the road. Now that the sound of her rapidly beating heart had stopped thundering in her ears, she could detect soft noises. A snore from Teach. A sigh from Lila Lorraine. A mumbled word from Happy.

What was that? She tilted her head, straining her ears, thinking she'd heard a tiny meow. Then she heard it again.

"Is there a cat on the bus?" she asked.

"No cat," Crunchy said.

"I thought I heard a cat." She glanced back in time to see a young black cat, scarcely older than a kitten, crawl out of Crunchy's shirt, climb up, and perch on the top of his head.

"What cat?" Crunchy asked.

"The cat that thinks it's a hat."

Crunchy reached up, took hold of the tiny creature, and cradled it in his huge hands. "This cat?"

"That cat."

Crunchy gently stroked the creature with one finger. "Not a cat, a kitten. I found it in the parking lot at the motel. Wet and shivering and crying. Dirty, too. And hungry. I fed him a roll I saved from the restaurant, but he didn't like it. His name's Journey."

"That's a good name," Mary said.

Journey crawled up Crunchy's torso and again perched on the ex-wrestler's head, looking pleased.

Seeing the same expression on Crunchy's face, Mary couldn't help smiling.

She stopped at a convenience store for gas and cat food without disturbing the sleepers, but at dawn, when she stopped at a restaurant, Kid Rags was instantly awake. One by one, the others opened their eyes, yawned and stretched. Mary saw them exchange gleeful smiles, but when they glanced her way, the smiles faded, though their lips still twitched and their eyes still twinkled.

Steeling herself against their infectious good humor, she stepped from the bus and led the way into the restaurant, which seemed busy for so early in the morning. They had to wait a few minutes until a busboy cleared a booth big enough for all of them.

Two cops drinking coffee at the counter turned around to study them. Although Happy and some of the others nonchalantly looked down at their hands or up at the ceiling, Mary forced herself to meet the cops' gaze. Hadn't she read somewhere that innocent people were curious about cops and guilty ones shied away from them? Or maybe it was the other way around.

After a moment, the cops turned back to their coffee, and the hostess came and ushered them to a still-wet table. Mary slid into the booth, surprised she'd made it that far on such wobbly legs. Well, she knew one thing—when this was all over, she'd go back to leading a squeaky-clean life. Anything else would give her a nervous breakdown for sure.

After the waitress placed Mary's hot chocolate and the elders' coffee on the table and took their breakfast orders, Kid Rags deposited a large, thick Manila envelope in front of Mary.

She narrowed her eyes at him. "What's this?"

"A present. I've been waiting for the right time to give it

to you."

She picked up the envelope, which felt much heavier than she'd expected, and pulled out a rectangular sheet of metal a little larger than a piece of notebook paper and approximately a third of an inch thick.

Teach's eyes widened. "Is that what I think it is?"

Kid Rags nodded.

Teach held out a hand. "May I see?" His tone sounded reverential.

Mary glanced at the metal plate before handing it over, unable to figure out why it inspired such awe. Sure, it had a pretty design etched around the border, but the letters of the words were backward and unreadable.

"Well, I'll be . . ." Teach touched the plate as delicately as Crunchy had touched his cat. "I can't believe you kept it all these years."

"What is it?" Mary asked.

"The printing plate for the share certificates for your grandfather's gold mine." Teach turned to Kid Rags. "You're a true artist, Kid."

"Thank you." Kid Rags spoke without pride or modesty, but quietly, as if it were his due.

"Am I understanding this correctly?" Mary said. "You were a forger?"

"Still am," Kid Rags said in that same quiet tone, "when I can get the work. People today don't seem to want to pay for fine workmanship, not when computers can do it cheaper and faster."

"Some swear he was the best in the business," Teach said. "Did all the paper work for the lamsters staying at your grandparents' farm."

"The ones that needed it," Kid Rags added.

"So you *did* know my grandfather," Mary said.

Kid Rags nodded. "We grew up in the same neighborhood in Chicago. He was a few years older than me, so we weren't close back then, but after I started doing the paper for his lamsters, we saw a lot of each other. I was sorry to hear he died. He was a stand-up guy all the way."

Mary ran the tip of a finger around the rim of her cup. "I wish I had known him."

"In a way you do," Kid Rags said. "You look a lot like your grandmother, but you're actually more like your grandfather—brave, fair, strong, ready for anything. And not above a bit of manipulation, I might add."

Mary gave him a dubious look. "Are you sure this is me you're talking about?"

"Hmmph," he muttered, lips twitching. "Beating down an old man's defenses using his favorite brand of bourbon. Whoever heard of such a thing?"

The waitress appeared bearing an armload of plates, which she dealt out as easily as a deck of cards.

They ate silently for a few minutes, then Iron Sam looked at Kid Rags and said, "I heard of you. You did Carlos Marcello's papers."

Kid Rags swallowed a mouthful of bacon and eggs. "That's right. I did."

Mary was about to take a bite of toast, but she paused long enough to ask, "Who's Carlos Marcello?"

"They called him 'The Little Man' because he was only five feet four inches tall," Teach said. "There were two others they called 'The Little Man'—Johnny Torrio and Meyer Lansky, probably the smartest guys in the business. People laugh at small men who want to be powerful, saying they have Napoleon complexes, but believe me, no one laughed at those three little men."

Happy glowered at no one in particular. "How come nobody makes fun of tall people who want to be powerful, or laugh at them for having a . . . a Goliath complex?"

"Good thinking." Teach pointed his fork at Happy. "Unfortunately, our society has a bias against short people."

"Tell me about it," Happy grumbled.

"Johnny Torrio came up with the idea of the Syndicate," Lila Lorraine proclaimed proudly, as if she had known the man personally.

And maybe she had, Mary reflected. She knew little about the old woman. Though not as obvious about it as the men, Lila Lorraine was as reticent to talk about her past as they were.

"Who's Carlos Marcello?" Crunchy asked. "I met Johnny Torrio and Meyer Lansky, but I never met no Carlos Marcello."

"Understandable," Teach said. "Carlos Marcello was a mob boss in Louisiana." He glanced at Iron Sam. "Perhaps you would like to tell the story."

Iron Sam hunched over his food without answering.

"How come you didn't ask me if I want to tell the story," Kid Rags protested.

Teach raised one eyebrow. "Would you like to tell the story?"

Kid Rags made a magnanimous gesture. "No. You go ahead."

Teach laughed and said, "Carlos Marcello was conceived in Sicily and born in Tunisia as Calogero Minacori, but he denied his Sicilian heritage. He never bothered to become a U.S. citizen, so in 1951 when he refused to answer questions before a senate committee, Estes Kefauver recommended he be deported, which he could do because of Marcello's 1938 conviction for possession of twenty-three pounds of marijuana. But neither Italy nor Tunisia would take him.

"From 1953 to 1961, Marcello was under a constant order of deportation, and he fought it with every legal weapon available. He decided that if he lost he didn't want to be too far away from his base of operations, so he got his name inserted into the record books of a jungle city called San Jose Pinula, which was the only Central American city he could find with a blank space in the appropriate time period."

"Then he had me make him a Guatemalan passport," Kid Rags said.

Teach nodded. "That way, if Marcello had to take a 'vacation' as they called it, he would be in close touch with his business associates.

"Robert Kennedy, the Attorney General at the time, decided that if Marcello preferred Guatemala to Sicily, he'd oblige him.

"When Marcello showed up for his quarterly visit to the New Orleans Immigration Department, he thought it was another routine appearance, but when he extended his arm across the desk to sign his Statement of Appearance, he was handcuffed, dragged to a waiting car and finally to an Immigration Department jet where he was the only passenger. Then, on Robert Kennedy's orders, he was dumped in the Guatemalan jungle.

"Marcello eventually made his way back to the United States and resumed his operations, but he always had a special hatred for the Kennedys, particularly Robert. Sam Giancana in Chicago also hated the Kennedys, but that's another story."

After checking out two addresses for Iron Sam in Springfield, Illinois and finding that both of them had been turned into parking lots, Mary drove to a third address, this one on McClure Avenue in Peoria.

Iron Sam stared out the window at the newly built apartment complex, which was decked out with huge banners proclaiming *NOW RENTING*.

After a long while, he rose, shuffled to the door, waited for Mary to open it, then struggled down the steps. Once outside, he hobbled slowly away from the bus. His stooped shoulders sagged more than usual, and his hands, one of which carried the paper bag containing his belongings, hung almost to his knees.

"Where's he going?" Lila Lorraine asked.

Mary jumped up. "I don't know, but it doesn't look like he's planning on coming back."

She ran after Iron Sam.

"It's no use," he said in his rasping voice.

"What's no use?"

"I don't know this world. Everything's changed."

Mary reached out an arm, but snatched it back, sure Iron Sam wouldn't welcome her pity.

"You don't have to leave. I'll drive you wherever you

want to go."

"Why? So I can talk to you about your grandfather? I didn't know him."

"I already figured that out."

He stopped and looked at her, his gaze as intense as ever. "You did?"

"Yes."

"And you still took me to all those places?"

"Yes."

"Why?" He shot the word at her.

"To be honest, I don't know. I guess I thought we'd find the guys you were looking for, and that would be the end of it."

"What guys?"

She shifted her weight from foot to foot and averted her eyes.

"You mean wise guys? Is that what you think this is about?"

Mary nodded.

He let out a snort of laughter that rattled in his throat, choking him. Coughing and hacking, he fell against a parked car.

Mary took a step forward and stopped, not knowing what to do.

Iron Sam coughed once more, then hauled himself upright and walked away.

"Where are you going?" she asked.

"To find someplace to die."

"Where? In the wilds of Peoria?"

He continued walking.

Mary kept pace with him. "Look, why don't you come on back to the bus. Maybe if we all put our heads together, we can figure out what to do." When he didn't even pause, she said, "There's a pizza place across the street. We can go eat. That should make Kid Rags happy, at least."

"Why would I want to make him happy? No one ever made me happy." Iron Sam took two more steps, then stopped and looked back at the bus where the others waited, various expressions of concern and curiosity on their faces. "Okay," he said at last.

When the pizza was set before them, together with a pitcher of beer Kid Rags liberally spiked with bourbon, they all grabbed a slice. As always, Iron Sam hunched over his food, but after a few bites, he leaned back.

"I did meet your grandfather once," he said.

Her mouth full, Mary could only give him a questioning glance.

"It was a long time ago—forty years, maybe. I was supposed to hit a guy by the name of Carmine 'The Snake' Rastelli, but before I could do the job, Rastelli disappeared. Someone told me he went to a safe house in Colorado run by a friend of us called Jimmy Boots. When I arrived, I saw two or three lamsters, but Rastelli wasn't one of them. Jimmy Boots let me hang around for a few days in case he showed up, but he never came. I think Lila Lorraine was there, too."

Lila Lorraine nodded.

Iron Sam coughed. "But I don't remember anyone taking my picture."

"So that's it," Teach said. "I've been wondering how you knew Jimmy Boots."

"Could Carmine the Snake have been hiding out in the secret room?" Mary asked, remembering the rollaway bed she had seen.

Teach raised his eyebrows. "Jimmy Boots had a secret room? Well, I'll be . . ."

Kid Rags laughed. "So there is something you don't know, Teach."

"I got the feeling Jimmy Boots wasn't comfortable having me stay there," Iron Sam said. "Maybe he did have Rastelli hidden away."

"He wasn't in the secret room," Lila Lorraine said emphatically.

"Did you ever find Carmine the Snake?" Mary asked.

"No. I found his car, but not him. Since I took the money

and the credit for the hit, it wouldn't have been good for business if he turned up alive somewhere, so I kept looking for him, but he had completely disappeared off the face of the earth." He frowned at Mary. "I don't know why I'm talking to you. I never told anyone this before."

"Don't feel bad," Kid Rags said. "We've all shot off our mouths. It's those wide, innocent eyes of hers that get to you after a while."

"So no one knows what happened to Carmine the Snake?" Mary asked.

"I doubt anyone cares," Teach said. "As I told you before, he was an unpleasant fellow. Not only did he rape women, there were rumors he also raped his male victims, but no one could agree on whether he did it before or after he killed them."

Lila Lorraine shredded a piece of pepperoni, then dropped the bits back onto her half-eaten slice of pizza.

Without looking up, she said, "I know what happened to him."

Chapter 14

They all gaped at Lila Lorraine.

"How do you know what happened to Carmine The Snake when no one else does?" Teach asked.

"I was at the farm one summer visiting the Stuarts when a fancy Cadillac pulled in front of the house." Lila Lorraine's voice was so soft Mary had to strain to hear. "A man stepped out of the car, and I bit my lip to keep from laughing. He was all duded up like Roy Rogers—ten-gallon hat, embroidered silk cowboy shirt, bolo tie with a huge chunk of turquoise in an ornate silver setting, silver belt buckle as big as a saucer, and linen pants tucked into high-heeled cowboy boots decorated with silver conchos. I got the impression he thought that's how people in Colorado dressed and wanted to blend in, but he looked out of place on that dusty, windy farm.

"He had a smug expression on his face and a cigarette dangling from a corner of his mouth. Any desire to laugh died when I looked into his eyes. They were hard, cold. I think they were light brown, but the way the sun hit them made them look red. He must have blinked, since it's something we all do automatically, but I don't remember ever seeing his eyelids move. His head jutted forward and his ears stuck out, giving him the look of a hooded cobra ready to strike.

"He mentioned the names of a few men who had stayed at the farm and said he also needed a place to hide out for a few days. At the time, we didn't know what Rastelli had done, otherwise Jimmy might have suggested he move on, but although Jimmy didn't take to the man, he had no reason to turn him away, so he agreed to let Rastelli stay the night.

"That night passed without incident except for several off-color stories Rastelli told around the dinner table, so the next day when Rastelli asked to stay another night, Jimmy said yes, on the condition that Rastelli watch what he said.

"That afternoon Jimmy worked in the barn where he had his workshop, Rastelli made phone calls in the living room, supposedly looking for another place to stay, and Gina and I canned wild plum jam in the kitchen. Pete—Jimmy and Gina's son, Mary's father—played outside by himself.

"Gina asked me to stir the pot of jam, said she had to go check on Pete. Pete was ten or twelve at the time and well able to look after himself, but he tended to hide when Jimmy had guests. They terrified him, poor dear. He had a tire swing attached to a cottonwood in the front yard, and he loved to climb the rope and hide in the tree, though Jimmy had forbidden him to go there. The tree was very old, and the branches tended to break easily, but Pete didn't care. He felt safe there.

"I told Gina I'd go check on him and try to talk him out of the tree—the last thing the poor kid needed was a scolding. As I passed through the living room, Rastelli grabbed me, clamped one of his hands over my mouth, the other around my neck, and dragged me to the couch. I kicked and hit him and tried to bite his hand, but it made him more excited. Finally he stopped choking me and started to rip off my clothes, keeping one hand over my mouth. I tried to get away, but he lay on top of me, crushing me. In my struggles, I managed to knock over a lamp. Gina came running. When she saw what was happening, she kicked him in the side, then hit him over the head with the fallen lamp. He shifted position long enough that I managed to wiggle out from underneath him. He jammed his elbow into my solar plexus, doubling me up, then hauled off and punched Gina in the mouth, sending her crashing to the floor.

"I heard the back door slam and the refrigerator being opened and closed. Jimmy called out, asking if there was any beer left. Then he must have heard us struggling because a second later he charged into the living room, grabbed a rifle out of a gun cabinet, and smashed the butt into Rastelli's face, knocking him out.

"He put an arm around Gina, helped her up, and asked if she was okay. After she said yes, he hugged her and hugged her, then turned to me and asked if I was all right. I hurt all over, but I nodded.

"Jimmy let go of Gina, stared at Rastelli for a moment, then grabbed him by the collar of his fancy shirt, dragged him through the living room, out onto the front porch, down the steps, and into the yard, where he let go. Rastelli fell face down and lay still.

"'Is he dead?' I asked hopefully. 'No,' Jimmy answered, kicking Rastelli. Rastelli groaned, shook his head, struggled to all fours, cursing and threatening.

"Jimmy pointed the rifle at Rastelli's head, pulled the trigger, and said, 'Now he's dead.' Without another word, Jimmy threw Rastelli in the back of his pickup, tossed a shovel and a pickaxe on top of him, got in the truck, and roared away.

"Gina and I clung together, assuring each other we were okay. As we walked toward the house, arm in arm, we heard a tiny whimper. We froze for a fraction of a second, then ran to Pete's tree. We could see him clinging to a branch, white-faced and wild-eyed. We tried to coax him down, but he was in shock, I think, and didn't seem to hear us. While Gina talked soothingly to him, I ran to the shed and got a ladder. Gina climbed up, managed to pry his hands free, and carried him down. We wrapped him in blankets, fed him hot chocolate, but he couldn't stop shivering.

"Gina explained that Rastelli did bad things to us, but I don't think she got through to him. All he knew was that he'd seen his father kill a man in cold blood.

"When Jimmy came back an hour or two later, he tossed me his keys, told me to follow him. He drove Rastelli's car to Stapleton Airport, left it in the long-term parking lot, got into his truck, and drove us back to the farm, not uttering a single word.

"Later, at dinner, he looked at each of us in turn and said, 'This is something we never talk about.' And, until today, none of us ever did."

No one spoke. Even if she knew what to say, Mary didn't think she could force the words through her constricted throat.

When she finally managed to speak, the words came out sounding strained. "You mean my grandfather murdered someone?"

"Of course not," Lila Lorraine said. "Killing a snake isn't murder."

"Neither is putting a bullet in the head of a corpse," Iron Sam added.

"But Lila Lorraine said he was still alive."

Iron Sam pinned her with his gaze. "As soon as the hit was sanctioned, Rastelli was dead. If your grandfather hadn't killed him, I would have. Your grandfather was simply the instrument of his death."

Mary shrunk back into her chair. "Is that how you justify what you did for a living?"

"I didn't need to justify it. All I had to do was carry out my orders."

"I don't understand how you can be so blasé about killing people."

"In essence, you witness a single death in a lifetime. Death makes its impact only once. And you become a killer only once. After that, it's a job like any other."

"It's not like any other job. You kill people."

"So do soldiers."

"That's different."

"Is it? How?" Iron Sam sounded more curious than combative.

Mary turned to Teach.

He shrugged. "Don't look at me. I'm with Sam on this one."

She tried to think of a cogent argument, but all she could come up with was, "When soldiers kill, they're authorized by the government."

"An authority they give themselves," Teach pointed out.

"Soldiers kill to protect us."

Teach stroked his chin with a thumb and forefinger. "They sure saved us from all the North Koreans and then later the North Vietnamese who were storming our borders, didn't they?"

Kid Rags laughed, but Mary couldn't even force a smile.

"Whether it is the government or the Syndicate," Teach said, "it's all about profits. People have the idea that wars happen, like floods or earthquakes, but they are always—always—a deliberate act by individuals for profit. Anything else is a con, a play put on for the benefit of us little people."

Mary looked at him as if she'd never seen him before. "You really do believe everything is a con, don't you?"

"Yes. Because it is." He slapped the table. "This is solid, right?"

"Right," Mary said hesitantly, wondering where this was leading.

"But according to physics, it's nothing more than a manifestation of the electromagnetic spectrum, as is everything we see or hear or feel. Our brains con us into believing this is a solid table, and Happy's shirt is that bilious shade of green."

Happy stuck out his chest, Crunchy scrunched his face in concentration, and Iron Sam finished eating his slice of pizza.

Kid Rags laughed. "Always the life of the party, huh, Teach?"

Iron Sam rose. "I'll be going now."

Mary held up a hand. "No. Wait. I told you we'd figure something out, and I meant it."

Iron Sam remained standing, but he didn't leave.

"You haven't told us what you're looking for," Lila Lorraine said.

Iron Sam turned his head to stare out a window. "All those years sitting in a cell that stunk like somebody died inside the cinderblock wall and was still moldering away in there, I kept sane by imagining myself smoking the world's finest cigar and drinking the best Irish whiskey among familiar surroundings. But everything I know is gone."

Lila Lorraine beamed at him. "Well, why didn't you say so? I know just the place—The Joker in Chicago."

"The Joker where you and Gina Dale and Jimmy Boots

and Crunchy used to work?" Mary asked, wide-eyed. "You mean it's still in business?"

Lila Lorraine nodded. "It sure is. It's been there since before prohibition and it will probably be there long after we're gone."

"Spaghetti doesn't own it anymore," Kid Rags said. "I heard he turned it over to his son to manage, and his son sold it."

"But it's still The Joker." Lila Lorraine smiled. "Those were good days. It'll be nice to see the place again." She turned her attention to Kid Rags and recognition replaced the faraway look in her eyes. "Now I know why you seem so familiar." She leaned toward Mary. "He was one of the slicks who used to hang around outside the stage door."

Kid Rags sat straighter, smoothed his mustache, and adjusted his polka dot bow tie.

Happy jumped up. "Come on, let's go. What are we waiting for?"

Kid Rags stopped preening and pulled his plate closer. "I'm not finished yet."

"Me either," Crunchy said.

Grumbling to himself, Happy sank back onto his chair.

After a moment, Iron Sam sat down and reached for another slice of pizza.

Apparently deciding to make the most of his enforced inactivity, Happy peered at Iron Sam. "What are you dying from?"

To Mary's surprise, Iron Sam didn't take offense, but spoke one word, sharp and clipped.

"Cancer."

Happy bounced in his seat. "How long you got left? You in a lot of pain?"

Iron Sam took a bite of his pizza, chewed it slowly, and washed it down with the bourbon-laced beer.

He sat back. "I could go at any minute. And no, I don't have a lot of pain."

"Really?" Mary blurted. "I thought cancer was agonizing."

"Sometimes it is," Teach said. "Other times it causes surprisingly little discomfort. All too often, the doctors who are trying to 'cure' the cancer create the pain and trauma. Since there is no cure, they try to kill it by burning or cutting or poisoning and hope they don't kill the patient in the process. Speaking of cons, as far as I'm concerned, so-called modern medicine is one of the biggest cons around."

Kid Rags groaned. "Don't get him started. He can talk for hours on the evils of the pharmaceutical industry and how doctors are their pimps, pawns, and pushers. Not that he's wrong. We just don't need to be reminded of it."

Happy didn't seem to be aware of this exchange. His bright eyes focused on Iron Sam. "What kind of cancer you got?"

"All kinds. I didn't know I had it until I vomited blood all over my food one day. The doctor told me it was so extensive he couldn't do anything. That's why they let me out of the pen."

Teach gave him a sharp look. "They don't let people out of prison because they're dying."

"In my case they did."

"I don't mean to be disrespectful," Teach said, "but why did they?"

"Two or three weeks ago I got a visit from a kid out of law school. Looked about fifteen. Said he was my new lawyer and that a doctor was going to be testifying to the parole board on my behalf. I thought he was trying to get money from me, or information so he could write a book. You'd be surprised how many young punks think they can write. But he told me he didn't want anything from me. It was all paid for."

"By whom?" Teach asked.

"I don't know. He said he couldn't tell me even if he knew, which he didn't. The client contacted him by email and paid with an anonymous wire transfer.

"I didn't think anything would come of it since the parole board didn't like me. I refused to apologize for what I did. I'm not the one who murdered those people. I was the weapon. But somehow he and the doctor managed to persuade the board that since I was dying I no longer posed a threat to society, and they let me out."

"Maybe someone in the Syndicate did you a favor," Mary said.

"Could be, but I doubt it."

Happy's eyes gleamed. "Maybe they wanted you out so they could take their revenge on you."

"For what? I didn't do anything to them. And almost everyone I knew is dead."

"What about the relatives of one of your victims?" Mary asked.

"It doesn't make sense since I'm dying."

"Maybe it's the guy in the blue car," Crunchy said.

Lila Lorraine put her fingers to her mouth. "He's not still following us, is he?"

"He is," Iron Sam said. "I can feel him."

"I see him from time to time," Mary said. "He stays way far back, but he's still there."

"So who is he?" Kid Rags asked. "What does he want? And what are we going to do about it?"

"Shoot him," Happy said with relish.

Lila Lorraine toyed with her pizza. "Maybe we should wait and see what happens."

"Action beats reaction," Teach said.

Mary looked from one to another. "What can we do? If we go looking for him, he'll see us coming a mile away and take off like he did yesterday. And we can't call the cops."

Crunchy shook his head vigorously. "No cops. Don't like cops."

"No cops," Happy echoed.

"But we have to do something," Teach said.

Although the men all nodded in agreement, no one ventured a plan of action.

"But don't worry," Kid Rags assured Mary. "Give us enough time, we'll think of something."

Mary groaned. "That's what I'm afraid of."

Chapter 15

"It seems odd you knew my father when he was a boy," Mary said that night when she and Lila Lorraine lay in their beds in a motel on the outskirts of Chicago.

"Odd how?" Lila Lorraine asked.

"I don't know. It's just that he doesn't talk about his childhood."

"He was a nice kid. Smart, too, although he didn't do too well in school. He liked fixing things. When he was eight or nine, he took all the sinks apart to learn about plumbing. Drove Gina nuts. She'd turn on the water and the next thing she knew the floor would be flooded."

Mary smiled at the thought of her father studiously, maybe even joyfully, taking apart the plumbing fixtures, but her amusement faded when the image of a trembling, white-faced little boy with shocked eyes slipped into her mind.

"I've known my father my whole life," she said softly, "but now I find out I never knew him at all. I had no idea he went through so much as a child."

"I don't think he wanted you to know. After that day, he spent more and more time away from the farm, throwing himself into extra-curricular activities at school. He tried out for all the sports, but he was too skinny to be good at any of them until he discovered swimming. At first he wasn't much good at that either, but he kept at it, spending hours after school swimming laps. He got so good he went to college on an athletic scholarship.

"He seldom returned to the farm during those years, but after graduation, he visited one last time. He had met a girl—Gwen—and planned to marry her. I think he wanted to reconcile with your grandfather, but when he got to the farm, he found two rough-looking lamsters on the premises.

"'What if Gwen and I have kids?' he asked Gina. 'How can I bring them to see you, never knowing who will be here or what will happen? It would be more than I can bear to have a child of mine see what I did.'

"Gina felt torn between the needs of her husband and her son, but she kept it to herself. 'You do what you have to do,' she told Pete.

"He kissed her on the cheek, said, 'Good-bye, Mom,' shook hands with Jimmy, and left the house.

"They never spoke to each other again.

"It about broke Gina's heart that she never got to know you or hold you in her arms, but she kept track of you. She and Jimmy went to your high school graduation. They would have gone to your college graduation too, but Jimmy was recovering from a heart attack and couldn't travel."

Tears stung Mary's eyes, but she brushed them away with a quick, impatient gesture. "You really did know my grandparents well, didn't you?"

"I spent a lot of happy days on that farm." A chuckle sounded in the darkness. "Jimmy used to say I visited there so often I might as well move in. He meant it too, but I still had some life in these old bones, so I laughed it off as a joke. And then, overnight it seemed, I grew old and frail and couldn't travel the way I used to, and we drifted apart, though I still talked to Gina on the phone occasionally."

There was a moment of silence followed by a long sigh. "One of the few regrets I have is that I didn't accept Jimmy's offer. It would have been nice living out my final days on the farm. Not that there's anything wrong with my apartment, but the walls do close in sometimes."

"Would you like to go stay there for a while?" Mary asked. "The house is a mess—it's run down, and whoever killed my grandparents trashed the place—but I think we could fix a couple of rooms so they'd be habitable.

"I've been trying to figure out what to do with Iron Sam. I don't feel right about letting him go off by himself to die, and he doesn't want to go back to the hospice, so I thought he could stay at the farm. Since you two have a history together, I wondered if you'd mind staying with him. He shouldn't be alone, even though I think that's what he wants."

"I accept," Lila Lorraine said without hesitation.

"Don't you want to think about it? I mean, you'll be out there in the middle of nowhere. I'll call and stop by as often as I can, but for the most part you'll be on your own, and you're not—"

"Not young anymore," Lila Lorraine finished when Mary stopped abruptly.

"Well, yes," Mary said, glad of the darkness that hid her blushing face.

"Maybe it's foolish, and I know it will be terribly sad for me to be there without your grandparents, but I'd like to do it. One of the worst things about growing old is having outlived your usefulness. It will be nice to be needed for a change." There was a smile in her voice when she added, "I won't have to worry about my blood pressure medicine. I have enough to last for years."

The next morning, watching Lila Lorraine put on her makeup, Mary said impulsively, "How about if I do that for you?"

Lila Lorraine smiled at her. "Would you, honey? I make such a mess of it, but I feel so naked without my face on."

Mary wiped away the smeared makeup and re-applied it with deft strokes.

Lila Lorraine nodded in approval. "You do that well."

Mary laughed. "You sound surprised."

"Because I've never seen you wear makeup. And you should. You'd be so beautiful. Mascara and liner and shadow would make those lovely gray eyes of yours stand out. And you're too pale. You could use a bit of color on your cheeks."

Mary flicked her wrist dismissively. "I don't like the way it makes me feel." She tilted her head to one side, studying her handiwork. She added a hint of blue eye shadow and a dusting of rouge. "There. All done."

Lila Lorraine leaned close to the mirror, gazed at her reflection for a moment, then rose and gave Mary a quick hug.

There was a knock on the door and the sound of Kid Rags' growling voice. "You ladies about ready? We're starving."

Mary opened the door and ushered out a suddenly shy Lila Lorraine.

Kid Rags whistled.

Teach took off his hat and, grinning, clapped it to his chest.

Iron Sam narrowed his eyes as if he couldn't figure out what she'd done differently.

Crunchy stared. "You look young, Lila Lorraine. And so pretty."

Lila Lorraine beamed.

Happy shifted his weight from foot to foot. "We going or not?"

After breakfast, Kid Rags directed Mary to North Avenue where he and Jimmy Boots grew up. Both of their houses, along with most of the original buildings on the street, had been bulldozed and replaced with modern townhouse developments already showing signs of age.

Mary drove slowly down the street, ignoring the honking horns of irate drivers, and wondered what it had been like when her grandfather lived there. Had there been so much traffic? So many people? So much noise?

"Turn right at the next light," Kid Rags said. "That will take us to River North where The Joker is located."

She parked the bus on New Orleans Street in front of the bar—a free standing red brick building ornamented with wrought iron grillwork, a stained glass window, and a carved wooden door flanked by brass light fixtures.

Accompanied by her entire entourage, she walked around the neighborhood waiting for the bar to open. Because of an absence of contemporary construction, she found it easy to imagine Jimmy Boots and Gina Dale, arm in arm, strolling along these very streets, perhaps glancing at the large rectangular structures, maybe marveling at the fancy brickwork or the stone carvings and bas-reliefs decorating many of the buildings.

Finally, noticing that the elders lagged behind, she returned to the bar, which had opened for business.

The Joker was larger than she expected and not as dim, looking more like an old dance hall than a neighborhood tavern. The long mahogany bar top and the brass foot rail were polished to a high sheen. An old-fashioned etched brass cash register perched on one end of the bar, and faded ads for long forgotten beers hung on the walls. Toward the rear of the room, a low stage faced a dance floor. Next to the stage stood a battered upright piano and an antique Wurlitzer jukebox framed in an arch of bubble tubes like the one she'd seen in that old movie *On the Waterfront.*

They found a table large enough for all of them and gave their orders for drinks and sandwiches to a pretty waitress who was dressed much like Mary in black slacks and a white shirt.

While waiting for their food, Happy went to the piano, sat down, pressed one of the high keys four or five times, jumped up and went to the jukebox, fished for change, then pushed some buttons.

Mary didn't pay much attention to the opening bars of the music, but she sat up straight when a gorgeous voice washed over her and turned her insides to warm honey.

"Who is that?" she breathed.

Lila Lorraine smiled. "Johnny Horton. 'All For the Love of a Girl.' One of my favorites."

Before the song ended, an old man with heavy jowls, a huge belly, and wild white hair—what remained of it— waddled into the bar and stood by the jukebox. As soon as the last note died away, he pulled the plug, sat at the piano, and played a tune familiar to Mary. What was it? Oh, yes. "Teddy Bear," an old rock-and-roll song her mother had sung to her when she was a child.

With a guilty start, she realized she hadn't given a thought to her mother or Bill in days. Maybe she should call them. And tell them what? That she was roaming the country with a busload of old gangsters? Bill had met some of them, of course, but he'd have a fit if he knew that she since added a hit man to her passengers. No, better wait until she got back to talk to them.

The waitress, followed by Happy, brought their drinks—ginger ale for Mary, bourbon for Kid Rags, beer with whiskey chasers for the others.

The piano player finished "Teddy Bear" and immediately segued into another rollicking old tune, which set Lila Lorraine to tapping her feet, bobbing her head, and jiggling her shoulders.

The bartender, a sandy-haired, hazel-eyed man in his late twenties or early thirties, approached their table. He was not nearly as handsome as Bill, but he had a nice open face and a ready smile.

"There's no way a beautiful woman can walk into my bar without letting me dance with her," he said in a voice as mellifluous as Johnny Horton's.

While Mary tried to think of a witty refusal, the bartender held out a hand to Lila Lorraine and whirled the beaming old woman onto the dance floor.

"How come I can't think of clever things to say like the girls in movies do?" Mary asked.

"Because you don't have a scriptwriter who spends hours formulating the perfect remark," Teach said.

"But you don't have a scriptwriter, and you never seem to be at a loss for words."

Kid Rags laughed. "You can say that again."

Watching the dancers execute a tricky-looking step, Mary frowned. "I'm not sure I trust that guy. He seems too smooth and charming to be real."

Kid Rags adjusted his bow tie. "He dresses well. That's a fine-looking shirt he's wearing."

Iron Sam, studying everyone and everything in the bar, made no comment.

"I like him," Crunchy said. "He's nice to Lila Lorraine."

"People who live next door to serial killers always say

they're nice," Happy commented darkly.

In the silence that greeted this pronouncement, the bartender returned a breathless but radiant Lila Lorraine to the table, seated her, then hurried off to wait on a ruddy-faced man signaling for a drink.

"His name is Tim. Timothy Olson," Lila Lorraine reported when her breathing returned to normal. "His father owns this place, bought it from Spaghetti's son."

The man at the piano started playing another song.

Lila Lorraine closed her eyes, smiling. "I love a boogie beat." Then her eyes opened wide and she swiveled around to stare at the piano player.

Mary followed her gaze, and watched the old man's fat fingers fly over the keys, jerk up during barely perceptible pauses, then immediately settle on the keys once more.

"I know this tune," Lila Lorraine said. "Spaghetti composed it. He called it 'Bootleg Boogie.' He played it like that, too." She stared at the man a while longer. "I think that is Spaghetti."

"Can't be," Kid Rags said. "Spaghetti was skinny. That's how he got his name, remember?"

"He really was thin," Lila Lorraine told Mary, "with a thin head and thin lips, but there was nothing thin about his smile. It was as big as the whole world. That's him. I'm sure of it."

She rose, went to the piano, and leaned against it until the song ended. Only then did the old man look up.

Mary couldn't hear what they said, but she did see him struggle to his feet, wrap his arms around Lila Lorraine, and give her a big hug. Moments later, Lila Lorraine led the old man to their table. She introduced Mary first, telling him that Mary was the granddaughter of Jimmy Boots and Gina Dale.

Spaghetti held out his hands and beamed at her. His age, his girth, his ungainliness all seemed to disappear as he enveloped Mary in the warmth of his broad smile.

"It's a pleasure to meet you, my dear," he said, huffing and wheezing. "How are your grandparents?"

Lila Lorraine stepped in and quickly introduced the

others, saving Mary the necessity of answering.

Spaghetti said he remembered Teach, Kid Rags, and Crunchy. He grinned at them and settled back in a chair, which creaked and groaned under his weight.

"It's so nice to be called Spaghetti again," he said, then added with a comical grimace of distaste, "All anyone calls me is Dom or Dominic or Mr. Galluccio, if they call me anything at all. Gee, it's great to see all of you. Too bad Jimmy Boots and Gina Dale couldn't make it. Maybe next time, huh? Do you see anyone from the old days? Of course you do," he answered himself, laughing with a burst of wheezing exhalations, "Whuf . . . whuf . . . whuf. You're all here, aren't you? What are you doing in Chicago? A trip down memory lane? Whuf . . . whuf . . . whuf. There's not many of us left from the old days."

The waitress brought a sandwich for Spaghetti along with the food for the rest of them.

"Well, isn't that sweet of you. Thanks, Judy," Spaghetti said, but he didn't pause in his recital to take a bite.

"I read in the obituaries this morning that Dottie Dixon passed away," he continued. "Do you remember her, Lila Lorraine? She took Gina Dale's place. Dottie married a Syndicate member who spent a lot of time in Las Vegas. One of the times when he was away, she had a brief affair with a lesbian. When he found out about it, he was furious, but he couldn't bring himself to kill Dottie, and since she wouldn't name her lover, he took revenge by killing the owner of the club where the two women met.

"Do you remember Harry Dorsey, the cop that came in every week to shake us down? I heard he moved to Palm Springs when he retired. Some of the cops must have been on the legit, but I never met one. Once when they found a man on The Corner with six bullets in him, the cops called it suicide. Whuf . . . whuf . . . whuf. And there was a beautiful girl that came flying off the roof of a downtown hotel and fell ten stories to the street. She was bound and gagged, but the cops called that suicide, too.

"Hey! Guess who I saw the other day. Benny Fingers.

Remember him? He was a busboy here way back when. Did a stretch in Joliet when Leopold and Loeb were there. He told me once even the mobsters in the joint didn't live so well. Dickie Loeb's cell was immense, and had shelves of books, filing cabinets, a huge glass-topped desk, two canaries. He and Leopold ate with the officers of the prison, not with the other prisoners, and they got special foods. The guards even allowed them outside the walls at times. And they wore white flannels instead of prison garb. Eventually, an inmate Dickie was trying to rape killed him. Dickie's family could buy off everyone but the grim reaper. Whuf . . . whuf . . . whuf.

"Remember Willie the Wolf? Big guy? Huge head? He died recently. On his wedding night. He'd buried four wives and decided to try for five, but she wore him out. What a way to go! What about you? Did any of you ever tie the knot?"

There was a moment of silence as if they weren't sure Spaghetti would be quiet long enough for them to respond, but when he took a big bite out of his sandwich and tilted his head expectantly, Teach, Crunchy, and Lila Lorraine all said no.

Iron Sam, draped over his mostly empty plate, didn't answer, didn't raise his head.

Kid Rags held up three fingers. "I got married three times, but none of them took."

"I was married once," Happy said. "She died of diabetes. I went to stay with my daughter Susan and her husband in Denver, but she died too, and he kicked me out." After a moment of silence, he said, choking, "Susan died in childbirth. No one's supposed to die having a baby anymore."

"No, they're not," Lila Lorraine murmured.

Spaghetti's mouth turned down and his jowls drooped. "My wife died ten years ago. We fought every single day. She made me furious with her airs and her terrible cooking and her nagging ways, but now I'd give anything to have one more argument with her."

Then, all at once, his mournful look disappeared and his affable grin returned. He reached into the pocket of his tent-like shirt for a handful of cellophane-wrapped cigars and passed them around.

Teach, Kid Rags, and Happy immediately began the ritual of lighting up.

Iron Sam glanced at the cigars, but didn't reach for one.

"Where can we get a good cigar?" Mary asked. "Something special?"

Spaghetti whacked his thigh and went into spasms of wheezing laughter. "You casting aspersions on my smokes?"

Mary wrinkled her nose at the smell of tobacco settling around the table, but she couldn't help smiling at him. "It's for Iron Sam—his first cigar since he got out of prison."

Spaghetti nodded. "I see."

When the waitress approached to clear off the table, he said, "Will you tell Tim we need one of the cigars from his private reserve?"

A few minutes later, the bartender came to their table with a wooden box he carried as if it contained a precious relic. "Which one of you is the connoisseur?"

They all nodded toward Iron Sam who, as usual, was sitting as still as death.

Tim opened the box with a flourish. After studying the contents, Iron Sam chose a dark brown cigar with a black and gold band. He lifted it to his nose and inhaled long and deeply.

There was no change of expression on his impassive face, no hint of satisfaction in his burning eyes, but as he lit the cigar with one of the wooden matches Tim gave him, the flame flickered as though his hand were trembling.

He puffed on the cigar, choked and coughed and sputtered, then puffed some more.

"Now all we need is a glass of your best Irish whiskey," Mary said.

"Anything else?" Tim asked, winking at Lila Lorraine.

"A beer for me," Lila Lorraine said, giggling softly.

Mary winced, wondering how the old woman could fall

for such a phony act. "Nothing for me," she said. She could have kicked herself when she heard herself add, "I'm driving." Why couldn't she be like the elders, she fumed to herself. They never offered excuses for anything they said or did.

Tim gave her a mischievous glance, as if somehow he knew exactly what she were thinking, then turned his attention to the old men. "What about you gentlemen? Anything from the bar?"

"Bourbon," Kid Rags said.

The others chorused, "Me too."

Smoking and drinking, the elders continued to discuss people from their past. Although Spaghetti did most of the talking, the others managed to get in a few words now and then.

Mary gazed about the bar, trying to picture her grandmother dancing on the stage, her grandfather polishing glassware as Tim was now doing.

The sound of the door crashing open drew her attention, and she saw a business-suited young woman rush into the bar.

"I forgot my anniversary today," she said, gasping. "I need a present for my husband."

Tim reached under the counter, pulled out a small gray jewelry box, and flipped it open.

The woman shook her head. "I don't think so."

"How about this?" Tim replaced the gray box and opened a brown one.

"Perfect," the woman said. "I'll take it. How much?"

Spaghetti's laughter drowned out Tim's response.

One of the men sitting at the bar called out, "Hey, Tim, that reminds me—my wife's birthday is tomorrow. You got any earrings?"

Tim set several small boxes on the counter. After deliberating a moment, the man chose one, then peeled a few bills off a large wad of cash.

A cop strolled into the bar. Tim slid an envelope across the bar top.

The cop slipped it into a pocket. Pointing a finger as if it were a gun, he said, "Catch you later."

Mary stood. "I have to get some fresh air." When Crunchy also rose, she said, "You stay here and talk to your friends. I'll be fine."

He made no response, but when she headed for the door, he followed.

Stepping outside into the harsh sunlight, she saw a vaguely familiar man peering into the windows of the bus. He was middle-aged, tall, and very broad. Though his muscles weren't sharply defined and his belly sagged, he gave off an aura of power, like a bodybuilder going to seed.

Without making a sound, Crunchy moved toward the man. When the man turned his head to look back at them, Mary recognized him as the one who had been sitting at the bar, impatiently signaling for another beer when Tim finished dancing with Lila Lorraine.

"Well, if it isn't Snow White and one of the seven old farts," he said, displaying his large, crooked teeth.

He took off running, faster and more gracefully than Mary would have expected from such a big man.

Crunchy gave chase, but the man jumped into his dark blue Grand Am and disappeared into the stream of traffic, leaving a panting Crunchy staring after him.

"Do you have any idea who that was?" Mary asked, hurrying to Crunchy's side.

"Never seen him before."

Mary shivered. "I don't like this."

"Me either."

"We should go back inside and tell the others."

"Got to check on Journey first."

Journey was sleeping on a seat in the bus, curled in Crunchy's sweater, but he jumped to his feet instantly when Crunchy pulled a napkin-wrapped piece of turkey out of his pocket.

Mary laughed. "Like Kid Rags."

She watched them, trying to forget the man she caught peering through the bus windows. Unable to put him out of her mind, she told herself he'd meant no harm—he'd run away, hadn't he?

But the worry kept poking at her.

Chapter 16

When Mary and Crunchy re-entered the Joker, she saw a huddle of men at the bar, Happy among them. With avid expressions on their faces, the men passed snapshots around and spoke in hushed tones.

"Steel boxed side members with cruciform bracing," Tim said.

"Also independent front wheel suspension with coil springs and a live rear axle with semi-elliptic leaf springs," someone else added.

Mary blinked when she realized it was Happy speaking; she'd never heard him use that quiet, authoritative tone before.

Crunchy joined the men, but Mary went and sat in her chair.

She tilted her head toward the bar. "What's all that about?"

"Classic cars from the fifties and sixties." Teach grinned. "What a guy, that Tim. He's got the sweetest operation I've ever seen."

Crunchy and Happy returned to the table.

Almost bubbly in his excitement, Happy said, "Tim told me we can go see the cars tonight at seven o'clock when he gets off work."

"That's nice," Mary responded, trying to sound enthusiastic.

Teach peered at her. "What's wrong?"

Mary blew out a breath. "The guy who's been following us was outside looking in the bus windows. He ran off when he saw us. Crunchy chased him, but he got away." She described the man. "Does he sound familiar to anyone? You might have seen him. He was sitting at the bar a while ago."

The elders all turned their heads to look at Iron Sam.

"I know lots of guys like that," he said, "but they're all still in the joint. And they have no beef with me."

"Do any of the rest of you know him?" Mary asked. "Maybe this doesn't have anything to do with Sam. Just because we first saw him in Leavenworth doesn't mean it's the first time he appeared."

"I'd of seen him if he showed earlier," Happy declared.

"Even without your glasses on?" Mary asked gently.

He slouched in his seat, muttering to himself.

"What's going on?" Spaghetti asked. "Why's someone following you?"

"I don't know," Mary said. With frequent interruptions and additions from the others, she told the story from start to finish. How she'd discovered that her grandparents hadn't died before her birth as she'd been told. How she'd set out to learn more about them and found herself traveling halfway across the country accompanied by the elders. How they'd picked up a tail somewhere along the way.

She didn't mention Happy's gun. Nor did she mention the drugstore burglary, thinking the fewer people who knew about that, the better for all concerned.

"Seems like you're having a real adventure," Spaghetti said, sounding envious.

Mary laid her hands flat on the table. "I'd invite you to come, but this is the end of the road for us. I think we should go back before something bad happens."

The elders looked at one another, then Lila Lorraine said, to the others' obvious relief, "You can't go back until you go see the farm where your grandmother grew up."

"You know where it is?" Mary asked.

"Sure. I've been there lots of times. It's not too far from La Crosse. Prettiest place you ever saw—rolling hills, green fields, cows. Of course, the DeBrizzi's don't live there anymore. Gina's older brother inherited the farm, and he went bankrupt. But the place is still the same. Or it was the last time I saw it."

Tim approached the table. "Are you and your friends ready for another round, Dom?"

Kid Rags ordered bourbon, then reached out and touched the younger man's sleeve, fingering the fabric.

"Nice cloth," he said. "I'd say it's Pima cotton, but I've never seen any like this."

Tim cocked his head. "It is Pima cotton. Grown in Arizona. Feels like silk, doesn't it?"

Kid Rags shot Teach a sly look. "Hard to believe anything so nice can come from Arizona, isn't it?"

Teach grinned at him, as usual refusing to rise to the bait.

"If you're interested," Tim said, "I have some shirts your size." Perhaps seeing the same wistfulness in Kid Rags eyes Mary did, he added quickly, "I can give you a good price. I'll show them to you later when you stop by to see the cars."

Spaghetti watched Tim leave. "He's a good kid. He lets me come here and play the piano whenever I want."

"I'll bet he doesn't pay you," Mary said.

Spaghetti looked at her in surprise. "No. Of course not. Why should he? He's my friend. And he doesn't charge me for my food or drink. Not that I can drink much anymore," he added glumly. "I don't need money. My no good son pays for my room at the home and gives me an allowance." He contemplated his pudgy fingers for a moment; then a smile brightened his face. "Hey! Guess where I'm living. North Lincoln Avenue and Clark Street."

Mary could tell by the gleam in Teach's eyes that he recognized the address, though no one else seemed to.

"SMC Cartage Garage," Teach said.

Spaghetti whacked his thigh and laughed his spasmodic laugh. "Give the man a cigar!"

Mary and Lila Lorraine exchanged glances, then raised their eyebrows and shrugged.

"It's where the St. Valentine's Day Massacre occurred," Teach explained.

Spaghetti nodded. "They tore the garage down, and it's now a grassy area next to the senior citizens home where I live. Looking out my window, I can see the seven bushes marking the place where those guys were killed."

"Only seven people were killed?" Mary said. "I thought there were more. Seven doesn't sound like much of a massacre."

"It does if you're one of the seven," Happy said.

Teach raised a finger. "Think about it. What if they told the truth and instead of calling it the St. Valentine's Day Massacre, they called it the Killing of Six Gangsters and One Gangster Groupie? Who would care?"

"So it's another OK Corral?" Mary asked.

Teach grinned at her. "Very good. You're learning. And it's a perfect analogy. In the old west, gunfights were most common in the 1870s and early 1880s, though they'd escalated right after the Civil War. During the war, they made important technical advances in firearms, and thousands of young men who served in combat became proficient in those new weapons. The same thing happened after World War One. The gangsters used to fight with fists and bricks and knives. Then, courtesy of the U.S. military, they all learned how to use guns."

"If your theory is true," Kid Rags said, "what happened after World War Two?"

"Biker gangs," Teach answered.

Spaghetti stood. "I have to get back to the piano now." He patted Mary on the shoulder. "I'm sorry to hear about your grandparents. They were good people." He waddled over to the piano, and played one sad song after the other.

Spaghetti was again sitting with Mary and the elders when Tim stopped by the table a few minutes before seven o'clock.

"I have to run an errand first," Tim said, "but Dom can show you the way to my warehouse. You don't mind, do you, Dom? I can drive you home afterwards."

Spaghetti beamed at him. "That's fine. I heard the DeSoto is back from the shop. I'd like to see it."

"Okay," Tim called over his shoulder, already heading back to the bar. "See you shortly."

A gorgeous young woman—statuesque, masses of curly red hair, sparkling green eyes—entered the bar, stowed her purse under the counter, and refilled the pretzel bowls.

Tim spoke to her for a few minutes, hugged her, gave her a kiss, and headed out the door.

Mary paid the bill with her credit card, trying not to think about how much she'd been spending, then she and the elders trooped outside.

She smelled rain in the heavy air, and her spirits quickened. Bill thought she was crazy, but she loved storms, the wilder the better.

Happy held out a hand, palm up, and gazed at the sky. "You don't think it's going to rain, do you?"

"It's supposed to," Spaghetti said.

Mary threw back her head and spread out her arms. "I hope it does." Then, feeling a twinge of guilt at feeling so good in the face of Happy's obvious anxiety, she dropped her arms and said soothingly, "It will probably be a quick summer shower."

"Spring shower," Kid Rags corrected. "It won't be summer for a while yet."

Lila Lorraine wrapped her arms around herself. "It feels more like fall."

"It better not rain," Happy muttered.

Kid Rags gave him a suspicious look. "I thought you liked rain."

"Not today I don't."

"Journey don't like rain, neither," Crunchy said.

Mary caught Teach looking at her. "What?"

"I was remembering how much Jimmy Boots liked storms. He even found the tornadoes out on the eastern Colorado plains exciting. I couldn't see it myself—all the wind and the eerie green sky and the noise—but he loved it."

"Come on, come on, we gotta go," Happy said, when it began to sprinkle. "What are you waiting for?"

Everyone but Iron Sam got on the bus. He stood motionless, head back, eyes closed, and somehow Mary understood that this was his first rain as a free man.

"What's he doing out there?" Happy grumbled. "I better go get him."

Mary caught his arm as he rushed by her. "He won't be long. Leave him be."

Chapter 17

Happy seemed to forget whatever had been bothering him once he entered Tim's warehouse. His eyes got as big as a child's at a toy store as he moved from car to car, speaking in that same authoritative tone Mary had heard him use in the bar.

He stopped by a red car that looked brand new and exclaimed, "A 1954 Ford Thunderbird!" He pointed to a pale yellow car with white trim that he said was a 1958 Desoto Fireflight, and to a cream-colored one he proclaimed to be a 1958 Oldsmobile Rocket 88.

"You know your cars," Tim said.

Mary watched Tim focus his attention on Happy as they discussed capacities and transmissions and engines and power and chassis, and she almost felt kindly toward him.

Happy caressed a bright orange car with a black top. "I can't believe it! A 1967 Dodge Charger! I had one exactly like this. I loved that car. It really had muscle—7210cc capacity. 375 bhp. Independent front suspension with wishbones and tension bar. And a classy sport oriented styling—recessed rear window, spoiler formed in the boot lid, retractable headlights. And it could go one hundred twenty miles per hour." He got a faraway look in his eyes as if he were remembering what it felt like to drive the car. "Vroom, vroom," he whispered.

Tim opened the driver's door, gestured for Happy to enter, then circled around to the passenger side.

Mary rushed toward them, envisioning the car and both men smashed beyond recognition, but stopped abruptly when she realized they were simply sitting and talking.

She backed away, stepping on Teach's toes.

Teach pointed his chin at the Charger. "Nice guy, that Tim."

"Yeah, right," Mary said, glancing around the warehouse. Shelves lined the walls, shelves full of new and used small appliances, power tools, and electronics of all kinds.

Teach wandered over to join Crunchy, Kid Rags, and Iron Sam who were examining the merchandise.

Spaghetti stood by the DeSoto, spouting off to Lila Lorraine about the virtues of the car.

Mary marveled at how interested the old woman seemed. She herself could not keep her eyes from glazing over when Bill and her father got on the subject of vehicles. She couldn't understand what they found so interesting. All she cared about was her car getting her where she wanted to go, though, come to think of it, the red VW Beetle in the corner there did look cute.

As she admired the shiny little car, Spaghetti, with Lila Lorraine in tow, appeared at her side.

"You wouldn't believe the terrible condition that 1962 Bug was in when Tim got it," Spaghetti said. "Some kid had turned it into a dune buggy or a hot rod or some such, but Tim restored it to its original condition."

"Does he do the work himself?" Lila Lorraine asked, sounding as if she wanted to know.

"No. He farms the work out to body shops. He has contacts all over the city." Spaghetti extended his arm in an expansive gesture. "All these cars have been restored." He pointed to a long, sleek, gray two-seater. "That one got wrecked in a high speed chase, but you'd never know to look at it now."

"What kind is it?" Lila Lorraine asked.

"A 1985 Morgan 8 Plus Roadster. It's more current than Tim usually deals with, but he liked the 1930s styling."

Seeing Kid Rags approach, Mary excused herself and went to meet him.

"No clothes," he said. "I don't see any clothes."

"Let's go ask." Mary headed for Tim, who was getting out of the Dodge Charger.

"I didn't forget the shirts," he called out to them. "Give me a minute." He spoke a few more words to Happy, then made his way to a door at the back of the warehouse. He unlocked it using a card key, then came out a few minutes later carrying an armful of pastel shirts folded and sealed in plastic.

Kid Rags casually sorted through the shirts, though Mary could tell he wasn't nearly as nonchalant as he seemed. He set aside three shirts, then studied them, obviously trying to choose among them.

"How much are they?" she asked. When Tim named a price that seemed ridiculously low, she ignored her misgivings—making an old man happy was more important than worrying about the dubious legality of the purchase, wasn't it?—and said, "We'll take all three."

"Since you're buying—" Happy began.

Mary held up a hand, silencing him. "No cars. I draw the line at buying anyone a car."

"Sheee," Happy said, kicking the cement floor, "how come I never get anything?"

Mary fished her checkbook out of her purse. "Anyone else want anything?"

Crunchy handed over an unopened package containing a blob of bluish-gray fur. "A catnip mouse. For Journey."

"Where'd that come from?" Mary asked.

"Found a whole box of kitty toys."

"Well, one catnip mouse isn't going to break the bank. Anything else for anyone?"

Teach shook his head. "No. We're fine."

While Mary wrote the check, most of the elders started straggling for the door, but Happy took another look at the cars, for once not hurrying everyone along.

Dusk had faded into night when Mary stepped outside, but floodlights illuminated the small parking lot where the elders milled around. She took a deep, appreciative breath of the rain-washed air, then froze, staring at the bus. She closed her eyes, thinking they were playing tricks on her, but when she opened them again, she could still see the lettering on the side of the vehicle.

"Happy!" she yelled.

He poked his head out of the door of the warehouse.

"Come here!"

He took a few cautious steps forward.

Mary pointed a finger at the bus. "Look!"

"What?" he asked with exaggerated innocence.

"It says Rocky Mountain Senior Center."

"Yeah? So?"

"Where did you get this bus?"

He shifted his weight from foot to foot. "Borrowed it."

Kid Rags whacked Happy on the side of the head with the back of his hand. "Idiot! You used water-based paint."

Happy launched himself at Kid Rags and started pummeling him. Kid Rags raised his fists in front of his face and jabbed back.

"Stop it," Mary shouted. "Stop it this instant."

Kid Rags and Happy moved closer together, and it looked to Mary as if they were trying to choke each other.

Lila Lorraine pressed her knuckles to her mouth.

Spaghetti hummed softly under his breath.

Teach leaned against the bus, grinning.

Iron Sam watched impassively.

Crunchy rushed to the two combatants, grasped each by an upper arm, and held them apart. Happy kept punching, but Kid Rags brushed off his jacket and adjusted his bow tie.

Crunchy let go of the two men and brandished a fist. "You do what Lady says or I crunch you."

"He started it," Happy mumbled.

Kid Rags repositioned his hat. "You're the one who used water-based paint."

"That's all I could find in the craft room. How was I supposed to know it would rain?"

Mary put her hands on her hips and glared at the two little old men. "Let me get this straight. You stole this bus from an old folks' home?"

"No," Kid Rags said. "It came from a senior center—a place where we sometimes go to eat and hang out during the day."

"We're senior citizens," Happy added, "so it sort of belongs to us."

Mary made balloons of her cheeks and blew out a breath.

"Now what are we going to do? I can't drive a stolen vehicle."

Happy's eyes lit up. "I'll drive."

"No one's driving this thing," Mary said, trying to remain calm. "What if we get stopped?"

"You've been driving it," Kid Rags pointed out, "so what's the big deal? We can buy some spray paint and paint over the sign again."

Hearing laughter behind her, Mary whirled around. Narrowing her eyes at Tim, she demanded, "What are you laughing at?"

Tim stopped laughing, but he couldn't seem to wipe the smile off his face.

"This isn't funny," Mary said, gritting her teeth. Mentally she added driving a stolen vehicle to her list of crimes. Perhaps she could serve all her jail sentences concurrently; then she'd be out while still fairly young.

"Do you have a phone I can use?" she asked Tim. "I'd like to call for a couple of cabs to take us to a motel for the night."

"No need. I can drive you. Wait here. Don't go away."

He trotted around the side of the building. A few minutes later, he drove up in a long white van. Though much smaller than the bus, there were ten seats, enough for all of them.

"I got this Chevrolet Express for a customer who wanted to go into business giving tours of Chicago," Tim explained, climbing out of the van. "But he reneged on the deal at the last minute, and I got stuck with it." He turned to the elders. "Why don't you load your things onto the van while I wipe down the bus."

Teach nodded. "Good thinking. I doubt the cops would dust for prints, but you never know."

Mary held up a hand. "Wait just a minute. I see no point in trading one stolen vehicle for another."

Tim jerked his head back. "Stolen? Whatever gave you the idea the van is stolen?"

Mary's cheeks reddened. "It's not?"

"None of his merchandise is stolen," Teach said. "That's

what makes this such a sweet operation. It's all legal."

Mary's eyebrows drew together. "But I saw him paying off a cop."

"Richard Brock, Tim's friend," Spaghetti explained. "Tim buys the cars and the rest of the loot at police auctions. Richard keeps him informed of when the auctions are and what the good stuff is, and Tim gives him a percentage of the profits."

Mary studied a rain puddle, wishing it were deep enough for her to dive into. When she finally glanced up, steeling herself against the laughter she thought sure she'd see in Tim's eyes, he was already in the bus wiping the steering wheel, the dashboard, and the rear view mirror with a white cloth.

The elders loaded the van with their belongings. Crunchy, accompanied by Journey, stowed Mary's bags.

"That's everything," he announced.

Tim hopped off the bus. "I'm finished here. You people ready to go?"

Mary hunched her shoulders against a sudden gust of wind and boarded the van.

As Tim drove away, she said, "What about the bus? Are you going to leave it there?"

Tim's lips twitched. "I'll take care of it later, but for now, how about if we go get something to eat? I'm starving."

Kid Rags chuckled. "I knew I liked this kid."

Tim pulled into a parking lot outside a cafeteria-style restaurant called Horn of Plenty. "My grandfather loved this place. He liked picking out his own food and not having to pay for more than he could eat." As they entered the restaurant, he added, "Order what you want. My treat."

"You sure?" Mary said. "It could run into quite a bit of money."

"It's just a late night snack."

Mary grinned impishly. "Very well. If you insist."

Kid Rags, leading the parade, took two trays and

immediately began filling them with his selections.

"I would have thought they'd all like to make their own choices," Tim commented, eyes focused on the dapper old man.

"Oh, they do," Mary said, still smiling.

He gave her a curious look, then turned his attention back to the serving line where Crunchy, not to be outdone by Kid Rags, also filled two trays.

"My God," Tim said, sounding awed. "What are those two doing?"

Mary laughed. "Picking out a late night snack." Then, taking pity on him, "I won't hold you to your offer to pay."

"No, that's okay." He gazed wide-eyed at the two old men. "Are they going to eat it all? Even I can't eat that much, and my mother claims I have a black hole instead of a stomach. I don't think they're going to be able to manage those trays. I better go see if I can get someone to help."

He made his way to the front of the line and spoke to the young man at the cash register. The young man called out, and two other young men emerged from the kitchen to carry the extra trays.

Happy went through the line next, taking his time making his selections, as did Spaghetti and Tim, but the rest of them slid through quickly, selecting a salad or a dessert and something to drink.

Tim paid without so much as flinching.

"I don't think I caught all your names," he said when they were seated at a large table in a semi-private alcove.

Spaghetti made the introductions, then launched into a long, rambling discourse, giving his version of the story they had told him earlier. When he finally wound down, Tim looked at Mary in surprise.

"So you've known these people only a few days?"

Mary nodded.

"And you're not related to any of them?"

"No. Why?"

He looked around the table, shaking his head. "You seem to have such rapport, as if you've known each other a long time."

"In a way we have." Mary smiled at the elders. "We've been through a lot together."

"Sounds like it. What did Dom mean about you being tailed? Is someone really following you?"

"Yes. Someone is really following us."

"We picked up the tail in Leavenworth," Happy said.

"You don't seem too concerned about it," Tim commented.

Mary shivered, remembering the man she'd seen peering into the windows of the bus. Had it been that afternoon?

"I'm very concerned. Scared, too, but there's not much I can do about it. We don't know who he is or what he wants, and we can't go to the cops."

Tim raised his eyebrows, but only said, "What's the license plate number? I have a friend who can run it through the computer for me."

"No cops. I mean it."

"I won't mention you. I'll ask him to do it as a favor for me. I can say the guy dented my car or something."

"I don't know the plate number."

"I do," Happy said. "It's a Kansas plate. WOC six . . . no, two . . . or maybe four . . . yeah, four. WOC four seven three nine six four."

"That's too many numbers," Kid Rags objected.

"Did you see the plate?"

"No."

"So how do you know it's too many numbers?"

Crunchy folded his arms across his chest. "It's WOC four six four."

Happy shot Kid Rags a triumphant glance. "That's what I said."

Seeing the befuddled look on Tim's face, Mary stifled a giggle. She had grown so used to the bickering, she barely noticed it anymore.

Tim took his cell phone out of his pocket, placed a call, and asked for Richard. After speaking to his friend for a few minutes, he set the phone on the table. "He'll call me back.

So, tell me. Where are you all planning on going next?"

"Wisconsin," Lila Lorraine put in before Mary could respond.

"Wisconsin?" Tim smiled. "Are you going to go look for the treasure?"

There was a moment of stunned silence, then the elders all began talking at once.

Laughing, Tim held up a hand. "Whoa. One at a time."

The elders looked at Mary. She forgot all about wanting to go home, forgot all about the man in the blue Grand Am.

"What treasure?" she asked breathlessly.

"Why the gold, of course. The gold your great-grandfather helped steal."

Chapter 18

Mary opened her mouth to speak, then closed it again without saying anything. So many questions rattled around in her head, she couldn't even begin to sort them all out.

The elders pelted Tim with questions.

"It's a long story," Tim said, "and it's getting late—the cafeteria will be closing soon. Maybe we should wait until tomorrow."

"Tomorrow might not come for some of us," Happy said ominously.

Glancing at Iron Sam, Mary had to agree. Each day, each hour, Sam seemed to get grayer, as if he were already turning to dust. The smell of decay was getting stronger, too.

"Why don't you give us the short version," Mary said.

The others nodded in agreement.

"The short version. Hmmm. Let's see. My grandfather Patrick O'Feeny and three of his buddies—Dugald Stuart, Charles Stuart, and Adam Kleinman—robbed a bank in southern Wisconsin, but things were so hot they buried the gold, and to my knowledge no one recovered it."

Iron Sam had been staring at his plate, but now he jerked his head up and fixed his gaze on Tim.

Mary wondered what in that bare recital caught the old man's interest. The thought of buried treasure? It even made her pulse race.

"What's the long version?" she asked.

Tim locked his hands behind his neck, stretched out his legs, and leaned back in his chair. "According to my grandfather, Dugald Stuart was the father of a kid they called Jimmy Boots because of the cowboy boots he insisted on wearing. If Jimmy Boots was your grandfather, Mary, that means Dugald was your great-grandfather. Charles was Dugald's cousin, but they were so close they were more like brothers. My grandfather, the Stuarts, and Adam Kleinman all worked for John Fitzhugh, known as The Shoemaker because he owned a shoe store. He was also part of the commission of gangsters controlling Chicago."

"When was this?" Teach asked.

"Late 1920s. Early 1930s."

"I thought Capone controlled Chicago back then," Mary said.

"No," Teach responded. "At his best, Capone did not control all of Chicago—there were rival gangs. He controlled the politicians, which is why it seemed he controlled the whole city. And actually, he didn't do it alone. A commission ran the rackets in Chicago. Capone just fronted for the commission. When Capone was serving a ten-month sentence in Pennsylvania for carrying a pistol, business continued as usual in Chicago—others on the commission picked up the slack. And when Capone went to prison for tax evasion, crime in Chicago didn't lessen. Capone was small potatoes, all things considered."

"So why did they talk about him like he was the main crime boss?" Mary asked.

"Who cares," Kid Rags growled. "I want to hear about the gold."

Crunchy folded his arms across his chest. "You hurt my ears." He nodded at Teach. "Why did they?"

"The mob had designated figureheads that were well known to the public," Teach responded. "By building the image of these men, the real power brokers remained invisible. Hoover and his men also built the image of these figureheads—the bigger the game, the more powerful the hunter seems. In the end, Hoover and Ness had little to do with Capone's downfall. It's been said the commission furnished the books to the IRS. With a national syndicate in the offing, the mob had to get rid of all the wild, high profile guys who wouldn't take orders, guys like Capone, Legs Diamond, Lucky Luciano, Dutch Schultz. The guys who stayed out of the public eye and were willing to go along to get along, like The Shoemaker, prospered."

"My grandfather and his friends were in their thirties at the time," Tim said after a respectful pause. "They were not at all pleased with the way their careers were going—they were still pretty low on the totem pole—and they could see their dreams of wealth slipping away. Like many on their level, they had a hard time living on what their boss grudgingly tossed them and they were looking for a way to climb the ladder.

"The Shoemaker offered to grant them small territories of their own for crap games, loan shark operations, or pinball machines, but he insisted the financing must come from him—at regular shylock interest rates, of course. He charged one dollar a week for every five dollars borrowed. Since the average loan period was six weeks, they would have had to repay eleven dollars for each of those five—a mere one hundred and twenty percent interest in forty-two days. Then they would be forced to borrow more operating capital for the next six weeks.

"The four friends told The Shoemaker they'd think about it, but they didn't intend to follow through. They had seen other guys fall for the scam and end up in eternal debt to the mob. They also had to be careful how they turned down The Shoemaker. Mob bosses do not take well to having their overtures rejected.

"While they were trying to figure out what to do, they heard about a cream puff bank in Racine, Wisconsin. Since the bank had no vault, only a safe, not much money was kept there, but they decided to rob it anyway, thinking it would be a quick, easy way to snatch some cash.

"They planned the job meticulously, trying to anticipate everything that could possibly go wrong, but they could not have anticipated the terrible problem they would run into."

"What problem?" Happy asked.

"Gold. Bags and bags of gold coins. Way too much for that little bank."

Kid Rags laughed. "Doesn't sound like a problem to me."

"I don't get it," Mary said. "How come the bank had so much gold?"

"Gold was still legal tender in this country at the time," Tim said.

"Really?" She glanced at Teach, who nodded.

"Thinking that three was a lucky number," Tim continued, "they had chosen to rob the bank on Monday, March thirteenth, 1933—"

Teach drew in a sharp breath.

Mary looked from Teach to Tim then back to Teach. "What?"

Teach raised his eyebrows. "You don't know that date?"

"No. Should I?"

Kid Rags got out his flask, took a slug, then passed it around. "Drink," he advised. "You're going to need it. I can hear another lecture coming on."

"It's hard to explain without giving you a history of the war on gold in this country," Teach said, "but I'll try to be brief. Gold made us free. When gold backed the dollar, we had a stable economy, no national debt to speak of, and control over the government.

"The United States government is a lot like the Sicilian Mafia. It started out working for the people and ended up working against them. In the beginning, no one feared the federal government. People knew the true power resided in the states. In 1917, the U.S. government announced they would shoot draft dodgers. They had to do something drastic, otherwise people would have ignored their draft notices. Nowadays people are so used to government control, they're unaware of all the freedoms they have lost."

Kid Rags smoothed his mustache. "This is what you call being brief?"

Tim smiled. "You sound like my grandfather, Teach. He used to talk about how everything bad happened after we went off the gold standard."

"It did," Teach said. "Money by fiat leads to inflation, then to massive national debt, and finally to bankruptcy. It's fashionable to dismiss this as being another conspiracy theory, but the truth is, other people's money means other people's control. People seem to have the idea that the national debt is something we owe to ourselves, when in fact we owe it mostly to bankers and financiers in other countries. We are the collateral for those loans. They own us.

"Meyer Lansky at his most visionary never came close to attaining a fraction of the power those people have. To me, they are the real syndicate, the real gangsters. Organized crime on such a grand scale they can steal entire countries and few are ever aware of it.

"We've been fighting that financial syndicate from the beginning. At least twice in the early days of this country, national banks were established which controlled the money supply, but when massive inflation resulted, their charters weren't renewed.

"Lincoln issued fiat money to finance the Civil War, but after the war he put us back on the gold standard. That, I think, is one of the reasons he was killed.

"McKinley insisted over and over again that if we were to remain free the gold standard must be maintained in America, we must never have a federal income tax, and we must never allow a Federal Reserve Board to be established. He was also assassinated.

"Then there was Franklin Roosevelt. On Sunday, March fifth, 1933, he announced that saving gold was prohibited, and that starting on the sixth, all banking transactions would cease for one week, except for people surrendering their gold. In some places, people lined up for blocks waiting to turn in their stash. On March thirteenth, when the banks reopened for business, armed treasury agents went after everyone known to have gold that hadn't been turned in.

"It must have been some of that gold those four men stumbled on."

"They couldn't figure out why there was so much gold in the bank that day," Tim said. "They knew about the Bank Holiday, of course, but they thought things would be back to normal by the thirteenth. The sight of all that gold stunned them. For a short time, they felt rich beyond their wildest dreams. Then the trouble started."

"It must have been a shock when they found out gold had become illegal in this country," Teach said. "From 1933 until 1974 when Nixon rescinded it, private ownership of gold was a crime punishable by ten years in prison and a ten thousand dollar fine. In the land of the brave and the home of the free, no citizen could own gold coins, gold bullion, or gold certificates.

"In June of that year, after Congress ratified it, the United States officially went off the gold standard, and the United States citizens elected Roosevelt to an unprecedented fourth term as president.

"The United States became insolvent, and the dollar—created out of thin air and the belief of its users—became the biggest con of all times."

"You finished?" Kid Rags asked when Teach paused to take a sip of water.

Teach set the glass back on the table and slumped in his chair, as if the weight of the whole world lay on his shoulders. He nodded without speaking.

"Good," Kid Rags said. "Now we can find out about the buried treasure."

Lila Lorraine, Happy, and Spaghetti, who all looked half-asleep, perked up.

"Yes, the gold," Happy said.

Before Tim could continue with his story, the cashier approached the table and said, sounding not at all apologetic, "I'm sorry, but we're closing now."

Chapter 19

Despite jaw-cracking yawns and dragging feet, the elders denied being sleepy.

"We can go back to The Joker," Tim said. "I don't think we have a private party scheduled for the back room tonight."

Mary rubbed her gritty eyes and wondered if there would be any vacancies left in the city by the time they went in search of motel rooms. And what about tomorrow? She'd about maxed out her credit cards. Would she have enough left to get them all back home by bus or train? If worse came to worst, she could borrow money from her fiancé, promising to pay him back when she sold the farm.

Disappointment stabbed at her, doubling her over, at the thought of having to give up the farm. Maybe if she went to work for Bill she could keep it. But after they married, he'd have as much say as she, and to keep the peace, she'd sell it anyway.

Tim's voice penetrated her dark thoughts. "Mary?"

She started. Glancing around, she noticed the elders were all looking at her with hopeful eyes. Waiting for her okay, she realized.

She smiled brightly. "The Joker it is."

On the way to the bar, Tim pulled up in front of one of the solid brick buildings with the fancy grillwork she walked by earlier that morning.

"I'll be right back," he said, jumping out of the van.

A few minutes later, a light shone through the windows of the top floor of the building. A loft apartment? Like in lower downtown Denver? If so, his various enterprises must be profitable.

The voices of the elders swirled around her as they discussed what to do with their share of the gold.

Mary smiled to herself. She knew exactly what she would do with her share. Assuming, of course, there was gold and that they could find it.

Tim returned fifteen minutes later carrying a large Manila envelope and a scrap of paper.

Glancing at the paper, he asked, "Do any of you know a Mario Vinzetti? Lives in Topeka, Kansas?"

They all looked at one another and shook their heads.

"Mario Vinzetti," Mary said. "Is that the guy who's been following us?"

"Yes. I got a call from Richard. He said he checked out Vinzetti, and there are no wants or warrants."

Mary turned around to ask Iron Sam if Vinzetti could be related to one of his wise guy pals, but when she caught the forbidding look in his eyes, the one thing about him not deteriorating, she held her tongue. If Iron Sam did know the man, he'd mention it, wouldn't he?

Yeah, right, she answered herself, remembering Teach's story about how he'd outlasted months of interrogation.

Tim parked behind the bar next to the dumpster, in a space marked: *NO PARKING. DELIVERIES ONLY.*

"Oh, Dom," he said. "I called the home and told them you'd be late."

Spaghetti beamed. "Thanks."

Mary gave him a curious glance. He didn't seem at all resentful of the way Tim took charge.

"I also took the liberty of making motel reservations for you, Mary," Tim said. "I got them to promise to hold the rooms until you got there, no matter how late."

Mary bristled, but secretly felt relieved they had a place to spend the night.

Tim unlocked the back door, ushered them inside, then locked the door behind them. He led them to a small room that had all the charm of a corporate conference room, dropped the Manila envelope on the table, then left, saying, "I better let Kirsten know we're here."

Kirsten. That must be the gorgeous redhead.

When Tim returned, he was carrying a bottle of bourbon and a tray full of shot glasses. Mary held up her hand in refusal when he placed a drink in front of her, but all the others, including Tim himself, tossed theirs back.

"I notice you don't have a computerized drink dispensing system," Mary commented.

"My father wanted to put one in," Tim answered, "but I like the ambience of an old-fashioned bar. I think people find the sight of all those bottles comforting, and you lose that when the bottles are replaced by a keyboard."

Kid Rags poured himself another drink. "The gold?" he asked.

Tim smiled at him. "Oh, yes. The gold. Where was I?"

"They went into the bank and found bags and bags of gold," Happy said.

"Right. My grandfather didn't go into the bank. Since he was the wheelman, he needed to remain in the car with the engine idling, ready for a quick getaway. He said his eyes bugged out of his head when his buddies left the bank pulling a small wooden cart piled high with boxes and bags of all kinds, not just bank bags. He could hear the clink of heavy coins and bars as they heaved the bags into the rear of the car, and he knew they had hit the jackpot.

"As planned, they drove to a garage in Racine they had rented under assumed names, wiped down the stolen car they'd used for the robbery, locked the garage door, then dispersed to their own vehicles and drove back to Chicago.

"During the next couple of days, they made a few discreet inquiries and discovered, to their horror, they had merchandise so hot no one wanted to handle it. Gold had been declared illegal, and anyone caught with even a single coin was in big trouble, like someone today caught with a lot of drugs, only worse, because the United States government had jurisdiction, not the local cops. A massive manhunt was set in motion but they kept it hush-hush since they didn't want anyone to know that robbers had stolen some of the confiscated gold. It might get people to thinking they didn't have to comply with the new laws.

"The connected guys, of course, knew what was going on—they always did—and The Shoemaker and some of the other bosses organized their own search.

"All of which made the four robbers very nervous. If the law got their hands on them, they could go to prison; if The Shoemaker got his hands on them, they could get dead.

"The mob had a saying, 'wet the beak,' which meant that whatever you did, you had to give your bosses a piece of the action, and if low level guys like Dugald, Charles, Adam, and my grandfather took down a score they were supposed to immediately turn everything over to their boss. Sometimes the bosses would remember to give the lower echelon guys their share, and sometimes they didn't. Since the four robbers hadn't 'wet the beak,' they were in real trouble."

"That doesn't seem fair," Mary said.

"It wasn't," Teach responded. "Mob bosses ran their businesses like fiefdoms—they demanded total loyalty, but felt no need to treat their underlings fairly. They thought they could rule by fear, but when fear is around every corner, people lose their fear of the fear. They sometimes even lose their fear of the ones administering the fear.

"All the bodyguards and all those layers of insulation the bosses surrounded themselves with weren't just to protect themselves from the law and from their rivals, but also from their own disgruntled employees."

"My grandfather never lost his fear of The Shoemaker," Tim said. "He knew the perfidy The Shoemaker was capable of, and he spent his whole life looking over his shoulder. But I'm getting ahead of myself.

"There they were with all that gold, and they couldn't do anything with it. They couldn't spend it like they would have been able to a few days before, and they couldn't fence it since the fences would report back to their boss. They also hated to walk away from it. They thought the ban on gold couldn't last forever, and even if it did, things would eventually cool down enough so they could find some way of turning it into cash, maybe by smuggling it into Canada.

"Knowing the risks of keeping the gold in the garage for any length of time, they decided to bury it. But where? Dugald thought of the perfect spot—an isolated section of The Shoemaker's property in northern Wisconsin, the one place in the entire world their boss would not think of looking."

Teach laughed. "Like father, like son. That sounds like something Jimmy Boots would come up with."

Tim tossed back another shot of bourbon and passed the bottle around. "Since they were scheduled to go to Siskiwit Bay in northern Wisconsin to get a load of Canadian Whiskey, they decided to stop for the gold on the way, bury it at The Shoemaker's place, then continue on to their rendezvous. Everything went as planned. Not a hitch. They got to Siskiwit Bay, made their contact, loaded the whiskey on the truck, then headed back for Chicago.

"After a mile or so, they started to get a bad feeling—nothing specific, just a tingling on the back of their necks—but they had learned to heed such feelings.

"They decided to take a different route than planned, so they called The Shoemaker's people to let them know of the change—The Shoemaker insisted on being kept informed of everything his employees did. An hour after the call, they ran into an ambush. The whiskey was destroyed, and Adam, Charles, and Dugald were all killed. In the confusion, my grandfather managed to escape. He hid behind a tree until all the commotion died away."

Mary's eyes widened. "The Shoemaker set them up!"

Tim nodded. "That's what my grandfather claimed."

"But why?"

"I'm not sure. All I know is that prohibition agents were paid off, but they still needed to make an occasional bust. A lot of times both the agents and the mob bosses arranged the busts. My grandfather once told me that when he crept out of the trees and went to survey the wreckage, he smelled no alcohol, but whatever had been in those bottles pooled on the road."

"Caramel-colored water," Teach said. "That's what they used. Whiskey was too valuable to waste on set ups."

"So your grandfather was the only person left who knew the whereabouts of the gold?" Kid Rags asked.

Tim nodded.

"Did he ever go get it?"

"No."

Kid Rags got a faraway look in his eyes. "Then it's still there."

"Could be."

"Well, what are we waiting for?" Happy got to his feet. "Let's go dig it up."

Tim lifted a hand. "It's not that simple."

Happy sat back down. "Didn't your grandfather tell you where to find the gold?"

"He did. He talked about the gold all the time, even more so as he neared the end of his life. He must have told me the story a hundred times, but here's the kicker—I don't know if any of my grandfather's story is true."

"What?" Happy yelped.

"No gold?" Kid Rags said.

"No gold?" Crunchy echoed.

Lila Lorraine and Spaghetti exchanged bewildered glances.

Iron Sam's spine stiffened slightly.

Mary looked at everyone in turn, not knowing what to think.

"Are you playing games with us?" Teach asked, sounding more amused than affronted.

"Maybe, maybe not," Tim said with a glint of mischief in his eyes. "My grandfather was crazy, and no one but me believed a word of what he said, and even I doubted him sometimes."

"Sheee." Happy slumped in his chair. "I thought we were all going to be rich. I wanted to buy me that Dodge Charger we saw tonight."

"Is any of what you told us true?" Iron Sam asked, an odd intensity in his voice.

Tim opened the Manila envelope, pulled out a photocopy of a newspaper article, and passed it across the table.

Iron Sam picked up the paper and stared at it for a long time. Although his face remained expressionless, Mary felt sure his still features masked powerful emotions.

"Let me see." Happy bounced in his seat. "Let me see." Iron Sam handed the article to him; Happy glanced at it, then passed it on.

When the article reached Mary, she studied the three men pictured, then read about the shoot-out that resulted in the deaths of "a gang of notorious bootleggers." She took another look at her great-grandfather's unsmiling face and thought it seemed familiar, but then so did the faces of Charles and Adam.

"This is the only other thing I have," Tim said, taking a snapshot out of the envelope. "A picture of my grandfather, Dugald, Charles, and Adam."

When Mary caught a glimpse of the faded photograph being handed around, she dug in her purse for the packet of snapshots she had found at the farm. With trembling fingers, she detached one depicting four men in old-fashioned clothes and hairstyles. She compared the two pictures. They were identical. No wonder the men seemed familiar—she had looked at this snapshot a dozen times. She passed both pictures to Tim. He glanced at them, then at her.

Their eyes met.

All at once Mary had a sense of time folding in on itself, a sense of the interconnectedness of all things, a sense of unfathomable mysteries hovering out of reach.

Spaghetti's laughter shattered the strange illusion. She averted her gaze. When she again looked at Tim, he was smiling at Spaghetti.

"It's so weird," Spaghetti said, "to think of your grandfather and Mary's great-grandfather knowing each other."

Lila Lorraine frowned. "I don't understand. If the story about the gold isn't true, why did you tell us about it?"

Tim shifted his smiling attention to her. "Because I like to think it is. And because it might be.

"After the ambush, my grandfather hitched his way back to Chicago. He made a report to The Shoemaker's people, not mentioning his suspicions. He could tell they no longer trusted him, and he knew he wouldn't get any more jobs, but a day or two later they ordered him to drive a crash car. Quite a comedown from his normal work.

"The mob guys liked to have someone ready to cause accidents to help insure they got away safe from whatever jobs they pulled. Often these crashes were no more than fender benders, but in this case the car was totaled and my grandfather badly injured. He was in the hospital a long time, and when he got out, he was not right mentally.

"'Crazy Pat', people called him. He did odd jobs, getting by as best as he could, and years later when his daughter— my mother—got married, she made her husband give Crazy Pat a job sweeping floors in his pool hall. As Crazy Pat got older, and Chicago tried to live down its gangster past, his stories seemed wilder and crazier than ever. He used to talk about Capone as if he'd known him personally. He called him Snorky and said he cooked a great stuffed steak. He also said Snorky didn't drink much, a little beer or wine, but that he sure liked females, was always chasing them—especially little girls, thirteen or fourteen years old. People laughed at my grandfather for his pretensions and dismissed his stories because he was 'Crazy Pat.'"

"That stuff about Capone is true," Teach said. "I read it in a biography about him."

Tim smiled wryly. "Wherever else my grandfather got his information from, it wasn't books. He couldn't read.

"I loved my grandfather, and after school every day I'd stop by the pool hall to listen to his stories. My father didn't like me visiting with Crazy Pat, but my mother told him to let me be. She said he and I needed each other. As I grew up and became more involved with school activities, I stopped going to the pool hall.

"Right before he died, I went to see Crazy Pat one last time. He lay in bed, too weak to move, but he gripped my arm with fingers that felt like steel.

"He looked me straight in the eyes and said, 'I hear what people call me. Crazy Pat, they say. Maybe I am. I can't always tell what's real from what isn't. But this story is true. I swear it.' And, once more, he told me the tale of how he

and three of his pals robbed a bank and buried the gold on
The Shoemaker's property."

Chapter 20

Mary woke from a restless sleep and lay listening to Lila Lorraine's soft snores. After a moment she became aware of another sound—Crunchy's voice outside her room.

She strained to hear, wondering if something was wrong. When she heard a tiny "mew," she realized he was talking to Journey.

Knowing she wouldn't be able to lie still enough to rest, let alone sleep, she dressed quietly and went outside. The lights in the parking lot were out, but in the pale gray illumination of dawn, she could see Crunchy looking at her, eyebrows drawn together in a worried frown.

"You okay, Lady?"

"Tired is all. I couldn't sleep."

She sat on the cold cement next to his chair and leaned against the tan bricks of the building.

Still frowning, Crunchy asked, "You want I should get you a chair?"

"This is fine. Maybe the cold will wake me up. Or put me to sleep." Crunchy gently transferred the limp cat from his lap to hers, then quirked his lips at the two of them, but said nothing.

Unlike Iron Sam's silence, which Mary found unsettling, Crunchy's seemed comforting, nonjudgmental.

She stroked the cat, feeling some of her tension seep away. "Do you think I'm doing the right thing by letting Tim take us treasure hunting?"

"Can't hurt."

"You sure? I mean, we don't know him."

"You didn't know us, neither."

"It's not the same. You are . . . Tim is . . ." She chewed on her lower lip, trying to think of a tactful way to voice her concern.

"You're afraid of upsetting the balance of power," Crunchy said.

Mary stared at him, unable to hide her surprise.

His eyes twinkled. "I don't talk so good as Teach or know so much from books, but I know some things. And I know people. Had to. A bouncer's gotta know when someone's causing trouble or when they're showing off for their girlfriend. You don't have to worry none—Tim's okay."

Mary scratched Journey behind the ears, and she could feel the rumble of his contentment through her fingertips.

"I hope so," she said. "I just can't figure out why he's doing this."

"Maybe he wants the gold. Or maybe he wants to vin . . . vindicate his grandfather."

"He could have gone any time. Why now?"

"We remind him of his grandfather."

Mary nodded thoughtfully.

"And he likes us," Crunchy added.

They sat in companionable silence for several minutes, then Mary asked, "Were you ever in love, Crunchy? I know you never got married, but did you ever love anyone?"

He remained silent for so long she thought he wasn't going to answer.

"Once," he said at last. "A long time ago."

"What happened?"

"She loved someone else."

"Was it Gina Dale?"

He studied her for a moment, then nodded.

"I'm sorry it didn't work out."

"I wanted her to be happy, and she was. Jimmy Boots made her very happy." He paused for several seconds, then said softly, "The world feels different with her gone."

The windows were closed against the early morning chill. The van smelled of fast food breakfast sandwiches and too many bodies confined in too small a space.

As Tim drove, Mary picked at her sandwich and looked at the scenery—if you could call miles and miles of suburbs scenery. It seemed strange not to be driving, to have become

165

a passenger on her own quest. The thing was, it didn't feel like her quest anymore.

Not liking the direction of her thoughts, she made a concerted effort to pay attention to the elders.

Spaghetti's wheezing laughter punctuated the story he told Lila Lorraine and Teach about an enterprising loan shark he used to know.

Kid Rags and Happy discussed the buried treasure and how they should divide it.

Crunchy fed bits of bacon to an ecstatic Journey.

Iron Sam gazed out the window, an uneaten sandwich loosely clasped in a skeletal hand.

Tim was also silent, a look of concentration on his face.

Mary wondered what he was thinking about. His grandfather? The gold? Traffic?

He glanced in his rear view mirror and smiled at her.

She smiled faintly in return. After a moment she asked, "What did you do with the bus?"

"I left it by a high school with the keys in the ignition and the doors unlocked. When I drove by this morning on my way to pick up Dom, I didn't see it."

"Do you think someone stole it?"

"I hope so. It will help muddy the waters."

She took a tiny bite of her sandwich, chewed it slowly, and swallowed. "Why are you being so good to us?"

He laughed, a mischievous look in his eyes. "Didn't want you having all the fun."

She nibbled on her sandwich some more. "I'm sorry about your grandfather. You were lucky. At least you got to know him."

"That's true." His smile faded. "I didn't tell you the whole truth yesterday. The reason I stopped going to see him when I got older is that I started to see what other people saw—that he wasn't someone special who had lived a fantastic life, but a crazy old man."

Mary nodded to herself. Maybe Crunchy was right. Maybe Tim was looking for vindication for his grandfather. And perhaps he was also looking for Crazy Pat's forgiveness.

"I did go hunting for the gold once," Tim continued, "but when I didn't find it, I decided it had been another of my grandfather's delusions. But somehow, while telling you the story and remembering the intensity of his look and the grip of his fingers the last time I saw him, I believe it. I think he and the others did rob a bank and bury the gold."

"I wondered why you hadn't dug the whole place up looking for it if you believed he buried it."

"I'm sorry you never got to know your grandparents."

"Yeah, me too."

He lapsed into silence, that same look of concentration on his face. She turned her attention to the elders.

"And once he paid off an employee at the Small Business Administration," Spaghetti said, "and got him to give a loan to a customer who had a hard time making his payments. The customer used the money from the loan to make payments to Tony Tuna. Another time Tony took a customer to a cabin in Wisconsin and held him prisoner while his guys maxed out his credit cards. When he finally let his customer go, Tony said, 'You still owe us the money. Pay up or the next time it won't be your credit cards we zero out, it will be you.'"

Mary dozed off; she awoke to the sound of Teach's voice.

"Not only were the odds vastly in favor of the casinos," he said, "they skimmed ten percent straight off the top. Those Vegas boys didn't miss a trick. Back when they made silver dollars from real silver, the casinos would collect them by the tens of thousands from their slot machines. They'd go through them, pick out any coins that had value for collectors, then send the rest to Switzerland to be made into money clips which they sold for a lot more than the one dollar value. Also, in the late 1960s when real silver dollars became scarce, the casinos minted their own coins to take their place. They cost seventeen cents apiece to make, and tourists bought them for one dollar each to use for gambling, the slot machines, tipping, et cetera. In the first few months after the initial minting, people took home more than six million dollars in so-called souvenir chips, leaving a profit of eighty-three cents per coin for the casinos."

Mary yawned and stretched. She glanced out the window and saw trees lining both sides of the road.

"Almost there." Tim smiled at her in the rear view mirror. "Have a nice nap?"

She smiled back, thinking he really did have a nice smile.

He gestured to the right side of the road. "The turn-off to Lake Arrowhead Road should be around here somewhere."

"I see a break in the trees ahead. Could that be it?"

Tim slowed the van.

"We there yet?" Happy asked, his voice squeaking in excitement.

"Not much farther," Tim answered, slowing the van even more.

The break in the trees proved to be Lake Arrowhead Road. It looked more like a path than a road, and the canopy of tree branches scraped the top of the van.

"A mile down this road is a huge boulder," Tim said, "and twenty yards beyond that is a deer trail."

Everyone grew quiet, scanning the side of the road for a boulder.

Happy, holding his glasses in front of his eyes, spotted it first. He bounced in his seat. "I see it! I see it!"

The boulder, as big as a house, must have been some sort of local landmark, because countless tire tracks matted the brush on either side of it, and broken beer bottles were strewn all around.

Tim pulled up to the boulder. Everyone scrambled out of the van and helped him unload two grocery bags of food and water, two shovels, a pickaxe, a blanket, and a strange-looking contraption with a long handle.

"A metal detector," Tim explained.

Teach paced off twenty yards.

Mary couldn't see a trail, only a narrow strip slightly less dense than the rest of the woods.

"This must be it," Teach said, stepping into the narrow

passageway.

In single file, Happy, Lila Lorraine, and Spaghetti followed him.

Kid Rags started after them, then backtracked, grabbed one of the bags of food, and hurried to catch up.

By the time Iron Sam picked up a shovel and, using it like a cane, disappeared into the woods, the narrow path looked like a trail, the underbrush trampled and skinny tree branches broken.

Tim handed a shovel to Crunchy, the other bag of groceries to Mary, and loaded himself with the rest of the gear.

Ten minutes after entering the woods, they emerged into a small clearing. Through the trees on the other side, Mary caught glimpses of a distant shimmering green lake and a huge chalet-style house.

Tim's mouth twisted in a wry smile. "The Shoemaker's cabin."

Mary laughed, then abruptly cut it off, thinking she heard a twig snap in the woods behind them. When the sound didn't recur, she asked, "Does The Shoemaker still own this place?"

"His heirs do. They keep it for a summer getaway, but they seldom use it. Too busy. They have a whole chain of shoe stores now, mostly here in the Midwest. Fitzhugh Shoes. Maybe you've seen their billboards."

"Can't miss them," Kid Rags said. "'Fitzhugh Fits You.' Makes you wonder what advertising genius invented that one."

Mary smiled at him, then took a deep breath. "Where do we start?"

"Three-fifteen," Tim answered.

Teach seemed to know what that meant, because he immediately started circling off to the right, the other elders close on his heels.

"Imagine the clearing as a clock," Tim told a puzzled Mary, "and the deer trail as the half hour."

Staring at the spot the elders were now examining, Mary

felt her heart beat faster. "That's where the gold is?"

"Supposedly."

"Wow!" She stood still, marveling at how her body tingled with excitement. Is this how the forty-niners felt? No wonder so many people had dropped everything and headed for California.

"Come on," she said. "Let's go dig up that gold!"

Chapter 21

The picnic was a quiet affair.

They were all stunned into silence by the sight of the treasure, Mary thought.

Then she giggled. Some treasure!

A bent spoon, a bullet casing, a rusty tin can. The last pass over the area with the metal detector had yielded a bit of gold—a signet ring—but nothing else.

"Before we quit," she said, "we should check the perimeter with the metal detector to be sure."

Tim looked up from the sandwich he had been brooding over. "Why? If there is any gold, it couldn't have shifted position all on its own."

"No, but a deer trail could have, and that's your point of reference, right? People talk about beelines and crows flying, but bees and crows meander all over the place. Maybe deer do the same. It's been what—more than seventy years since they buried the gold? Isn't it possible in all that time the deer changed their course?"

Teach nodded thoughtfully. "Good thinking."

Tim smiled for the first time since they sat down to eat.

Iron Sam leaned against a tree and closed his eyes.

The rest of the elders started laying bets on where they would find the gold.

Although they spoke with the same enthusiasm as before, Mary thought she detected a touch of reluctance in their manner. Perhaps they had decided they preferred the dream to the reality? Well, she certainly hadn't. The thought of the gold didn't dazzle her, but she needed it. She had to find it.

She stuffed the last of her sandwich in her mouth and jumped to her feet. "The rest of you can laze around if you want, but I'm going back to work."

She wielded the metal detector, making mental notes of where she found small metallic items in case anyone wanted to dig them up.

When the detector emitted a steady noise, and the gauge went haywire, she stopped in confusion. What was wrong with the thing? Then all of a sudden it hit her like a physical blow, taking away her breath.

"I found the gold," she whispered.

"I found the gold," she said a little louder. Then, forgetting for the moment she was trespassing, a misdemeanor not worth adding to her list of crimes, she shouted, "I found the gold!"

She opened her mouth to repeat the astonishing message, then froze.

What was that?

Footsteps?

She turned around slowly and peered into the woods.

All was still.

She strained her ears, but only heard her own furiously beating heart.

"You found the gold?" Happy asked from behind her, making her jump.

The gold!

All thoughts of a possible intruder fled.

She pivoted to face the elders and Tim. "I think so. I found something."

"Let me see." Tim relieved her of the metal detector. He fiddled with it for a moment, then swept it over the ground at his feet. When he got the same results as Mary, he let out a triumphant laugh.

He set down the detector, bounded across the clearing, and soon returned bearing the tools.

He offered a shovel to Mary. "Will you do the honors?"

Accepting the shovel, she had the foolish idea she should make a speech as in any other groundbreaking ceremony. When no words came to mind, she stuck the shovel in the ground, stomped on it, and managed to remove a small clod.

Crunchy took possession of the other shovel, but he couldn't dig more than a small amount, either.

Tim hefted the pickaxe. "That's why we have this." He brought the tool down with an earth-shaking thud.

Mary found the loosened dirt much easier to dig. Though she was not the least bit tired, she soon relinquished the shovel to Happy, who demanded his turn.

With Tim using the pickaxe and everyone else sharing the shovels, it didn't take long for them to dig a hole three feet wide and two feet deep. They worked in silence, their excitement so great it seemed to shimmer in the air like a heat mirage.

Mary was standing off to the side, curled hands itching for another go at the shovel, when she heard the distinctive sound of metal hitting metal. Her fingernails dug into her palms as she watched the dirt flying.

Then, in unison, Tim and the two shovelers, Teach and Spaghetti, stopped and stared into the hole.

"Do you see it?" Mary asked, unable to bear the suspense.

Tim looked over at her, a distracted expression on his face. "I don't know."

Mary stepped forward and peered into the hole. A patch of rusty metal with flecks of lime green paint showed through the dirt.

"That's not gold," she said, feeling betrayed.

"Maybe it's a chest they buried the gold in," Kid Rags said.

Mary brightened. "Maybe."

Teach and Spaghetti cleared away more dirt. Tim swung the pickaxe. There was a hollow ping. The pickaxe went through the metal and tore a hole in it. Mary caught a glimpse of green and something that looked like ivory before she had to move back out of the way of Tim's frenzied onslaught.

When Tim finally stopped to mop his brow, Mary and the elders stepped forward again and ringed the excavation.

No one spoke.

Mary barely even breathed. She stared into the hole. It couldn't be real—could it?—that skeleton dressed in a tattered, moldy suit sitting on what looked to be a rotting green sofa? Then she noticed the steering wheel.

She blinked, telling herself she'd been listening to too many gangster tales the past few days, but when she focused her eyes again, she realized she truly was looking at the remains of a person in a buried car.

"Well, I'll be . . ." Teach said softly. "I think I know who that is."

Happy started jiggling. "I gotta take a leak," he said in an anguished voice.

Kid Rags gestured toward the skeleton. "He's not going anywhere. He'll be here when you return."

Happy galloped into the woods. Moments later he came running back, his shriveled penis dangling out of his fly.

"Give me my gun," he screamed. "I need my gun."

"What's wrong?" Mary tried to keep her voice calm. "What happened?"

Kid Rags gave him a significant glance. "Little Happy's exposed."

Happy looked down. Stuffing his penis back in his pants and zipping up, he said in a high, excited voice, "I peed on some guy's shoes. He was hiding. Watching us."

Mary and Tim stared at each other, then Tim charged into the woods, with Kid Rags, Teach, and Iron Sam fanned out behind him. Mary followed, but stopped at the tree line, not wanting to leave the other elders alone.

She stood listening to the men crashing through the underbrush, to Crunchy lumbering toward her, to Spaghetti and Lila Lorraine speaking in low voices.

Not hearing Happy, she looked back—he was heading her way, fumbling with his gun. He seemed to be trying to point it at the woods, but his hands shook so badly, it wobbled all over the place.

She stalked toward him, hand outstretched. "You had no right going in my purse. Give me that before you hurt someone."

"But—"

"No buts," she said sharply. Realizing she sounded like her mother, she softened her tone. "Please? I don't want you to hurt yourself."

"I'm not going to hurt myself." He scuffled his feet, "Oh, all right."

Mary took the gun from him. She was holding it loosely, pointing it at a spot on the ground well away from them, when she heard a crackling of twigs. She whirled to see a lean, white-haired man with a trim white mustache stepping out from among the trees, both hands grasping a rifle held at an angle across his chest. Though he wore running shoes and a dark green velour sweat suit, she detected something militaristic about his stance, something that said the whole world was his for the taking.

He stared at Mary, his dark eyes cold and hard. "You going to use that gun, lady?"

"Don't call her lady." Crunchy moved toward him.

The man gestured with his weapon. "Stay where you are."

Crunchy stopped, one foot still in the air.

"Shoot him, Mary," Happy squealed. "Shoot him."

Out of the corner of her eyes, Mary could see Crunchy slowly setting his foot down, then inch toward the man.

She tightened her grip on the gun, but didn't raise it.

"Who are you?" To her surprise, her voice remained steady.

"I'm the caretaker here."

Mary looked from Happy's gun to the caretaker. Gasping, she dropped the weapon. What if she had shot him?

"What are you doing here?" the caretaker asked.

Happy bounced on the balls of his feet, jabbing the air. "Having a picnic. What's it to you?"

At that moment Tim and the others returned.

Tim smiled reassuringly at Mary. "We didn't see anyone." Then, apparently catching sight of the rifleman, he recoiled. "Who are you?" he demanded.

"The caretaker. You people are trespassing. Get your stuff and clear out."

Tim held up his palms. "Sure. Anything you say." He walked over to where the shovels lay on the ground, seized one, and turned.

The caretaker leveled his rifle at him.

"Don't you want us to fill in the hole first?" Tim asked.

"No. Get your stuff and go. Or leave it. I don't care. Just go."

Mary bent to pick up the gun.

"Careful with that thing, Mary," the caretaker said.

Chills ran up and down her spine. How did he know her name?

Oh, right. Happy had used it.

When Mary straightened, gun in hand, the caretaker swung his rifle around and pointed it at her.

"Go," he said.

Though she wanted to run—run as fast and as far as she could—she walked sedately to the blanket, tucked the gun back in her purse, and started packing the remains of their picnic.

Tim gathered the tools, then came to help her. One by one the elders followed suit. Crunchy stood studying the man for a while longer, but when the caretaker trained his rifle on him, he slowly plodded toward Mary, though he kept looking back.

"Whew," Mary said when they drove away. "I was afraid he would call the sheriff, or shoot us, or something."

Kid Rags made a show of dusting off his suit jacket. "I was afraid he would make us fill in the hole."

They all laughed except Crunchy, who said, "Why didn't he?"

"Probably because there were too many of us to keep track of," Tim answered.

Mary smiled at Happy. "Maybe he thought Happy would shoot him."

Happy puffed out his chest. "I would of, too, but you took my gun."

Noticing how intently Iron Sam regarded her, Mary realized he hadn't known about the gun. They must not have mentioned it since he joined them. She nestled the purse closer to her side, wishing she'd left the weapon back in the clearing—better yet, that Happy hadn't seen fit to bring it in the first place.

"Something's fishy," Crunchy said. "That guy's fingernails looked too neat and clean."

"He wore an expensive warm-up suit," Kid Rags added.

Mary shivered, remembering the odious way he said her name. "You think maybe he wasn't just a caretaker?"

Crunchy and Kid Rags nodded.

She wrapped her arms around her waist. "Then we're doubly lucky to have gotten out of there without any trouble."

"Someone didn't," Lila Lorraine said softly.

"Once when I was a kid I saw a car that color," Spaghetti said. "My dad told me it was owned by a bookkeeper for the commission. 'Numbers' they called him."

Teach stroked his chin with a thumb and forefinger. "That's who I think it is. Numbers disappeared before I got to Chicago, but people still mentioned him and his car from time to time. A lime green Packard, they said. A custom job with brass trim that shone like gold."

"How come I don't remember?" Lila Lorraine asked.

"You were probably too young," Spaghetti answered.

Lila Lorraine beamed at him.

"I think I mentioned before," Teach said, "that the commission furnished the IRS with Al Capone's books. Emboldened by the success of the Treasury Department in putting Capone away, other agencies started nosing around, wanting to make a name for themselves, too. Numbers, in his ostentatious car, made an easy target for them. When he disappeared, people said that, to protect themselves, the commission took him out."

"They killed their own man?" Mary asked. "Whatever happened to honor among thieves?"

"In the Syndicate, like in the military, everyone is expendable—no one is a trusted ally. It all depends on the next deal. The one thing all highly successful people have in common is a total self-absorption which allows them to sacrifice anyone, no matter how dear, for the greater good— their greater good, that is."

"Jeez," Mary said, wondering what it would be like to be so ruthless. Probably very lonely. Or maybe not. Maybe rich, egotistical people didn't need anyone. Maybe their money satisfied them.

She stared out the windows watching her dreams recede further and further into the distance. Wishing she'd found her great-grandfather's gold.

Her gold.

All at once she felt exhausted, and her eyes felt sore as if she had been crying for a long time. If it hurt so much to have your dreams destroyed, was it worth having any?

"Dreams are overrated," Teach said.

Startled, Mary turned to stare at him. Her cheeks red-dened when she realized she had spoken aloud. She bit her lip, but curiosity got the better of her.

"How come you think dreams are overrated?" she asked.

He smiled at her. "Everyone has a dream. Stalin had a dream. Ted Bundy had a dream. So did Juan Corona and David Berkowitz. They all followed their dreams, but the world would have been better off if they hadn't."

"Jeeminy Christmas, Teach," Kid Rags said. "You're getting as weird as Happy."

Happy straightened his shoulders and said in his deep voice, "Over five hundred serial killers are roaming America right now."

Kid Rags adjusted his bow tie. "I rest my case."

"What dream of yours was destroyed, Mary?" Lila Lorraine asked.

Mary sighed. "It's not important. I'm disappointed we didn't find the gold is all."

Teach gave her a sidelong glance. "Somehow I didn't expect you to succumb to gold fever."

"It's not fair. I finally decide what I want to do with my life, and the means of getting it is dangled in front of my face, then it's snatched away."

Though she'd not intended to tell them any of this unless

they'd found the gold, the words spilled out. "You all know I inherited my grandparents' farm. The other day I told Lila Lorraine my idea of letting Iron Sam stay there until, well, you know."

"Until I croak," Iron Sam said.

Mary nodded. "And I asked Lila Lorraine if she'd stay there with you, and she said yes, partly because she was tired of the walls closing in on her and partly because she was tired of being useless. While we talked, I had a—not a vision exactly, more like an idea that popped into my head fully formed.

"I saw us all living there, along with others your age. We'd remodeled the house and enlarged it, and we built a few small cottages for those who wanted to live alone. We had crops growing in the field, and Happy drove the tractor—"

"Did we have a baby bulldozer?" Happy asked. "I saw one once. It was no bigger than a car. I bet it would be fun to drive."

Mary smiled. "A baby bulldozer and any other machinery we needed." Her voice grew dreamy. "We had flowers growing all around the house and cottages, lots of trees, and a roadside stand where we sold the produce we grew plus all kinds of other things, like the jewelry Kid Rags made."

Kid Rags pointed to his chest. "I? I made jewelry?" His eyes narrowed. "What is this? You trying to reform me?"

"No. Well . . . I guess, but it's not what you think. You sounded so sad the other day when you said people didn't want to pay for fine workmanship that I got to wondering if you could use your talents some other way. I was admiring the scrollwork you did on the share certificates when it dawned on me that you could make stunning gold or silver jewelry using that same design. You could forge other designers' work if you feel more comfortable doing that, but I don't think you'd need to. You're a real artist. Somewhere on the farm is my grandfather's gun smithy—we could turn it into a jewelry workshop for you."

"Jewelry," Kid Rags said as if rolling the word around on

179

his tongue. "I could do that." Then his face broke out in a broad grin, and he repeated, "I could do that."

"I know you can. I saw you doing it. I also saw us printing those share certificates, framing them, and selling them as a novelty. It would be a shame to waste such artistry."

"What did me and Journey do?" Crunchy asked.

"You protected us. Kept us safe. When Lila Lorraine or I or whoever worked in the produce stand, you made sure the customers didn't get out of hand."

Crunchy nodded, causing Journey, who was sitting on top of his head to emit a small meow and jump into his lap. "Me and Journey can do that."

"What else did I do?" Lila Lorraine asked.

"Whatever you wanted to. You made jam or cooked special treats. Sometimes you helped look after the ill, and in the summertime you took care of the flowers."

"Flowers! Oh, I'd like that."

"And me?" Teach asked.

"You were our overseer. You told us how to do things, conned your way into getting us the permits we needed, and helped me hire the people to do the things we couldn't do ourselves. Iron Sam sat in the sun, pitching in if he could, and Spaghetti kept us entertained—playing the piano and regaling us with all the local gossip."

Spaghetti beamed at her. "You saw me in your dream?"

"Not the original vision—I didn't know you then—but you are in it now. Every one of you is in my dream, but that's all it is. A dream. It would take a fortune to do it, and I'm broke. I doubt I'll be able to keep the farm."

After a long silence, Crunchy said, "I have my social security. You can have that."

Mary swallowed. "I can't take money from you."

"Me and Journey want to live at the farm. The hotel in Pueblo don't allow cats."

"I have my social security check, too," Lila Lorraine said, "and some jewelry my mother left me. Since I don't have anyone else to leave it to, I planned to give it to you anyway."

"I have a little money I was saving for my old age," Kid Rags said.

"So do I," Teach acknowledged.

Then, except for Iron Sam who stared out the window, they all talked at once, expanding on the dream.

Mary noticed Tim looking at her in the rear view mirror.

"I'd like to contribute too," he said.

Her original distrust of him came flooding back. "Why would you do that? What's in it for you?"

"It sounds like a good investment."

He grinned at her, and suddenly she felt exposed, as if one too many buttons were undone. She glanced down, and was reassured to see her white oxford shirt still decorously fastened and tucked securely into her forest green jeans. When she glanced at him again, his smile had broadened, and she got the impression he knew exactly what she was feeling.

Chapter 22

Mary's stomach roiled. It was one thing to conceive of grandiose dreams while under the warm influence of gold fever, quite another to consider them in the cold light of reality. Perhaps with the contributions mentioned they could all manage to live at the farm—assuming, of course, the elders actually wanted to and weren't patronizing her—but it wouldn't be the storybook farm she envisioned, where the unwanted and unneeded could help to the best of their waning strength and abilities, with paid employees doing the hard work and round-the-clock nurses caring for the sick and feeble.

Maybe she could apply for grants, but as Teach said, other people's money meant other people's control. Would the grant-giving foundations subvert her dream and substitute their own agendas? Probably.

And what about Tim? If she accepted his offer to invest in the farm, would he want to have a measure of control?

She stole a look at him. His eyes met hers in the rear view mirror, and her treacherous stomach seemed to do a flip.

"We're almost there," he said.

"Almost where?" They hadn't been driving long enough to be nearing Chicago.

He decelerated. "You'll see."

"Why are you stopping?" Kid Rags called out. "There's no place to eat around here."

"I think there's a sandwich or two and a piece of chicken left from lunch if you're hungry," Mary said. If he was hungry—of course he was hungry. Doubt gnawed at her belly once again. What if she couldn't keep him and the others fed? What if they all died of starvation on that hard-scrabble farm?

Tim slowed the van to a crawl, found a break in the woods, and pulled into a small clearing beside one of northern Wisconsin's ubiquitous lakes. The trees cast long shadows, and the setting sun turned the water to molten gold.

"It's beautiful," Lila Lorraine breathed.

"Looks like something from another planet." Kid Rags waved a half-eaten chicken leg for emphasis.

Tim gave a vague look around, as though he'd never contemplated the aesthetics of the place. His normally pleasant, open face seemed shuttered.

Happy bounced in his seat. "What are we waiting for? Let's go if we're going."

Tim nodded, but a minute passed before he climbed out of the van. The rest of them followed, shivering in the rapidly cooling air.

Tim opened his mouth to speak.

Iron Sam, his stillness compressed to a high degree of tension, stared at the younger man as if he knew what was coming.

All at once Mary also knew. She had the irrational urge to clap her hands over her ears to block out Tim's words, but she forced herself to listen.

"They didn't stand a chance," he said quietly. "The ambush was conducted like a military exercise. Most of the agents waited here in their vehicles, but a few hid in the trees across the way."

He led them out to the road, looked down the long stretch of straightaway, and pointed to a hill in the distance.

"My grandfather drove down that hill. He felt that itch between his shoulder blades warning him something was not right, so he paid particular attention when a car pulled in behind him from a side road. But the car kept well back.

"As Pat neared this spot, the agents' cars swarmed out of their hiding place, blocking the road. The car behind him accelerated until it hugged his bumper, hemming him in.

"Then the shooting started.

"Dugald, sitting in the cab with Pat, managed to get off a short burst from his tommy gun before he died.

"Since Pat drove, he had a revolver rather than a bulky submachine gun. He emptied his weapon at the agents through the shattered windshield. He felt a sting from a piece of flying glass and thought they'd hit him. He inched opened the door and dropped to the ground. Choking on the stench of gunpowder, he crawled into the trees away from the raining bullets. This is what hell must smell like, he thought as he hunkered down and tried to reload his revolver.

"It happened about this time of night—past sunset, getting dark—but the headlights of the vehicles made the scene as bright as a stage play. It felt like a stage play to Pat, too. Like it wasn't real. Still fumbling with his gun, he noticed that the firefight had turned one-sided. No answering shots came from the back of the truck where Adam and Charles had been protecting the cargo. And Pat knew his friends were dead.

"The gunfire stopped. For a second all was still, quiet. Then an agent let out a whoop, ran to the truck, jumped inside, and came out holding two bottles of whiskey. Laughing, he smashed them against the side of the truck. One or two of the other agents joined in the laughter, but the rest of them did their work in silence, breaking some bottles, but mostly emptying them onto the road. Flashbulbs went off as other agents recorded these heroic deeds."

"Sticky with Dugald's blood, tears streaming down his face, Pat lay hidden in the trees and waited until long after the truck—now containing only the bodies of his friends, empty bottles, and splintered crates—had been hauled away.

"When he finally staggered to his feet, body wracked with grief and adrenaline shakes, he stumbled to the spot where his friends had been murdered. Broken glass glinted in the moonlight. He sniffed, wondering why he couldn't smell any alcohol. That's when he realized The Shoemaker had sold them out to the prohibition agents, and that Dugald, Charles, and Adam had died protecting a shipment of colored water."

Tim stopped, took a deep, ragged breath, but no one else made a sound.

Sick to her stomach, mind curiously empty, Mary stood staring at the place where government employees had murdered her great-grandfather. She couldn't even begin to imagine how Pat had felt as he contemplated the senseless deaths of his friends.

Iron Sam's cough broke the silence.

Lila Lorraine and Spaghetti began speaking quietly to each other.

Mary made a helpless gesture. "I don't understand how Pat could have gone back to work for The Shoemaker."

Tim smiled sadly. "He didn't have much choice. If he let on by so much as a flicker that he knew The Shoemaker had set them up, The Shoemaker would have had him killed. As it happened, the next job The Shoemaker sent him on was driving a crash car. I don't think they intended for Pat to survive the 'accident', and in a way he didn't. He never acted the same afterward."

One by one the elders drifted away until only Mary, Tim, and Iron Sam regarded the massacre site.

Mary shot Iron Sam a curious glance. Why did this particular spot disturb him so?

Then, with a flash of intuition, she knew.

"Adam Kleinman was your father, wasn't he?" she said softly.

"Yes," Iron Sam answered with a barely perceptible movement of his lips. After a moment he added, "My mother insisted I take my stepfather's name. It didn't make any difference to me. One man's name is the same as another."

Mary glanced from Iron Sam to Tim then back at the road, goose bumps stippling her arms. How odd to think this nondescript bit of tarmac bound the three of them together.

"How odd," Tim said, echoing her thoughts.

Mary looked at him. Their eyes met. Once again she had the disorienting feeling of time folding in on itself, and she thought she could see, out of the corner of her eye, the shadowy figures of four men.

Her great-grandfather and his cousin. Tim's grandfather. Iron Sam's father.

"The ambush may not have been The Shoemaker's idea,"

Teach said as they headed back to Chicago. "People have the idea the gangsters corrupted the politicians when, in actuality, the politicians were all over them, demanding their due."

Spaghetti nodded. "That's for sure. I remember what one of my customers told me. He said, 'Clear your mind about us trying to corrupt public officials. We are fighting them off all the time to prevent them from asking for more.'"

"It seemed everyone wanted a piece of the action," Teach said. "I'm not saying prosecutors and judges and other officials were completely corrupt. They were willing to serve the public at their convenience, but when they received a better offer, they went with it.

"In bootlegger days, beer bought more sunshine friends than money did. The brewers usually sold their beer in kegs, but one enterprising fellow set up a bottling plant that could handle eighteen thousand bottles a week. He didn't sell so much as a single bottle. It all went to pay off the government employees.

"Mayor William O'Dwyer of New York once said, 'It doesn't matter whether it is a banker, a businessman, or a gangster—his pocketbook is always attractive.' Fraudulent contributions to political campaigns play a pivotal role in American politics. They devised the hundred-dollar-a-plate dinner, and later the thousand-dollar-a-plate dinner to give such donations the appearance of legitimacy. Mobsters and businessmen often bought as many as a hundred tickets to such affairs, a lump sum contribution of ten thousand dollars for every dinner—and there were many dinners."

As much as Mary liked hearing Teach talk, her attention wandered. She couldn't help marveling at the remarkable coincidence that she and Iron Sam—and Tim, of course—had ended up at that fateful spot.

But maybe it wasn't such a remarkable coincidence. This journey had been a direct result of her grandparents' murders. Her resolve to talk to Iron Sam came about when she discovered that someone had also murdered Robert Stuart and his wife. If Iron Sam had remained in

186

Leavenworth, they probably would not have met, but some mysterious benefactor—Mario Vinzetti, perhaps?—arranged for his release. The two murdered old men and Iron Sam had all been the sons of the men massacred on that lonely Wisconsin road. Could the murderer and Iron Sam's benefactor be the same? It was possible. But why? Revenge? No. All the fathers had been victims themselves.

According to Tim.

Mary narrowed her eyes as she gazed at the back of Tim's head. What if he hadn't told them the whole story? What if Crazy Pat had convinced him that the other three men had conspired against him, and now Tim was trying to get even?

As if he felt Mary's gaze on him, Tim turned around and grinned at her.

Cheeks burning, she ducked her head. The thing was, she felt sure he'd told them the truth, at least the truth as he knew it. And she couldn't see him killing anyone, especially not two elderly couples.

"Where to next?" Tim asked.

"Topeka, Kansas," she said without hesitation. "I need to find out who Mario Vinzetti is and what he wants with us."

Chapter 23

"When are we going to stop for food?" Kid Rags asked.

"We're not," Mary answered.

"We're not?"

"We're not?" Tim echoed.

"Not until we need gas," Mary said.

"But I'm hungry," Kid Rags said in an aggrieved tone.

Mary handed him a bag of sandwiches, granola bars, and apples she had bought at the convenience store when they last stopped for gas. "Here, help yourself."

"What if I get tired driving?" Tim asked. "It will be a long time before we need to refuel."

"Then I'll drive," Mary said briskly.

Tim groaned. "You better give me one of those sandwiches, Kid Rags." He sounded as put upon as the old man, but the corners of his mouth quirked up.

Mary ignored him and went back to figuring out when they would arrive in Topeka. She wanted to be there by early evening, but it didn't look as though they'd make it. Tim had been late picking them up that morning. He had some business to attend to, he'd said—*yeah*, Mary thought, picturing the gorgeous Kirsten, *monkey business*—and then he had to swing by the retirement home for Spaghetti. On top of that, it took hours to get out of Chicago. Now that they sped along the interstate, she hoped to make up for lost time.

One good thing: they were taking I-80, which meant they could bypass most of Missouri. Although they were in a different vehicle, she still felt conspicuous. After all, how many gangs of octogenarian desperados could there be?

Shortly after they turned south on I-35 outside of Des Moines, Mary called a halt. If they kept going, they could probably reach Topeka by midnight, but everyone was getting cranky and restless.

Even me.

They checked into a budget motel flanked by a family restaurant and a honky-tonk, a popular spot for locals, judging by all the Iowa license plates on the vehicles in the communal parking lot.

When Mary saw Kid Rags cast a longing glance at the restaurant, she said, "You go ahead." She rotated her shoulders, which felt as tight as if she had been the one doing the driving. "I'm going to take a shower first."

With a chorus of "Me too"s, the elders disappeared into their rooms, leaving Kid Rags in the parking lot, looking as forlorn as a child with a lump of coal in his stocking on Christmas morning.

Taking pity on him, Mary opened her purse, extracted a granola bar, and tossed it to him.

Eyes lighting up, he plucked it out of mid air and began ripping off the wrapper as he headed for the room he would share with Teach.

Mary entered her room, plopped on the bed, and lay back.

"You want to take your shower first?" Lila Lorraine asked.

"No, you go ahead. I don't think I can move."

Hands behind her head, Mary stared at the ceiling and wondered what tomorrow would bring. Even if, as Happy claimed, Vinzetti started tailing them when they left Leavenworth, she felt sure the surveillance connected somehow to the mystery of her grandparents' deaths. Would she finally learn why they had been killed, and by whom?

Lulled by the sound of running water, she drifted off to sleep and dreamt she sat by a lovely moss green lake in the middle of a Wisconsin forest. The light dimmed, and it seemed as if the trees advanced on her, grasping branches outstretched.

She awoke with a start when she heard Lila Lorraine's voice calling out, "I'm done. Bathroom's all yours."

She tried to shake off the dream, but as she stood under the soothing fall of hot water, she could feel the menace that emanated from those nightmarish trees.

When Mary emerged from the bathroom, she found Lila Lorraine sitting on her bed, photographs spread all around her.

"I thought I had a picture of Gina Dale. Yes. Here it is." Lila Lorraine's hand darted out to pick up a snapshot. She gazed at it a moment, a far away look in her teary eyes. "I do so miss your grandmother."

She blinked rapidly, then handed the photograph to Mary. In the picture, three identically dressed young women, with their heads touching, smiled at her.

Lila Lorraine pointed to the dark-haired beauty in the center. "That's me."

"You were stunning! You look like an actress I saw in an old movie, Claudia something or other."

"Claudette Colbert." Lila Lorraine smoothed her non-existent eyebrows. "And didn't I know it. To enhance the resemblance, I plucked my eyebrows the way she did, and eventually they stopped growing back. I'm so pleased to see that you don't pluck yours. Gina Dale didn't either. That's her on the right. The other girl is Cokey Flo."

Mary tilted the picture toward the light to get a closer look at Gina Dale. Though not as striking as either Lila Lorraine or Cokey Flo, Gina had a quiet beauty all her own. Her jaw line was strong enough that in some lights she might look masculine, but the radiant smile brightened her face and softened her features.

"I still have that dress," Lila Lorraine said.

Mary tore her gaze away from her grandmother's face and threw a questioning glance at the old woman.

"The dresses we wore for that picture. I still have mine. It doesn't fit anymore, hasn't for years, but I like having it around. It's something of a good luck charm for me. In fact, I brought it with me."

"You did? Really?"

"Sure. Want to see it?"

"I'd love to."

Lila Lorraine gathered the pictures, tucked them into a side pocket of her suitcase, then removed a tissue-wrapped bundle, which she carefully laid on the bed. She unfolded the sheets of tissue paper to reveal a glittering red dress. She held the dress in front of her body and swayed to music only she could hear.

"Isn't it gorgeous?"

"Very pretty," Mary answered, though, in truth, the dress was too flashy for her taste. The long-waisted bodice was sequined, the thin shoulder straps were linked ruby rhinestones, and the short, flirty, multi-layered chiffon skirt was shot through with scarlet metallic threads.

Lila Lorraine stopped swaying and gave Mary an appraising look. "I'll bet it would fit you." She held out the dress. "Here. Try it on."

Mary put her hands behind her back. "No. I couldn't. I wouldn't feel right."

Again that appraising look. "You'd be beautiful."

"What if I ruin it?"

"You won't ruin it." She continued to hold out the dress. "Please? For me?"

"Oh, all right."

Lila Lorraine beamed, apparently unfazed by Mary's ungracious tone. She watched bright-eyed while Mary slipped on the dress, then stepped back and clapped her hands.

"I knew you'd look lovely!"

Mary twitched her shoulders and tugged at the bodice, trying to cover more of her breasts. "It's too small."

"It's perfect." Lila Lorraine gazed at Mary a moment, then said softly, "It does bring back memories." She sat in front of the mirror. "Are you going to help me put on my face?"

"Sure. Let me get this dress off first."

"Leave it on a little longer. Please?"

Mary fidgeted, but finally nodded. If it would make Lila Lorraine happy, she could manage to wear the flashy dress a few more minutes.

When she finished applying Lila Lorraine's makeup, the old woman stood and said, "Your turn."

"My turn for what?"

Lila Lorraine pointed to the cosmetics strewn across the surface of the dressing table.

Mary backed away, but Lila Lorraine caught her hand and drew her forward.

"We don't have time to play any more dress-up," Mary protested. "The guys will be getting hungry."

"Let them wait." Lila Lorraine put her hands on her hips. "If you don't do it, I'll do it for you."

"This is just plain silly." Mary brushed her lashes with the mascara wand. *To say nothing of unsanitary.* After a few quick strokes of the eyeliner pencil and a touch of blue eye shadow, she stood. "There. All done."

Lila Lorraine gave a satisfied nod, then all at once she gasped.

"What?" Mary asked, alarmed. "What's wrong?"

Lila Lorraine pointed to the old pair of sneakers on Mary's feet.

Mary laughed, but Lila Lorraine didn't crack a smile.

"You can't wear those shoes. Don't you have any others?"

"No, but what difference does it make? Nobody but you is going to see me like this."

A knock sounded on the door.

Before Mary could make a dash for safety, Lila Lorraine opened the door. Kid Rags, followed by Teach and Crunchy, entered the room. All three gazed at Mary for what seemed like a long time.

Crunchy spoke first. "Gina Dale!"

Teach nodded. "You look exactly like her when she was young."

Kid Rags bowed slightly. "Real pretty."

"Hey, come on!" Happy shouted from outside. "What's taking so long?"

Tim crowded into the room. "Yeah, what's taking so—" He stopped abruptly and stared at Mary. "Wow!"

Mary's face felt so hot she was sure it matched the red of the dress. "I'll be right out, I need to get changed."

"Why?" Tim asked. "You look great. I like the shoes. Makes a statement."

His eyes gleamed, and her knees unaccountably felt weak.

"Don't change," Crunchy said. "I like you in that dress."

"And anyway," Kid Rags put in, "I'm hungry."

Without knowing how it happened, Mary found herself outside, surrounded by the elders, on her way to the restaurant. Spaghetti, she noted with amusement, looked only at Lila Lorraine. Iron Sam kept to himself.

They had taken but a few steps when Tim broke away from the group.

"Be right back," he mumbled. "Forgot something."

He went into his motel room, and when he came hurrying out a minute later, he wore a tie and had put on a brown herringbone sport jacket over his faded blue jeans.

Chapter 24

The roast beef special at Big John's Family Restaurant tasted delicious, but Mary did not enjoy a single bite. Every time she lifted the fork to her mouth, she imagined herself dribbling gravy on Lila Lorraine's cherished dress.

Finally, shooting a look of defiance at a grinning Tim, she tucked her napkin into the skimpy bodice and managed to finish her meal.

To her relief, no one in her entourage lingered in the well-lit restaurant after dinner, and they soon trooped across the parking lot. She cast a wistful glance at her room as they passed the motel, but let herself be swept along to Honky-Tonk Heaven.

A live band wailed about somebody done somebody wrong as they made their way to the only available table. It was too small to accommodate such a large party, but Tim rounded up enough chairs for all of them.

A waitress, whose hat and boots covered more of her than all the rest of her cowgirl outfit put together, approached. Mary ordered a club soda with lime, thinking if she spilled it in the tight confines, it would do the least damage to the dress. The others ordered beer or bourbon or both.

Leaning back in her chair, drink in hand, Mary felt herself relax. The band was good and so were the dancers, though Kid Rags didn't seem to agree. He watched them with a pained look on his face.

Draining his double bourbon, he rose and held out a hand to Lila Lorraine. "Let's show them how it's done,"

Lila Lorraine immediately got to her feet and took his hand.

As the two glided around the floor, the other dancers made way for them. Many stopped to watch.

Tim caught Mary's eyes and winked at her. "You'd think they were Ginger Rogers and Fred Astaire."

Mary giggled. "Fred Astaire, maybe, but not Ginger

Rogers. Ginger would never wear a get-up like that."

Lila Lorraine had abandoned her jellybean colored warm-up suits for a subdued challis dress, but she piled on more rings, bracelets, and necklaces than usual in compensation.

"They seem so young out there," Tim said.

Teach lifted his shoulders and let them drop. "Not surprising. Except for ballerinas, who suffer with foot and knee problems, most dancers age well."

"Was Kid Rags a dancer?" Mary asked.

"Not a professional, but I understand he spent a lot of time on the dance floor. He liked the ladies."

Mary smiled. "I figured as much."

Teach cleared his throat. "I'm not in his league, but I do a pretty mean two-step. I'd be honored if you'd dance with me."

Mary's smile broadened. "I'd love to."

Teach's touch was light as he steered her around the dance floor, and she had no trouble matching her steps to his.

"It's a nice thing you're doing," he said after a moment.

"What? Dancing with you?"

He chuckled. "That, too, but I meant the farm. Have you thought of how hard it will be on you?"

Mary stiffened. "I'm not afraid of hard work. The only reason I haven't wanted to settle down and get a real full-time job is that until now I haven't found anything I thought worth doing."

"I never doubted it for a moment. I'm just afraid you've overestimated how much work we can do. This trip has been magical for all of us, like dipping into the fountain of youth, but it won't be long before we all slip back to our old decrepit selves."

"I did take that possibility into consideration, and that's why I wanted the gold—to make sure we had enough money to hire all the help we needed. I may have understated it when I told all of you my dream, but I didn't want any of you to think you were going to be doing busywork. I wanted you to know that no matter how much or how little you could do, you'd be a vital part of the operation."

"You have given this a lot of thought, haven't you?" When she nodded, he continued with an uncharacteristic hesitancy, "There's one other thing—what I meant when I mentioned about it being hard on you. Speaking *in loco grandparentis*—have you thought what it will be like watching all of us . . . pass away?"

Mary swallowed. She had been trying hard not to think about that. "I know one thing," she said in a small voice. "It will be easier than not doing the farm and knowing all of you are going to die alone."

They danced a few steps in silence; then Teach said softly, "Your grandparents would be proud of you." He drew her close and gave her a hug. "*I* am proud of you."

Tears welled up in Mary's eyes.

When Teach led Mary back to the table, Kid Rags rolled his eyes. "Jeez, Teach, what did you do to the poor girl? This is a dance, not a funeral."

He turned Lila Lorraine over to Spaghetti and held out a hand to Mary. "Come on, I'll put a smile on your face."

Mary dabbed at her eyes. "I'm not sure I can keep up with you."

"No problem." Taking her hand, Kid Rags whirled her into his arms, then away from him. The next thing she knew, she swung behind him, at his side, in front, and into his arms again. Within a short time she was gasping for breath, while he seemed remarkably composed.

She laughed. "Why you old fraud. You're making me do all the work."

"Of course I am. The secret to being a good dancer is to make your partner look even better."

"Did you ever think, when I first knocked on your door in Denver, that we'd be dancing together in Iowa?"

"I thought I'd never see you again."

"I'm glad I came back."

"Me too."

Mary spotted Lila Lorraine dancing with Spaghetti, her head on his shoulder, a dreamy look on both their faces.

"Somehow I expected you to end up with Lila Lorraine."

"Nah, she's not my type." Kid Rags raised and lowered his eyebrows and flicked the ash from an imaginary cigar before reclaiming both Mary's hands. "I like them young and nubile."

Mary laughed, then leaned forward and kissed him on the cheek. "You are an old fraud."

When they returned to the table, Kid Rags dropped onto his chair and wiped the back of a hand across his forehead. "Whew! Now I remember why I gave up women—they wear me out." He signaled for the waitress to bring him another drink. "From now on, I'm sticking with bourbon."

As Mary started to sit, she noticed a wistful expression on Crunchy's face. She went to him. "Would you dance with me, Crunchy?"

"I'm not so good a dancer as you." He sounded reluctant, but he rose to his feet before the words were completely out of his mouth.

It was a slow dance. Crunchy held her gently, shifted his weight from foot to foot, and gave her the shy smile that until now he reserved for Journey.

They did not speak. At the end, Mary said gravely, "Thank you, Crunchy."

"Thank you, too."

They were halfway back to their table when Mary noticed Tim making his way toward them. Tim pointed a finger at Mary, then at himself. At her nod, he beamed and took a few rapid steps forward. She noticed his smile disappear at the same time she felt a heavy hand clamp onto her shoulder.

All at once someone jerked her around and pulled her into a boozy embrace.

Not again!

Although this man was leaner than the truck driver who assaulted her, he was big. 6'2". Maybe 220 pounds. And he had that same self-satisfied smirk on his clean-shaven face.

Mary tried to squirm out of his grasp. "This dance is spoken for. My partner will be here any second."

The man tightened his grip. Crushed against his chest, she could smell the cheap laundry detergent that had been used to clean his fancy cowboy shirt, the mousse he'd used to slick back his dark hair, the lime-scented cologne he'd spilled all over himself.

She felt more than heard his sharp intake of breath.

She turned her head in time to see Tim bending back the hand that rested on her shoulder. Tim kept wrenching the hand until it looked to Mary as if the man's wrist might snap.

"You can go now," Tim said, staring into the man's eyes.

One, two seconds ticked by. Tim still held on to the wristlock.

When Tim finally let go, the man rubbed his wrist and stared back at Tim.

Another second ticked by. The man turned and walked away.

Tim kept staring after him.

Mary let out a breath she hadn't realized she'd been holding. She looked around, expecting everyone to be watching them, but it had all happened so fast only a few people cast curious glances their way.

She summoned a shaky smile. "It seems as if lately I'm always needing to be rescued."

Tim turned to her, the harshness fading from his eyes. "I didn't rescue you. I was claiming my dance."

He held out his arms.

Mary walked into his embrace. "You look like you do that rough stuff all the time."

"Not all the time, but working in a bar I occasionally meet people who need to be shown the error of their ways."

"Have you always worked in a bar?"

"I used to be a stockbroker."

Mary stopped short. "You what?"

He smiled. "That's right. A stockbroker. My mom felt so proud. She was the one who insisted I get an education. She was the one who made sure I went to Wharton."

"And your dad?"

"He wanted me to go into the family business."

"The bar?"

"No, no. Dad was a bookie. Worked out of his pool hall.

Mom didn't want that life for me, didn't want it for herself, either, even though it was all she ever knew. When I began working at one of the fancy downtown brokerage houses, she sat my dad down and told him she wanted him to retire. He tried to talk her into letting him keep the pool hall, but she said the book was too much a part of it, so he needed to get rid of the entire business. 'What am I going to do?' he asked her. 'I'm too young to stop working.' 'You'll think of something,' she said."

"Your mom sounds tough."

Tim laughed. "Mom? Not at all. Well, maybe she is, but in a velvet glove sort of way."

"What did your dad do?"

"Oh, he moped around, spent a lot of time at various bars drowning his sorrows, then one day he wandered into The Joker and met Spaghetti's son. The son kept complaining about how hard he had to work. My dad, who has no sympathy for anyone's problems but his own, said, 'So, sell the bar.' 'Easy for you to say,' the son whined. 'Who'd buy a dump like this?' My father took a good look around, then said, 'I would. How much you want?' After he completed the sale, he discovered that Spaghetti, not his son, owned the place."

"If the son didn't own it, how could he sell it?"

"Spaghetti had given him his power of attorney. My dad now owns a whole string of neighborhood bars. Never been happier. Me? I was miserable. Even though I made a pile of money, I hated being a stockbroker. Several years ago, I told my dad it was a sleazy racket. I felt as if I was running a numbers game, making money for big investors on the bodies of small investors. He said, 'Whatever you do, don't tell your mom. She's so thrilled you're a success in a supposedly honest business.' He suggested I work for him until I figure out what I want to do. When I asked, 'What about Mom?' he patted me on the back and said, 'Don't worry. I'll take care of her.' I've been at The Joker ever since."

He moved closer to her. "Enough about me. Let's just

dance."

For a moment Mary felt herself floating, suspended between the melody and his touch.

Then the music ended.

When they got back to the table, Crunchy was standing, waiting for them.

"You okay, Lady?"

"I'm fine, Crunchy. Really I am."

He turned to Tim, looked into his eyes for several seconds, then nodded once.

Teach pointed his chin at the dance floor. "You handled yourself smoothly out there. Are you an athlete?"

"No. I never developed an interest in sports. See, my father was a bookie, and he explained to me how the system works. When you grow up knowing outcomes are often fixed and that gambling is the real reason for professional sports, it seems unimportant."

Teach stroked his chin. "I can see that."

"What do you mean gambling is the real reason for professional sports?" Mary asked, wondering if she was missing something. A Y chromosome, perhaps?

"Without gambling," Tim explained, "there would be no professional sports. Not many college sports, either. It's like horseracing. No one goes to the track to watch the pretty horses run. Everyone wants a stake in the action. Winning one for the Gipper is fine, but when it comes to the crunch, it's the cash that counts."

"It's what I keep telling you, Mary," Teach said. "Everything is a con."

"And it's usually the small bettor who gets taken in," Tim added. "Things like the point spread were invented to give gamblers the feeling that the odds are even." He shook his head. "If they only knew what steps are taken to beat the point spread. When I was a kid, my dad used to tell me a story about a pro football game that's considered to be one of the greatest games ever, because it drew huge TV audiences for the first time."

"Hey, I remember that game," Kid Rags exclaimed. "It

was between the—"

Tim held up a hand and continued, "The owner of one of the teams gambled big—we're talking major bucks here. He wouldn't allow the coach to go for a field goal that would have won the game because it would have ruined the point spread. The team eventually made a touchdown in overtime, winning the game, and the owner got his money."

"So what was the team?" Mary asked.

"I'll give you the same answer my dad gave me—any team, any time, anywhere."

"Individual athletes, too," Teach said. "In the early 1960s, the mob forced the heavyweight champion of the world to take a fall during a title fight. He hated the idea, but the mob controlled—and exploited—him, so he had to do what they said. One day while drinking heavily in a Vegas hotel restaurant, he saw one of the bosses of the Cleveland Syndicate. He walked over to the guy and got into an argument with him. He drew back his fist. The boss did not move. In careful words, spoken clearly and distinctly, the sixty-four-year-old boss said, 'If you hit me, nigger, you'd better kill me, because if you don't, I'll make just one phone call, and you'll be dead in twenty-four hours.' The boxer walked away without a word, checked out of the hotel, and left town."

Mary stole a glance at Iron Sam, who seemed to be listening intently. Is Iron Sam the one the boss would have called? She shivered. Strange how every time she got to thinking these were ordinary old men, something happened to remind her of what they had once been.

"About ten years later," Teach said, "this same boxer died of an overdose, but he was not an addict—he hated needles. He had been making a comeback and wanted another chance at the heavyweight championship—a straight up fight this time—but the mob wanted him to take a fall again. He refused, so they hot-shotted him."

"What's going on?" Happy asked, returning from a circuit around the honky-tonk.

Before anyone could answer, Lila Lorraine and Spaghetti

also returned.

Mary stood. "I don't know about all of you, but I'm exhausted. I think I'll turn in."

Lila Lorraine and Spaghetti looked at each other. "We're staying awhile," she said.

Kid Rags raised his glass. "I'm going to have another drink."

"Me too," Happy said.

Iron Sam coughed and hacked.

Crunchy started to rise, but sat back down, eyes twinkling, when Tim jumped to his feet.

Once outside, Tim took off his jacket and draped it over Mary's shoulders.

She smiled. "I didn't realize men still did things like that."

"I didn't realize women still let them."

"Well, I appreciate it. It's chilly out here."

They walked in silence for a moment, then she said, "It sounded to me as if you prescribe to Teach's view of life. That it's all one great big con. Don't you believe in anything?"

"In a way I do. I grew up knowing the lower end of the con, and then as a stockbroker I learned about the higher end. What I'm looking for, and what I believe I can find, is a civilized life somewhere in between."

"That's beautiful, but I'm not sure I understand what you mean."

Tim chuckled. "I'm not sure I understand either."

A few more paces took them to her door.

"Oh." She looked around. "We're here." She shrugged off his jacket and handed it to him.

He smiled at her, holding her gaze.

Her cheeks grew hot. She ducked her head and rummaged in her purse for the room key. After opening the door, she turned to face him.

"There's something else I believe in." He took one of her hands in his, placed a kiss in the palm of her hand, and curled her fingers around it.

She felt a light shock radiate up her arm and down to her belly.

"Good night, Mary," he said softly.

She could only nod.

He plucked the key out of the lock. "Do you want me to give this to Lila Lorraine so she won't disturb you later?"

Another nod.

Backing into the room and shutting the door behind her took unexpected effort, as though she had to push through masses of jelly.

She stumbled to her bed, sat down, and slowly opened her tingling hand.

Amazing.

It still looked the same.

Chapter 25

Tim pulled up behind the blue Grand Am parked in front of the pale yellow frame house. "You told me Vinzetti was following you."

"He was," Mary said, "but I haven't seen him since I caught him looking into the bus windows."

Tim put on the parking brake, then tapped his fingers on the steering wheel. "Maybe this isn't such a good idea. Have you considered the possibility that he killed your grandparents?"

Mary's stomach muscles tightened. "I've thought about it."

"And?"

"And nothing. I've come too far to turn back now."

"We could go to the cops."

"With what? That Vinzetti followed us? I doubt they'd care. And he isn't following us now."

"We going or what?" Happy asked.

"I'm going," Mary said, climbing out of the van. "The rest of you can stay here if you want."

When Mary rang the doorbell, Crunchy stood beside her, the other elders and Tim ranged behind them.

The door opened part way; Vinzetti peered out at them. He scowled, then started to close the door.

Crunchy stuck out a foot. The door slammed against his heavy shoe.

Vinzetti kicked Crunchy's foot once, twice. Crunchy didn't budge.

"We want to talk to you," Mary said.

Vinzetti glanced at her, but did not respond.

She took a deep breath. "Why did you follow us?"

Directing his gaze behind her, he stiffened. She glanced over her shoulder, tracking his gaze, and saw Iron Sam standing motionless, looking grimmer than the grim reaper himself.

Vinzetti shifted position, but Mary could see that Iron Sam was still in his line of sight, staring at him.

"What do you want with us?" Mary asked.

Vinzetti blinked as if awakening from a trance, squinted at her for a moment, then continued watching Iron Sam.

No wonder. Even though she had grown used to him, that silent, immobile figure still commanded her attention. And gave her goose bumps.

Resisting the urge to rub her arms, she opened her mouth then closed it when she couldn't think of anything else to ask. It appeared so easy on television and in movies. You asked questions. They answered. But what did you do when they didn't answer? Let someone else take over the interrogation?

She threw back her shoulders. *No. My grandparents are the ones who were killed. It's my responsibility.*

"Did you murder my grandparents?" she asked.

Vinzetti wrenched his head around and stared at her. "Murder? What are you talking about? I didn't murder anyone."

"Well, you've been following us, and I thought—"

"Listen up, Little Miss Muffet. That had nothing to do with you. Or your grandparents."

"Then why were you following us?"

Glancing at Iron Sam, Vinzetti stuck a finger beneath his collar and pulled the fabric away from his neck.

Mary felt like stamping her foot and screaming at him; instead, she curled her dangling hands into fists and enunciated slowly and firmly, "Somebody killed my grandparents, and I want to know who and why. You became a player when you started following us, and now you're a suspect. Our only suspect. You talk to us, or we go to the police."

Vinzetti choked out a semblance of a laugh. "The cops won't get involved in anything as ludicrous as this."

"They're already involved," Mary said in that same firm voice. "How do you think we found you?"

Tim stepped forward. "We'll start with the Chicago

police—I know people there. All it will take is one call, and the local cops will be at your door. Do you want to go down for multiple murders?"

"Multiple murders?"

Mary nodded. "Four that we know of."

Vinzetti closed his eyes. "Look," he said, opening them again. "I don't need this grief. It was a simple tail job. I was hired to keep tabs on Samuel Bornstein when he got out of the joint. That's all. I don't know anything about any murders."

"What are you?" Mary asked. "A private detective?"

"Something like that."

"So who hired you?"

"Can't say."

"Can't, or won't?"

"Can't. We set it up over the Internet. He contacted me through an online remailer, so I don't know his identity."

"What about when he paid you? Did he put a return address on the envelope?"

"No envelope. Direct deposit."

Tim took out his cell phone. "We have no time for games, and we are not going to negotiate. You give us the name of your employer, or we call the police and let you explain everything to them."

"I told you—"

"I know what you told us," Tim said. "Now you can tell us the truth. I'm sure a smart operator like you found a way around the remailer. Perhaps a tracer on an email you sent him?"

Crunchy clenched his hands into fists. Iron Sam seemed to grow even more menacing.

Vinzetti looked at each man in turn. "Maybe I did. Maybe I traced it to an Albert Hoffman on Ohio Street in Racine, Wisconsin."

"What address?" Tim asked.

Vinzetti spit out a number.

"What does Albert Hoffman want with Sam?" Mary asked.

"He didn't say."

"Are you still working for him?"

"He terminated my services when you caught me checking out your bus. That's all I know. I swear."

Thinking how silence seemed to make Vinzetti nervous, Mary emulated Iron Sam and stood still without saying anything.

Vinzetti looked from Iron Sam to Tim to Mary, and cleared his throat. "I don't know anything about your grandparents or who killed them. I told you all I know, so take your pet gorilla"—he jutted his chin at Crunchy—"and the rest of your sideshow freaks and get the hell out of here."

Crunchy shot Mary a questioning glance.

She nodded.

He withdrew his foot. Vinzetti slammed the door.

"Do you believe him?" Mary asked when they settled in the van once again.

"I think so," Tim answered.

"He looked to the right when he talked," Teach said. "That usually indicates a person is remembering. People generally look to the left when they're making things up."

Kid Rags laughed. "Our own private lie detector."

Mary sighed. "I believe him, too. He seemed genuinely stunned at being accused of murder. Maybe we better get out of here before he calls the police and complains of being harassed."

"He won't call the cops," Teach said. "He might have been telling the truth about Hoffman, but he was hiding something. He acted too skittish to be entirely innocent of any wrongdoing. I doubt it has anything to do with us, though."

"So, who's Albert Hoffman?" Mary asked.

"I don't know," Tim said.

"Anyone?"

All but one of the elders shook their heads.

"What about you, Sam?"

"Never heard of him." Iron Sam slumped against the seat as if drained. He coughed, then drew in a ragged breath. "Don't know what he wants with me."

"So we're back where we started," Lila Lorraine said.

"Not quite." Spaghetti held up first one pudgy finger and then another. "We know who followed you and who hired him." He held up a third finger. "And we know where to find him."

Lila Lorraine nodded wearily. "In Wisconsin."

Mary buried her face in her hands. This could not be happening. It should have been over once they'd talked to Mario Vinzetti.

She raised her head, which felt as heavy as a bowling ball, and rubbed her eyes. "We should get something to eat. Maybe we'll feel better with food in our bellies."

"I'll second that," Kid Rags said without his usual enthusiasm.

Happy bounced in his seat. "Let's go if we're going. What are we waiting for?"

Noticing that his bounce seemed forced and his voice strained, Mary realized he was wearing down. They all were.

She glanced at Tim. Even he seemed tired. Did he have as restless a night as she? Every time she had thought of his kissing the palm of her hand, her heart thumped and tiny explosions of heat pulsed through her body.

She averted her eyes when he turned around and grinned at her. Drat that man! Did he always know what she was thinking?

Sitting in a fast food restaurant and watching Kid Rags pick at the single hamburger he had ordered, Mary said, "I think it's time for us to go home."

"What about Albert Hoffman?" Crunchy asked.

Mary took a bite of her chicken sandwich and munched slowly. What about Albert Hoffman? Why was he so interested in Iron Sam? Had he arranged Iron Sam's release from prison? And what did that have to do with her grandparents' deaths? Probably nothing. Except for a waning gut feeling, she'd found no evidence linking the two occurrences, and in the end, it was all about the evidence, wasn't it?

She stole a look at Iron Sam, who was laboriously chewing on a French fry. Since he appeared to have no interest in Hoffman, she didn't see any point in putting the elders through the exhausting ordeal of returning to Wisconsin.

And she had another, more pressing reason for ending the journey.

"I'm tapped out," she said. "I might have enough to get us back to Denver, but that's all. I'm not sure I can scrape up enough for gas to drive Teach to Arizona."

"Don't worry about me," Teach said. "If need be, I can find a way to get extra cash."

Mary bit her lower lip. "I doubt that will be necessary."

"I realize this is your project," Tim said, "but if you want to go back to Wisconsin and talk to Albert Hoffman, I'll be glad to finance it." He held up his hands as a protest formed on her lips. "Consider it a loan if you wish, or part of my investment in your farm."

Mary narrowed her eyes. "Weren't you the one who thought talking to Vinzetti was a bad idea? Why are you so gung-ho about talking to Hoffman?"

He smiled at her. "It's not about what I think, but about what you want. I know if you don't follow through, all the rest of your life you'll be kicking yourself for quitting."

You don't know me. You don't know the first thing about me.

But he was right. *Dadgummit.*

"It's not my decision to make," she said. "This affects all of us."

Happy raised his right hand as if taking an oath. "I say we go to Wisconsin."

Mary gave him a searching look. "You sure?"

"Sure, I'm sure. I want to know where Hoffman gets off putting a tail on us."

"I vote yes." Kid Rags took a surreptitious sip from his hip flask. "Anyone want a drink?"

They all shook their heads in refusal.

"Journey likes riding in the van," Crunchy said. "We want to go."

Spaghetti folded his arms and rested his elbows on the table. "I abstain. Since I live back that direction, it's no skin off my nose."

Lila Lorraine looked at him with shining eyes. "Then I'm going, too."

"I think it's a good idea to go where the trail leads you," Teach said. "If that means returning to Wisconsin, so be it."

"What do you think, Sam?" Mary asked when he didn't bother to comment.

He struggled to swallow the food in his mouth. "Wisconsin," he finally managed to gasp.

"It's unanimous, then." Mary plastered on a bright smile. "Wisconsin, here we come."

While they waited at a red light on their way out of Topeka, Teach pointed to a pawnshop wedged between a video arcade and a thrift shop.

"See that pawn shop? It used to be a barbershop back in the sixties. A guy by the name of Hoot Bobben was killed there."

"I think I met him once when he visited Chicago," Spaghetti said. "They called him Hoot because of his flat face, round glasses, and the two cowlicks on the top of his head that stood up like the horns of an owl."

"That's Hoot, all right," Teach said. "He was a button man for the mob—"

"What exactly is a button man?" Mary asked, more to make conversation than because she wanted to know.

"Books and movies often use the term to mean hit man," Teach responded, "but a button man is more of a soldier— similar to a corporal or a sergeant—with others under his command and with ties to the higher echelons. The term 'button man' is of Sicilian derivation. The Italian Carabinieri originally wore large shiny brass buttons and were, of course, men of authority, so the Mafia, which was organized along military lines, called its men of authority 'button men.'"

The light turned green. As they drove off, Teach turned around to take one last look at the erstwhile barbershop.

"Hoot is famous for being the first to dispose of a rival in the crusher."

"I worked in a junkyard once," Happy said in the confident tone he used when speaking about cars. "That twelve foot high hydraulic press had two powerful rams, each with a striking power of a million pounds. It could crush a car in ninety seconds and turn it into a metal cube less than three feet square. We shipped the cube to a steel mill where it got melted down to make steel for new vehicles.

"If someone left a body in the trunk of one of those cars, it would of disappeared forever."

The moment of speechlessness that usually greeted one of Happy's pronouncements dragged on and on. In fact, no one said much of anything for the rest of the day.

That evening they checked into a motel on the outskirts of Davenport, then headed for a nearby restaurant. Conversation during dinner consisted of such terse comments as "Good soup," and "Pass the salt."

After they trudged back to the motel, Mary paused at her door, reluctant to face another anonymous room.

"I think I'll take a walk," she said.

"Mind if I come with you?" Tim asked.

"If you want."

When the others declined to join them, Mary and Tim strolled around to the back of the motel where a narrow stream coursed between grassy banks. As they silently followed the stream, Mary couldn't help worrying. Although the elders all voted to continue the journey, she didn't think they were up to it.

Tim's voice startled her. "Everything will work out okay

in the end."

"Will it?" she asked, wishing she believed him.

"Yes. You'll see."

He stopped and held out his arms to her. Without a thought, she went to him and laid her head on his chest. He rocked her gently. All the tension drained out of her body, leaving her feeling limp and weak-kneed.

They stayed together for what seemed like a very long time, then he leaned away from her. When she looked at him, he lowered his head until she could feel his warm breath on her face.

"Wait," she murmured. "What about Kirsten?"

He pulled back. "Kirsten?"

"That gorgeous redhead I saw you kissing at The Joker."

He chuckled. "Kirsten's my bartender. And my friend. Nothing more."

Mary settled her head against his chest again. "That's all right, then."

"Don't you have something to tell me?"

"Like what?"

"Lila Lorraine let your secret slip last night."

Thinking she could happily stay in his arms for the rest of her life, she said, "I don't have a secret."

"If I remember correctly, his name is Bill."

"Bill? Bill who?"

She listened to his heart, which seemed to be beating in time with hers. Then she sprang away as if she'd been touched with a cattle prod. "Omigod! Bill!"

Chapter 26

The mat on the porch of the steep-roofed two-story brick house stated *WELCOME*, but Mary saw no welcome in the hard brown eyes of the well-dressed woman who answered the door. Although her skin looked smooth and tightly drawn over her cheekbones, the ropy veins and liver spots on her clenched hands led Mary to surmise she was about sixty years old.

"I've already been saved," the woman said.

Mary's brow furrowed. "What? Oh, no. We're here to—"

"And I tithe at my church." She started to close the door.

"Is Albert Hoffman here?" Mary asked quickly.

The woman paused. "You friends of Albert? Well, any friend of Albert's is not a friend of mine." She continued closing the door.

"Not friends. We've never met him. We just want to talk to him."

"He doesn't live here anymore," the woman said through the remaining crack.

"Do you know where we can find him?"

"No." She clipped the word.

"Then maybe you can help us."

"I don't see how."

"Please. Can we talk?"

The woman didn't answer. Nor did she close the door the rest of the way.

"My name is Mary Stuart. We—"

The door opened wider. "Did you say Stuart?"

"Yes, and we—"

"Any relation to James or Robert Stuart?"

"James Stuart was my grandfather. But how did you—"

"Was?"

"Someone murdered him not too long ago."

The door was wide open now, and Mary could see the muscles working in the woman's jaw.

"Did you know my grandfather?"

"Not exactly."

Mary glanced at Tim and Teach, but they looked as confused as she felt. "I'm sorry," she said to the woman. "I don't understand."

The woman moistened her lips as she studied Mary. She raised her shoulders in a tiny shrug and unlatched the screen door.

"This could take a while. You better come in."

Mary hesitated. "You don't mind letting strangers into your house?"

The woman's eyes were bright, feverish. "Believe me, no Stuart is a stranger here."

Mary felt a chill that had nothing to do with the cool breeze rustling the leaves of the maple tree in the woman's front yard, but that didn't stop her from entering the house when the woman held open the door.

Tim and the elders filed in behind Mary.

Wrinkling her nose, the woman recoiled as Iron Sam passed by, but with a visible effort, she managed to collect herself and lead the way into her large, spotlessly clean living room.

"I'm Janice Hoffman," she said. "Albert's my ex-husband. At least he soon will be."

Mary introduced everyone, though Janice seemed uninterested in learning their names.

When they all found places to sit, Janice perched on the arm of the remaining empty chair, then immediately rose to her feet.

"Would you like anything to drink?" she asked, sounding distracted. Without waiting for an answer, she sat back down and pressed her lips together.

Mary twisted a lock of hair around a forefinger. When she realized what she was doing, she laced her hands, rested them in her lap, and waited for Janice to speak.

"I don't know where to begin," Janice said at last.

"The beginning is a good place," Teach told her.

Janice narrowed her eyes at him; then obviously deciding

he wasn't ridiculing her, she nodded. "The beginning. That would be the bank robbery back in the 1930s before Albert and I were born."

No prima donna ever had a more rapt audience. Even Happy, for once, remained still.

"Eli, Albert's father, worked as a teller at that bank. A young man starting out. I heard the story so many times over the years that I have it memorized. He always began the same way by saying, 'We weren't equipped to handle all the gold pouring into the bank that day. The old-fashioned safe was so full it could not be closed, and bags and boxes of gold were piled on a cart in front of it and even on the floor.'"

Her eyes clouded and a vertical line appeared between her perfectly sculpted eyebrows. "I don't understand why there was so much gold. Something about the government confiscating it from local farmers who'd saved it, I think.

"Eli would go on to explain that the bank manager sat in his office, making calls, trying to find out why the armored car hadn't yet come to take away the gold.

"The guard, an elderly man hired for the occasion, nodded off at his station by the door. At times, apparently remembering his duties, he would jerk himself upright and try to look alert, but soon he'd yawn and nod off again.

"There were no customers in the bank at the time. According to Eli, the bank had been closed the week before, and people didn't seem to be in any hurry to resume normal banking relations, though several people came by to turn in their gold before the government agents could seize it.

"Eli was staring out the window, trying to decide where to go for lunch, when he noticed a long, dark red car park in front of the bank."

Happy sat up straight. "What kind of car?"

Janice's eyes moved restlessly; her gaze did not settle on anyone or anything. "Eli said it was a 1932 Lincoln KB V12."

Happy nodded. "Good choice. A three-speed manual. Twelve cylinders. Capable of accelerating from a standstill to sixty miles per hour in twenty-six seconds in top gear alone."

Janice's eyes kept moving. "Eli watched the car idling at the curb. He couldn't see anyone in it—the windows were in shadow. He felt a prickling on his scalp and thought for sure something was about to happen, but no one got out of the car."

"They were trying to gather their courage," Tim said quietly. "They hadn't expected to see a guard—there hadn't been one when they'd cased the joint—and it made them hesitate."

All at once it seemed to Mary as though she herself sat in that dark red Lincoln, feeling the acrid nip of fear on her tongue. Had the cops somehow found out their plan? If she allowed herself to give in to this sort of paranoia, she wouldn't be able to get the job done. She took a deep breath and slowly expelled the fear welling up inside her. She took another deep breath and felt her self-confidence returning. *We can do this.*

Tim's voice brought her back to herself. "In the end, they decided to follow through with their plan."

Janice crossed her legs and re-crossed them. She continued her narrative as if she hadn't heard a word Tim had spoken. "Eli had just decided there was nothing to worry about when the three men climbed out of the car. They wore trench coats with turned up collars and fedoras pulled low on their foreheads. Before Eli could raise an alarm, they entered the bank, whipped their Tommy guns out from the folds of their coats, and disarmed the guard. Eli held up his hands, too excited to be afraid. It was like the movies, he claimed.

"The men went through the swinging gate that led behind the teller's cage and stopped short. Their eyes widened when they caught sight of the safe standing ajar and the bags and boxes piled in front of it. One of the men went to a box and opened it. From where Eli stood, he could see the gleam of gold bullion. The man immediately began piling the cart with as much of the loot as possible. Another of the robbers went to help, while the third kept his gun trained on Eli and the guard. Through it all, the only thing Eli could hear was the sound of the manager's voice begging someone to come take the gold off his hands.

"All three of the robbers were needed to move the heavily laden cart. Eli kept his hands in the air as he watched them transfer the gold to the car. He expected them to return for the remaining gold, and he didn't want to take a chance on getting shot. After they emptied the cart, however, they jumped in the car and took off. Moments later the armored truck arrived.

"In the days that followed, Eli was interrogated extensively. He got the impression they thought he was an accomplice, but they never charged him.

"A week or so after the robbery, Eli came across an article in the paper about three bootleggers who had been killed in a shoot-out with prohibition agents. Examining the pictures of those three vaguely familiar men, he concluded they were the ones who robbed the bank, but he didn't tell the authorities—he was so sick of them and their questions and insinuations, he wanted nothing more to do with them.

"Weeks passed, then months, then years. Though Eli studied the newspapers, he didn't find any mention of the gold, and he said he could feel it out there somewhere, waiting for him.

"The only legacy he passed on to his son was his obsession with the bootleggers' gold. Instead of the three bears, Eli told Albert stories about the three robbers—Adam Kleinman, Dugald Stuart, and Charles Stuart."

Janice's hard eyes focused briefly on Mary, then her gaze wandered again.

"Albert went into banking after college. In fact, he ended up working at the same bank his father had. A few months ago, the bank was sold for the third or fourth time, and Albert got downsized. That's when his obsession with the robbery took hold. He went on the Internet and somehow managed to find the sons of the two Stuarts, thinking one of them might have a clue to the whereabouts of the treasure. Then he went to visit them. And now you say James was murdered?"

Mary nodded. "His wife, too. Also Robert and his wife."

"Oh, Albert," Janice whispered.

Mary swallowed the lump in her throat and wondered why she'd thought knowing who killed her grandparents would make it easier for her to accept their deaths. She still didn't know why Albert had killed them, though. Did he want to eliminate anyone with a claim to the gold? Or—she went rigid at the thought—had he tortured them to find out what they knew?

Janice gritted her teeth. "I haven't seen Albert since, but when large sums of money disappeared from our savings account, I got into his computer and discovered what he was up to. Since neither Robert nor James had the gold—Robert's wealth came from his wife, and James lived on a dirt farm—Albert realized there was only one other possibility. Adam Kleinman's son. He found the man in prison, dying of cancer, and paid a lawyer, a doctor, and a member of the parole board to get the son released, hoping he would head for the gold."

Mary glanced at the impassive Iron Sam, but everyone else seemed to avoid looking at him.

Janice stood and began pacing. "I forgave Albert when he didn't live up to my expectations. I forgave him when he got passed over for promotions. I even forgave him when he got laid off." Her voice rose toward hysteria. "But when I found out he spent our savings, cashed in our IRAs, and remortgaged the house so he could get a hit man released from prison, I changed the locks and started divorce proceedings."

"Do you happen to have a picture of Albert?" Mary asked.

Janice had been glancing up, down, everywhere, anywhere, but now she looked at Mary. An eerie sound crawled from her throat. It took a moment for Mary to recognize the sound as laughter.

"Do I have pictures?" Janice said, her voice at hysterical pitch. She reached into a cabinet beneath a bookcase and pulled out a photograph album. "I have all the pictures you need."

Mary gulped and tried to control the shaking of her hands as she leafed through the album. Many of the snapshots included a man who might be Albert, but in every case the eyes had been gouged out and the face mutilated, as if stabbed repeatedly with a sharp object.

Chapter 27

It was Kid Rags who asked the question on all their minds.

"Well, do you know where the gold is?"

Iron Sam looked up from his untouched meatloaf. "You talking to me?"

Kid Rags nodded.

"I never heard of the gold until Tim told us about it."

"But your father—"

"I don't remember him. I was only four or five when he died."

"You have a brother, don't you?" Mary asked.

Iron Sam's head swiveled in her direction. "What of it?"

"Seems to me it would have been easier for Albert Hoffman to go after him than to go through all the trouble and expense of getting you released from prison."

A ghost of a smile played on Iron Sam's gray, cracked lips. "David's dead."

Remembering Teach's story of how the three-year-old Sam had gripped a knife while standing over his sleeping brother, Mary became very interested in her own meatloaf. She took a tiny bite and chewed it slowly. When she realized she was counting her jaw movements, the image of Bill doing the same flashed through her mind.

She sneaked a peek at Tim. He was gazing at her, an unreadable expression on his face.

She tried to swallow, but her throat felt constricted. A sip of water helped; she finally managed to get the food down.

"So this is the end," Happy said gloomily.

Mary pushed her plate away. "We could go back to The Shoemaker's place and look for the gold again. It has to be there someplace."

"Unless Albert found it," Kid Rags pointed out.

"There is that," Tim said, "but it's worth taking another stab at it. I still have the metal detector and the tools packed away in the van, so nothing's stopping us."

"What if the caretaker's there?" Crunchy asked.

Mary gave him a tired smile. "Then we leave, but we'll know we tried."

With the exception of Iron Sam, the elders kept up a desultory conversation as they rode north after their early dinner. Neither Tim nor Mary joined in. Several times Mary caught Tim looking at her in the rear view mirror, but she let her gaze slide away before their eyes could meet.

The sun hung low on the horizon when Tim finally stopped at The North Woods Inn, a cluster of tree-shaded cabins on the shore of a small lake.

"I'm going to stretch my legs," he said after they checked in. "Anyone want to come?"

Though the elders pleaded exhaustion, they urged Mary to accept.

As the two walked beside the lake, Mary tried to keep her distance, but somehow she and Tim kept managing to bump into each other.

After a while, Tim stopped, picked up a pebble, and skimmed it across the water. He picked up another pebble, jiggled it in his palm, then tossed it aside.

"Where do we go from here?" His tone sounded light and careless, but his eyes looked grave.

"We already decided. The Shoemaker's place."

He gave her a sidelong glance. "That's not what I meant."

"I know," she said in a small voice.

With volition of its own, her hand swung out and brushed against his. A spark of electricity jumped between them.

They exchanged smiles, then spoke simultaneously:

"I shouldn't have tried—"

"I should have told you—"

They stopped at the same time, then started over, still in concert:

"I should have asked—"

"I shouldn't have let—"

221

They laughed, and all at once the shyness that had sprung up between them the previous evening disappeared.

Mary held out her arms as if embracing the lake, the trees, the gathering darkness.

"Isn't it lovely?" she exclaimed.

"Lovely," he said, gazing at her.

Returning his look, she let her arms fall slowly to her sides.

He reached out and touched her cheek with the back of a hand. "Very lovely."

She stepped away from him; the simple movement took astonishing concentration.

He nodded as if he knew what she was thinking, but how could he know when she herself didn't?

At first glance the clearing looked the same, then Mary realized the pile of displaced dirt rose much higher than when they'd left it.

"Looks like someone's been doing some digging," Spaghetti said as they traipsed across the clearing.

Slowly, so as not to disturb the small cat perched on top of his head, Crunchy looked around. "Where's the caretaker?"

Mary stopped to listen. She heard no sounds out of place, no snapping of twigs, no rustling in the underbrush, no stealthy footfalls.

"I don't think he's here."

"Me and Journey will keep watch."

"Good idea."

While Crunchy scanned the tree line, Mary went to join the rest of her party at the excavation site.

"Jeez." She stared at the fully exposed car. It was long, much longer than modern cars and must have been beautiful at one time, but now it looked ready for the crusher. The roof of the car had been ripped away, and the rotting upholstery hacked to pieces. The hood, the sagging doors, and the lid of the gutted trunk all gaped open. If the gold had been hidden in the car, it certainly wasn't there now.

"The caretaker must have done this," Lila Lorraine said.

Tim's eyebrows drew together. "Or Albert Hoffman."

Teach nodded. "Or both."

Mary shot a questioning glance at Teach. "What do you mean—both? You think they worked together?"

Teach stroked his chin. "A good offense is the best defense. I think Hoffman followed us here, hid in the woods, and watched while we searched for the gold. Instead of running away when Happy discovered him—"

"He confronted us, claiming to be the caretaker, and demanded to know what we were doing," Mary finished.

Teach smiled. "Exactly."

Mary felt a tickle of sweat on the back of her neck. "So that was Albert Hoffman we saw?"

"I think so. Yes."

Mary wrapped her arms around herself and rocked heel to toe as she thought of how the man calling himself the caretaker had pointed his rifle at her. Had smiled and called her by name. Had killed her grandparents, then had killed again.

"We have to go," she said. She heard a quick, rasping noise and realized it was the sound of her own breathing. "We have to get out of here. Now. What if he comes back?" Her voice rose. "He could kill us all!"

"He didn't before," Kid Rags pointed out. "By now he's probably on a tropical island somewhere spending our gold."

Crunchy hailed them. "Journey's found something!"

They all hurried over to where Journey was sniffing at a pale object gleaming in the grass.

Happy squatted to take a closer look. "It's a skull."

"Numbers," Spaghetti and Teach exclaimed in unison.

"The guy from the car?" Lila Lorraine asked. "What's he doing way over here?"

Happy straightened. "He didn't walk here on his own two feet, that's for sure."

Journey batted at the skull with a forepaw, then, apparently losing interest in it, he stalked into the woods, followed by Crunchy.

"Journey found more bones," Crunchy called out.

The rest of the skeleton, Mary realized a moment later when she surveyed the scattered bones.

Teach picked up one of the larger bones, turned it this way and that. "Well, I know one thing. Hoffman didn't find the gold."

"How do you figure?" Kid Rags asked, adding hastily, "short version."

"It looks to me as if someone took the skeleton, flung it against the trees, then tried to smash it. Some of the smaller bones are broken, but others, like this one, have nicks on them, the kind you'd get if you stabbed at them with a spade. Whoever did this was more than a little angry."

"Angry because he didn't find the gold," Tim said.

Teach pointed a thumb and finger pistol at him. "You got it."

Mary peered deeper into the woods. "So Albert Hoffman is still out there, watching us, waiting for us to lead him to the gold?"

Teach spread his hands. "Could be."

Forgetting how panicked she had been moments before, Mary said, "Well, that's not going to stop me from finishing the job. I need to know, once and for all, if there's any buried treasure."

It took hours, but they covered the entire clearing with broad strokes of the metal detector. Although they heard several blips indicating small metal objects, which no one bothered to dig up, they did not find the gold.

"So that's that," Mary said, a strange emptiness sweeping over her.

Without speaking, they packed their gear and returned to the van. As they drove away, Iron Sam broke the silence.

"I know where we can get some money," he said, the words rattling in his chest. "Not a lot. About twenty thousand dollars. But it should still be there."

Chapter 28

"Kentucky?" Mary blurted out before she could stop herself. "Why hide your money in Covington, Kentucky?" When Iron Sam turned his steely eyes on her, she said, "I don't mean any disrespect. I'm surprised is all."

"It's where I lived," he rasped, his voice sounding more gravelly than ever.

"Oh. I thought you lived in Cleveland." Floundering under his forbidding gaze, she continued weakly, "Since you worked for the Cleveland Syndicate, I mean.

Iron Sam's eyes closed, and his head lolled to one side. He sat still—no perceptible rise and fall of his sunken chest, no sound of his labored breath.

Mary froze. Before she could collect herself enough to go check on him, his lips parted and a few words floated out on a wheeze.

"Worked for the D.I. Syndicate."

When he said nothing more, Mary looked at Teach.

"The D.I. Syndicate was the Cleveland Syndicate," he explained. "They changed their name after opening the Desert Inn in Las Vegas, but long before that they had expanded far beyond the Cleveland city limits.

"Johnny Torrio was the first to move his enterprise to the suburbs, having decided it was cheaper to bribe a small town than a big city, and others soon followed suit. That's why Newport and Covington were such hotbeds of gambling and prostitution—they were right across the Ohio River from Cincinnati and had plenty of bribable government employees. A barrier of hills and bad roads cut off northern Kentucky from the bluegrass part of the state, so it grew closer to Cincinnati for economic survival. The Cleveland Syndicate, of course, was right there to help.

"It was brilliant, actually. Though not far apart, Covington and Newport were in separate counties. When the heat was on in one county, gamblers could go to the neighboring county. By switching back and forth, the Syndicate didn't miss any of the lucrative convention business from Cincinnati."

"You sound like you admire those people," Mary said.

In the silence that greeted her remark, she could hear Spaghetti and Lila Lorraine murmur softly to each other. Looking around to check on the rest of the group, she noticed that Iron Sam, Crunchy, and Journey all appeared to be asleep. Kid Rags and Happy passed the hip flask back and forth. Tim cocked his head while he drove, as if listening for Teach's response.

"Not at all," Teach said finally, his voice harsh. "People tend to romanticize prohibition, to romanticize the so-called Mafia, but they don't get it. It's about the unholy trinity—criminals, politicians, and businesspersons—all working together to sell out the little people. And make no mistake about it—no matter how rich and successful we might be, the vast majority of us are the little people.

"Prohibition and the Syndicate seem to belong to our mythical past, but the forces that created them are very much alive today. Take illegal drugs. They're flooding into this country as we speak. Why? It's not that the drug cartels are too powerful to be stopped. It's that the very people who profess to protect us have sold us out. Government employees are pocketing millions, perhaps billions of dollars every day. You don't believe me? I could give you a long speech detailing past government connections with drugs—Trafficante and the CIA, Oliver North and the Contras, the Cuban connection, MK-Ultra, Mena, Arkansas—but I'll keep it simple. Ask yourself this—who has the most to lose if illegal drugs are stopped or even legalized? Give up? The DEA, that's who. Willingly deprive themselves of all that money and power? I don't think so."

For a second Teach looked almost as forbidding as Iron Sam. "A leader of the Shan, one of the opium tribes of the Golden Triangle, once proposed to the DEA that if the DEA would give them a small percentage of the money spent on the war on drugs, he would educate his people, bring them into modern times, and get out of the opium business altogether. The DEA refused."

"Even more telling, the DEA had an office in Chiang Mai, a city in Thailand located on the edge of the Golden Triangle. A branch of the Nugen-Hand Bank had adjoining offices. They even shared a secretary. The Nugen-Hand Bank, in case you don't know, was a bank created by two Australians for the sole purpose of laundering drug money."

Seeing an unfamiliar emotion wrinkling Teach's face—sorrow, perhaps, or maybe anger—Mary reached out and touched his sleeve.

He gave her a vague, unfocused look.

"Why did you learn all this if it doesn't make you happy?" she asked.

Out of the corner of her eyes, she saw Happy sit up straight and peer at them.

"Happy?" Teach repeated, as if it were a word in a foreign tongue. "Is happiness so important?"

"Isn't it?" she asked, confused.

Teach smiled faintly.

Happy, apparently deciding they weren't talking about him, took the flask from Kid Rags and raised it to his lips.

"You want to know why I learned all this?" Teach said. "I witnessed something back in the early 1960s, nothing important at the time, just a tiny piece of a puzzle, but I got curious. I knew I, we, the entire world had been conned, and I wanted to know why. So I started talking to people and reading, and eventually I discovered another piece of the puzzle, then another. And another. Each piece led to another piece, sometimes several, and I saw, for the first time, that everything was connected. I learned something else, too. That nothing important in the way of human affairs happens by accident. There is always someone, somewhere, pulling the strings. And with total disregard for us little people."

"What did you see?" Mary asked.

"I was in Dallas in November, 1963—"

Kid Rags let out a loud guffaw. "Don't tell me you saw the rifleman on the grassy knoll!"

Mary had to admire Teach's impeccable sense of timing. He waited until Kid Rags' smile faded, until Crunchy and Iron Sam opened their eyes, until everyone focused their attention on him.

"No," he said at last.

There was a collective whoosh of exhaled breath.

Another pause. "I saw a man talking to another man. That's all."

"That's all?" Lila Lorraine said. "What do you mean, 'that's all'?"

"Exactly that. It was early November. I was in a nightclub having a drink with a guy I knew from my Chicago days. He'd been a go-fer for the mob like Jimmy Boots and me. In fact, Jimmy Boots introduced us. I'd heard he'd done well for himself, owned a couple of strip joints in Dallas, and I went to see him, thinking we might do some business together. I had set up a poker game in a nearby hotel—a real fancy place—and I asked him if he knew of any juicy pigeons he could shoo my way. For a percentage, of course. He seemed interested, and I thought he'd agree, then he shook his head. He didn't want to risk it, he said, explaining that cops and politicians hung out at his club, often using it as a place to hand off bribes. Though it was undoubtedly true, I suspected he turned me down because my deal was too small for him.

"We chatted a few minutes, nothing important. 'How about them Cowboys,' he said. 'Looking good this year,' I said. You know, bar talk. When two men walked in the door, he excused himself and went to greet them. They obviously knew each other well, maybe even exceptionally well. I'd heard rumors that my Chicago acquaintance was gay, and it looked to me as if these men were too. That's the extent of what I saw. See what I mean? The whole thing was insignificant and would have remained so except two or three weeks later I was in a bar in Oklahoma City, and I happened to glance at the television screen in time to see that club owner shoot one of those two men.

"Of course, by then I knew the man was Oswald. It was

months before I learned that the man with him was David Ferrie, but that has no bearing on this story."

Mary pressed her fingers to her temples. "You saw Jack Ruby talking to Lee Harvey Oswald weeks before Kennedy was assassinated? I thought there was no connection between the two of them."

"That's what we were all led to believe. The media made it seem as if Jacob Rubinstein—Jack Ruby—was so overcome with grief at the death of his president he felt compelled to take out the monster who had killed him. The whole thing was too weird. The Rubinstein I knew didn't respect politicians—few, if any, gangsters did—so why would he kill someone he knew over a little thing like an assassination? Whatever suspicions I had, I kept to myself. Wisely, it turned out. One of the women who worked at the strip club told the FBI she saw Oswald and Ruby together, and she died in a fatal car crash soon afterwards, as so many witnesses to the assassination did."

Teach glanced around with the searching gaze of a man accustomed to looking over his shoulders. "Even now that everyone knows the truth about Kennedy's death—or at least think they do—it feels strange to be talking about this. I've kept quiet about it all these years."

An ache formed in Mary's throat at the sight of the fatigue etched on the old man's face. What had it cost him to keep his secret locked inside for a lifetime?

Random snatches of thought flashed through her mind like a meteor shower. Without any warning, one blazed brightly.

She clapped a hand to her mouth and stared at Teach. "Are you saying my grandfather knew Jack Ruby?"

Teach nodded, a quizzical frown on his face.

"That seems so bizarre. I mean, somebody had to have known him, right? I never expected it to be someone related to me." She contemplated that for a moment. "Everything really is connected."

The throb of music from a passing car drowned out Teach's words, but she thought she heard him say,

"Welcome to my world."

When the music faded into the distance, she said, "One thing I don't understand. You seem to have such sympathy for the little people, but you prey on them too, like your unholy trinity."

"Not all of them. Not the nice ones, not the innocent ones. For example, I would not have tried to con you. You have kind eyes."

"Thanks."

"I didn't mean it as a compliment. Merely an observation."

"Oh." Then, "I don't think you answered my question."

Teach smiled. "I hoped you wouldn't notice."

"Well?"

"I may be sympathetic, but I have no respect for the little people. In the end, the power resides with them. If they didn't buy illegal substances, go to prostitutes, and gamble, organized crime could not have become a force. If they didn't allow themselves to be conned into needing unnecessary products, big business could be held in check. If they didn't allow themselves to be kept ignorant—and here I'm talking about the educated people—the government wouldn't have been able to control them as easily.

"Now that I think about it, maybe it's not a trinity keeping one foot on our necks, but a quadripartite, with the little people making up the fourth side."

"We have met the enemy and it is us?"

"Something like that."

"Give the poor girl a rest," Kid Rags called out.

Mary held out a hand to Teach. "Don't pay any attention to him. I like hearing you talk. You know so much and you phrase it well. Have you ever considered writing a book?"

"I plan to. I've been doing the research for it my whole life. I just haven't found the time to get it on paper."

Mary's eyes gleamed.

Teach gave her a sidelong glance. "Why are you looking at me like that? Oh, no. You're not going to reform me now, are you?"

Mary smiled.

Kid Rags laughed. "Face it, Teach. You're toast."

Teach stared out the window as the miles rolled by. Mary supposed he was upset with her, but when he finally turned to her and said, "I have a title picked out," she realized he had been gathering his thoughts.

"What are you going to call it?" she asked.

"*A Tale of Two Lawmen.*"

"What's it about? Wait, I know! Wyatt Earp and Eliot Ness."

"Who else? There were so many similarities, the major one being that both men were bigger in death than they were in life. Wyatt lived out his remaining years travelling from town to town, sometimes working one side of the law, sometimes the other. Eliot became Safety Director for Cleveland, Ohio. He had a reputation for being a drunk—"

Mary burst out laughing.

Teach stopped. "What?"

"Nothing," she said, still giggling. "It struck me as funny is all. Capone, the bootlegger, drank almost nothing, but his nemesis, the lawman, drank to excess."

Teach smiled. "I didn't make that connection. To me, the irony is that while Ness lived in Cleveland, the mob grew more powerful, and in the end, they left on their own, moving to Las Vegas and Florida.

"Highly imaginative biographies of both Wyatt and Eliot were published after their deaths, ensuring the immortality of their legends. I often wonder—if they had lived to see the publication of these books, would they have gone for it, or would they have tried to set the record straight?"

It was way past dark when they stopped for the night. Lila Lorraine fell asleep immediately, but Mary lay awake for a long time. She had the itchy feeling she'd forgotten something. When she was finally dropping off, it came to her: she and Tim hadn't spent a single moment alone together all day.

Chapter 29

The single story brick building could have housed any business—a doctor's office, a bank, an insurance agency. Without the sign over the doorway, Mary would not have identified it.

"A library?" she asked. "You hid your money in a library?"

"I was going away for a long time," Iron Sam said, as if that explained everything. He coughed, then added, "The mason owed me a favor."

As sick as he was, he maintained enough mastery over his body to keep still, eyes steady, hands motionless while talking. Every day, though, he drooped more—the only indication that his iron control might be slipping.

Happy gazed at the building. "Where is it? Behind the cornerstone?"

Noting the lack of animation in Happy's voice, Mary squinted at him. He looked old—so very old—as if he'd aged a dozen years overnight. She sighed. They all seemed to have aged. Teach's face was drawn and Crunchy's eyes lacked their usual sparkle. Kid Rags swayed as if at any moment he'd topple over, and Lila Lorraine leaned on Spaghetti.

Not having been on the road as long as the others, Spaghetti had held up well. During the long drive today, he'd monopolized the conversation, regaling them all with the exploits of his erstwhile customers, but now he looked as worn as the rest of the elders.

Tim looked spent, too. Well, no wonder; he'd been doing all the driving, and they had not stopped except for the short time it took to refuel and buy food no one, not even Kid Rags, had been interested in eating.

"Maybe we should turn in early," she said. "Get a good night's rest and come back tomorrow." She paused, waiting for Happy to make a portentous remark, but he gazed listlessly at the building.

A coughing fit racked Iron Sam's body. When it finally left him, he said, gasping, "Today. Won't take long. Need hammer. Chisel."

"I might have a hammer," Tim said, "but I don't have a chisel. Will a screwdriver do?"

"Should."

While Tim trotted back to the van, which he'd parked halfway down the block, Iron Sam lurched toward the library. Beads of sweat glistened on his forehead as he struggled to open the heavy glass door.

Mary started to go to him, but stopped, not knowing if he'd welcome the help. As she hesitated, she saw Crunchy surreptitiously stick a foot in the door and give it a nudge to open it wider.

Iron Sam led the way through the door into the vestibule. On the far side, a second glass door led to the library proper. A uniformed guard, stationed on the other side of the door behind a podium, rummaged through a girl's backpack. A woman tapped her foot and glared at him.

Mary and the elders moved aside when the woman came crashing out, the little girl in tow.

"Its okay, Mom," the girl said as the woman opened the outer door. "They always check—"

The closing door cut off the rest of the words.

Mary glanced back at the guard and saw him giving them the once over. When he finally looked away, she scanned the vestibule. It was lined with blond bricks, each bearing a name; some included a date or other inscription. A center plaque explained that each memorial brick had been purchased to help finance the construction of the library. According to the date, the library had been built around the time Iron Sam had been sent to prison. One name caught Mary's attention, and all at once she knew where Iron Sam had hidden his money.

In a sickening moment of clarity, she also understood why he'd used that particular name. Clutching her stomach as the waves of nausea washed over her, she reeled to the door, pushed it open, and stumbled outside.

Their only bond, the only thing she and Iron Sam had in common was that strip of road in Wisconsin where his father and her great-grandfather died. How then could she understand him? Somewhere, deep down, were they the same?

When a new wave of nausea threatened to overwhelm her, she forced herself to breathe deeply and evenly.

Teach and Crunchy appeared at her side.

"You okay, Lady?"

Mary nodded, then stopped when even that small motion made the nausea flare again.

"He didn't know who he'd be when he got out," she whispered. "He was afraid he'd lose himself, so he chose the one name he would never forget. His brother's birth name. David Kleinman."

"Hate endures," Teach murmured.

Mary squared her shoulders. "I'm okay now, really. I got spooked for a moment."

Teach gave her a flicker of a smile. "Getting a glimpse into a stone killer's mind would spook anyone."

Mary's laugh sounded like a sob, and ended in a hiccup. "Anyone? Even you, Teach?"

He nodded. "Even me."

"What's wrong?" Tim jogged to them, hammer and screwdriver clutched in one hand.

Mary smiled, absurdly pleased at the concern she heard in his voice.

"A moment of claustrophobia," she said, gesturing to the library. Catching sight of Lila Lorraine and Kid Rags peering through the door, she turned the gesture into a wave.

When Mary, Tim, Crunchy, and Teach entered the vestibule, Spaghetti was touching one of the bricks, and saying to Happy, ". . . football player for the Cleveland Browns. He was a Catholic, had a pretty wife, a bunch of kids. A family man. He didn't believe in gambling, drugs, and prostitution. When he ran for sheriff of Campbell County, the mob drugged him, dragged him to a hotel, ripped off his clothes, put him in bed with a prostitute, and took pictures. In the past when they'd done this, the candidate always backed down, but he called their bluff. The mob released the photos, but for once the voters weren't suckered, and he got elected."

Tim held out the tools to Iron Sam who sagged against a wall.

Iron Sam closed his eyes. "You do it. Behind David Kleinman."

Tim looked around, a puzzled expression on his face.

Mary showed him the brick, then placed herself between him and the guard. She stood sideways so she could keep an eye on both of them.

"We'll cover you," she said.

Except for Iron Sam who remained propped against the wall, everyone clustered around, hiding Tim from the guard's sight.

Tim poked at the grout with the screwdriver. "Feels solid." He tapped the screwdriver with the hammer. The sound seemed to echo in the small chamber.

Holding her breath, Mary peeked at the guard. He didn't appear to have heard a thing.

Tim tapped the screwdriver again. A tiny piece of grout fell out.

Tap. Tap. Another piece.

Mary felt her fingernails digging into her palms, but couldn't relax enough to uncurl her hands.

"Someone's coming," Lila Lorraine hissed.

Tim dropped his arms. They all froze.

The outside door opened. A teenage boy ran through the vestibule and into the library. Mary could see the guard confronting him, but could not hear what he said.

Tim repositioned the tools. He hit the screwdriver, harder this time. A big piece of grout fell out.

Happy moaned. "This could take forever."

Tim hit the screwdriver once more. A piece of the brick broke off, tumbled to the ground, and shattered.

Spaghetti laughed softly, with tiny exhalations of air.

"Whuf . . . whuf . . . whuf. Looks like the grout is harder than the brick."

"You're right," Tim said. He placed the flat end of the screwdriver in the letter V, then glanced over his shoulder at Iron Sam. "Do you mind if the brick gets destroyed?"

Iron Sam gave no indication he heard or cared.

Tim pounded the screwdriver; the brick cracked.

"Uh, oh," Kid Rags said. "The guard's looking at us."

Teach detached himself from the group. "Leave this to me."

He entered the library.

Mary saw him flash a smile at the guard and move his lips in speech. The guard raised one shoulder in a disinterested shrug. Teach spoke again. Another shrug.

Tim tapped the screwdriver. Pieces of brick rained down.

The guard's head shot up, turned in their direction.

Mary's breath caught in her throat.

Teach appeared to stumble, clutched at the podium. The guard jerked his head toward him.

Another piece of the brick fell, but Crunchy, holding his open hands beneath where Tim worked, managed to catch it before it hit the floor.

Teach's lips moved. His arms made broad gestures.

The guard grinned and bobbed his head. Before long, the two men were deep in conversation.

Teach put a hand behind his back and pointed his thumb at the ceiling.

Kid Rags chuckled. "Teach could charm a crocodile."

Mary let out her pent-up breath and managed to uncurl her fingers.

Tim gave the screwdriver one final whack. The rest of the brick crumbled. He scooped the shards into Crunchy's hands, reached into the hole, and pulled out a packet wrapped in foil and sealed in plastic.

Mary stared at it. It looked so small. The height and width were the right size to be paper money, but it was only about an inch thick. It seemed impossible that it contained twenty thousand dollars. The seal hadn't been broken, though, and Iron Sam didn't seem to see anything amiss, so it must all still be there.

Tim took the packet over to Iron Sam.

Iron Sam looked at Mary, pushed himself away from the wall, and staggered to the door.

"Give it to her," he said, stepping outside.

Tim extended the packet toward Mary.

Mary took the packet, started to put it in her purse, then paused. What if her purse got stolen? What if Albert Hoffman was watching and thought the packet had something to do with the gold and tried to grab it?

"Come on," Happy said. "We gotta get out of here." He followed Iron Sam through the doorway.

Crunchy stuffed the pieces of brick into the hole, then stood waiting for Mary. She dropped the money into her purse and clutched it to her chest, thinking that with Crunchy guarding her, it should be safe until they got back to the bus.

It was.

The hum of excited voices rehashing the heist barely intruded into Mary's thoughts. She knew there had to be a way of protecting the money until she got back to Denver, but what?

"Do you have a scarf I can borrow, Lila Lorraine?" she asked finally.

Lila Lorraine pulled a large square of ecru silk out of her purse. "Will this do? It's not very pretty, but it goes with everything."

"It's exactly what I need."

Out of her own purse, she took the bundle of money and a few safety pins that had been tucked into an inside pocket. She wrapped the packet in one corner of the scarf, pinned it securely, then rolled it over and over, forming a sash. She tugged her pale yellow shirt out of her black jeans and tied the sash around her waist with the packet in the front, off to one side.

"How does it look?" she asked.

Tim smiled. "Perfect." In his voice she heard a world of meaning.

"No, silly. The money belt. Can you see it?"

"That's perfect, too."

"Hey, here comes the man of the hour," Kid Rags exclaimed.

"What took you so long?" Happy asked as Teach climbed into the bus.

"Oh, we got to talking, you know how it is."

"No, I don't," Lila Lorraine said. "I never understood how you could get total strangers to open up to you so quickly."

Teach ducked his head with feigned modesty. "Tricks of the trade, ma'am."

"No, really," Mary said. "How did you? You only spoke a few words and then he acted as if you were lifelong buddies."

"It's all in the eyes."

"Whose eyes? Yours, or his?"

"His, mostly. I asked if he knew where I could find books on sports, thinking he might be a sports fan. I didn't see the tiniest spark of interest in his eyes. Then I asked if he knew where the outdoor books were located. His eyes told me I was getting close, even though his body still said he wasn't interested. Considering the nearby river, I took a chance and said I was looking for tips on fishing. Bingo. His eyes lit up. Once you know what makes a man's eyes light up, the rest is easy. Flatter him, ask his advice, make expansive gestures, and he's yours."

"Easy for you, maybe." Tim started the van. "If no one minds, I'd like to get out of the metro area before we stop for the night."

Mary squirmed trying to get used to the feel of the sash. "Sounds good to me."

The elders, the adrenaline rush having dissipated, mumbled their agreement.

They made good time, and before long they were on I-74 heading northwest toward Indianapolis.

"Keep your eyes open for a motel," Tim said.

"Every silver lining has its cloud," Happy intoned.

Mary put her elbows on her knees and rested her head in her hands.

After a moment, she straightened. "I can't even begin to guess what you mean."

"Well, we found the money, and now he's dead."

"Dead?" Mary whipped her head around to look at Iron Sam.

She started when her eyes met his.

His lips twisted in a sardonic smile.

"Not him." Happy pointed to Kid Rags, who was slumped in his seat, tie askew, hat resting on the bridge of his nose. "Kid Rags is the one that's dead."

Chapter 30

Mary stopped pacing the waiting room and sat next to Teach on a hard plastic orange bench. "Will you talk to me? I can't stand being alone with my thoughts a minute longer."

Teach laid aside the magazine he'd been reading. "What do you want me to talk about?"

"Anything as long as it's far removed from here."

"Far removed? Let me think . . . Egypt's far. Did I tell you that regular dice made of ivory have been found in the ancient temples of Egypt? And loaded dice and gaming tables were found beneath the ashes of Pompeii."

Mary leaned back and let his words breeze through her mind.

"Card games also go way back. The French had a game known as *Pogue.* Yankee sailors combined it with an ancient Persian game called *As Nas,* which offered more combinations for betting. They called this new game Poke, which later turned into Poker."

"Hmm," she murmured, feeling her muscles relax.

"Pool was modified from an older game, too. The pool hall originally was a place to buy lottery tickets. Lottery was called pool because of the way winnings were paid off. Since some ticket holders would hang around these poolrooms all day waiting for the drawings, the owners installed billiard tables to keep them occupied. Billiards was either too slow or too difficult for the customers, so they devised their own game—pocket billiards. It became known as pool. Should I keep talking?"

"Only if you want to." Her voice seemed to be coming from a long way off.

He reached out and gave her hand a gentle squeeze. "Everything's going to be all right, you'll see."

She tried to smile, but her face felt stiff, as if coated with cement. "That's what Tim told me the other day and look where we are now. Actually," she continued after a moment's reflection, "he said everything will work out okay in the end. And it's not the end yet, is it?"

"Kid Rags is a tough old bird. He'll pull through."

"He scared me. He looked so white and still, I can see why Happy thought he died. I should never have embarked on this quixotic quest." She winced, remembering that Bill had used those very words back in Denver . . . a lifetime ago. Realizing her mind had wandered, she pushed the thought of her fiancé aside and turned her attention back to Teach.

". . . the adventure of a lifetime," he was saying. He smiled. "And you wouldn't have met us."

Mary blinked, then her eyes opened wide. "I'd forgotten that. It feels like I've known you my whole life. I can almost remember you telling me bedtime stories when I was a child."

She thought she saw the glint of tears in his eyes, but it might have been a trick of the light.

"Do you believe in ghosts?" she asked.

It was his turn to blink. "Ghosts? What brought that on?"

"It seems to me as if my grandfather and great-grandfather are on this trip with us. Sometimes I think I see them out of the corner of my eye, but when I turn to look, no one is there. And I have these flashes of, not intuition exactly, but . . ." She paused, searching for the word. "Transcendence, as if the past and the present are not stretched out in a line, but are wrapped together, like a big ball of yarn. Back at Janice Hoffman's house, I felt as if I were actually in the car with the robbers. I could feel what Dugald was feeling—his fear, his dwindling self-confidence, his determination to continue."

She stole a look at Teach, expecting to see him staring at her as if she were crazy, but he stroked his chin, a thoughtful expression on his face.

"The past is the present," he said. "Your grandfather, great-grandfather, all your ancestors are a part of you. They are in your genetics, and genes do remember."

"So you don't think I'm nuts?"

"Not at all."

"It can't be genetic memory. Jimmy Boots had already been born when they did the robbery. And my knowing about Iron Sam can't be chalked up to genetic memory, either."

"But the presentiment does come from your Scottish genes. Jimmy Boots was intuitive. I recall him telling me once he hated having such a worthless gift. The feeling came when it did the least good and disappeared when he needed it. Too bad. We could have made a fortune at the track."

Mary leaned over and rested her cheek on his shoulder for a moment, then struggled to her feet.

"I'm going to see if anyone knows anything yet," she said, stifling a yawn.

Before she took more than a step or two, she saw the doctor approaching. She froze in mid-stride, then set her foot firmly on the ground and went to meet him.

Mary couldn't help drawing a sharp breath when she saw Kid Rags lying in the hospital bed, an intravenous drip attached to his arm. He looked pale and insubstantial, as if about to fade away.

"Kid Rags?" she said softly.

He turned his face toward her. "Give it to me straight. I can take it."

She smiled. "You're going to be fine. There's nothing seriously wrong with you."

"I'm not a mushroom to be kept in the dark and fed manure," he growled.

"You really are fine. Or you will be when you get some rest, start eating again, and stop drinking so much bourbon. Oh . . . and take your blood pressure pills."

"If I'm fine, how come I passed out?"

"The doctor says you have hypoglycemia. That means you're tired and underfed."

He frowned at her. "Is this on the level?"

"Would Jimmy Boots's granddaughter lie to you?"

He stared at her a moment. Apparently seeing the truth in

her eyes, he nodded. "How long do I have to stay here?"

"A day or two. They want to keep you for observation to make sure your blood sugar and blood pressure get back to normal."

"Oh." He looked beyond her. "Hey, where is everyone?"

"Teach is in the hall. The nurse would only let one of us in. Lila Lorraine and Spaghetti are sleeping in the waiting room. Happy got tired of waiting for you to 'croak for real' as he put it, so he and Tim went out to work on the van—it developed a strange noise while we were speeding to get you here. Crunchy and Journey are holding the flashlight for them, and Iron Sam is still in the van. He refused to come inside the hospital."

"Smart fellow. Where are you going to spend the night? Here?"

"Tim got rooms for us at a motel called The Wooden Horse."

Kid Rags closed his eyes. Mary smoothed back his sparse hair, thinking he looked so vulnerable without his hat.

When he began to snore softly, she tiptoed from the room.

Mary was brushing her teeth when she heard Lila Lorraine say, "I'm going next door to tell Spaghetti good night."

"Don't forget the key," she called out.

Lila Lorraine must not have understood the gargled words, because a few minutes later a knock sounded on the door.

Mary pulled it open. Her lips parted in surprise.

"I didn't want to scare you by just barging in." Holding up the key, Tim sidled into the room and looked around. "Nice digs."

He tossed the key on the desk, then went to the bed nearest the window and bounced on it as if testing the springs.

"What are you doing here?" she asked, still holding the

door open.

He laughed. "What do you think?"

"It's almost two o'clock in the morning. I'm in no mood for games."

He propped the pillows against the headboard, leaned back, and stretched out his legs. Grinning, he said, "Lila Lorraine and I exchanged rooms."

"You what?" Mary closed the door and leaned against it. "You think you can waltz in here, announce we're sleeping together, and expect me to fall into your arms?"

His eyes sparkled with mischief, giving him a charming, boyish look. When she found her lips twitching in response, she turned and busied herself with the lock.

"It would have been nice," he said, "but no, I didn't expect it."

"Then what—"

All amusement faded from his voice. "Kid Rags' hospitalization got Lila Lorraine and Spaghetti to thinking about how little time they might have to be together, and they didn't want to waste any of it."

Mary opened her mouth, but before she could utter a word, he said, "No, I can't change rooms back—they were nearly asleep by the time I left. And no, I can't get another room. There aren't any vacancies."

"So what do we do now?"

He looked at her through half-closed eyes, making her heart beat wildly.

"Anything you want," he said. Then, unexpectedly, his expression changed to one of solicitude. "It's mean of me to tease you. You've had a long, hard day, and you need to get some sleep or you'll end up in the hospital with Kid Rags. I'll be a good boy. I promise. You won't even know I'm here."

She gave him a searching look and nodded, though she knew with him in the same room, she wouldn't be able to sleep at all.

* * *

Mary awoke, feeling remarkably refreshed. She lay under the covers a minute longer, luxuriating in the feeling, then sat bolt upright and glanced over at the bed Tim had slept in. It was neatly made.

She jumped up, ran to the window, and pulled aside the drapes. The sun blazed on the lot where they'd parked the van. She checked her watch—almost ten o'clock. Tim must have taken the elders to get something to eat.

She started to chide herself for being derelict in her duty, but stopped, deciding she felt too good to make herself feel bad. In fact, she felt so good she thought she could handle a phone call to her parents to let them know she was okay.

She dialed the number for Stuart's Plumbing Supply; Gwen answered.

"Hi, Mom," Mary said.

There was a long pause on the other end. "Mary?"

"Who else?" Mary giggled. "I mean, how many people in the world can call you Mom?"

Another pause. "Is something wrong? You sound—I don't know. Different."

"I feel great. How about you and Dad?"

"We're fine." Gwen's voice sounded stilted. "Your dad's at a meeting with a contractor." She paused for a beat, then burst out, "When are you coming home? We have to start making plans if you're going to get married in September. It's June already."

June? Mary counted out the days on her fingers. Almost a month had gone by since she'd heard about her grandparents' deaths and two weeks since her father visited her at her apartment. Despite all that had happened, it didn't seem as if that much time had passed.

"Mary? You still there, Mary?"

"Still here, Mom."

A plaintive note crept into Gwen's voice. "I don't understand what's gotten into you. You were such an obedient little girl."

"I'm not a little girl any longer," Mary said quietly.

A moment of silence followed by a loud exhalation.

"Your father said I should let you work this out on your own, but it's time you came back and settled down."

"I'll be returning soon. Say 'hi' to Dad for me. Bill, too," she added, surprised at how difficult it was for her to speak his name.

After hanging up, Mary continued to sit on the edge of the bed. She reached for the phone, then snatched her hand back. Finally, biting her lower lip, she picked up the receiver and dialed Bill's work number.

When his secretary answered, Mary opened her mouth, closed it.

Hung up without saying anything.

Chapter 31

Every morning the elders squabbled over whose turn it was to sit in the front passenger seat, but now it remained strangely empty.

Mary opened the door and poked her head into the van. "Doesn't anyone want to sit in front today?"

"It's your place." Crunchy folded his arms across his chest and regarded the others as if daring them to argue.

But they all nodded in agreement.

Looking at each in turn and meeting their bright gazes, Mary felt a blush creep up her neck. They thought she'd slept with Tim!

She peered at him from beneath her lashes. He grinned at her, a wicked gleam in his eyes.

"You're enjoying this, aren't you?" she muttered, climbing into the van.

"Immensely." He leaned over and spoke into her ear. "Look at it this way—when we do finally sleep together, it will be without fanfare."

She scowled at him. "You're awfully sure of yourself."

He smiled his mischievous little boy smile. "Admit it. You find me irresistible."

She tried to look withering, but couldn't keep the corners of her mouth from turning up. "I'll admit no such thing."

"Come on," Happy said. "Let's go. What are we waiting for?"

Tim turned the ignition key. The engine roared to life, then settled down to a low rumble.

"I almost forgot," he said. "I brought you breakfast—a carrot muffin and apple juice. Hope that's okay."

Mary smiled. "Sounds good."

As he handed her the small paper bag with a restaurant logo on it, their fingers happened to touch. The smile on her face stilled, and the breath caught in the back of her throat. She barely managed to keep from dropping the bag.

Tim winked at her, put the van into gear, then drove out of the motel parking lot.

Mary devoured the muffin and guzzled the juice, as famished as if she really had spent the night in his arms.

They turned onto the street leading to the hospital. A rusty old Chevrolet sped past, veered into their lane, then stopped.

Tim jammed on the brakes. The tires screeched. The van slowed.

Teeth clenched, Mary gripped the dashboard and stomped on a phantom brake pedal.

All at once there was a jolt accompanied by a muffled crash. The Chevy jumped forward a foot or two. The van shuddered to a halt.

Mary's breathing was rapid and shallow. Her heart pounded. "Is anyone hurt?" she called out in a voice she did not recognize as her own.

There was a chorus of subdued "No"s.

Tim's head hung down, his shoulders slumped. After a moment he lifted his head and shook it, as if to clear it.

A young woman wearing hip-huggers and a cropped top got out of the Chevy, walked to the rear of her car, and stood surveying the damage.

Although there was nothing threatening in the woman's stance, Mary felt an unaccountable chill. Aftershock, she told herself.

Tim opened the door, glanced over at Mary, then hopped out and approached the woman.

"Why don't you watch where you're going?" the woman yelled, waving her arms about. "Look what you did to my car!"

Tim held up his hands, palms facing out. "Let's keep calm. I'm sure we can discuss this in a rational manner."

"Don't tell me to keep calm, asshole. It's your fault. You're the one that doesn't know how to drive."

The Chevy passenger door opened. Another young

woman emerged. Shouting obscenities at Tim, she headed in his direction.

Mary jumped out of the van and looked from one outraged young woman to the other. Neither appeared to be interested in what Tim was trying to say.

Something in her peripheral vision grabbed Mary's attention.

A man. Moving toward Tim and the first woman.

A curiosity-seeker or perhaps a fellow driver coming to help.

Then she noticed that the man gripped a thin metal bar. A tire iron?

The man raised his arm.

"Tim!" she screamed. "On your left! Look out!"

Tim's forearms came up as he turned his head to the left.

Mary tried to go to him, but the second woman blocked her way. Mary flicked a glance at the van. The elders were all trying to get out at once, and Crunchy was trapped behind the knot of bodies, an agonized expression on his face. Mary kicked the woman in the shin, shoved her aside, and dashed between the cars.

The man swung the tire iron. It grazed the side of Tim's head at the hairline and thudded against his left forearm.

Tim crumpled to the ground, blood pouring from his scalp.

The man raised his arm again.

"Noooo," Mary screamed, charging at him.

Her head butted him in the armpit. He stumbled, wheeling away from her.

She jumped on his back, wrapped her arms around his throat.

He staggered toward the vehicles and fell backward, ramming her against the side of the van. He righted himself, moved forward a few steps, then hurtled backward again.

She felt the breath whoosh out of her lungs.

He rammed her against the van once more. Her arms loosened. He shook her off. She slid down the side of the van, gasping for breath.

She tried to lift herself up. The world began to spin.

She closed her eyes for a moment, hoping to control the dizziness, but that made it worse.

Opening her eyes again, she saw Tim curled into a fetal position in the middle of the street, Lila Lorraine kneeling beside him.

Teach, Happy, and Crunchy chasing the assailant.

Iron Sam watching the rusty Chevrolet speed away from the scene.

Spaghetti standing over her, holding out a hand.

He helped her rise to her feet. She reeled, grabbed hold of him to steady herself.

Then ran to Tim.

Mary pulled up to the emergency entrance, bringing the van to a halt as gently as she could to keep from jostling Tim. She got out and hurried around to the passenger side to help him, but he was already standing when she arrived.

He gave her a faint smile. "I'm fine."

She let out a humph of unamused laughter. "Yeah, real fine." His face was pale, blood still seeped from his head wound, and he cradled his injured left arm against his blood-soaked chest.

"It looks worse than it is," he said.

"Well, we'll soon find out."

Mary led the way into the hospital, stopped at the desk, and waited for the nurse to look up from the computer. The elders, minus Iron Sam who still refused to enter the building, clustered around her. Tim kept walking.

She dashed after him. "Where are you going?"

"To get cleaned up."

"The nurse can do that after they take X-rays."

"No X-rays."

Mary rolled her eyes. "I don't believe this. Why are you being so stubborn?"

Tim paused outside the door to the men's restroom and turned to her. "You sound like my mother. She calls me a stubborn Swede. But I'm not being stubborn. There's no need for X-rays—my arm isn't broken. Look." He gently punched his right palm with his left fist. "No pain."

Mary put her hands on her hips. "Then why are you wincing?"

"There's a dull ache, but no shooting pains."

He pushed open the door to the men's room. Mary followed him inside.

"What about your head?"

"What about it?"

"You might have a concussion."

Opening his eyes wide, he peered into the mirror. "No concussion. Both pupils are the same size."

Mary chewed on her lower lip, wishing she remembered more of the first aid class she'd taken back when she worked as a lifeguard at Congress Park. She thought uneven pupils signaled concussion, but did matching pupils indicate that everything was okay?

She watched him dab at his bloody hairline with a dampened paper towel. Well, she remembered one thing—you didn't clean a wound that way.

"Here, let me." She reached for the towel.

To her surprise, he handed it to her without a fuss.

The door opened and Teach walked in. Lila Lorraine followed, took a quick look around, then backed out again.

"This is the men's room," she whispered loudly.

Mary shrugged her shoulders. "So?"

"So you're not supposed to be in here."

Mary held the paper towel under hot water to soak it, added a dollop of soap, and began to wash the blood from Tim's face.

"Believe me, this is the least of the crimes I've committed since embarking on this journey."

Tim's head had been hanging over the sink, but now it snapped up.

"What crimes?" he asked, a gleam of laughter in his eyes.

Mary pushed his head back down. "Never mind."

"Tell me," he said, his voice echoing in the basin.

She got a clean towel, soaked it, and continued washing his wound. "I can't. It's not my story to tell."

The door to the restroom opened again. Happy, Spaghetti, and Crunchy entered. Wide grins stretched Happy's and Spaghetti's faces.

"Look what we got." Crunchy held out his big hands, which were heaped with bandages, gauze, cotton balls, antiseptic ointment, and a pair of surgical scissors.

"Where did you get this stuff?" Mary demanded. She wiped a forearm across her brow. "Forget I asked."

Happy puffed out his chest. "They were practically giving it away."

Tim started laughing. The elders joined in.

Mary shook her head, but helped herself to the proffered supplies.

After she cleaned Tim's face and bandaged the wound, she had to admit he didn't look too bad. The color was even returning to his cheeks.

"Now let me look at your arm," she said.

He rolled up his sleeve. She found no break in the skin, but an extensive bruise was already forming.

"Want us to go back and find something for that?" Spaghetti asked.

"No!" Mary exclaimed.

Tim laughed.

"It's a good thing you have a nice chunk of muscle on that forearm," Teach said, "otherwise the bone would have been broken."

Tim inspected the bruise, then rolled down his sleeve. "I have some ointment I can put on later."

Mary pointed at the three scavengers, then at the door. "Go take that stuff back where you found it."

Happy scuffed a foot. "Do we have to?"

"Yeah." Tim grinned. "Do we have to?"

Kid Rags took his gaze off the television when Mary, Tim, Teach, and Lila Lorraine entered, then he turned back to the television and continued to flip channels.

"Did you talk to the doctor?" he asked, his gaze focused on the flickering screen.

"Not yet," Mary answered.

"He says I have to stay another day or two. Something to do with my age." He threw the remote on the bed. "It's discrimination, that's what it is."

Happy, Crunchy, and Spaghetti crowded into the room. Taking note of their bulging pockets, Mary realized they hadn't returned the purloined supplies, but she didn't say anything. The way this trip was going, they'd probably need them.

"We got ice for Tim," Happy announced, holding a partially filled pillowcase.

Mary pressed her lips together. She wasn't even going to ask where they got it.

Spaghetti tugged at Mary's sleeve. "Kid Rags is bleeding."

Two strides took Mary to the side of the bed where Kid Rags had yanked out his IV. She held out a hand to Spaghetti.

"Quick. A Band-Aid."

Smiling sheepishly, he reached into a pocket and pulled out several small bandages. She took one, ripped it open, and slapped it on Kid Rags' arm.

Kid Rags swung his skinny legs over the side of the bed and gave Mary a defiant look.

"I'm blowing this joint."

Mary nodded. "Good idea."

His jaw dropped. "You mean you'll let me?"

"You're a grown man. I have no authority over you, and anyway—" She bit off the words, not wanting to express her worry.

But Happy did it for her.

"A moving target gathers no moss," he intoned.

Kid Rags narrowed his eyes. "Something happened, didn't it?"

"We'll tell you later, but now you have to get dressed,"

she said. "Where are your clothes?"

"Here they are." Lila Lorraine thrust them into Kid Rags' arms. "I found them in the closet."

Kid Rags slid off the bed and took his clothes into the tiny bathroom. He emerged a few minutes later looking like his old self. He touched a finger to his hat brim, smoothed his mustache, brushed a bit of lint off his navy pinstripe suit.

"What are we waiting for?" he said, straightening his red polka dot bow tie. "Let's go if we're going."

"Hey," Happy protested. "That's my line!"

Chapter 32

"So what gives?" Kid Rags asked when they'd exhausted the topic of his "jail break."

Mary's fingers tightened on the steering wheel. "We had an accident."

Happy hooted. "That was no accident. I know a crash car when I see one."

Tim repositioned his pillowcase ice pack. "I saw hardly a dent in either of our bumpers, yet those girls carried on as if I'd demolished their car. I was waiting for them to try something when Mary shouted at me to look out. I turned and managed to deflect most of the blow."

"He swung his arm back, getting ready to clobber you again," Spaghetti said. "I thought for sure you were a goner—it all happened so fast, we couldn't get out of the van in time to help."

"But Mary dived at him," Lila Lorraine said, "and pushed him away."

Tim reached out and touched Mary's cheek. "You did that? For me?"

Mary tilted her head toward his hand. "I didn't plan it. I just did it."

"That makes it even more remarkable."

"She jumped on his back," Crunchy said.

Tim's eyes widened as he looked at Mary. "You did?"

She nodded. "I can't believe it, either. I don't know what got into me."

"He banged her against the van until she fell off him," Happy said.

"We chased him, but he got away," Crunchy added.

"It's not fair," Kid Rags grumbled. "I missed all the fun."

Tim studied Mary, his eyes graver than she'd yet seen them. "Did he hurt you?"

"I don't think so." She rotated her shoulders. "I'm a bit sore is all."

"I never saw him," Tim said. "Did anyone get a good look?"

"It was the caretaker," Crunchy responded. The elders murmured their agreement.

"Albert Hoffman?" Tim paused, looking reflective. "I should have known, but to be honest, I didn't expect him to try anything. Since he seems to think we're leading him to the gold, it makes no sense for him to try to kill us before we get there."

"Not us," Teach said. "Only you, Tim."

"Me? Why me? He doesn't know I have any connection to the gold. His father knew of three bank robbers. He might have guessed they had a driver, but he couldn't have known about Crazy Pat. His father didn't see the driver, and Crazy Pat's name didn't appear in the article about the bootleggers."

"It has nothing to do with your grandfather," Mary said. "Albert's trying to even things up. I bet he followed us to the library, and he thinks that whatever we dug out of the wall will help us find the gold. He wouldn't be concerned about having to handle a few old people and a wimpy girl, but a strong young man is something else. After all, Albert is getting on. He has to be in his sixties."

Tim smiled. "You're not exactly a wimpy girl."

Mary slowed the van as they passed a road construction crew working on the side of the highway.

"He didn't know that. Until today even I didn't know."

"So what happens now?" Spaghetti asked. "As long as we're on the move, we should be safe. He can only set up another ambush if he knows ahead of time where we'll be. But we can't stay on the road forever."

"We assume he's tailing us," Kid Rags said, "but we never see him. We don't even know what car he's driving."

"I do," Happy said. "I saw him drive off in a bronze Lexus this morning."

Lila Lorraine cleared her throat. "Tim's been using his credit cards everywhere, even to pay Kid Rags' hospital bill. Maybe Albert's been following the paper trail. Since he's a banker, he'd know how to do that."

"It's possible," Teach said. "It wouldn't hurt to switch to cash now that we have some."

"Now that Sam has some," Mary corrected. "It's up to him what we do with it."

Iron Sam coughed and hacked and coughed some more. "It's Mary's money. She can do whatever she wants."

My money? Blood money? Mary pushed the thought out of her mind. Whatever the source, the elders needed it.

"Cash it is," she said. "Listen, everyone. I mean this. Be very, very careful. Albert Hoffman has killed four people we know of, and today he almost succeeded with a fifth. There's no telling what he might do when he discovers we don't know where the gold is."

Mary glanced around the motel room in Iowa City. It looked like all the others she had stayed in, giving her the disconcerting feeling that no matter how far they traveled, they always ended up in the same place.

The only difference was that, once again, Tim and Lila Lorraine had exchanged rooms.

Mary peeked at Tim. He was leaning back against the pillows, smiling at her.

The smile disappeared when her gaze met his.

"You saved my life today," he said softly.

She tried to shrug, but her sore body had stiffened, and her shoulders didn't move.

"It was nothing."

"It was everything."

She reached out to touch him, but stopped herself with an effort she hoped didn't show.

Putting her hands behind her back, she said, "I'm going to take a very long, very hot shower. Do you need to use the bathroom first?"

He laced his fingers together and turned his palms toward her, cracking his knuckles. "I'm fine." He grinned lazily. "Let me know if you need someone to wash your back."

She puffed out a cheek with her tongue. "And who might that someone be? You?"

He raised his eyebrows in mock innocence. "Me? No, but I'm sure I can find someone who'd be willing to volunteer."

Smiling to herself, she went to take her shower.

When Mary came out of the bathroom, feeling only a bit better, a strong odor tickled her nose.

She sniffed. Menthol, camphor, eucalyptus, and something else. Clove, maybe.

Tim held out his left arm. "It's the ointment I'm using."

Mary went over to inspect the bruise, which had turned a dark purple. Gently laying a finger on his discolored skin, she asked, "Does it hurt?"

He winced. "Only when it's touched."

She snatched her hand away. "Sorry."

"No problem."

He stood.

Finding herself staring at his naked, beautifully muscled chest and the line of reddish-gold hair disappearing into his jeans, she ducked her head, cheeks flaming.

"Take off your shirt," he said.

She jerked her head up. "I beg your pardon?"

Suddenly conscious of her naked body beneath flimsy pajamas consisting of pink boxer-style shorts and a matching tee shirt, she wrapped her arms around herself.

He showed her a small white jar with a purple label. "The ointment. I want to put it on your back. You've been doing a good job of hiding it, but I know you're in pain."

She searched his eyes. What she saw in them did nothing to reassure her. She raked a hand through her hair. The resulting twinge in her back settled the matter. Turning away from him, she slipped her shirt over her head and lay face down on the bed

She flinched when she felt his hands on her back. "Ow! That hurts. Ow. Ow. Ow. Oooh . . . that feels good."

As the soreness and kinks receded, her back became

warmer.

And warmer.

The heat seeped inside her, into the very depths of her being. Her body became liquid fire, consuming all thought.

She didn't know how she got the strength to move, but all at once she jumped up, ran into the bathroom, and leaned against the closed door.

Her heart slammed against her chest so hard she felt sure it would burst right out of her body. And her lungs seemed to have forgotten how to function.

She finally managed to draw in one deep breath, then another, and another. When she gained possession of herself, she clutched a towel to her chest and opened the bathroom door.

As she caught sight of Tim standing there waiting for her, something flipped in her stomach.

Woo!

She grabbed hold of the doorjamb to steady herself.

"What's wrong?" he asked.

Her eyes filled with unshed tears. "This is a real mess we've gotten ourselves into."

The look on his face was just short of pain. "You mean Bill?"

She shook her head. "I can't marry Bill now. I didn't know . . ." *Didn't know what? Didn't know you were in the world? Didn't know I could feel this way?*

Although she could not find the right words, Tim nodded as if he understood.

She tried to smile, but only managed a poor, lopsided thing. "I had to hang up when I called Bill's office this morning—I couldn't bear talking to him, knowing how I feel about you. I realize I'll have to talk to him eventually to let him know it's all over between us, but since it doesn't seem fair to do it on the phone, I'll have to wait till I get back to Denver. Not that I think he'll be all that upset. In fact, I'm sure he'll be relieved, especially when I tell him my plans for the farm."

Realizing she was babbling, she took a deep, shuddering

breath. "If we had met two weeks ago, even one week ago, things would have been different, but I have responsibilities in Colorado now. I can't move to Chicago to be with you."

"That's not an issue," he said quietly. "I go where you go. Besides, I like what you're going to do with your farm. I want to be a part of it."

"Won't it be boring for you?"

An impish smile lit his face. "I have a hunch it will be anything but."

"Oh," she managed to say.

He touched her forehead with his own.

Needing to feel his skin against hers, she dropped the towel and slipped into his embrace.

They clung to each other as if they would never let go.

"Do you know when I first fell in love with you?" he murmured into her ear a long moment later.

She nodded against his chest. "The red dress."

"No. When you walked into The Joker with all those aged gangsters."

"They're not all gangsters."

"Maybe not, but I know the type. I used to see them at my father's pool hall. And there you were—sweet, confident, innocent."

She gave him a wry smile. "Not as innocent as you might suppose."

"Despite whatever crimes you seem to think you've committed, you're still innocent compared to those old rogues, but you treat them with respect, and they all clearly adore you."

"Not all. Not Iron Sam."

"Even Iron Sam. Sometimes he looks at you as if you're the daughter or granddaughter he never had."

She laughed. "You're making that up."

"No, I'm not. That's the way they all look at you, especially Crunchy."

"I do know Crunchy thinks of me that way—he was in love with my grandmother, and I remind him of her. It's odd—I never used to be aware of old people as real persons.

I'm not stupid. I know they weren't born old, but it didn't occur to me that heroes and villains, killers and great lovers could be hidden in those feeble bodies."

He smiled at her, his heavy-lidded eyes gleaming, and suddenly the room felt much too warm and still, like the calm before a summer storm.

He bent and brushed her lips with his.

A bolt of lightning flashed through her body, buckling her knees and curling her toes. She held him tightly, too dazed to do anything else.

He kissed her again, deeper this time.

"I love you," he said. "Even before I knew you, I loved you. And I always will."

Chapter 33

Sitting at two picnic tables pulled together, Mary and her companions studied the people who entered the park-like rest area.

They did not see Albert Hoffman.

Tim folded the map he'd been studying. "Tomorrow, or the day after at the latest, we'll be in Colorado. We need to start making plans."

"You're right," Mary said, marveling at how calm he seemed, as if eluding death and making earth-trembling love were common occurrences for him. Her whole body ached from the effort of trying to maintain her composure.

She stood and started clearing away the debris from lunch. She didn't feel ready to face whatever waited for them at journey's end—too many things worried her. Albert Hoffman, of course. The logistics of getting everyone moved. Whether the house would be habitable until they could renovate it, though perhaps it wasn't as bad as she remembered—after all, her grandparents lived there until a few weeks ago.

Arms filled with trash, she headed for the dumpster.

"I'm still hungry," Kid Rags announced.

"There's a granola bar in my purse," she said over her shoulder.

When she returned to the table, her purse lay open in front of Kid Rags, and he was staring at something cupped in his palm.

He glanced at her, a puzzled expression on his face. "I thought you said you were broke."

"I am. I mean, I was before Sam gave me his money."

"But you have this gold."

"What gold? You mean the signet ring we dug up at The Shoemaker's place?"

"No. These two coins."

"Oh, those. I found them in my grandfather's desk.

They're my good luck charms." She smiled at Tim and the elders. "They work, too. I've had a lot of good luck lately."

"Good luck? I'll say." Kid Rags extended his arm. "Do you know how much these are worth?"

"Gold sells for—what?—four hundred dollars an ounce? And together they weigh about half that."

"Weight! Who's talking about weight?" He held up the smaller coin. "This is a 1929 Indian head five dollar gold piece in 'about uncirculated condition'. It's worth at least six thousand dollars."

Mary gulped. "Six . . . thousand . . . dollars?"

"Maybe more. There are various classifications of near mint state coins, and it's almost impossible to tell the difference between them with the naked eye. It would have to be authenticated by a professional grading service, but I do know it's worth at least six grand."

Everyone crowded around them, making it hard for Mary to breathe.

"What's the other one worth?" Happy asked, his voice squeaking in excitement.

"A 1933 ten dollar Indian head coin in 'about uncirculated condition'? Forty-nine thousand at a bare minimum."

There was a moment of stunned silence, then a babble of voices.

Mary sat down, unable to think of anything except that she'd been casually toting around a small fortune.

She could hear Teach talking, but it took a long time for his words to register. When they finally sunk in, she lifted a hand to her mouth.

"What did you say?"

Teach shrugged. "I asked if these coins could have come from the Racine bank job."

Tim gave him a doubtful look. "I don't see how. They buried it all, every single coin. They wanted to make sure it couldn't be linked to them in any way. Don't forget—the treasury department wanted to get hold of the robbers, and so did the Chicago commission."

"Jimmy Boots coulda dug it up," Crunchy said.

Tim shook his head. "No one but Crazy Pat knew where to find it."

"Could Jimmy Boots have overheard him talking about it?" Spaghetti asked. "You said Crazy Pat always used to tell the story."

"Of the robbery, yes. But I think I'm the only one he told where they'd hidden the loot. And none of the other three could have told anyone before they died. They didn't know ahead of time where they were going to bury it."

Mary grew still. "Dugald knew. Don't you remember, Tim? You said Dugald thought of the perfect spot."

Tim blinked. "So I did. You're right—he would have known."

"And he told Jimmy Boots," Crunchy said, "and Jimmy Boots dug it up."

Teach laughed. "Well, I'll be . . ."

Mary looked off into the distance. "I don't think Jimmy Boots ever intended to dig it up. He wanted to make his own way in the world, but Gina Dale got pregnant. She wanted to raise her child away from city influences, and since Jimmy Boots didn't have enough money to buy a farm for her, he went and got the gold."

"That does sound like Jimmy Boots, Mary," Lila Lorraine said. "It's as if you knew him."

"She should," Kid Rags said. "It's all we've talked about for two weeks."

"No it isn't," Happy protested. "We talked about cars, too."

Kid Rags glowered at him. "Who cares about cars?"

"Where's the gold now?" Iron Sam rasped.

They all stared at him.

Coughing, he stared back. "Well, where is it?"

"Maybe Jimmy Boots spent it," Spaghetti said, "and those two coins are all that's left."

"It's possible," Lila Lorraine said hesitantly. "But spent on what? Except for the farm, he and Gina didn't own much."

Kid Rags looked at the coins still nestled in his palm.

"Maybe he buried it again and forgot where he put it."

Teach didn't join in the ensuing laughter. "It happens more often than you might think—that's why there are so many legends about buried treasure."

Happy bounced on the balls of his feet. "So, what are we waiting for? Let's go find it."

"How many acres did Jimmy Boots own?" Tim asked.

"Eighty," Mary responded.

Tim whistled. "That's a lot of ground to cover with a metal detector."

Teach looked preoccupied, as if trying to figure out how long it would take. "Maybe Jimmy Boots put the gold in a post hole bank. If so, it would make the job a lot more manageable."

"Post hole bank?" Mary asked.

Kid Rags handed her the gold coins and reached for his flask.

Mary caught his eye. "You just got out of the hospital."

"The doctor said I shouldn't drink so much bourbon. He didn't say I couldn't drink any." He took a tiny sip and passed the flask around.

"In the old west," Teach said, wiping his mouth with the back of a hand, "banks were few and far between, and highly untrustworthy, so whenever the ranchers got their hands on any gold or silver, they hid it in remote corners of the house or buried it, often in a fencepost hole to make it easier to find again. I remember one particular story that interested Jimmy Boots. A rancher went out to his cow pen one moonless night, removed a fencepost, dropped his bag of gold in the hole, then replaced the post and headed for bed, satisfied he'd protected the coins. A couple of years later, the rancher needed the money so he went to dig it up, but time had obliterated the small identifying mark he'd made on the post, and he couldn't remember which one marked the gold. He dug up half his pen before he found the right post. People today hunt for treasure around the abandoned corrals of the old southwestern ranches, and sometimes they find it."

"Maybe that someone will be us," Happy said. "Then I

can still buy me that Dodge Charger Tim has."

Crunchy folded his arms across his chest. "If Jimmy Boots found the gold, then it belongs to Mary."

There was a pause, as if they were waiting for Mary to say it belonged to all of them, but she could not force herself to speak the words. In the end, she knew, it would be better to have a single arbiter. Fewer problems that way.

Kid Rags shrugged. "Okay with me. All I want is a nice place to live, plenty of good food to eat, lots of bourbon, and a little work to keep me busy."

Teach smiled at Mary. "Someplace quiet to write my book would be nice."

"I don't have anyone but Mary to leave it to, anyway," Lila Lorraine said.

Spaghetti winced. "I sure wouldn't want my no-good son to get a hold of it."

Iron Sam coughed and hacked. "Doesn't make any difference to me."

"As long as I can have the Dodge Charger," Happy said. "That's all I care about."

Mary tried not to shudder at the thought of Happy in a car on public streets. "How about one of those little four-wheeled ATVs instead? You could drive all around the farm without having to worry about traffic."

"I guess." He kicked at the grass, but Mary could see a tiny smile playing on his lips.

"And I promised you a baby bulldozer."

"Aren't we getting ahead of ourselves?" Tim asked. "We haven't found the gold yet, and there's a chance we won't. Keep in mind, this is all supposition."

Back in the van, speeding toward Omaha, Mary put all thoughts of the gold out of her mind. Tim was right: except for the two coins now secured in her makeshift money-belt, it was supposition. And they did need to start making plans.

They decided to pack Lila Lorraine's things and lock them in a storage unit. Later, when Tim rented a truck for his and Spaghetti's move to the farm, he could stop in Omaha and pick up Lila Lorraine's possessions.

"I already have a storage unit," Lila Lorraine said. "The apartments at the residence come furnished, and they're so small there's no room for my own furniture. I couldn't bring myself to get rid of any of my things, even though I never thought I'd get a chance to use them again."

"There will be plenty of room in the truck," Tim said. "Spaghetti doesn't own much, and I'm only going to bring my personal belongings. I'll arrange for Kirsten to run the bar and take over my side business. She can sell the existing inventory for me on a consignment basis."

"What a dreary place," Lila Lorraine exclaimed the next morning when they drove into the parking lot of the Wide River Senior Citizen Residence. "You can't imagine how thrilled I am to be leaving here."

They carried the boxes they'd scavenged to her apartment. She set the men to packing her knickknacks and kitchenware, seemingly unconcerned with the possibility of breakage, then led Mary into her bedroom.

As they started clearing out the closet, Mary said, "If you have the slightest doubt about moving to the farm, we can do this another time. I feel as if I'm rushing you into something you might not want to do."

Lila Lorraine smiled. "No doubts whatsoever. I know it won't be the same without Gina Dale and Jimmy Boots, but I'll have you and Spaghetti and all the others. The thought of dying alone didn't make me sad—no matter how many people are with you, you still die alone. What made me sad was living alone." She gave Mary a one-armed hug. "And now I won't have to."

She bent to place a gray winter coat in a box, then straightened. "What do your parents think about all this?"

Mary kept her eyes focused on the blouse she was folding. "I haven't told them yet."

"I never met your mother, but I'm sure she'll be proud of

you. And even though Pete might not tell you, I know he will be too. He tends to be reserved, but he's a good boy. It will be nice to see him again. Did I tell you he used to call me Auntie Lila?"

Lila Lorraine lapsed into silence.

Mary tried to picture her father's reaction when she announced that a bunch of her grandfather's old cronies would be living at the farm. And Tim. Would he like Tim? She smiled to herself, unable to imagine anyone not liking him. She strained her ears, listening for the sound of his voice; instead, she heard Teach.

"It amazes me that people are so willing to throw away their hard-earned cash. They don't seem to understand they're playing someone else's game. The only way to win is to play your own game."

"Didn't I hear you say you sometimes run a game?" Tim asked.

"I have an arrangement with one of the saloons in Tombstone. During the busy season I dress like an old-time gambler, a Dapper Dan, and play poker with the tourists. Gives them such a thrill, they don't seem to mind so much about losing. Of course, the games aren't as long now as they used to be—when I was younger I could play twenty or thirty hours at a stretch by 'sleeping out' an occasional hand. I'd lean back in my chair, close my eyes and doze off a few minutes, then wake, refreshed and ready to . . ."

The sound of Lila Lorraine's laughter startled Mary.

"Listen to Teach," Lila Lorraine said. "You're going to have your hands full with that one. It's always something with him. Gina Dale used to call him a mile a minute thinker. We often marveled at how Teach and Jimmy Boots could be such good friends—they were so different."

Mary paused, her arms full of dresses. "What do you mean, different? I got the impression they had a lot in common."

"Oh, heavens no. Your grandfather hated scams. He understood the need for simple lies—not everyone deserves the truth—but he could not tolerate the con. That's why it was strange that he liked Teach so much."

Mary stared at her. "But I thought . . ."

"Thought what?"

Shaking her head, Mary dumped the dresses on the bed, picked one up, folded it, and placed it in the box, wondering where she'd gone wrong in her assessment of Jimmy Boots. As she continued folding the dresses and packing them, she mulled over everything she'd learned about her grandfather. She could feel the tumblers in her mind falling into place one by one, as if Lila Lorraine's revelation held the key to unlocking his character.

She had no blinding flash of inspiration, just a slow realization she did know him after all.

And she knew something else, too.

She folded the last dress—a lavender shirtwaist—placed it in the box, and sat on the edge of the bed.

"I know where the gold is," she said in a conversational tone.

"Mary figured out where the gold is," Lila Lorraine called out.

The men gathered at the bedroom door.

"Where do you think it is?" Kid Rags asked.

Mary glanced at them. "I don't think. I know."

Chapter 34

About twenty miles past Gunnison, Teach directed Tim to a dirt road angling off Highway 135. The van bounced over the ruts, rattling Mary's teeth.

"Stop past this curve," Teach said.

"We there yet?" Happy asked.

"No, but I think we should wait before going farther in case Hoffman is still tailing us."

Teach got out of the van and climbed a small hill.

Only Mary and Tim followed.

From the top of the hill, Mary could see the dirt road they had traveled, the highway beyond, and a panoramic view of the mountains.

The voices of Spaghetti and Lila Lorraine drifted upward, and Mary could hear them oohing and aahing over the scenery. Though she was used to the grandeur, she had to admit the mountains looked spectacular today. The rocks and trees, the patches of snow on distant peaks, all stood out in stark relief against the deep blue cloudless sky.

Tim put an arm around her shoulders. She snuggled into his embrace.

He kissed the top of her head.

"None of that," she said with mock severity. "We have work to do." But she didn't move away, not even when he pushed her hair aside and nuzzled her neck.

She sighed contentedly, thinking she'd never been so happy. The two days of travel since Omaha had been uneventful, but the nights in Tim's arms had been . . . her mind went blank. She could not think of a single word to describe the marvel of their lovemaking.

Tim let out a groan, as if sharing the memory of those nights, and stepped back.

"You're right," he said. "We have work to do. We're so close to finding the gold, and with a killer stalking us, this is no time to get distracted. I'll meet you at the van."

Mary breathed deeply of the heady, pine-scented air, and watched him leave. After a moment she went to join Teach, who stood several yards away, peering through a pair of binoculars.

The binoculars, a dozen powerful flashlights, and plenty of rope—which Crunchy had insisted they needed—had been purchased that morning at a discount store in Gunnison.

"Any sign of Albert Hoffman?" Mary asked.

"No." Teach lowered the binoculars.

As they descended the hill, he pointed out two parallel dirt strips disappearing into the distance. "That's our road."

Doubt tinged her voice. "Do you think the van can make it? It looks more like a cart track than a road."

"We're not going far." He gestured to a cluster of scrubby, boulder-strewn hills. "It's in there."

Tim parked next to a couple of blue spruce. When they got out of the van, a crow squawked at them from a high branch, then flew into the hills.

"I can't climb those," Lila Lorraine said, sounding tearful.

"You don't have to." Teach parted the scrub brush. "There's a passageway here someplace."

Noticing all the litter and the crisscrossing tire tracks, Mary felt her first twinge of misgivings. She had not realized the place would be so public; maybe someone already found the gold.

"We're surrounded by national forest," Teach said, still searching for the path. "People don't know this bit of land is private property, and even if they did, they wouldn't care. It seems to be a popular area for all-terrain vehicles, though I doubt they'd be riding in these hills—too many boulders."

Mary dragged a foot over one of the tire tracks, obliterating it. "I read somewhere that in the past few years ATVs have done more damage to delicate mountain ecosystems than loggers did in the past century."

Not hearing a comment from Teach, she glanced at the

empty spot where she'd last seen him.

"Teach? Where are you?"

He stepped out from behind a stand of spindly scotch pines. "I found the path. It's rougher going than I remember, but it's only about fifty feet long."

The path was nothing more than a V-shaped cleft between two hills. Sharp rocks made walking difficult.

The elders, refusing to be left behind, picked their way through the opening, using the rock facings of the hills to balance themselves. Mary and Tim, burdened with the rope, shovels, and other equipment, had no easier time of it.

Emerging from the passageway, Mary found herself in a small clearing barely big enough for all of them. An overhanging rock blotted out the sun. She shivered, grateful to Teach for reminding them to bring jackets.

"I don't see the mine," Spaghetti said.

Teach pointed to some tall, thick-stalked weeds growing out of a pile of rock and dirt. "It has to be behind there."

Mary felt her spirits rise. One thing for sure—no one had entered this mine in a very long time.

She pulled the weeds, which weren't as firmly rooted as they looked. Once she got rid of them, she could see the lintel above the mine entrance. Bursting with energy, she grabbed a shovel and began attacking the dirt pile.

With Tim wielding the other shovel, they soon demolished the mound.

Tim unhooked a hammer from his belt, pried away the boards covering the entrance, then took a few steps backward.

"Aren't we going in?" Kid Rags asked.

Crunchy moved in front of the entrance to block it. "Needs to air out. Don't know what's been building up in there all these years."

Mary relaxed, glad of the respite. The idea of going into that pit, with tons of rock poised above her head, did not thrill her.

"You want me to carry you over the threshold?" Tim asked.

She laughed. "No thank you. I prefer to go to my doom on my own two feet."

Lila Lorraine glanced at the mine. "It's not dangerous, is it?"

"Mines are always dangerous," Crunchy said.

"Rotting timbers," Happy said with great relish. "Cave-ins. Bats."

Crunchy poked his head into the entrance and sniffed. "No bats. And anyway, bats don't hurt nobody. But you have to watch out for cave-ins. That's why we need rope."

"How come you know so much about mines?" Kid Rags asked.

"Worked in one once. Didn't like it."

"I think we can go in now," Tim said.

Mary stepped into the mine.

Light penetrated a few yards along the rock-walled tunnel; beyond that lay darkness so thick she thought she could reach out and touch it. The air felt dank and had a strong, musty smell. Somewhere nearby water dripped.

She turned on her flashlight. The darkness swallowed the beam. The others clicked on their flashlights, and the tunnel brightened enough for her to get a good look.

Bits of quartz, like stars, twinkled on the rough rock walls. About forty feet away, the tunnel ended in a pool of blackness. A drop of water condensed on the rock ceiling and fell into the pool. Hearing only a faint, distant plink, Mary realized the blackness was the opening of a deep shaft. At one time, boards must have covered the hole; the few remaining jagged pieces of wood looked like the fangs of a menacing beast.

In front of the shaft, two tunnels angled off the main one, forming a Y.

Happy darted toward the tunnel on the right, but Crunchy caught hold of his belt and yanked him back.

"Hey," Happy yelped. "What's the big idea?"

"We gotta tie ourselves together."

"Why?"

"So we can pull you up if you fall in a hole."

Mary studied the floor of the tunnel. What she could see of it beneath fallen stones and chunks of rotten timber looked like solid rock.

"Crunchy's right," Teach said. "It is dangerous. There's at least one tunnel beneath these, and in a couple of places the dynamiting caused the upper ones to become unstable, but the adit is safe except around the mineshaft."

"That's the place for me," Lila Lorraine said. "Where's the adit?"

"This entrance tunnel is the adit." Teach pointed to the pool of blackness. "That's the mineshaft."

Crunchy went back outside and got the rope from where Tim had dropped it when he helped clear the entrance. He tied the rope around Teach's waist first, then Tim's and Happy's, leaving about ten feet between each man.

"I'll stay here," Iron Sam said, coughing.

Lila Lorraine moved to stand beside him. "I'm staying, too."

"And me," Spaghetti said.

Kid Rags hesitated. To Mary's relief, he also declined to come with them. Though he seemed to be doing well, she couldn't forget how deathly pale he had looked when they'd taken him to the hospital.

Crunchy wrapped the rope around Mary's waist, then tied himself to the end of the line.

Teach led the way into the right hand tunnel. It was narrower than the main tunnel, but here and there, room-size holes had been blasted out of the walls.

They hadn't gone far, perhaps thirty yards, when a pile of fallen rocks blocked their way.

Tim gave a laugh. "I sure hope your grandfather didn't bury the gold under all that. There must be tons of rock to move."

"I could do it," Happy said, "if I had my baby bulldozer."

Mary directed her flashlight beam on the walls, the ceiling, back down the tunnel they had traveled. She didn't know what she'd expected, but it wasn't this echoingly empty expanse with no hiding place except the rock pile.

"Jimmy Boots couldn't have hidden it in there," Teach said. "There's not a lot of sand and dirt built up on top of the rocks, which means it's a recent cave-in."

A muted rumbling caught Mary's attention. A moment later a rock crashed onto the top of the pile, rattled down the side, and came to rest at her feet.

"Very recent," Teach said.

"What do we do now?" Tim asked.

Mary eyed the rock pile. "The only thing we can do—climb over it."

Teach took one wary step, and then another. "Seems stable enough."

All at once the rock he was standing on gave way; he lost his balance. Tim put out a hand to steady him.

"Maybe Tim and I should go by ourselves," Mary said.

Crunchy folded his arms across his chest. "Everybody goes or nobody goes."

Happy began clambering up the rocks. When he got as far as the rope allowed, he looked back. "Come on, what are you waiting for?"

Sand and pebbles showered them as they helped one another over the pile. On solid footing again, Mary brushed herself off and looked around. This stretch of the tunnel looked as dreary and as devoid of obvious hiding places as the first part.

She hadn't taken more than two or three steps when she heard a low moan like that of a tormented soul, and the ground moved. Her stomach gave a sickening lurch. The rope tightened around her waist as Crunchy yanked her to safety.

Tim released a pent-up breath. "I don't think we should go any farther. It feels like the tunnel is getting ready to cave in."

"We've gone about as far as we can." Teach shined his flashlight down the tunnel. "As you can see, it ends a few yards ahead."

They climbed back over the rock pile and retraced their steps to the adit.

Spaghetti came to meet them. "Did you get it?"

Mary shook her head. "The gold must be in the other tunnel."

But they didn't find it there, either.

When the five explorers returned from searching the left hand tunnel, which was shorter but even more treacherous than the right one, Kid Rags said, "You didn't tell us where you got the idea to look for the gold in this mine."

Mary freed herself from the rope. "From something Lila Lorraine told me." She glanced apologetically at Teach. "She said Jimmy Boots hated the con."

Teach chuckled. "Didn't have much use for gamblers, either."

"Yet he agreed to go in with you on the gold mine scam."

"He was a good friend. As I told you before, I don't think he wanted to do the scam, but he knew I needed the money, so he went along with it. We didn't plan on him actively participating. I intended to do all the work."

"It got me to thinking that if he put some gold in the mine, then it wouldn't have been a complete lie, would it?"

"Where would he have hidden it?" Iron Sam asked between coughs.

Mary spread her hands. "I don't know, but I'm sure it's here."

"There's one place we haven't looked," Tim said. "The mineshaft."

Remembering how long it had taken the water drop to hit bottom, Mary put her hands on her hips. "No one is going near the shaft. It's too dangerous."

"No it's not," Kid Rags said. "We've already been over there and checked it out."

Mary blew out a breath. "Why am I not surprised?"

The men trooped to the mineshaft, ignoring Crunchy's suggestion that they secure themselves with the rope.

Mary trudged after them, Lila Lorraine close on her heels.

Standing next to Tim and holding his hand, Mary peered into the shaft. Even with all their flashlights trained down the vertical tunnel, she could barely see the bottom. Feeling dizzy, she tightened her grip on Tim's hand and stepped back, but not before she caught a glimpse of white.

"What's that?" she asked, unable to keep a quaver out of her voice.

"A skeleton," Happy said, holding his glasses to his eyes. "No. Two skeletons."

Mary shivered. "I know one thing. If the gold's hidden down there, it's going to stay there. No way in hell would I climb down to get it."

"I'll go," Tim said.

She stared at him, picturing a third skeleton on the bottom of the shaft. "No. Absolutely not."

"You want the gold, don't you?"

She shook her head so hard her ears popped. "Not that badly, I don't. With Sam's money and the two gold coins, we have enough to fix up the house and keep the farm going for a while."

"And when the money's gone?"

"I'll figure out a way to get more." Seeing him gaze down the shaft in what could only be described as a calculating manner, she turned his body so it faced hers, and looked him in the eyes. "No amount of money is worth risking your life for. I couldn't bear it if anything happened to you."

He cupped her face in his palms. "Nothing's going to happen to me."

"What about your arm?"

"What about it?"

"It's injured, remember? You can't climb down there with only one good arm."

"Sure I can." He laughed. "I may not be able to get back up again, but I can climb down."

"That's not funny," she said crossly.

He touched her cheek with the back of his hand. "I've gone exploring in old mines before. I know what I'm doing.

But you'll have to pull me up."

"For my sake, please don't go."

"For your sake, I have to go."

"I can't talk you out of it?"

"No. I'll be fine, you'll see. First I'll need to find something solid to tie the rope to."

Kid Rags pointed to a large eyebolt pounded into the base of the tunnel wall on the other side of the mineshaft. "Will this do?"

Tim tugged at the bolt; it held fast. He threaded the rope through the eye and lashed it securely. "I'd be willing to bet someone placed the bolt here for this very purpose."

"Jimmy Boots?" Spaghetti asked.

"Or whoever dug the shaft," Iron Sam said.

Tim tied knots every twelve to eighteen inches along the length of the rope, then tied the end around his waist.

Mary wanted to put her arms around him and hold him close one last time, but she kept her hands to herself. She could tell, from the faraway look in his eyes, that he was preparing himself for his descent, and she didn't want to break his concentration.

She held her breath when he finally lowered himself into the shaft and began climbing down his rope ladder. About fifteen feet below the rim, he came to a narrow protrusion. Seeing him pause on the ledge, she allowed herself to inhale. The breath caught in her throat when he pushed away from the side of the shaft with his feet, swung out into empty space, then swung back underneath the ledge and disappeared.

"Tim?" The word came out as a croak. She tried again. "Tim?"

"Mary?" His voice resonated as if he were speaking into a barrel.

"I hear you."

"I'm in a large excavation. Looks like someone started to blast out a tunnel, then quit. I see something I want to check on."

"Be careful!"

There was no answer.

Straining to hear, Mary didn't make a sound. Neither did any of the elders, who were gathered around the mineshaft, peering into the pit.

After a moment Mary heard the sound of rocks clacking together and a hollow "Oops."

Oops?

"Tim? You okay?"

"I'm fine. A rock rolled onto my foot. You won't believe this, but I found something."

"The gold?" Happy squeaked.

"Maybe, I don't know. I'm tying the rope around one of the packages."

Mary unslung her purse from across her shoulders, set it against the wall next to the eyebolt where no one would trip over it, and returned to the mineshaft.

"Okay," Tim yelled. "You can pull it up now."

They lay down their flashlights to free their hands. With all of them tugging on the rope, it took only seconds to haul the bundle to the surface.

They crowded around while Crunchy and Kid Rags untied the rope. Then, as one, the elders stepped back.

Mary knelt before the package and removed the heavy plastic wrapping. Finding an ancient olive drab rucksack, she undid the buckles and laid back the flap.

A few gold coins spilled out.

"Oh . . . my . . . God," Lila Lorraine breathed.

Crunchy's eyes grew wide.

"What's going on up there?" Tim called out.

"You did it!" Spaghetti shouted. "You found the bootleggers' gold!"

"Well, throw the rope back down. There's five more packages."

Mary jumped to her feet, but Crunchy had already dropped the end of the rope down the mineshaft.

Teach stared at the gold. "I don't believe it."

Kid Rags grabbed a coin and lightly ran his thumb across its face. "Believe it. It's real."

Laughing gleefully, Happy picked up a handful of coins and let them slip through his fingers.

Iron Sam coughed and coughed.

Mary gathered the spilled coins, stuffed them back into the rucksack, and re-buckled the flap. Maybe later she'd feel excited about the gold, but for now all she could think about was getting Tim back safely.

They hauled up the rest of the gold without incident.

As Mary untied the final bundle so she could toss the rope down to Tim, she heard a faint metallic click. She stiffened. "What was that?"

Before any of the elders could answer, a voice boomed out, "Put your hands on your heads and back away from my gold. Now!" The voice rose. "I said now! I have a gun, and I will not hesitate to use it."

Chapter 35

Feeling as if she'd been socked in the stomach, Mary turned her head and saw a man silhouetted in the glare of the mine entrance. She could not discern his features, but still she knew him.

Albert Hoffman.

He advanced into the mine, light glinting off the gun he aimed at her and the elders.

"I said, back away from my gold."

No one moved.

"How did you find us?" Teach asked.

"A transmitter. Don't worry," Hoffman added, sounding almost kind. "It's so small you wouldn't have found it even if you had thought to look for it."

The tone of his voice shifted. He didn't yell, but the low-pitched urgency was more commanding than a shouted order. "Keep your hands where I can see them, and back away. Now."

They raised their hands and slowly backed away from the gold.

Mary noticed that Crunchy was trying to put some distance between him and the rest of the group, but Hoffman stopped him with a reproving wiggle of the gun.

"Stay together," he said in that same deadly tone. "Except for you, Mary."

Bile rose to Mary's throat at the sound of her name, but she managed to give him a steady stare.

"Go untie the rope. If you try anything, I will shoot the senior citizens."

Mary returned to the packages of gold and squatted to finish untying the knots on the final parcel.

"Untie it from the wall first," Hoffman said.

She gasped. "I can't do that. How's Tim supposed to get up here?"

He smiled benignly, never taking his eyes off the elders.

"He's not. Now be a good girl and do as you're told."

Looking over her shoulder at him, Mary scuttled to the eyebolt. She crouched with her right side against the wall so Hoffman couldn't see what she was doing, and groped for her purse. Pretending to untie the rope with her left hand, she opened the purse with her right, reached in for Happy's gun, and tried to pull it out. It caught on something and didn't budge. She fumbled to get a better grip, and gave another yank. It still wouldn't come out.

"What's taking so long, Mary?" Hoffman demanded.

She glanced at him. His eyes were still focused on the elders.

She tugged at the gun. "The knot's too tight."

He flicked a look in her direction.

Iron Sam staggered toward Hoffman, gathered his strength with a visible effort, and leapt at him.

Hoffman fired his weapon.

Iron Sam went flying backward, hitting the ground with a sickening thud.

The shot echoed and reechoed in the tunnel, sounding like a barrage of gunfire.

Her hand still in her purse, Mary gripped the gun and pointed it at Hoffman. She curled her index finger around the trigger and pulled. Meeting resistance, she held her breath and increased the pressure.

Crack!

The jolt traveled up her arm and slammed into her shoulder.

Blood welling out of his chest, wide-eyed disbelief frozen on his face, Hoffman spun around. Teetered on the edge of the pit for an eternity.

Then tumbled into the great maw.

The final echoes of gunfire died away, but the smell of burnt gunpowder and singed leather hung in the air.

Disentangling her hand, Mary dropped the still smoking purse, ran to untie the final parcel, and tossed the end of the rope to Tim.

Though she could hear him shouting, she could not make

out the words. Pain stabbed at her eardrums, and everything sounded muffled.

Feeling Tim's weight on the end of the rope, she tried to haul him up, but with nothing to brace her feet against, she couldn't do it by herself.

Happy and Lila Lorraine stayed with Iron Sam, but Crunchy, Teach, Kid Rags, and Spaghetti came to help Mary.

When she saw Tim's anxious face appear above the mineshaft, she clenched her jaw and tightened her grip on the rope. It wasn't until he stood on solid ground, with his arms wrapped tightly around her, that she let herself sag in relief.

"You always thought you should die like this," Lila Lorraine told Iron Sam. With Spaghetti's help, she struggled to her feet.

"Now what?" Tim asked. "Do we leave him here?"

Mary scanned the mine, wondering if they should bury him under a pile of rocks. No. That would take too long. What if someone heard the shots and came to investigate?

Her gaze rested on the mineshaft. "We put him down there."

"That's where Hoffman is," Kid Rags objected. "You can't have them together."

Happy squinted at him. "Why not? Iron Sam won't care. Dead is dead."

"We do what Lady says." Crunchy seized one of Iron Sam's arms and started dragging him toward the shaft.

Tim hesitated, then took hold of the other arm.

Before they rolled him into the pit, Lila Lorraine called out. "Wait!"

She went over to where Mary had flung her purse, wrestled with the gun and managed to free it. She wiped it on her fuchsia sweatshirt, then wrapped Iron Sam's fingers around the grip.

"So long, Sam." She gave him a push.

Iron Sam turned a lazy somersault as he fell.

After an impossibly long time, Mary saw him land in a sprawl on top of Hoffman. She stared down at him, thinking she should say some final words, but nothing came to mind. After a moment, she stepped away.

Tim shouldered a rucksack. She bent to pick one up.

"Here, let me help," he said.

He held it while she slipped her arms into the straps and settled it on her back. When he let go, she swayed, barely managing to keep her balance.

"Maybe we should lighten the pack," Tim said.

"No." Hearing the harshness in her voice, Mary softened her tone. "I can do it."

Almost doubled over under the heavy load, she stumbled toward the entrance. Hands and pockets filled with the contents of a third rucksack, the elders followed. Tim brought up the rear.

It took two trips.

After secreting the gold in the van, they resealed the mine, piled dirt and rocks against the entrance to hide it, then swept the area with the thick-stalked weeds to obliterate their footprints.

As they drove away, Mary said, "I have the awful feeling we've forgotten something."

"Your purse?" Lila Lorraine asked.

"No. I have that."

Tim gave her a reassuring smile. "We brought back all our equipment."

"And the gold," Kid Rags contributed.

Mary smacked herself on the forehead with the palm of a hand. "Hoffman's car! We can't leave it here."

"Where is it?" Spaghetti asked.

Happy pointed to a flash of bronze hidden in the brush. "There."

Tim stopped the van. They all climbed out to investigate.

Happy tried the driver's side door. It opened. "Aw, shucks," he said, kicking the dirt. "I hoped I'd get to jimmy it."

Tim slid into the driver's seat, reached under the dashboard, and in less than a minute the engine purred.

He handed the keys of the van to Mary. "When we were in Gunnison this morning, I noticed a tavern called The College Inn. I'll leave the car in the parking lot behind it, and meet you at that place where we got gas."

He drove off, trailing a cloud of dust.

Mary stopped in Gunnison long enough to pick up Tim and refuel the van, then headed east on Highway 50.

No one spoke—or if they did, she couldn't hear them— until they were seated around a table in a Salida diner.

"You okay, Lady?" A worried frown crumpled Crunchy's face.

She nodded.

"Back there with Hoffman," Teach said. "What you did—"

She raised a palm.

He fell silent.

She glanced around the table, looking at Tim and each of the elders in turn.

When all eyes focused on her, she said in a low, clear voice, "This is something we never talk about."

Epilogue

The rooster crowed.

Mary awoke, rolled over to nestle next to Tim, and found his side of the bed empty. Befuddled by sleep, she groped for him, unable to figure out why he was gone.

"Good morning, Sleepyhead."

Yawning, she sat up and gazed blearily at him. "You're awake early."

He placed a breakfast tray in front of her and gave her a kiss. "Teach and I had some final preparations for your big day."

She laughed. "*My* big day?"

In Tim and Teach's hands, the small roadside stand she'd envisioned had blossomed into a major undertaking. They'd purchased an old double-wide trailer at a public auction in the next county, gutted it, fitted it out for a store, and stocked it with local crafts: homemade jams and jellies, cornhusk dolls, wildflower wreaths, quilts, and, of course, Kid Rags' creations.

Old-fashioned peddler's carts filled with produce, also locally purchased because the farm could not yet sustain itself, lined the front of the building. Lilac bushes, forsythia, and tubs of flowers grown in their greenhouse blossomed around the periphery. A chain link fence surrounded the whole area, making the place seem at once intimate and inviting.

And today was the well-advertised grand opening.

Tim grabbed a piece of toast off the tray and started to leave. "Oh, I forgot to tell you." He turned around and grinned at her. "The Allisons next door are thinking of selling out. They promised us the first option."

Mary returned his smile. "You're not going to be satisfied until we own the whole county, are you?"

"Now there's a thought." He took a bite of toast, chewed it slowly, then swallowed. "Actually, I'll be satisfied with owning all the land up to Jack's place." He tilted his head. "Speaking of Jack, I think I hear his truck now. Interesting how he comes earlier and earlier each day."

"Good." Mary sipped her orange juice. "I worry about him all alone in that big, decrepit house. The sooner he moves into the cottage we built for him, the better."

"He'll come soon enough. The lure of good food, his goats, and you is too much to resist."

She pretended to pout. "I come last after food and goats?"

"Not with me." Tim took another bite of toast and chewed it thoughtfully. "Personally I can do without the goats, so you'd come in a solid second."

She threw a pillow at him.

Chuckling, he tossed it back and left the room.

Mary continued to sip her orange juice, remembering the first time she'd met Jack. He'd driven to the farm in a rattletrap pickup truck almost as ancient as he and about as ill kempt. The man's clothes had not seen the inside of a washing machine in a long time, and his yellowish white hair, beard, and mustache stuck out in all directions, giving him the appearance of an albino lion. His faded brown eyes seemed half-crazed until she realized that grief made them look so wild.

He'd twisted his baseball cap in his gnarled hands and shifted his weight from foot to foot. Finally, he'd blurted out an incoherent tale of a son dead in Vietnam, a daughter dead of breast cancer, a wife dead of diabetes, and goats in need of a place to live.

"I've heard you're taking up farming," he said. "Have you thought of angora goats? They're sturdy, eat almost anything, even the forage horses and cows won't touch, and do well in drought conditions. And their hair is valuable."

"The county's going to take my farm. Doesn't matter about me. I'll eat a bullet or go to a nursing home, one or the other, but I'm worried about my goats."

Glad she could help the sad old man, Mary had bought all thirty of his goats and hired him to tend them. She'd also purchased his farm for little more than the back taxes and a promise he'd always have a place to live. He'd watched with bright-eyed interest the building of his new cottage next to Spaghetti and Lila Lorraine's, but for now he preferred to remain in his old house.

Mary made a sandwich with her scrambled egg and a slice of toast and settled herself on the window seat. This was her favorite view, especially so early in the morning when all things seemed possible. She couldn't help smiling as she surveyed Happy's crooked rows of corn shoots, the angora goats in the field of wildflowers, the sheep nibbling on the lawn of native grasses, and the recently planted mature shade trees standing guard over her domain, including the secret places where they'd buried the gold.

One thing she'd learned this past year: the adage was wrong. Money could buy happiness.

Spaghetti was whistling "Bootleg Boogie" and stirring a huge pot of vegetable soup when Mary entered the kitchen with the tray of empty dishes.

She inhaled appreciatively. "Smells delicious."

He nodded and smiled without missing a note.

The fountain of youth, Mary had come to realize, was not just love and security, but being useful, having a reason to get up every morning. Until Spaghetti had discovered an unknown talent for cooking, he'd moped around the farm, disrupting everyone's serenity.

"This tastes terrible," he'd complained one evening, coming in to sample Mary's spaghetti sauce. "My mother put the basil in at the end. She said if you put it in too early, the flavor cooks out. And you don't add enough garlic."

"Then you do it!" Mary had thrust the spoon into his hand and stomped out of the kitchen.

Ashamed of her outburst, she'd returned a few minutes later to apologize and found him crooning to himself while he'd seasoned the sauce.

Ever since, he'd shared the cooking duties with Mary and Deanne.

"Isn't Deanne awake yet?" Mary looked around the kitchen as if expecting the young woman to come popping out of a cabinet.

Still whistling, Spaghetti pointed to the dining room.

Deanne and Crunchy were helping themselves from the chafing dishes on the sideboard. Journey, Marmalade, and Spitting William were entwined around their legs, waiting for the handouts they knew would be forthcoming.

All five looked up at Mary's approach. Crunchy and Deanne beamed at her, but the three cats gave her baleful looks, displeased with the delay of the expected treats.

Crunchy, of all the elders, had proved to be a safe, capable driver. Equipped with a new driver's license—a valid one—he ran errands in town whenever Mary or Tim were too busy to go themselves. As often as not, Crunchy would return with a stray cat, earning himself the title of Cat Wrangler.

One day he'd gone to the hospital to visit Happy, who'd had a bout of the flu, and returned with a shy young blonde wearing a nurse's uniform and a painful-looking shiner.

"Can we keep her?" he asked.

The farm had worked its magic and now Deanne was strong and vibrant, though undergoing a bitterly contested divorce from her abusive husband. Never returning to her old job at the hospital, she seemed content with helping to care for the elders.

Mary chatted with Crunchy and Deanne for a moment, then fixed herself a cup of hot chocolate and took it outside. As she did most mornings, she proceeded to the stand of trees she'd fertilized with her grandparents' ashes. She set the cup on a white wrought iron table and plopped on a lawn chair. A calico cat shot out from underneath the chair, tripping Lila Lorraine who headed her way.

"Sheesh," Lila Lorraine said. "If Crunchy isn't bringing a cat home, then Journey is. There was a time many years ago when I thought I'd end up in a cathouse, and now look at me—it's come true."

Mary laughed. "You may not be fond of cats, but you have to admit they do help control the mice."

Lila Lorraine stroked her chin in unconscious imitation of Teach. "You've got a point."

After a moment of companionable silence, Lila Lorraine said, "We never did drive by the farm where your grandmother grew up."

"I don't need to see where she lived as a child." Mary spread out her arms. "This is what's important—where she chose to live as an adult. She lived out her life here. And so will I."

"There you are, Lila Lorraine." Teach strode toward them. "You promised we could have some potted plants for the store."

"They're in the greenhouse."

"I didn't know which ones to take."

Lila Lorraine rolled her eyes. "Come on. I'll show you."

Before following her, Teach smiled at Mary. "You look lovely this morning."

Mary glanced down at her black jeans and ivory blouse, then back at him.

He tipped his hat. "The clothes don't make the woman. The woman makes the clothes."

"You say the sweetest things."

"You make it so easy."

He looked over his shoulder as he walked away. "Now that the store is ready, I'll be able to get a start on my book."

Mary smiled at his retreating back. He'd been saying words to that effect every day for the past year.

Excited at first with the thought of writing, he'd helped her set up a library in a new wing of the house, furnishing it with all of his books plus the many thousands he'd since purchased at estate sales and auctions. He'd even learned how to use the new computer she'd bought him, but he soon abandoned that means of research.

"Nothing but gossip and propaganda," he'd said with a sniff.

Someday he might write his book, but she doubted it. A social being, he'd probably always find something more stimulating to do than spend hour after hour with only his typewriter or the computer to keep him company.

"Hey, let go of me!"

Mary turned toward the yelp and saw Bessie, like a sturdy tugboat, towing the much larger Jack along in her wake.

Bessie's sparse gray hair was tucked under her straw gardening hat. She had dirt stains on the knees of her overalls and an expression of outrage on her face.

"You tell her," Bessie ordered.

"Tell me what?" Mary asked.

Bessie released Jack and put her hands on her hips. "That man has got to go!"

Mary gave her a puzzled glance. "Who? Jack?" Bessie had always seemed tolerant of Jack since he was the only other member of the group who knew anything about farming.

"Not Jack." Bessie threw out an arm and pointed at Happy, who rode a tractor in a distant field. "Him."

Jack, clean-shaven and wearing a new chambray shirt, winked at Mary. It was all she could do to keep from laughing, but somehow she managed to maintain a straight face.

"What's he done now?"

"He drove that four-wheeler of his over my runner beans this morning," Bessie exclaimed. "And he's plowing that field all wrong. I've never seen anyone plow the way he does. Tell her, Jack. Tell her the rows are supposed to be straight."

"I'll talk to Happy," Mary said soothingly.

Jack edged away. "Can I go now?"

"Have you eaten breakfast?" Mary asked.

"Not yet. Had to see to my goats first."

"Well, you go on and get something to eat. I noticed we have those sausages you like so much."

"Yes, ma'am," he said, ambling toward the house.

Mary shifted her attention back to Bessie, thinking of all they'd accomplished in the past year.

To her surprise, the easiest thing had been to get the permits and zoning variances they'd needed. Everything fell into place when they'd given the County Building Commissioner what he wanted.

He'd put his mother-in-law, Bessie, in a nursing home, but his wife had begun complaining that Bessie was fading away, losing interest in life, and she wanted to bring her home to live with them. The Commissioner promised to grease the wheels if Mary took the crotchety old woman off his hands.

It was the best bargain Mary ever made. Not only had she been able to renovate the old farmhouse, bringing it up to code and adding two extra wings; she had permission to build as many cottages on the farm as she wished.

And she had Bessie.

Bessie brought a lifetime of knowledge on farming to the operation. She taught them about vegetable gardening and how to can the excess. She insisted on having a flock of chickens, which gave them all the eggs they needed, and she even took care of wringing the necks and plucking the ones for dinner.

Bessie's daughter, grateful that her mother had regained an interest in life, stopped by every week to give the house a good cleaning.

Mary smiled at Bessie. "I don't know what we'd have done without you."

The old woman stuck her thumbs under the straps of her overalls. "I'm sure you would have done well," she said with patent insincerity. "Now if you'll excuse me, I have to get back to my weeding."

A few minutes later, Happy drove up on his ATV, leaving the tractor parked haphazardly in the field.

"I didn't do whatever that old witch said I did."

"You didn't drive over her runner beans?"

"No. Well, maybe, but only a little. What else did she say?"

"Not much. Just that she'd never seen anyone plow the way you did."

He puffed out his chest. "She said that?"

Mary nodded.

"Maybe she's not as bad as I thought."

"Keep away from her garden, okay?"

Happy sped away, his answer lost in the roar of the engine.

Mary shook her head. So much for the moment of quiet contemplation she'd hoped for. She gulped her now cold chocolate and went in search of Kid Rags, who was sure to be in his workshop.

All the guns had been cleared out of the smithy in the barn and locked in the refurbished secret room. They now used the tools and equipment for nothing more deadly than jewelry making. Kid Rags had designed a line of earrings that were light and delicate, mere traceries of gold. He'd given his first pair to Mary; it was one of her prized possessions.

As expected, she found him at his workbench, hunched over a huge lighted magnifying glass on a stand.

She knocked on the open door and stepped inside.

Kid Rags' face lit up when he noticed her. "Just the person I wanted to see. I have a present for you."

He handed her two tiny gold discs on earwires.

"Very nice," she said.

Her tepid tone seemed to amuse him. He stepped aside and gestured to the magnifying glass.

Holding the discs under the glass, she gasped. "Oh, my God! They're fantastic!"

She turned the discs this way and that, studying them from every angle. They were exact miniatures of her lucky coins.

"I can't believe you got so much detail on such tiny things!"

"It's what I do," Kid Rags said matter-of-factly.

Mary admired the earrings a moment longer. Then she remembered why she had come here.

"It's time for you to eat breakfast."

"In a minute. I have something I want to do first."

"Now," she said, knowing that when he got involved in working, the minutes could stretch into hours.

"But I—"

She held up a wagging forefinger.

"Oh, okay. I guess I am hungry." He turned off the lights and ushered Mary out of his workshop.

After watching to make sure he actually went into the house, she headed for the store. When she got there, her parents were stepping out of their car.

Her father opened his arms for a hug. "I know I've never said it before, but I'm proud of you." He cleared his throat. "Any problems with the plumbing?"

Mary smiled. He asked that every time she saw him, though he knew perfectly well there were no problems; he had supervised the work himself.

"It's fine. Everything's fine."

He glanced around. "The old place is looking good."

She held her breath, wondering if he planned to ask where she got the money to remodel, but all he said was, "There's Lila Lorraine. Be right back. I have to go say hello."

Mary turned to her mother and kissed her on the cheek. "You're looking well."

"You, too." Gwen smiled. "Guess who we brought?"

For the first time, Mary noticed a couple in the back seat. "Bill!"

Bill stepped out of the car and extended a helping hand to his hugely pregnant wife. He hadn't been the least bit unhappy when Mary broke off their engagement. He married his secretary within the month, but he remained a friend of the family. Mary suspected her mother still entertained hopes the two of them would get back together someday, even though she seemed fond of both Bill's wife and Tim.

"Welcome," Tim said, coming out to greet everyone.

After hugs all around, Gwen pointed to the road. "Look at all those cars. I've never seen so much traffic out here."

First one car pulled into the parking lot, then another. When the lot filled, people stopped along the side of the road.

Mary smiled at Tim.

This was going to be a very good day.

Other Titles available from Pat Bertram and Second
Wind Publishing.

A Spark of Heavenly Fire
Pat Bertram
In quarantined Colorado, where
hundreds of thousands of people
are dying from an unstoppable,
bio-engineered disease,
investigative reporter Greg
Pullman risks everything to
discover the truth: Who unleashed
the deadly organism? And why?

More Deaths Than One
Pat Bertram
Bob Stark returns to Denver after
18 years in SE Asia to discover
that the mother he buried before he
left is dead again. At her new
funeral, he sees . . . himself. Is his
other self a hoaxer? A
doppelganger? Or is something
more sinister going on?

Light Bringer
Pat Bertram
Thirty-seven years after being
abandoned on the doorstep of a
remote cabin in Colorado, Becka
Johnson returns to try to discover
her identity, but she only finds
more questions. Who has been
looking for her all those years? And
why?

Excerpt from Light Bringer

Tracks led to the house where a small gray creature huddled against the door.

She clapped her hands. "Shoo. Shoo."

The creature did not stir.

"Go on. Get," she shouted.

The creature still didn't move. Was it dead? This wouldn't be the first time a dying animal had been attracted to the warmth seeping from beneath the front door.

She approached gingerly, relaxing when she saw what appeared to be an old gray blanket that had somehow ended up on the stoop. She bent over to collect the wad of fabric, then straightened. Bad idea. Who knew what vermin had taken refuge in the folds.

Before she could figure out what to do, the blanket moved. She jumped back and stared at it. The blanket moved again, giving her a glimpse of a coppery curl.

She lifted the bundle, cradled it in her arms, and drew back the blanket. Two dark eyes, shining with intelligence, gazed at her.

She sucked in a breath. An infant, no more than nine months old.

As the infant continued to gaze at her, its eyes brightened to gleaming amber. Then it beamed at her—a welcoming smile, both joyous and knowing, as if it had recognized a dear friend.

Helen's face felt tight. "Who are you?"

The baby chortled in response.

"And who left you here?" She glanced at the tracks. They led in only one direction—toward the house.

Feeling dizzy, she crouched to examine the tracks more closely.

They were footprints. Tiny footprints in the snow.